Southwest Georgia Regional Li
Decatur-Miller-S
Bainbridge, GA

S0-BDA-562

SWGRL-DEC STACKS
31052006040269
CRO 2005
TOUCHED BY VENOM

WITHDRAWN

HEADQUARTERS-101

They came into [...] o-
crats burning w[...] he
potters' work sh[...] re
the smoke from [...] air
chalky. One br[...] er
against the wal[...] he
dropped her. They began searching for her man.

He was in the men's ceramic studio and they dragged him into the courtyard. With the leather laces from his own sandals, they bound his hands and ankles, then gagged him with a clot of clay and chaff.

They led a yearling over, man height and twice as long, wings a-tremble and scales contracted, its claws fully intact: one of the warrior-lord's own dragons. They cracked bullwhips against the yearling's hide to drive it into a frenzy. It attacked the bound man. Between drawing one breath and another, the man was disemboweled.

Let this be a lesson to you, roared the blue-eyed, blond-haired aristocrat, as blood from a woman's mouth dried upon his boot heels. *Let this be a lesson none of you forget!*

I can assure you, blue-eyed, blond-haired one, no one forgot. Not the pottery clan men, who ever after were the most brutally devout upon Clutch Re. Not the women, who suffered blows for misdemeanors imagined and real. And certainly not the potters' children, who witnessed the horror of that day. They, most of all, lived lives haunted by the only two screams the bound man had time to utter, a man who'd been a master potter, a claimer, and a father.

[...]y father.

[...]e woman with the broken jaw, my mother.

[...], I can assure you, blue-eyed, blond-haired one, that was a [...]n no one forgot. Least of all I, Zarq Kavarria Darquel. That [...]n made me all that I am today.

WITHDRAWN

TOUCHED
by
VENOM

BOOK ONE OF THE
Dragon Temple
Saga

JANINE CROSS

A ROC BOOK

ROC

Published by New American Library, a division of
Penguin Group (USA) Inc., 375 Hudson Street,
New York, New York 10014, USA
Penguin Group (Canada), 90 Eglinton Avenue East, Suite 700, Toronto
Ontario M4P 2Y3, Canada (a division of Pearson Penguin Canada Inc.)
Penguin Books Ltd., 80 Strand, London WC2R 0RL, England
Penguin Ireland, 25 St. Stephen's Green, Dublin 2,
Ireland (a division of Penguin Books Ltd.)
Penguin Group (Australia), 250 Camberwell Road, Camberwell, Victoria 3124,
Australia (a division of Pearson Australia Group Pty. Ltd.)
Penguin Books India Pvt. Ltd., 11 Community Centre, Panchsheel Park,
New Delhi - 110 017, India
Penguin Group (NZ), cnr Airborne and Rosedale Roads, Albany,
Auckland 1310, New Zealand (a division of Pearson New Zealand Ltd.)
Penguin Books (South Africa) (Pty.) Ltd., 24 Sturdee Avenue,
Rosebank, Johannesburg 2196, South Africa

Penguin Books Ltd., Registered Offices:
80 Strand, London WC2R 0RL, England

First published by Roc, an imprint of New American Library,
a division of Penguin Group (USA) Inc.

First Printing, November 2005
10   9   8   7   6   5   4   3   2   1

Copyright © Janine Cross, 2005
All rights reserved

 REGISTERED TRADEMARK—MARCA REGISTRADA

LIBRARY OF CONGRESS CATALOGING-IN-PUBLICATION DATA:

Cross, Janine.
Touched by venom / Janine Cross.
p. cm. (The Dragon Temple saga; bk. 1)
ISBN 0-451-46048-0
I. Title. II. Series: Cross, Janine. Dragon Temple saga; bk. 1.
PS3603.R674T68 2005
813'.6—dc22   2005014310

Set in Weiss
Designed by Ginger Legato

Printed in the United States of America

Without limiting the rights under copyright reserved above, no part of this publication may be reproduced, stored in or introduced into a retrieval system, or transmitted, in any form, or by any means (electronic, mechanical, photocopying, recording, or otherwise), without the prior written permission of both the copyright owner and the above publisher of this book.

PUBLISHER'S NOTE
This is a work of fiction. Names, characters, places, and incidents either are the product of the author's imagination or are used fictitiously, and any resemblance to actual persons, living or dead, business establishments, events, or locales is entirely coincidental.
    The publisher does not have any control over and does not assume any responsibility for author or third-party Web sites or their content.

The scanning, uploading, and distribution of this book via the Internet or via any other means without the permission of the publisher is illegal and punishable by law. Please purchase only authorized electronic editions, and do not participate in or encourage electronic piracy of copyrighted materials. Your support of the author's rights is appreciated.

To Zach and Faren
(even if I won't let you read this
till you're older)

ACKNOWLEDGMENTS

Huge thanks to Linda Demeulemeester, a brilliant writer and amazing friend whose insights and humor not only shaped this book but have supported me through some intensely interesting times.

Many heartfelt thanks also to Michel Nadeau, whose decades of friendship gave me the time and resources to realize a great deal, this book not the least.

Thanks also to my agent, Caitlin Blasdell, and editor, Liz Scheier, for their patience and hard work, and Therese, so new and wondrous in my life, whose support has been monumental.

PROLOGUE

They came into the yard on a cloud of red dust, four young aristo-crats burning with indignation and wine, and they went into the pot-ters' work shed and hauled the woman out by her hair. They dragged her along the floor, through shards of shattered statues, out into the yard, where the smoke from the kilns was only just beginning to turn the air chalky. One man broke her jaw beneath his boot heel, then stood her against the wall of a mud-brick hut. Her knees sagged, so he dropped her. They began searching for her man.

They mistook Twisted Foot Ryn for the one they wanted, and it wasn't until Ryn's flock of children, all shrieks and small, balled fists, threw themselves upon the four that the aristocrats realized they'd erred. Weeping, Ryn's woman told them where to find the man they wanted.

He was in the men's ceramic studio. Blue powder covered the hairs on his brawny arms and filled the mortar on the table before him. He said nothing. Slowly, he placed his pestle down in the mortar. Just so.

They dragged him into the courtyard even though they needn't have, for he put up no resistance. With the leather laces from his own sandals, they bound his hands and ankles, then gagged him with a clot of clay and chaff, but one of the four said *No, take it out. She needs to hear him scream.*

When they were ready, they led a yearling over, man height and twice as long, wings a-tremble and scales contracted, its claws fully in-tact: one of the warrior-lord's own dragons. They lashed the man up-right against a water-filled barrel, then stacked an empty one atop it and ordered it filled with stones to prevent it from tipping. They cracked bullwhips against the yearling's hide and hurled platters at its head to drive it into a frenzy. It attacked the bound man.

Between drawing one breath and another, the man was disemboweled. But the aristocrats had difficulty bringing the yearling under control, and by the time they managed to subdue the beast with muzzle poles and blow darts, the ribbons of white sinew and meat strewn across the courtyard came not just from the once-bound man, but from a potter's child and one of the aristocrats.

Let this be a lesson to you, roared the blue-eyed, blond-haired aristocrat, as blood from a woman's mouth dried upon his boot heels. *Let this be a lesson none of you forget!*

I can assure you, blue-eyed, blond-haired one, no one forgot. Not the pottery clan men, who ever after were the most brutally devout upon Clutch Re. Not the women, who suffered blows for misdemeanors imagined and real. And certainly not the potters' children, who witnessed the horror of that day. They, most of all, lived lives haunted by the only two screams the bound man had time to utter, a man who'd been a master potter, a claimer, and a father.

My father.

The woman with the broken jaw, my mother.

No, I can assure you, blue-eyed, blond-haired one, that was a lesson no one ever forgot. Least of all I, Zarq Kavarria Darquel. That lesson made me all that I am today.

I write this so the people of my new land—these gruff, impulsive foreigners—will understand and learn without ever witnessing such as I and the rest of the potters' children did, so many mountains, so many scars, and so many years ago.

ONE

My first memory: white dust.

Cool and airy, drifting down upon my head like a blessing. The taste of it a fine, gritty tang I later knew to be kaolin. The soft thud of hammers crushing lumps of dry clay into small pieces, the crunch of rolling pins reducing the granules to powder. The unbroken rhythm of hands kneading air pockets out of damp clay, the thuds as steady and resonant as a heartbeat.

I was born a danku rishi via, a pottery clan serf's girl, on the dragon estate known as Clutch Re. I could claim none as my navel aunties, however, for my mother was born not in Clutch Re, but in Clutch Xxamer Zu, the very same dragon estate infamous for reckless wagering during Arena events. When of a day the Xxamer Zu estate owed Re a sum it could ill afford, my mother was among the serfs given in lieu of lucre.

She arrived in Clutch Re late one Fire Season evening, ill and filthy from the monthlong march from her birth Clutch. Due to her skill with clay, she was placed in the pottery clan, and no sooner did my father lay eyes on her then he claimed her as his roidan yin, his garden of children.

Within days, it became obvious she would have difficulties in her new home: She would not, could not, be piously servile. Even to her claimer. She wanted to create with clay whatever she wanted, whenever the whim took her.

So she did.

Mother's defiance against the men's daily Proclamations about what could be sculpted, when, was tolerated for three reasons only: my father's mastery of clay, mother's own impressive skills, and her sweet, light nature.

For yes, contrary to how many have painted her, my mother was the softest creature I have ever known. Soft-spoken, soft-stepping, her face alight with a kindness that drew children to her knees. Almost a sacrilege, that, to have such a benevolent countenance upon a lowly Clutch serf. Yet there it was; the calm eyes, the gentle smile, the infinite patience of the dragon-blessed shining from my mother.

The immensity and population of Clutch Re helped conceal her oddness. A fertile, hill-pebbled valley sprawling between jungle-choked mountains, Clutch Re was home to almost a hundred serf guild clans, or rishi kus. It boasted an enormous infirmary, several smaller hospices, three mills, a plethora of apothecaries, an infamous dragonmaster who was the best in the nation, though admittedly the most eccentric, and enough egg workers to form a veritable regiment, all necessary for the welfare of Re's seven thousand brooder dragons. Our pottery clan, danku Re, was just a blot on the huge map of Warrior-Lord Re's Clutch. Mother was invisible—and safe—as long as she remained quiet.

My second memory: my father's arms.

Ruddy, brawny, thick, with coarse black hair, his hands from the wrists down pale, soft, and hairless from the endless hours immersed in clay solution.

Throughout our childhood, my sister, Waisi, insisted this could not be a real memory, not so young in my life as I claimed, and perhaps she was right—really, she must be—for my childhood was spent with the other potters' children in the women's barracks. I had little close contact with my father. Indeed, I only understood him to be such when I was about four.

Like all women regardless of clan and status, my mother lived separate from the men and saw her claimer privately only when summoned to the mating closets. Otherwise, all conversation with him was in the manner of orders received or words exchanged in the course of a day's work. My intimate memory of his hands so early in my childhood must therefore be fabricated or transposed, lifted from later in my life and transplanted back to the time when I still crawled on all fours.

Was my father, Darquel, as weak as history portrays him? Or bewitched by the evil spirit that supposedly inhabited my impious rebel mother? Neither. Merely obsessed. Obsessed with my mother, who was called Darquel's Kavarria, Darquel's Obsession, after father claimed her, though others called her his Djimbi whore when out of his earshot; obsessed with his eldest girl-child, Waisi, who was determined to rise in status somehow, anyhow; and obsessed with me, his youngest, Zarq.

Yes, that was my father: obsessed with three vastly different women.

I remember the first time I heard the word *Djimbi* applied to my mother. I was nine years old, and my mother, sister, and I were watching Mombe Taro, the annual ceremony when chosen boys are publicly inducted into apprenticeship to the dragonmaster. Dono stood beside me, shoving and elbowing and leaning forward for a better view. He and I had been playmates when younger, and I was enjoying his company, despite his insistence that I address him only by his full name, Yeli's Dono.

He should not have been standing beside me, young Dono. Although only nine years old, he was regarded as a man, and men are supposed to line one side of the Lashing Lane, the road used during Mombe Taro, and women and children the other. But as the men have to stand behind the monks, they are deafened by the gonging of the monks' ceremonial water bowls, and blinded by the reflecting tin and water of the same. Thus, while approximately half the men observe the segregation, the rest crowd onto the women's side of the 'lane of pain.' This is all conveniently overlooked by attending Temple wardens.

Never do the women stray over to the men's side, need I point out.

We had walked all morning to reach the Lashing Lane by high noon. The stable stench of dragon dung, decomposing nests, and maht, regurgitated dragon food, coated my tongue like thick jelly. Waisi stood on my left, pinching my neck and complaining she couldn't see. Dono stood on my right.

"Look, look!" he screamed. "They're coming!"

The cries of the crowd lining the lane momentarily drowned out the noise of the water bowls.

The First Holy Wardens of Clutch Re came out of the largest stable, resplendent in their robes of iridescent porphyry, indigo and green. They walked with eyes straight ahead. Each carried a bronze crucible of holy oil and a whisk, which they dipped in the oil and flicked over the whipping bar that ran down the median of the lane. They moved with such grace that the feathery antennae atop their three-cornered hats barely quivered.

I know now what I didn't then: Those antennae aren't real. The real ones, reverently removed from the corpse of whatever male dragon has died, are horded by the Ashgon himself, the sacred advisor to the Emperor and titular head of Ranon ki Cinai, the Temple of the Dragon. But back then, I was dumbstruck to see the graceful, iridescent antennae arcing above the heads of those men.

"They can thmell better when they wear them," Dono shouted, his lisp pronounced in his excitement. "They can thmell just as good as a bull dragon, hey-o!"

I doubted the truth of that. Wearing a dead bull's olfactory antennae hardly seemed likely to improve the senses of the wardens' fleshy nares. But I held my tongue. Clutch women are taught young not to dispute the male word.

"I can't see," Waisi shouted, though her cries were just one more noise in a storm of excited shouts and babble.

Only the monks remained impassive, their faces made flat and silver by the harsh reflection of tin and water. They sat cross-legged on the ground, lining the entire lane, their water bowls before them. Naked save for their loincloths, their bony bodies were coated in dust stirred up by the crowd. They never ceased moving their thin arms; each left hand held a metal rod, which was struck against a water bowl, while each right hand constantly nudged the bowl, making the water within swirl. This produced an eerie, atonal noise, a quavering *wong* that was both metallic and liquid.

It was not a noise you'd wish to hear at night.

Following the First Holy Wardens came the Temple Superior of our Clutch, and behind him the Ranreeb of the Jungle Crown, the Holy

Overseer of the collective of Clutches to which Clutch Re belonged. It was a mark of Re's status that the Ranreeb was present; Mother said he'd never attended Mombe Taro at her birth Clutch.

The Ranreeb had a vast disdainful face skirted by thick, turgid chins that bulged obscenely fore and aft of his neck. I stared at that face above its magnificent robe of iridescent bull scales, these ones real, not fake.

"How can such an ugly man be holy?" I wondered aloud.

Waisi ignored me, save to cry, "Move out of the way, Zarq. Move over!"

"Hey-o, hey-o!" shouted Dono, capering like a rabid monkey. "Here they come!"

And so they did: the apprentices.

The inductees came first, some stumbling and ashen in terror, others lock-jawed and stiff-necked, eyes fixed not on today or tomorrow or even the near future, but on some distant time when they might earn this crowd's awe and reverence. A dreamtime, that, a phantom time.

The servitors came next, several years older, much fewer in number, as fearful as the inductees but able to control it with discipline and bravado. Their necks, backs, chests, arms, and calves all bore the snakelike scars of previous Mombe Taros. They knew what they had to endure that day and knew it intimately.

Last came the veteran dragonmaster apprentices, the ones who'd walked the Lashing Lane many times and whose bodies were bas-relief maps of scars. There were only seven of these, all between age sixteen and twenty. All had entered Arena and survived. All burned with the fervor of achieving master status, of becoming the next dragonmaster of Clutch Re. Chances were, they wouldn't. A dragon claw or fang or a fellow apprentice would put them early into a sepulchral tower. Maybe this year, maybe the next.

But such cogency has no place in the mind of a veteran apprentice.

Right away, I noticed their erections. Truth, I'd been looking for them, as had Waisi and Kobo's twins, Rutvia and Makvia. All four of us poked each other and tittered. Behind us, Mother yanked on Waisi's and the twins' braids with her strong potter's hands. She even yanked on my own scabby bristle, causing instant tears. We paid heed. Unwise while in the presence of so much masculinity to mock the phallus.

Yeli's Dono still pranced beside me like one crazed.

"Lookit the thize of that one!" he bellowed. "That'th a cock, hey-o!" He tugged on his own little thing beneath his dirty loincloth.

A venom cock, they're called. I'd heard the words grunted respectfully among pottery clan men. I'd also heard the words mentioned by women wearing a carefully blank expression cultivated to hide opinion. Understand, women do not revere the venom cock as men do. They see it for what it is: an uncontrollable reaction to an impending event, and a slightly foolish reaction at that.

Dono's reverence was a mystery to me back then, made all the more mysterious by his assertions about what a venom cock could do: slay a woman! Cripple a baby! Turn pleasurers into deaf, blind, barren idiots!

The only truth I knew about the subject was what my eyes told me: The veteran apprentices looked mighty silly waddling up the lane to the whipping bar, their penises pointing the way.

The dragonmaster, the cinai komikon himself, came last, a suitable distance from his underlings. He wore no Temple finery, just a loincloth and a multitude of furious white scars. In his arms lay the venom whips, oily black in the sun's rays.

The noise of the crowd died to respectful murmurs as he strode down the lane. Even Dono stopped capering. The eerie *wong* of the water bowls reigned supreme.

He was grinning, the dragonmaster. A big, gap-toothed grin. Occasionally, he cackled, his sinewy neck taut with rivers of veins. He looked demented despite his awesome tolerance of venom, built up from years of contact with uncut dragons; he was clearly intoxicated by the venom-soaked whips that lay in his bare arms.

Now and then he paused and nodded to someone in the crowd; everyone in the vicinity of the nod looked at each other in panic. You? Me? Was he nodding at me? What does it mean?

He terrified me with his scars, his grin, his whips and his cackles. Waisi's grip on my arm grew tighter. The twins pressed close.

Wong. Wong. The atonal wavering of the monks' bowls vibrated in my chest.

I knew the dragonmaster would stop before me. I knew. I held my breath, throat swollen, heart galloping, vision clouding.

But he walked on, oblivious to the potter's brat about to faint from fear.

His passing was like a wind rolling through the crowd. Immediately, everyone shifted, shivered, smiled, joked, and resumed jeering at the servitors and inductees stationing themselves along the whipping bar.

The bar ran down the center of the Lashing Lane and was elaborately carved into the shape of an impossibly long, undulating bull dragon. The posts that supported the bar had also been carved, these with vaguely human shapes. They glistened with tears of consecrated oil.

The servitors and inductees jostled each other as they gathered along the bar, trying to stand before a section of the crowd comprised of clan and not a rival ku. Thus stationed, they gripped the bar with both hands, eyes fixed on air, legs braced. Most shivered as if fevered. Some openly sobbed.

I felt cold myself. That happened every lashing, the empathetic shivering, the lightheadedness, the fearful anticipation of blood.

"Don't be such a baby," Waisi said, and I clamped my back teeth together. She nudged Dono. "Get ready to run, you. You promised me a whip."

"I will. I'll get one! Watch me!"

The Ranreeb and the Holy Wardens stood at the far end of the Lashing Lane, out of sight from where we stood in the popular halfway mark of its length. The dragonmaster still walked the lane, whips draped across his extended arms.

The sun bore down. The wind died. Heat reflected off the dirt road. Small biting flies nipped necks and ears.

It was *hot*. The skin on my arms felt as if it were shriveling. The press of bodies, the musk of so many men, the incessant clang of the monks' bowls . . .

"Stop leaning on me!" Waisi hissed, and she pinched me with heat-sticky fingers.

By craning my neck and squinting, I could just see the dragon-master reach the end of the road. He stood there, motionless. Time stretched.

The crowd grew restless. Some of the men started to grumble. Oh, was it hot!

Then a trumpet blast! An answering roar from the crowd! The huge double doors of the stable at the lane's end groaned inward.

A yearling burst out, all tassels and oiled scales and jangling bells. The crowd roared anew and pushed forward, chanting the name of our bull dragon, the title also granted the warrior-lord of our Clutch: "Re! Re! Re!"

I half turned and clung to Mother, who fought the surge of the crowd to protect us from being pushed onto the road. Dono, Waisi, and the twins had no such fear of being trampled; they leaned out, arms waving madly, as the warrior-lord of our Clutch rode his year-ling up the lane, fist raised.

"Reaaaaay!" His cry became one long roar, joined by the cheers from the crowd.

A ruby-studded muzzle held shut his yearling's foaming snout. Brass hobble bolts held her wings clamped folding-fan style against the length of her body; if not for those clamps, leathery wings with a twenty-foot span would have hoisted our warrior-lord aloft.

Though muzzled and pinioned, the dragon had not been declawed—no yearling a warrior-lord rides ever is—and as she thundered toward us, those thick, curved talons boiled up a cloud of dust from the red earth. I held my breath and closed my eyes as the chestnut and green yearling drew near, her short forelegs churning, her strapped-down wing fingers flexing, her powerful hindquarters thrusting her forward in the distinctive lunging gait of a dragon.

Clud-thrish, clud-thrish; the sound was both a ripping and a pounding. *Clud-thrish, clud-thrish,* and then *whoosh!*—the dragon shot past, and I was coughing and sputtering, burrowing my head into my mother's bitoo to hide from the dust.

The men in Warrior-Lord Re's family followed, mounted upon smaller dragons, all of which were female, of course; domesticated dragons never laid eggs that hatched bulls. Never. All bulls were therefore jungle caught and rare indeed. One bull per Clutch was the norm, though even that was impossible for small Clutches; nanwan-bak cinai, or expeditions to seize a male dragon, often took upwards of ten years before success and were outrageously expensive. Mother's birth Clutch had never been able to afford another bull after their first male dragon had died, and the lord of that estate paid sorely each year to rent the stud services of bulls from elsewhere.

Clutch Re suffered no such problem. Our warrior-lord was canny with coin and politics, as had been his predecessors; our Clutch had never lacked for a bull. The current reincarnation of Re, our male dragon, was reputed to be the most virile yet. Thus, our pride and cheers.

Warrior-Lord Re's sons came first down the Lashing Lane, riding fast side by side, the eldest boy, Kratt, bellowing as fiercely as his fa-ther, one fist raised. Ghepp, the younger—hair and eyes as dark as Kratt's were light—also shouted as he raced up the lane, but his voice had not yet matured and his holy cry kept cracking. *He* rode with two hands on the reins.

The uncles, nephews, and cousins rode out next. After a suitable pause, the open carriages holding the warrior-lord's claimed women and female relatives followed.

Dust coated the seated monks so thickly by now that their hair was as red as pallum bark; even their lips were as red as wet earth. Dust likewise coated the apprentices braced along the bar. One poor mite who looked about seven years old had already fainted. He would be picked up and tied, semiconscious, to the bar, and would come awake with a scream at the first lashing. The same thing happened to at least a clawful of apprentices during each Mombe Taro.

I tried to distance myself from his terror by telling myself he only *looked* seven years old; he must really be much older. Only adult males can be chosen as apprentices, see, and unless that boy had become an adult by losing *all* his milk teeth early, he had to be older than seven. Had to be. I kept repeating that to myself, loath to think the words *dragon bait*, and with them acknowledge the reality that the boy had been chosen merely as a sacrificial toy for our bull dragon.

The Re carriages rolled down the lane on either side of the whip-

ping bar, pulled by paunchy, declawed females on the cusp of becoming brooders. Each oval-bodied dragon stood five feet tall at
shoulder and more than twice as long. Their scaled hides were the
color of mossy redwood, save for on their throat, where blue-gray
crop dewlaps hung. Their bony tails flicked this way and that, the
diamond-shaped membrane at the end of each tail russet. They had
no wings, those dragons; had undergone wing amputation at birth.
Scars of citrine flesh marked where a holy knife had cut wing webbing
from the length of each scaled body.

The dust began to settle. The crowd pushed forward yet again,
hands outstretched. Glittering in finery surely too hot for such a day,
the Re women began throwing paddam into the crowd. Torn from old
Mombe Taro gowns and weighted with sugared nuts knotted at center, the gaily colored paddam rained down. Lemon linen, blue gossamer, purple silk . . . treasure! I pushed and scrambled with the rest
of the children to get as many as I could.

By the time the carriages reached the end of the long Lashing Lane,
my cheeks bulged with sweetened nuts and my grimy hands triumphantly held no fewer than four paddam of the finest silk.

Waisi and I compared.

I gawked. *Nine*, she had *nine*, and one bearing gold-shot trim as well!
That someone had willingly torn up a gown like that, and that Waisi
had had the luck to get a paddam of it, seemed the ultimate injustice.
Sulking, I refused to trade any of mine, even though Dono had a
turquoise one I liked, and one of the twins had two green silks she
wanted to exchange for my one crimson.

I was so piqued by my misfortune that I didn't pay much attention
to the beginning of the ceremony. But I knew from the blood roars of
the crowd when Warrior-Lord Re started the whipping, gauntlets
shielding his hands from the dragon venom on his whip. His sons,
brothers, uncles, and what have you joined in, theatrically striding up
and down the lane, taking their time before choosing which apprentice they wished to lash eight times, standing behind the chosen boy
and provoking the crowd to roar approval until the poor apprentice's
knees shook and he longed for the whip to fall, just to end the
wretched anticipation.

I paid little heed to any of it. All I saw were Waisi's nine paddam and my own pitiful four. *And* she would wield a whip, if Dono was fast enough to secure her one!

Then I started to wonder. . . . Why had my old playmate promised my sister a whip? Why indeed?

It wasn't until later that I learned the truth: Waisi had promised to perform sexual favors for Dono in front of his adolescent peers, *if* he secured her a whip. And Dono, desperate to earn the respect of his male peers and shed the double shame of virginity and being a bastard child, had boasted the favors were a certainty. Waisi hadn't been attracted to Dono, understand; he was barely half her age. But she *had* wanted a whip, and for two years running, Dono had won one from the drag-onmaster, thereby earning himself, and our clan, much respect for being one of the few rishi to induct a chosen boy into the dragon-master's apprenticeship.

Why my sister's sudden interest in obtaining a whip? Simple. She was a ripe fruit determined to be picked by an aristocrat. Her only chance of catching the eye of a bayen lordling was at Mombe Taro, when serfs and aristocrats alike mingled, and she knew the best way to get the attention of every man present was to wield a whip.

There's something about a full-figured adolescent girl using a whip that has always attracted Malacarite men.

But I knew none of that back then, when I was nine years old and the world seemed a safe and simple place. Though an unjust place: as Mombe Taro progressed, I continued to sulk furiously over my paltry four paddam.

Waisi brought me out of my sulk. "He's going to claim me," she screamed in my ear. "I'll be his forever!"

"Yeli's Dono?" I said in disbelief.

She shot me a withering look. "No, yolk brain, *him*." And she pointed.

The warrior-lord's First Son, Waikar Re Kratt, stood at the whip-ping bar not far from us, his adolescent, muscle-corded back glis-tening with sweat as he plied his whip. He'd removed his shirt and tied it artfully about his hips, vain thing, and tied a bandanna of the same fine cloth about his forehead to prevent sweat running into his blue eyes.

Mirth immediately shattered my sulk. "Funny Waisi! He's bayen—you're rishi! A first-class aristocrat never claims a serf, ever!"

"They do. Sometimes." She glared at me. "*He* will, anyway. You'll see."

I studied him, then, that golden-skinned adolescent with eyes like lapis lazuli. Or at least I started to. But I couldn't watch for long; I was distracted by the one he was lashing, for he had chosen to whip the semiconscious seven-year-old boy.

What I saw must not have been what Waisi saw. While her eyes glittered and her lips parted as if from overwhelming thirst, my mouth turned as dry and sour as lime dust.

This is what I saw.

Seven-year-old legs, thin and smooth and slightly knock-kneed, coated with red dust save for where rivulets of urine had created grimy trails. Shiny black flashed through the air behind those knees in a swift, near silent flicker. The skin on those small calves—they could be cupped in a woman's hands, they were that slender—split. I thought of old cloth, the kind that's been in the sun and rain too long and shreds apart at the merest pull. Now obscene red poked through the skin, and I hadn't realized it until then but that's what happened when flesh was exposed by a whip; it protruded in a meaty welt.

Eight times I saw skin as soft as mine, on a body just as slight, divided.

I prayed the boy would faint again. He never did. "Mama," he gasped in a snot-choked scream, over and over and over and over. "Mama! Mama!"

My head cleared after I vomited. Good thing I hadn't had much to eat for breakfast; the woman whose foot I retched across might have noticed. As it was, like Waisi, she watched that golden aristocrat as if hypnotized.

Then it was time for the whips to be returned to the dragonmaster, for all the apprentices' backs and calves bled freely, their eyes rolled with delirium from the venom, and the expected clawful had fainted but not, abstrusely, that seven-year-old boy. Children in the crowd danced with anticipation at the race about to take place, and parents shouted at their progeny to run fast, get a whip, go, go!

I'm ashamed to admit I tossed aside my empathy for the seven-year-old as if it had been an empty nutshell. I was instantly caught up in the excitement.

I always ran in those races, loving the competition and cheers from the crowd. I'd never won a whip, but then, never before had I wanted to. I'd been born forlornly short of the desire to whip an apprentice from a rival clan. Today—nine paddam to my four!—I was determined to get a whip, just to spite Waisi.

All along the Lashing Lane, especially at the popular halfway mark, we children jostled and wrapped our hands in the sticky paddam swathes we'd collected, eyes riveted on the dragonmaster of Clutch Re.

The dragonmaster again strolled down the Lane. As he drew nearer the halfway mark, I could see his grin was as fierce and demented as before. The whips draped in his arms dripped blood as well as venom and consecrated oil.

The metallic *wong* of the water bowls hit a higher note than previously —less water within—and the moans and babbling of the poisoned apprentices ebbed and swelled in rhythmic waves.

Waisi crouched beside Dono and whispered in his ear. Whatever she said made his cheeks flush. It also strengthened my resolve to best them.

The dragonmaster drew nearer us. Re, show us mercy, he was *slavering*. He was truly mad, that sinewy, half-naked man with shaven head and rotting teeth and a chest crisscrossed with scars. . . .

That repulsive chest inflated. I knew then, I *knew*, he was going to give cry. I burst from the crowd just as he threw back his head and howled.

With shrieks shrill enough to revive the apprentices slipping into stupor, the children lining the coveted midway point of the lane launched toward the dragonmaster. I was fast, yes, but if the dragonmaster had not been so close, and if I had not had that head start, I would not have reached him when I did, which is to say I was among the first children to stand before him, panting and triumphant. Dono came pounding up shortly after me. Full-figured Waisi could never have run so fast.

"Ah, me, me, me!" Dono cried, elbowing me aside.

The dragonmaster ignored him and calmly handed out whips to the others who had arrived alongside me.

"Me, me!" Dono shrieked as the crowd of children around us thickened to a lice-ridden clot.

The dragonmaster had but one whip left, and the noise about him increased. He held the whip aloft; a long, beaded string of saliva dangled from his chin and touched Dono's shoulder.

"So you would have this whip, rishi hatchling?" he cackled.

"Yeth!" Dono cried. The lisp ever present in his speech—he had no teeth, not a one—became markedly pronounced in his agitation. "Yeth, I would!"

"But I think one was faster than you, hey-o?" The dragonmaster's eyes fell on me. "You would use this whip, rishi brat?"

I swallowed, shrugged. He roared with laughter. "You have to do better than that to convince me!"

"I would. *I* would!" Dono shrieked. "I wath here firth—"

"*Liar!*" the dragonmaster bellowed, his nose suddenly a hairsbreadth from Dono's. "You think I'm blind? An idiot? A dupe? The brooder brat was before you."

I remembered my fear of the man.

I looked about; all the other children were scurrying back to the sidelines, except those with whips, and these now plied them eagerly against their chosen apprentices. The crowd cheered them on, oblivious to the little drama taking place between the dragonmaster, Dono, and me.

"Well?" The dragonmaster thrust his face before me.

I stared into brown irises marbled with white, and white sclera marbled with blood.

"Take the whip. You ran for it; you use it." He grasped my left hand—my unswathed hand, my unprotected hand—and pressed the whip against it.

The effect of the venom was immediate.

It was slick, that leather, and warm, like something freshly killed, and my palm tingled strangely. My fingers began throbbing, a peculiar expanding and contracting sensation that instantly was the focal point of my attention, for they pulsed in precise counterpoint to the water bowls, and the water bowls rang in harmony with the moans of the apprentices. No, they talked, those water bowls, *talked*, and the apprentices chanted back replies, their voices melodic and full of joyful mystery so that I wondered how I hadn't noticed before or maybe I had noticed but because my arm was pulsing I hadn't thought about it and if my neck would just stop throbbing as if it were an oozing heart then I might understand why the sky moved and the sun stood still and the ground imparted such hard heat beneath my back. . . .

I hit the ground back first, faceup.

The fall jarred the whip from my grasp. I heard Dono whimper and sensed him fleeing to the safety of the crowd.

The dragonmaster's face loomed over me. For the first time, I noticed the thin beard sprouting from his chin. It was the exact color of his skin, a brown-splotched dull green, like mud-spattered sage. The beard had been plaited and at the end of the thin plait hung a green wooden toggle. It swung to and fro, to and fro, grotesque as a clot of mucus.

Dono whimpered again—no. It was *me* whimpering. Dono was gone.

"Next time you run, little brooder bitch, be prepared to use the whip," the dragonmaster sneered. He picked up my fallen whip and then he, too, was gone.

A woman appeared, a cascade of fire for hair. She stood above me, looked out at the crowd, her flaming hair licking at a short, sudden breeze.

A toss of the head: a profile. Haughty. Breasts outthrust. Hands on hips, long, full legs spread wide. Defiance and invitation radiating outward.

This was no ordinary being, no. This was a carnal creature, a magnificent silhouette, all lush curves and proud stance. I couldn't see a face amid that fiery hair, for the sun glared directly in my eyes. But I was certain the woman possessed a striking, almost terrifying beauty.

She was demanding to be chased, daring to be captured.

Was any man worthy of her? I thought not. Would any obtain her? No. How to conquer such a feral sensuality?

Then the figure crouched beside me, blocked the sunlight from my eyes. Spoke.

"Stupid Zarq. Stupid, stupid little brat."

No otherworld creature, this, but Waisi, my sister, determined to catch the attention of every aristocrat present by carrying me off the lane. Yes, I may have stolen her opportunity to impress everyone by her use of a whip, but she would capture their attention nonetheless.

As she heaved me into her arms—her long, tawny hair caressing my cheeks—she loosed another string of curses at me.

I turned my head slightly, saw with venom-blurred vision that she had indeed caught the attention of every man in sight. It was not just *I* in my drugged state that could smell the hot, spicy scent of seduction wafting from Waisi. Oh, no. Every nose along the lane twitched from the fragrance of her, and the eyes of women as well as men were, for a brief moment, on none but my sister.

And then the moment was over, and we were back among the crowd, and Waisi unceremoniously dumped me at my mother's feet. By then, tiny bubbles of pus had formed on my palm from where the dragonmaster had pressed the venom-coated whip against my unprotected hand.

Mother crouched above me and furiously rubbed at the venom with a strip of cloth. Dono fumed beside her.

"Bathtard! *I* would have uthed that whip. Djimbi crap—"

Mother clouted him so hard he ended up facedown in the dirt. "You dare talk so of the cinai komikon?"

Fury emanated from Dono: She shouldn't have struck him; a woman never strikes a man, and because of something he'd done several years ago, nine-year-old Dono *was* regarded as a man. But he'd gone too far cursing the dragonmaster, so he suffered the indignity quietly. Almost quietly.

As Mother returned to treating my hand, he spat this at her, his lips pressed against dirt:

"Whore. Just like him. Yolk-brained Djimbi filth."

"Ignorant little brat, you," Mother snarled at him. "We have more wisdom than all ludu din din combined. You are nothing beside us, nothing—"

We. She had said *we*. As if she were like the dragonmaster, born from the loins of a despised jungle native.

I must have jerked or tensed, perhaps gasped, even. Mother broke off midtirade; our eyes met. A frantic, pained look flashed across her face.

And it was then that I saw her for what she was.

It was as if an invisible veil, magically placed over my eyes at birth, had blinded me to the obvious. But her admission, spoken so vehemently in my presence, had jerked free that veil, and suddenly beneath the sun-kissed bronze of my mother's skin I saw the dappled tan-and-sage pigmentation of a deviant, of a pervert, of a dragonwhore. Of a Djimbi.

My heart rate sped up and my accelerated pulse pumped the last dregs of venom through my veins.

I fainted anew.

TWO

When next I became aware of my surroundings, it was dark, that stifling blackness that devours Re valley when the mountains swallow twilight. The humid air was thick with the musky smells of jungle: rotting humus, moist foliage, sweet night blooms. The scent of damp greenery was so different from the dry smells of the exposed, sunbaked Lashing Lane. We were near the eastern edge of Clutch Re, not far from our pottery clan compound. Each guild within a Clutch forms its own clan; each clan lives within the walls of its own compound. We potters of danku Re—the pottery guild clan of Clutch Re—were no different.

I came to slowly, resuscitated by the familiar jungle smells. Then I remembered my mother's admission and the abrupt revelation it had brought. I whimpered.

"Hey-o, Zarq. No fear, no fear, almost home."

"I had a bad dream."

"Just a dream."

"You said you were Djimbi."

She grunted and shifted my legs a little, which were latched round her waist.

"Mama?" I whispered. "You're not Djimbi."

"I am." She dropped the words from her mouth as if they were hot stones. "Your navel Greatmother, my mother, is jungle-born Djimbi. She was raped during capture and brought with her mother to Clutch Xxamer Zu as a slave. Shortly after, I came into the world. I, too, am Djimbi."

"My Greatmother came from the jungle," I said in disbelief. "My Greatmother in Clutch Xxamer Zu."

"Yes."

"But you're only half-blood Djimbi, yes?"

"By the color of my skin, it matters little whether I'm half or full blood. And I speak the language, have certain Djimbi skills. I am Djimbi."

"But—"

"We'll talk more of this in the morning," she said shortly. "Hush now, hey-o. Hush."

But we never did. Talk of it, I mean, her Djimbi blood, my Djimbi ancestry. Not until the day she died did she discuss her mother again, and then not by words. And I, too ashamed of what I'd learned—me, part Djimbi!—I never found the courage to break her silence before then.

That night I visited the mating closets. Mother carried me. Not because I couldn't walk without fainting, but because she didn't want me waking anyone else in the women's barracks. I knew it was very late by the damp coolness of the air, but was too sleepy to be concerned with questions.

The cubicles within the stilt-raised mating shack were always hot, airless, and close smelling. Mother set me down on the mats in one cubicle and softly slid the door closed. She left it unlatched and returned to my side. I drifted back to sleep.

I awoke to find my father looming over me, stinking tallow candle in one hand. He was crouched on his haunches, and his hairy shins pressed against my tummy as he reached over and gently lifted my injured hand. He growled in his throat, a noise I instinctively knew was directed at the dragonmaster.

"What've you done for her?" he grunted.

Mother's voice came out of the darkness near my feet. "Bathed it with cooled boiled water, applied a poultice—"

"It'll scar."

"I hope not. I was quick."

"What did he do it for?"

"Because he could."

"Crazy bastard."

"Yes."

My father sighed and reached awkwardly to stroke my brow. "Don't race again next year. Or go slowly if you do. Hear?"

"Yes, sir," I murmured.

"Sleep," he ordered, and patted my head again. I turned on my side and closed my eyes, with the intention of feigning sleep so I could listen to what they might next say. But the day's events and the late hour defeated me. My parents remained silent the short time it took for me to drift back into slumber.

I awoke sometime later to the hiccup-gasps of my mother and the heavy, wet breaths of my father coming from the cubicle across from mine, and, comforted by the familiar, I fell immediately back to sleep, dragonmasters and Djimbi lineage completely forgotten.

The Djimbi. The Mottled Bellies. If Malacar, my birth nation, has any true-blood natives, they are to be found in the Djimbi. *If* you can find the Djimbi, that is. They are an elusive people.

As children, we were terrified those green-haired half-demons would slink out of the jungle, slide snakelike over our walls, and steal us from our sleeping mats. They would cut out our tongues and eat them raw, then bind us and blind us and drag us deep into the jungle, where they'd hoist us into the jungle crown using pulleys and ropes. There, among the decomposing nests of a dragon colony, they'd feed us limb by limb to sharp-toothed hatchlings.

The Djimbi did that. Oh, *we* knew. Didn't matter what the adults would or wouldn't admit. We knew. The Djimbi loved feeding children to hatchlings. They did it to tame the hatchlings, see, and accustom them to the Djimbi scent.

Then, when the hatchlings were sated, they would touch them. Sure, sure they would. Stroke the hatchlings' scaled heads and gristle-packed crops and cool, dirty bellies. They'd reach beneath their whip-thin tails and slowly insert fingers where fingers shouldn't go, then tongues and cocks and whatever else our imaginations could come up with. . . .

There's some truth to all that.

That's what titillated us and repulsed us and fueled our terrible, terrifying fantasies.

It was not only we children who feared the Djimbi, though. The Archipelagic people—the Emperor's Own—also feared them, their fear based not just on stories of kidnap, cannibalism, and bestiality, but on cultural prejudices.

Understand, five hundred years ago, when the blond-haired Xxeltekers first crossed the glacial range that separates their nation from Malacar, they flourished as nomads upon Malacar's fertile plains and never once caught sight of the Djimbi, for the Djimbi live solely in the rain forest. Indeed, the Mottled Bellies weren't discovered until 130 years later, when Emperor Wai Soomi-kun from the Archipelago launched a concerted coastal invasion upon Malacar's shores, and in doing so entered the jungle.

Without discrimination, the Emperor's warriors raped women they came across from both the Xxelteker and Djimbi tribes. Those bastards born from the loins of raped Djimbi women stubbornly bore the mottled green-and-brown pigmentation of their mothers, while those born from the loins of Xxelteker nomads bore pale ivory skin. These latter children were deemed acceptable of recognition by some of those who had sired them; the Xxelteker nomads were soon absorbed by the Archipelagic invaders.

It did not take long—seventy years or so—for the notion to flourish that the ivory-skinned children of those invaders were Malacar's true natives. The Djimbi, with their bizarre pigmentation that was so difficult to breed out, with their incomprehensible jungle culture, their singsong language, and their intimacy with dragons, were viewed as subhuman intruders.

Thereafter, pockets of Malacar were invaded many times by various island tribes. Indeed, the land was not yet called Malacar, but was known by numerous names, depending upon which people you spoke with, where, during which decade. From coast to mountain range, from jungle valley to fertile plain, the nation was peppered with slowly diverging cultures. But throughout, revulsion toward the Djimbi remained constant.

Two hundred and seventy years after the first Xxelteker nomads, the great Zarq Car Mano united the various cultures and peoples of the land into the nation it is today: Malacar, the Land of Iron. However, little changed for the Djimbi under Car Mano's rule, and they remained as elusive and reviled as ever.

Even the great Car Mano could not prevent the warlike, millennia-established peoples of the Archipelago from coveting our land. A mere sixty years after the forging of our nation, the Archipelago once again invaded Malacar, this time under the direction of Emperor Wai Fa-sren. Using a formidable militia fortified by his own brand of religious doctrine, Emperor Wai Fa-sren soon conquered Malacar. He ruled by means of a rigid theocratic dictatorship: Ranon ki Cinai. The Temple of the Dragon.

The landed gentry favored by Emperor Wai Fa-sren—those with the strongest allegiance to the Emperor, wealth in their coffers, and easily traced Archipelagic ancestry—soon rose to various levels of power. Known as bayen, aristocrats of First-Class Citizenship, their prosperity, status, and political sway soon separated them from the bulk of the populace. Only they were allowed to own dragons.

One hundred seventy years later, when I was but nine, Emperor Wai Fa-sren's successor continued to rule Malacar by means of the Temple. As a rishi, a Clutch-born unindentured serf, I was almost at the lowest level of Temple hierarchy. But there was one group of people considered much lower than mine.

The Djimbi.

I was lucky indeed that my skin was like my father's and showed none of the pigmentation of my Mottled Belly mother.

I awoke just before dawn on the day following that memorable Mombe Taro. I was back in the danku women's barracks, the domicile where women and children of the pottery clan slept. I didn't remember being carried back. I *did* recall Mother whispering something odd in my ear, though, something like "Run ever, my Zarq. Run fast."

Dream nonsense.

Predawn is a dusky time, a watery otherworld moment suspended between light and dark. Edges are blurred. Everything looks liquid. Back then, on that morning, I kept still, savoring the calm.

My reed sleeping mat, which at night was furred with old sweat and stuck like honey to my body, now felt clean and crisp and smooth. Waisi's arm felt cool where it touched mine, not thick with fleshy heat. The night had transformed the snores and farts and whines of a barrackful of women and children into light, even breaths. No crickets stirred within the walls, no cockroaches skittered over the raised wooden floor. Outside, stars melted into murk while dew silently beaded huts, temples, and stables alike. Gray silence reigned, cool air its consort.

The stillness was so rare I couldn't feast enough on it. I didn't just listen to it; I drank it in through every pore.

Then a flametail gave its signature *tee-tee-wheet!* from the jungle. A pause, then it repeated its cry. Its soliloquy continued for a short time before another flametail joined in.

The dense gray around me lightened to a pale ash. Someone stirred and coughed to my left. A basabird screeched. Abruptly, the entire jungle erupted into raucous birdsong.

I groaned and sat up.

I saw my hand, caked with cloth bandages stained yellow. In a rush I remembered the previous day: the dragonmaster, the race, the whip thrust into my palm. Today—the day following Mombe Taro—was Sa Gikiro.

My heart skipped like a bead of water dropped upon a red-hot skillet. I grabbed Waisi's arm in terror. "Wake up, wake up! Day of Doom!"

She groaned in her sleep.

"Waisi, the dragonmaster will pick me for sure. He'll see my hand and remember me and pick me—"

"Shut up, Zarq," she growled, and rolled away from me. "Don't be such a shitball. You're a *girl*."

I was a girl. Ergo, I was safe. I stared at her long braids and wondered what had come over me.

"Paak time, Waivia," Mother mumbled from her mat beside me. When she called Waisi by her proper name, Waivia, she meant business. At all other times she called my sister by the fond diminutive Waisi, as did I. "Hey-o, girls, *up* you get."

Others stirred, too. The mothers of young men rose quickly. As one, they knelt, folded arms behind backs, foreheads pressed to the ground, in Supplication to a Dragon position, and started chanting.

Their drones drew the air out of the barracks and replaced it with tension. Some of the babies started to whimper.

I rolled up my mat, eager to be out of there.

"What's all the fuss for?" Waisi said grumpily, rubbing sleep pebbles from her eyes. "The dragonmaster never comes into this zone, anyway."

"He *might*," I said, but low, so the chanting mothers couldn't hear me; the last thing they needed was their fears spoken aloud. "There's always a chance he might."

Waisi dismissed the possibility with a disdainful wave of her hand, hauled herself to her feet, and trudged before me, down the worn wooden stairs of the women's barracks, into our compound's court-yard. The red dust of the courtyard smelled rich with dew, and at our approach a flock of tiny mitewings burst from the ground, into the sky. Although the sun had not yet crested the eastern jungle ridge, the threat of its coming turned the air heavy with humidity. Waisi began unraveling her plaits as she walked.

"I hope the dragonmaster *does* come," she said. "I hope he comes and takes Dono out of here."

"Shhh!" I hissed, and pointed at the humped mud huts directly across from us. They belonged to old Yeli; he and his sons, including Dono, all lived within. "They're probably awake."

"So?" Waisi sniffed. She lowered her voice, though, not so brave as to express her opinion within earshot of men. "It's so stupid. While the women are praying our zone won't be visited, the men are praying it will. Do you think my hair is beautiful?" She shook out her thick hair and wrapped it about her bosom. "My breasts are going to be bigger than Mama's. Not like *you*. That's what you get for being named after a man."

I didn't like to be reminded of my angular figure and masculine name, and tried to draw the conversation back to the significance of the day. She would have none of it.

"Soggy Carrot Day," she said, deliberately mispronouncing the Emperor's tongue.

As we hitched the wooden paak ramp to its barrel, she mocked the solemnity of Choosing Day by listing in a singsong all the other names the day goes by: Dragonmaster's Snatch, Day of Re, Dawn of

Reckoning, Doomsday, and, of course, our favorite: Soggy Carrot Day, which, if pronounced correctly, is Sa Gikiro. Her litany annoyed me, not because of its irreverence, but because I envied her her clever sarcasm.

"You shouldn't laugh, Waisi. Sa Gikiro is *important*."

She made a rude noise with her lips and gestured at me to help lift the egg cradle. We bent, grunted, and hoisted the rusted egg cradle onto the mixing barrel and locked it into place.

"I know how important it is," she said, thumping a latch shut. "That's why I hope the dragonmaster *does* come and choose Dono as one of his new apprentices. I want some silk for a proper gown, and jewels—"

"I thought you liked Dono."

She shrugged.

"He could *die*, you know. Some of them do. Look what the venom did to my hand, and I hardly even touched the whip." I brandished my bandage under her nose and a flake of yellow landed on her foot.

"Does it still hurt?"

"It's kind of numb, like I slept on it all night."

She shrugged again. If I'd confessed to excruciating pain, that might have held her interest. Truth, the whole arm throbbed queerly, as if I'd whacked my elbow against a table corner. But there was no point in complaining; I wouldn't be relieved of work unless dying. A harsh reality of rishi life, that.

But Waisi's indifference piqued me, and as we walked toward the egg cellar, I voiced my indignation.

"You're not nice, Waisi, not *at all*. If Dono was one of the boys chosen, he'd be whipped at next year's Mombe Taro. He'd suffer, maybe die—"

"Shut up. You don't know anything. Little brat."

"Am not."

"Are too."

"Am—"

"Just think a bit, hey-o? All the men right now are praying the dragonmaster will choose a boy from our clan as apprentice, and why? 'Cause they know it'd improve our clan. We'd be rich *overnight*."

We entered the cellar; she banged the heavy wooden door closed behind us. I squinted in the darkness.

"So don't act like all the other pottery clan women," Waisi said contemptuously, "sniveling and carrying on like it would be a tragedy. Use your brain."

The cellar smelled of sour green featon chaff and earth that had never seen the light of day, a damp reek of slow decay and fat worms. In the gloom, the pumpkin-sized dragon eggs at the bottom of the cellar's steep earthen ramp huddled beneath their protective blanket of chaff. To me, those cloaked shadows looked sinister, half alive. The cellar scared me—

"She doesn't have a brain to uthe," a voice spat out of the dark. "Zarq'ths yolk headed."

I shrieked at the voice; Waisi merely crossed her arms over her chest.

"What are you doing here, Dono?"

A short, lithe shape rose from the eggs huddled at the bottom of the cellar.

"Waiting for you." A wheedling note crept into Dono's voice. "I thought I'd help you carry eggth—"

"I don't need your help," Waisi said curtly.

Dono started up the ramp toward us, hands outspread, lisp exacerbated by his wheedling. "Awww, don't thay that—"

"You didn't get me a whip, Dono."

"I'll make it up to you."

"I'm not keeping my part of the deal. You can forget all about that."

Dono stopped before us, an ingratiating smile upon his narrow face. "You can't back out now. I've told everyone—"

"Once a year, Dono, once a year. That's how often Mombe Taro takes place. When else am I going to have the chance to impress a bayen lordling, hey-o? You ruined it, so you're *not* going to get anything from me."

"You know what'll happen to me if you don't do thith? You know what they'll say?"

"I don't care."

"It's your sister's fault, not mine. That was my whip—"

"Hey! I won that whip fairly," I cried indignantly, forgetting completely that Dono was considered a man and his word was therefore not to be refuted. "I was fastest. I reached the dragonmaster before you."

"I could beat you any day," Dono said, his face undergoing a rapid change.

"But you didn't beat me yesterday, did you?" I said hotly. "So the whip was mine. Not yours, *mine*."

"You cheated. No girl beatth a man. Ever."

I should have kept my mouth shut; I could not.

"Even the dragonmaster said I was faster than you," I said, hands on hips. "I've *always* been faster than you—I've just always let you think you're faster. So there."

Dono glared at me, quivering with fury. Then his arm shot out, slender and smooth as a bark-stripped twig, and his fist landed deep in my belly.

I doubled over; couldn't breathe, couldn't scream, couldn't move. Then I drew in a breath and pain roared across my abdomen. Dono dug his fingers into my bristle-brush hair, yanked my head back, and landed a stinging blow across my face.

I shouldn't have fought back; I did.

I clawed at his eyes, shrieking, felt skin shred under my nails. He kicked my legs out from under me. I landed hard on my rump, reached for his ankle to yank him down. But his foot landed in my ribs, then against a kidney, then in my belly.

I scrambled away, went sprawling down the ramp into the shadows, my teeth jagging through my lower lip. I thudded against the eggs huddled at the cellar's bottom; featon chaff lifted into the air and settled about me.

"Leave her alone!" Waisi shouted, and from where I lay, stunned and hurting all over, I watched two silhouettes grapple at the top of the cellar ramp, backlit by the nimbus of light shining from the cellar door.

The two figures parted, chests heaving. The smaller, thinner of the two flicked his thumbnails against his throat in a gesture of insult.

"You think you're so fine, danku Re Waivia, with your big ass and big tits? You think an aristocrat is going to claim you and get you out of here? Not a chance. You're kiyu material, born to be a sex slave. A lowly rishi Djimbi whore."

"Get out of here, Dono," my sister growled. "Get out of here before I tear your puny balls off with my teeth."

He held a finger before her face. "You'll beg me to claim you one day. You'll thee."

He whirled, yanked open the cellar door, and disappeared into the blinding morning light. After a moment, Waisi descended the ramp. I started sobbing.

"Stop your sniveling! You don't see me crying, do you? *Zarq*. Boy without a penis."

I bit my lip and held my breath as she knelt before me. Why was she angry at *me*? But angry she was; she radiated heat and fury as she stared down at me.

"I'll make this easy for you, hey-o?" she spat out. "You take what I want, I hurt you. You hurt me back, and I hurt you worse. Understand?"

I didn't.

"Do you?" she said brittlely.

I nodded, kept nodding as she flared her nostrils, sucked in a breath, and rose to her feet. "Fine. Let's see if you broke any eggs."

I obeyed, moving jerkily upon my knees, a wooden puppet completely unable to think for itself, let alone identify a cracked egg. But I went through the motions nonetheless, shuffling through the featon chaff, seeking sticky goo. Waisi likewise went from one egg to the next. Finally, she straightened and nodded: no leaking albumen present.

"Get up, then," she said. Not unkindly. Her voice, if anything, was husky with unshed tears. "We've got paak to make."

Waisi pushed a wheelbarrowful of dragon eggs uphill in silence. I trudged after her, in a daze.

Once outside the cellar, we both stopped, blinking in the rosy yellow of early morning. I felt as if I'd climbed out of a night terror that had turned, mid-dream, into reality.

I glanced at Waisi. Her cheeks looked like roasted coranut shells, shiny teak brown, and her eyes stared straight ahead. Sweat beaded her neck and bosom as if she had coughing fever. I looked away.

Over by the cluster of mud-brick huts where the Leishu men slept stood Mother and Leishu's Caan. The two women worked in rhythm, thumping their long wooden pestles into narrow barrels as they ground featon grit into flour for Sa Gikiro holy cakes. My playmates, Rutvia and Makvia, were barely visible among the muay fronds of our First Garden; the plants swayed as the twins crawled about, popping yellow maggots between their thumbs. Their mother, Kobo's Dash, was crouched in her usual spot at the garden's southern end, grinding sesal nuts into paste. Nearby, Korshan's Rutkar shoved eggshell and muay fodder through the bars of the hutches that contained our meat source, the lizardlike renimgars.

Normality reigned.

It confounded me that everything looked ordinary despite what had just occurred in the cellar. Surely, *everyone* should have been affected by the aura of violence and upheaval coming from the cellar's dank depths. . . .

"Come on," Waisi said, and I hastily obeyed.

We pushed the egg barrow over to the paak-making nook at the northern end of the women's barracks, then placed the five eggs we'd collected into the snug depressions in the cradle we'd earlier latched atop the paak barrel.

Waisi lifted the corak off its wall hook, while I fished a hard curl of pallum bark from the dusty urn that perpetually sat in the paak-making nook. I crouched on the ground and began grating the bark into a fine red powder, my belly knotted with emotion, nausea threatening with each wave of pain that radiated from where Dono had landed his blows.

"I'll show him," Waisi growled. "I'll get out of this place one day." And she stabbed the corak into the base of an egg.

She withdrew the instrument smoothly and swiftly, the triangular prongs of the corak leaving behind three neat holes. Not a single shard of shell broke off into the barrel; she was good at stabbing, Waisi. Albumen began thudding into the barrel in heavy ropes as she stabbed all five eggs.

"I'm going to be a pleasurer, the most famous in all of Malacar—"

"A pleasurer?" I squeaked. "You?"

Her dark eyes turned as moody as the jungle in twilight. The corak in her hand twitched.

"You don't think I'm pretty, little brat?"

I did not. Pretty is light, sweet, pleasing. Waisi was none of that. She was a full moon and dark shadows, a she-cat in heat, all claws and swollen vulva.

Her hair lay thick and motionless to her rump until the sunlight caught it, whereupon it blazed mahogany and gold. I'd seen men stop stupid with the sight of Waisi's hair in full sunlight, and they always stumbled away as though drunk. Greatfather Maxmisha himself walked straight into a wall once after coming upon Waisi bent broad hipped and flame haired over the paak molds.

And that was just her hair.

Her eyes were as black as a burnished smoke-fired jug, yet excitement could light candles behind them, whereupon they gleamed a gold-flecked russet. Her lips were like the marinated chilies we brought to temple on holy days, red and plump with honeyed vinegar. Her skin looked as warm and tasty as a fresh holy cake. She moved as if boneless.

No, I did not think her pretty. She was another word altogether, one that wasn't even in my nine-year-old vocabulary. But I was wise enough not to say so.

Dry mouthed, I merely husked, "I wish I looked like you."

She bent and hugged me. I winced as she pressed against my angry bruises, but all Waisi did was squeeze once more, release me, and return the corak to its hook on the wall. She crouched on the ground beside me and began chopping chilies on a slab of granite stained red from caustic juice. She didn't care that her embrace had caused me pain. Just like she didn't care about leaving me, leaving to become a sex slave.

I didn't understand. Why would she *want* to be kiyu?

Even I had overheard enough chat in the pottery shed to know what abject misery such a girl suffered, locked permanently in kiyu stables, a disdained plaything for dozens of men, none of whom belonged to her clan. Death came when the stinking mass of mating pustules in her womb turned gangrenous. Death came sooner if she was successful at suicide. . . .

I burst into sobs.

"What is wrong with you *now?*" she asked, throwing down her chili knife in exasperation.

"I don't want you to go," I blubbered. "You'll die. All kiyu die—"

"Kiyu!" She sprang to her feet. "Who said anything about kiyu?"

"You said—"

"I really think you're intentionally stupid, I really do." She rapped my forehead. Her hands smelled bitter and tangy from the chilies. "Try to *think*."

"I'm trying—"

"I'm not going to die a dirty serf, Zarq, no matter what Dono said. I'm going to be Wai-ebani bayen, a private pleasurer for an aristocrat. Not *kiyu*. I'll leave this vomit pit far behind."

Her lower lip puckered, and her front teeth—white, even, and the envy of the pottery clan—bit down on it. They sank deeper. Deeper. My pulse sped up.

"Wai-ebani bayen," she said, though it sounded like a threat, not an ambition. "Foremost First-Citizen Pleasurer. That'll be me."

She gestured at the eggs sitting in the cradle on the barrel. "Help take these off."

My hands shook as we removed the albumen-drained eggs from the cradle and placed them gently in the wheelbarrow, careful not to break the yolks still whole within the shells. Korshan's Limia came over, her baby cradled snugly upon her back in the cowl of her bitoo, and wheeled away the yolk-filled shells.

I tried to picture Waisi as an ebani.

Understand, an ebani is *not* like an Archipelagic concubine. An ebani lives in the women's barracks of her claimer's clan, or, if an ebani's claimer is an aristocrat, she lives in the women's wing of his mansion. Unlike a concubine, she retains no independence nor receives lucre for services performed; she therefore doesn't have to worry about water taxes, building tithes, or other such tawdry fiscal details.

And unlike a concubine, any child an ebani accidentally bears with her claimer is legitimate, though far lower in status than the children begotten from the claimer's household roidan yins. Some bayen men claim upwards of five or six women as roidan yins, or gardens of children, so as to produce many children; that is a roidan yin's duty, after all, to beget children.

An ebani, on the other hand, is expected to produce only devotion, allegiance, and exquisite pleasure. In my limited nine-year-old's point of view, I could not see proud, temperamental Waisi doing a very good job at that.

And, too, there was the rather large hurdle of her status: she was rishi, a freeborn Clutch serf. Very few aristocrats claimed a rishi as their ebani. There were too many fine young women from aristocratic households to fill such a station.

Waisi worked the lid off an urn of lime. I tossed my grated pallum bark into the barrel of albumen, and a spicy cloud puffed into my face. Waisi threw a bit of lime into the barrel, then added a generous amount of salt.

"Get the bung. Wipe your nose first, before it drips all over it," she ordered.

I dragged my bandaged hand across my face, leaving a smear of yellow poultice on my nose that made me feel cross-eyed. I hefted the slightly rancid-smelling cork bung onto its side and rolled it, wheel-like, over to the barrel. Together we lifted off the egg cradle and thumped the bung into its place, effectively closing the hole.

I stood next to her, and for once pulled my weight as we both grasped the leather straps on the barrel's sides and tipped the barrel over. The straps creaked, our arms strained, and then *thump!* The barrel thudded onto the ground.

We began rolling it between us, finding the necessary rhythm and the right distance from each other to keep the barrel in constant motion. The albumen within sloshed through and rattled the waffle grids slatted in different sections of the barrel's midriff.

"Kiyu," Waisi snorted in disgust. "I'm going to be far better than that, little Zarq. Despite your mess yesterday, I'll still get his attention. I'll still be claimed as his ebani."

I wondered if I dared speak. *What* mess? And who would claim my sister as First-Citizen Pleasurer, who?

My expression must have asked the question for me. Waisi laughed.

"You want to know who'll take me as Wai-ebani, don't you? I told you already. Yesterday."

The moment she said that, I saw again eyes like lapis lazuli beneath long, flaxen hair. I saw again a sun-bronzed arm wielding a whip against a young boy's calves.

"Ah, you know who I mean," Waisi said, as realization flooded my face. "So some things *do* seep into that brain of yours! Say it, Zarq. Go on. Say it."

Obediently, I whispered, "The warrior-lord's First Son. Waikar Re Kratt. He'll claim you as Wai-ebani bayen."

She nodded, and her expression turned glutted and smug.

THREE

We finished making paak in silence, rolling the barrel until the albumen within whispered, indicating it had turned into froth. By then the soft pink of dawn had turned into the bright, hard yellow of full morning; we sweated freely, and my bandaged hand throbbed. Mother helped grease the long, rectangular paak molds with gharial oil, fill them with our frothy paak mixture, and carry them to the kilns where embers still glowed from firing ceramics two days previous. Usually Waisi and I did such alone. That morning we were running behind.

Small wonder.

All the pottery clan men already milled about the courtyard, exchanging greetings. Their limbs shone from the palm oil they'd rubbed into their skin. Two women set out tureens of sesal nut paste before them, followed by platters of another day's paak, cold and neatly sliced.

It's what we ate every morning, every day, every season: dragon eggs, in one form or another. Unfertilized dragon eggs, understand; the eating of dragon flesh is forbidden to all but a dragon, and a fertilized egg is considered dragon flesh.

Evening meal was the same as what we ate in the morning, paak and sesal nut paste, with the addition of yanichee soup, rishi style: the yolk boiled into threads instead of fried, and floating in a broth made from renimgar meat and the ubiquitous green muay leaves found in every Malacarite serf's diet.

Oh. And featon grit.

Yes, we ate those kernels fed to brooder dragons. Hard as pebbles, they were, yet we ate them. Morning and noon soaked in water, at night, in yanichee. A lean diet, or so I thought in my youth. But experience would teach me that although the pottery clan had little variety, our cellars were never empty and our bones were strong and straight, and that such could not be said of others living a life of labor elsewhere. Really, we were well fed. By rishi standards.

Dono glared at me as Mother and I joined the women and children settling around the outskirts of the men, who by now had seated themselves upon the swept courtyard floor. To Waisi, Dono gave a look of mingled anger and appeal. She ignored him.

Moments later, Greatfather Maxmisha cleared his throat.

I craned my neck to see his wiry figure in the center of the men, for I loved how the growth above his left ear wobbled when he talked. It was a horrible thing, the size of a fist. On cool Wet Season mornings, he wrapped a turban around it.

"I'm waiting for wings to bless the herd of Re," he rasped.

"May your waiting end. May the wings hatch," everyone replied.

Ritual greeting out of the way, he nodded to Father and blood-Uncle Rudik, who served him a large slice of paak spread thickly with sesal paste. He took a bite, grimaced as was his wont, and the rest of the men began eating. Mother fidgeted, as impatient as the youngest children. When all the men had served themselves, we began to eat. Mother shamelessly took two slices of paak. I was not so brave and stuck to my one, augmented by a bowl of grit and water.

Greatfather Maxmisha tottered to his feet and began the Proclamation before my grit was properly soaked, so I had to swallow the mess down while it was still hard. Again, Mother didn't bother with protocol, nor did the women who needed the grit thoroughly softened for their babies. Greatfather always overlooked those transgressions, whether from empathy or myopia, I don't know. I suspect myopia. He wasn't the empathetic sort, Greatfather.

"Today is Sa Gikiro," he husked. "Our clan will perform this to please the dragon: We'll go to temple, we'll return, we'll burn offerings. A work party will slash vines while chosen potters make coil bottles: symmetrical, bayen quality, to be smoke fired."

A groan went through all present. Smoke-fired bottles took several painstaking days to complete, especially ones of bayen quality, and slashing vines from our compound's outer walls for fuel was hot, hard work. The only person pleased was Mother. She flushed and beamed. She loved working in the jungle and focusing afterward on the intricate work of creating a coiled bottle fit for aristocrats.

Even at age nine, I knew Greatfather must have chosen that Proclamation to please her, for she only obeyed his Proclamations if they suited her. By choosing a Proclamation she'd like, he'd guaranteed that no defiance of his dragon-directed will would occur on holy Sa Gikiro. It made me uneasy, understanding that, yet I didn't know why.

The Proclamation over, the men rose, stretched, and returned to their respective huts. Usually, a trail of pipe smoke followed them, but temple demanded abstinence on Sa Gikiro, so that day the air smelled sweet.

Twisted Foot Ryn's brood gathered the empty food bowls and platters and scurried over to the washing corner to scrub them down. Leishu's Caan set to sweeping the courtyard smooth again. The rest of us returned to the women's barracks and readied ourselves for the trek to temple. The mothers of young children carried bowls of soaking grit discreetly tucked under a fold of their bitoos.

"Hey-o, Zarq," Mother sang, bending to link an arm through one of mine. "Vine-slashing day! We'll have fun, no?"

The last thing I felt like doing was swinging a scythe through insect-laden vines. But loath to dampen Mother's pleasure, I nodded.

Mother and I always accompanied the slashing parties, her to comb the outskirts of the jungle for medicinal barks and pigment sources, and I to do the miserable work of a young boy. Boyhood was always the gender ascribed me when my nimble arms and legs were needed to ease the workload of those with a genuine claim to the male sex.

Mother loved picking through the jungle's edge and often consumed the most embarrassing things with great relish. Olingo termites and the translucent goo inside brallosh leaves, for instance. Today her pleasure was increased knowing that when she returned from vine slashing, a dozen coiled bottles would await her in the pottery shed, made by hands unwilling to tackle the intricate designs the aristocrats desired on their ceramics.

As we climbed the barrack steps, Waisi tossed her hair. "You wouldn't catch me joining a work party. *Ever*."

Mother laughed. " 'Course not, Waisi! No girls allowed. Only our Zarq."

"And you," Waisi said accusingly.

"Close your fast lips," Big Grum Grum's Li said over her shoulder. "Talk so much and you'll get someone in trouble."

She was wise, Big Grum Grum's Li.

But Mother just winked at Waisi and said serenely, "We need fresh dyes and pigments. Someone who knows the proper things to gather must go search jungle's edge. Sacrilege, to make temple tiles with lackluster colors; only fresh will do."

Mother's serenity faltered while cleaning my face with a spittle-dampened corner of her bitoo. "Where-how these bruises, little one?"

"I hit her," Waisi immediately responded, not pausing as she brushed her hair to an enviable sheen. "She was capering about the egg cellar. Wouldn't stop. Almost broke an egg. I slapped some sense into her."

Mother clucked reproachfully at me. "You know better than that, Zarq. Ah, child. Now let me see your hand."

I held it out, and she unwrapped the crusty bandage. The center of my palm was a little bubbly and oily, like the deep-fried renimgar skin I so loved.

"Kiiiyew!" Waisi made the Malacarite sound of disgust that's also the term for the sex slaves whose wombs end up stinking from pus. "No man will claim you for sure now."

"By chance, our Zarq won't need a man, hey-o?" Mother said as she washed and dressed my palm with an unguent. "Maybe she'll claim herself."

"Nonsense," Waisi sneered, but Mother tweaked my nose as if we shared a secret.

The woven-reed walls of the barracks suddenly shook and rattled from a gust of wind. Odd, that, for the weather was hot and still, and at once my pulse accelerated with dread, an instinctual reaction shared by any creature experiencing an unnatural and sudden change in the climate, and Mother's hands fell still upon my new bandages, and we all in the barracks held our breath.

Hurricane?

From the courtyard came a peculiar flapping sound, growing rapidly louder, somewhat like wind through palm fronds, but not clearly demarcated as such. Then a hail of men's voices, the excited cries of young boys. Commotion. A baffling, explosive snorting sound. More voices.

All of us within the women's barracks stared at the woven-reed walls, breath held, limbs tensed. Footsteps thudded up the barrack stairs. . . .

My playmates, Rutvia and Makvia, burst inside, babbling and gesturing wildly.

". . . Outside, in the courtyard, they flew here—"

". . . Speaking to Greatfather right now—"

". . . On a *winged* dragon!"

A pause as this disjointed information sank in, then we all rushed to the barrack doors and pushed and jostled for a view. The sight that greeted us caused many to stuff fists into mouths and rear back, eyes wide with alarm.

A magnificent yearling dragon fretted in our courtyard's center, green- and rust-colored scales as glossy as enamel despite the clouds of dust stirred up the leathery, claw-tipped wings folding and refolding nervously along its flanks. The beast dwarfed our courtyard, its long, twiggy tail with diamond-shaped membrane at the end brushing the ground in front of the mating shack, its oval body, higher at shoulder than some of our men, reaching halfway across the courtyard's length.

Two strangers stood either side the yearling's arrow-shaped snout, wicked muzzle poles hooked through the dragon's nostrils to hold it steady. Even had the winged dragon not been present, it was obvious the two men were bayen; the shiny black of their knee-high boots, the rich turquoise and generous cut of their pantaloons, and the artfully unlaced fronts of their white silk shirts were unmistakably the garments of First Citizens, of Clutch aristocrats. Of bayen.

One of the two appeared to be concerned only with the dragon, from what little I could see of him behind the yearling's neck and bluish dewlaps, for he looked at none but the dragon and spoke steadily to it. But the other aristocrat ignored the dragon completely and instead gestured to one of our clan men to take his muzzle pole. The chosen man—Big Grum Grum—came forward with spine stiff from fear of the dragon. Neck locked and eyes glassy, he took hold of the proffered muzzle hook and stood straight as a temple spire.

With the repose of the truly privileged, the lordling sauntered toward Greatfather Maxmisha, strolling as casually through the dusty courtyard as if through an immaculate garden. Greatfather bowed low even as he tottered forward to meet the young lord.

I recognized him at once, that nonchalant, flaxen-haired young man. As did every woman crammed in the barrack's doorway.

The First Son of the warrior-lord of our Clutch. Waikar Re Kratt.

Striking a lazy pose that best showed the sun-browned muscles visible beneath his unlaced shirt, Waikar Re Kratt spoke with our Greatfather. He spoke briefly, gestured once with his chin at the women's barracks, whereupon we all shrank back into shadow. Greatfather bobbed his head. Bowed. Gestured brusquely for a boy to approach, whereupon he barked an order at him. The boy immediately whirled and ran toward our barracks.

With an alarmed murmur, we all fell back from the doorway. The boy clattered up the stairs and darted inside, eyes huge and shiny with excitement. He was a resident of the barracks, and not yet having reached manhood, could therefore so readily enter our domicile.

"Danku Re Darquel's Waivia," he barked. "Come forward!"

A collective intake of breath; ice water in my veins.

With a slow, hip-heavy walk, my sister pushed by the young boy and went outside. She stood there a moment in the sunlight, lush and flame haired, every limb replete somehow with indecency. Then she slowly descended the stairs and approached Waikar Re Kratt.

We all surged toward the doorway again, whispering and exchanging flushed looks. Not so flustered was our Waisi, not flustered in the least. She cat-walked toward Kratt as though she owned time and sunlight itself.

He remained in his casual stance, not a muscle flicking. But something in the air changed, all right. Oh yes. Something in the air changed. The tension was nigh on unbearable.

Waisi stopped several feet away from Kratt. I held my breath; would she not get on her knees and kowtow?

She would.

Slowly, with a sensuality that made me squirm, she knelt. She moved in a way that was as titillating as if she were unclothing herself for a mating. She was not submitting to this lordling, no. As she knelt with face pressed to earth, her fine, full rump and her lush hips high, her too-short bitoo exposing her long, smooth legs, she was taunting the lordling. Mocking him with all that she possessed.

Then she rose to her feet. Tossed her flaming hair. Lifted her chin at him—yes! she did!—and turned away. Walked back to the barracks with that rolling gait of hers that no man could ignore.

Kratt watched her as she mounted the stairs, watched her as she entered our barracks. The women gathered at the doorway pulled back as she came in, stepped away from her, aghast and dumbfounded by her outrageous behavior. Waisi sailed through them as if they did not exist. She returned to where she'd been kneeling, readying herself for temple, and continued to comb her magnificent hair as if nothing untoward had occurred.

My attention snapped back to Kratt. Unlike the other women, I'd not moved an inch from my post at the door. So I saw his reaction to Waisi's departure, and it chilled me to the marrow and aroused me, both.

He smiled, a lazy, feral smile that grew slowly and lingered. His eyes, so blue, so piercing, remained intently upon the barracks for several heartbeats. Oh, to be looked at that way!

Then he returned to the dragon.

Whatever words he exchanged with his peer were curt; within moments, the two were upon the yearling's back, muzzle hooks telescoped small and notched in the thick leather belts at their waists. Kratt sat in the fore, upon the dragon's stout neck, reins in hand; his friend sat directly behind him. I say *sat*, but in fact they half lay upon the dragon, so that Kratt's companion looked to be embracing Kratt while half lying atop him.

How would they get the yearling airborne with no space for the beast to run and launch itself upward?

By beating it, of course.

With a bamboo crop that cracked like a thunderclap against the yearling's neck, Kratt caned the yearling. The yearling flapped its vast wings, lashed its tail, reared up, and clawed the air with talons as thick as my arm and as bright as new steel. Dust billowed up, red and gritty. The yearling trumpeted. Kratt caned the beast once more, holding tight onto the reins, keeping its head back. Those great claw-tipped wings beat the air into a dusty gale; I squinted, held my breath, clung hold the doorframe as my bitoo snapped about my body.

Then *whoosh!* Kratt gave the dragon its head and the beast sprang upward. It was airborne.

It seemed impossible, a miracle, a feat of skill that only a demon could possess, that Kratt had launched the dragon skyward in such a small space. Now I know that the warrior-lord's yearlings are rigorously trained to do just such a thing, for use in combat, but back then, at age nine, I was unencumbered by knowledge. The miracle of seeing such a beast burst into flight was all that I knew.

And, of course, the marvel of the warrior-lord's First Son coming to view my sister, in our humble clan compound.

FOUR

After washing ourselves thoroughly, we potters set out for our zone's temple, the men carrying bamboo boxes filled with warm holy cakes, the women carrying urns of fermented chilies.

Of course, we were all abuzz with the unprecedented visit of Roshu-Lupini Re's First Son to our compound. The honor! The distinction! The fame! Everyone looked at my sister anew, though not necessarily with friendly intent; her behavior had been reprehensible; what had she been thinking? Mother berated her loud enough for all to hear.

"What did you, turning back upon Waikar Re Kratt so? What good comes of that, hey-o?"

"I know what I'm doing, Mother," Waisi said coolly. "I got his attention in the first place, didn't I?"

"But Waivia, this opportunity . . ."

Waisi's look silenced Mother. But we all knew what Mother had been about to say.

Although Waikar Re Kratt could pluck my sister from our clan and claim her as his ebani without recompensing us in the slightest for her loss, the fame garnered for danku, our pottery clan, would increase our status immeasurably. Temple would favor us in market transactions; rival clans would defer to us, seek our council, pay higher for our wares; men throughout our Clutch would view our young women as highly desirable. Having a clan woman in the household of the Roshu-Lupini would bring no end of esteem to us, certain.

However, if Waisi were chosen as a kiyu to join the warrior-lord's stables, she'd be just one more forgettable girl doomed to sexual slavery.

Waisi seemed not in the least concerned with this latter possibility.

She walked with head high, chin up. I was in awe of her. I knew word was spreading quickly through our sor about Waikar Re Kratt's visit.

Every Clutch is divided into trade zones, or sors. Each sor is comprised of a temple and a market square, around which various clan compounds have been built. Clutch Re was no different. The pottery clan compound was situated in the Zone of Precious Baubles, or, in the Emperor's Tongue, Wabe Din Sor. The trades practiced in our zone were regarded as frivolous by clans elsewhere in Clutch Re. For reasons unknown, only the leather tanners' clan had escaped the undeserved taint, though I ask you, why should an amphora for oil be considered frivolous when a leather loincloth was not?

Walls are necessary on a Clutch, not just to separate clan from clan. Jungle cats and feral dogs hate walls, and if they venture within, they can readily be trapped and killed. Of course, no Clutch is comprised solely of walls; such a dense network of alleys exists only near each sor's temple. The sesal fields, the gharial basins, the Zone of the Dead . . . those are all vast, unwalled spaces. At nine, I didn't like even the thought of them. Walls I knew. Unenclosed space scared me.

We reached the temple before long. Immediately, our clan fractured and swelled the mass of people already circumnavigating the temple. Those born during the Season of Fire turned to circle the temple east to west, mimicking the rising sun, while those born during the Wet, the Season of Rains, walked in the opposite direction. Mother and Waisi, born during Inbetween, walked east-west but faced backward, to recognize the hardships of the seasons that followed and preceded theirs.

As I was a fire child, I walked beside them, also east to west. But I faced forward.

Like all temples throughout Clutch Re, Wabe Din Temple was more than a temple. It was a marketplace and well-water place. It was a place for schooling those lucky enough, and a place for flogging those unlucky. It was where the daronpuis, the Holy Wardens, lived in tiled and gilded grace, administrating, admonishing, and ruling our lives. And meditating. They did that, too, though in my nine years I'd never seen it.

As I walked, I kicked up as much dust as I could and spat with gusto, loudly echoing Waisi's repertoire of invective. The only time a female may curse while in the presence of men is while circumnavigating the temple, so we all cursed heartily. Even Mother defamed Re, our Clutch bull, so vigorously her face turned red as a fire-baked brick.

Those curses fool the evil kwano spirits into thinking a male dragon is worthless, and thus the evil ones left alone our bull, Re. But also much jockeying takes place during circumnavigation, as each person tries to follow his current antagonist, be it sister, uncle, or someone from a neighboring clan. It is very cathartic to scream expletives and kick dust at one's opponent under the guise of piety. Though some of the pious occasionally came to blows. From time to time.

"Stinking Djimbi afterbirth!"

The yell came from directly behind me. I turned, and a heartbeat before dust bit my eyes, I saw Dono glaring at me.

Blinded, I stopped and balled my knuckles into my eyes.

"Dragon-sucking Djimbi whore!" he yelled, and his foot connected with my knee. I almost went down; Mother's grip around my arm kept me upright.

"Keep walking," she ordered, and I knew by her tone that she realized the kick hadn't been accidental, that this wasn't the usual competition between me and my old playmate in our quest to create the most shocking expletives.

Blinking gritty tears, I obeyed. Dono followed right behind.

"Hatchling fondler! Jungle deviant—"

"Limp-dick fuckless cuckold!" I countered, but Mother shot a look at me that bade me be silent and not inflame Dono further. There was more than anger in Dono's voice. There was malice. I was badly bruised and still sore from his attack that morning; I wanted no repeat of his frightening fury. So I obeyed Mother's look and bit my tongue.

I didn't glance back after that. I tried to ignore Dono and failed. Waisi and Mother stationed themselves either side of me, while still walking backward, and hooked their arms through mine to prevent Dono from kicking my knee backs again.

It was a long circumnavigation, that one.

When at last it was complete, we entered the temple with visible relief. With one last bitter curse hurled after me, Dono separated from us to enter the men's section of the temple. He descended to the ground tier, as befitted his age, and sat among the eldest boys there.

Wabe Din Temple was an open structure roofed with domes. Pendentives allowed the square plan at ground level to carry a dome above. Wabe Din had just the three requisite domes: one to shelter the men, one for the holy fire, and one for the women. From the apex of the central dome, the altar chimney exited as a magnificent four-headed dragon that glared over our entire zone from its perch. Smoke billowed out its four mouths in the four compass directions.

Mother, Waisi, and I entered the temple under the central dome and descended its eight amphitheater tiers to the sunken floor. Mother lifted the lid off the urn she carried as we approached the altar fire. We stepped close, but not too close, crammed our hands into Mother's urn, and cast a fistful of marinated chilies onto the smoldering flames.

Fizzle, hiss, belch! Smoke that burned the lungs and made the eyes and nose stream spewed up to thank us. Already a pile of shriveled, charring chilies sprawled like a dismembered corpse upon the fire, creating a peppery vinegar reek. An acolyte about Waisi's age and riddled with oozing acne repeatedly hoisted a long fork into the fire and raked off the chili offerings into a row of seed-splotched buckets.

Coughing and sputtering against the sting of the burning chilies, and our wombs now cinai-blessed from our offering—for the chilies represented human ovaries, and the fire the blessing of the bull dragon—Mother, Waisi, and I ascended to a tier in the women's pendentive. We sat.

And waited.

Ack, how I hated the waiting! It went on and on while people came and went, while women threw chilies onto the fire and the acolyte raked them off again. Throughout, the temple daronpuis strolled from tier to tier, pendentive to pendentive, cracking dragon whips over our heads to remind us of our fealty and subservience to Re, and bellowing statutes aloud, some from rote and some reading scrolls. Each daronpu wore a clackron, the holy dragon mask with the large, flared mouth that amplifies and sends the wearer's voice booming through temple. Those words rolled over the whip snaps and the white noise of the crowd circumnavigating the temple.

Headache coming, as usual. Mouth dry, eyes and nose membranes outraged by the burning chilies.

Gong! Gong! Every here and there, a daronpu struck a gong and we women obediently picked up the urn of remaining chilies sitting at our feet and passed it to whomever sat next to us.

Gong! Gong! The men likewise passed around their bamboo boxes of holy cakes. Thus we spread harmony, goodwill, and wishes of fertility from clan to clan. All the time, my bandaged hand throbbed and occasionally twitched like a beheaded pigeon.

Still, we waited. Waited for a daronpu to notice Greatfather Maxmisha sitting stern and straight among the men crowded on the tiers in the men's pendentive. Only when Greatfather was acknowledged with a somber daronpu nod would he rise and leave temple, the rest of the pottery clan following.

It was that way always on holy days. One entered the temple at will and left so also, as the statutes were recited throughout the day until sundown. However, the daronpuis took note of who stayed until acknowledged, informed their temple superior, and chits were handed out accordingly on chit days.

I know what you think. Chits should be distributed according to how many goods and services each clan has provided to temple and Clutch. And so and so and so, I say! In an ideal world, perhaps. But no, we sat upon those hard tiers and waited, prisoner to the whims of masked daronpuis.

I played games while I waited. With my eyes I connected the thousands of three-dimensional porcelain palm fruits decorating the pendentive columns. I examined the finely chiseled stonework on the arcing dragon-neck chimney and the legs supporting the huge, raised fire altar. I concentrated on the cracks in the cobalt blue tiles covering the massive stone hood that gaped over the fire and directed the smoke up the chimney. I critically regarded the colored glass tesserae of the ground-floor mosaic.

I forgot it was Sa Gikiro.

I first became aware of the noise as a lack, and I came out of my reveries with a violent jerk, instantly cognizant of the tension throughout temple. Mother, Waisi, every man, woman, daronpu, and child sat or stood rigidly, and I felt as if I were the only one not holding my breath, so I did that, too.

The source of this collective tension was apparent: the cinai komikon. The dragonmaster was the only one now moving within the temple as he descended one tier, then another, humming. Or perhaps the humming was only blood rushing through my ears.

Subtle movement outside as word spread. The crowd inched forward, each individual eager to watch yet unwilling to draw attention from the dragonmaster, despite his unprecedented visit to our zone on Sa Gikiro, despite the fact that this visit offered a chance for a clan to leap into prosperity if one or more boys should be chosen to apprentice to the dragonmaster. The reluctance stemmed from the knowledge that the chosen boys would be publicly flogged with dragon venom during next year's Mombe Taro, and suffer much worse should they survive. Much worse.

While everyone longed for the prosperity, no man wished such a fate upon himself or his sons.

So the crowd outside inched cautiously forward, an entity filled with trepidation, curiosity, and desperate hope. I felt hemmed in.

The dragonmaster stopped descending at the fifth tier in the men's pendentive and strolled along it, his every movement watched by the adolescents seated there. They watched as a mongoose watches a shadow that may be either rat or kwano snake, meal or death.

Suddenly, he stopped. Swatted the air once, twice, thrice. Crouched, then leapt upward with a blood-congealing roar. Midleap he spun, landing in the same spot yet facing the other direction, in the same half-crouch as he'd leapt from.

Several women shrieked. *I* shrieked. The boys seated nearest him jerked, poised to flee, to scramble away, to will themselves invisible. Or perhaps not. Perhaps I projected my fear onto them and read their wide, glistening eyes and open mouths and rapidly moving chests not as hope but as terror.

The dragonmaster remained crouched for several pulse beats, then tilted his head. This way. That way.

He's forgotten where he is, I thought, recognizing the manner of a dazed tree rat that has fallen to the ground.

Snap! The spell that held him broke, and once more he ambled along the tier, whistling. Yes, he *was* whistling.

He didn't seem to be examining the adolescents seated alongside him, yet all of a sudden he yanked one up by an earlobe. He prized the young man's mouth open, looked up his nose, pulled down his lower eyelids to examine the pink flesh underneath. His prey looked stunned stupid.

Judging by the glass bangles encircling the young man's biceps, I guessed he was a glass spinner's boy. I was right; the glass spinners in the women's pendentive shifted in barely suppressed excitement.

The young man was about Waisi's age and oddly shaped, with wide shoulders, a bulbous torso, and hairy arms that hung to bowlegs. Heavy flesh padded his rather pale frame, and that slack jaw of his threatened to catch flies.

"Dragon bait," Waisi breathed beside me, and from the corner of my eye, I saw her lip curl contemptuously. I knew what she meant: Here stood a boy being chosen merely as a toy for Re, our bull dragon. I refused to think of that seven-year-old boy at Mombe Taro. *Refused*.

The glass spinner's blocky frame was the exact opposite of the lithe, athletic kind needed to survive against a bull dragon, and he looked to not have the wits to know it. His apprenticeship would be short and his death spectacular and inevitable, witnessed by two hundred thousand Malacarites jeering at him from the stands of Arena.

If the dragonmaster chose him.

"You," the dragonmaster said, choosing him.

Just like that, a yolk-brained glass spinner picked as apprentice! Now his guild clan would be wealthy. Incredulity rippled round the temple. Would anyone else be picked from our zone? Would another clan be as lucky?

No.

The dragonmaster climbed the tiers to leave, to continue his search for apprentices in another part of our vast Clutch. He crooked one finger in the air for the yolk brain to follow him. The dazed glass spinner had to be nudged by a fellow to follow.

A cough sounded. Loud. Deliberate. Clear. The dragonmaster froze. *I* froze.

Again the cough, a throat-clearing summons from somewhere near the ground tier in the men's pendentive.

Slowly, the dragonmaster turned around.

His eyes darted to and fro, his nostrils flared; he tasted the air with the tip of his tongue. All right. Maybe he stood too far away for me to see all that, but this is what I imagined him doing as he stood brittlely tensed. The glass spinner also froze, having not moved more than two steps from where he'd been seated. His was a look of such utter bafflement that I wondered if he truly might be simple.

Cough.

My eyes shot to where the third cough had originated, and as fast as they moved, so too did the dragonmaster. He looked as tensile as a potter's cutting wire, as fluid as water, as he swiftly descended the tiers to stand before . . . whom? What boy had dared break the silence in temple, had deliberately drawn upon himself the cinai komikon's wrath? For I had no doubt that the youngster the dragonmaster now confronted was indeed the cougher. I doubt anyone else questioned it, either.

Beside me, Waisi sat straighter.

I think she was the first of all potters to realize who the boy was. In retrospect, I'm not surprised.

My name, Zarq, is an aberration for a girl.

To grasp the enormity of how strange the name is for a female, one must first understand how we name our babes in Malacar, and in every nation long under the Emperor's rule.

All sons upon birth are called First Son, Second Son, Third Son, and so on, or, in the Emperor's language: Wai Kar, Kazon Kar, and so forth. Naturally, the boy also takes the name of his father. He keeps that birth name until he loses all his milk teeth, whereupon he leaves the women's barracks and undergoes Tazik Masimutian, Call-the-

Name-Out Ceremony, during which all the men of his clan choose a name for him that reflects some trait, hoped for or existing, in the boy's nature.

For female babies, it is much the same.

A girl child, however, is not called a father's daughter. No such word exists in the Emperor's tongue. She is instead called so-and-so's girl, or via. That name is kept until the girl is claimed by a man, whence she is called so-and-so's whatever—desire, cook, temptress, and so forth.

So there you have it; the conventions that dictate how a Malacarite is named.

My name flouts these rules. Blatantly.

I was never called Kazon, though I was the second child to leave my mother's womb, and I was never via, or girl. I was Zarq. Zarq. That harsh, brusque Xxelteker name so common among Malacarite men.

In all the history of our pottery clan, and I daresay the nation of Malacar itself, never before had a girl been so named. When my mother gave birth to me and bestowed that travesty of a name upon me, another pottery clan woman was also laboring to push a babe into the world. A squalling boy was born the eve after.

Again, a strange naming took place, though not nearly as strange as mine.

The babe's mother died after a terrible labor, and because she was ebani-basa, a woman claimed as pleasurer by more than one man in our clan, no one could say for certain that the babe was Yeli's, as she'd stated. The boy was therefore referred to as Ebani-basa Caldekolkar. Caldekolkar: womb-ripping son. A terrible name to curse an innocent babe with.

You might think that, over time, the moniker would have been shortened. But not so, for boys will be boys, and when sensing a weakness in another, they will pounce; they reveled in calling Caldekolkar by his full, inglorious name: Womb-ripping son of a many-men pleasurer.

So in lieu of a father's name, the boy grew up with *ebani-basa* preceding his birth name. Not rare. Ebani-basas do conceive, after all. But such a name is not loved by any boy bearing so ignoble a title.

By the time both I and Ebani-basa Caldekolkar reached our fifth years, it became clear that the boy's mother had been correct: Yeli was the father. The wide, almost astonished eyes, the narrow face, the short legs, and restlessness of the boy all marked him as Yeli's get. And he resented his name with a hatred that surpassed the average child's loathing of a shameful parental burden.

So the days passed, and with each one Ebani-basa Caldekolkar yearned for the time when he could leave the women's barracks and be given his true name. He vowed to have his father's name precede it. I was sorry for how much he wished to leave the barracks, for he was an energetic playmate able to invent exhilarating games and increase the risk of old ones.

Then, when he was nearly seven, Ebani-basa Caldekolkar disappeared from our compound.

He returned at nightfall, his face ashen, his cheeks swollen, his chest soaked in blood. Not content to wait for his remaining milk teeth to fall out, and his name jeered at one too many times the day previous, he'd sequestered himself in the jungle's edge and pulled every remaining milk tooth from his mouth. Weak and triumphant, he returned to the pottery clan a man.

Infection set in, the kind so prevalent and feared by those who live in tropical climes. He was not expected to survive.

He wasted away, trapped in pus and delirium. The half-dozen adult teeth he'd had prior to extracting his milk teeth blackened and fell out. His fevered mutters haunted the women's barracks. I wept in fear nightly.

But, dragon blessed, his fever broke.

At the cusp of his seventh birthday, Ebani-basa Caldekolkar left the barracks and was given a mat in one of his father's huts. He was also given his true name: determined one. As vowed, he asked that his father's name precede it. His request was granted on the condition that he drop the paternal prefix when he claimed a woman of his own, for no adult man bears his father's name, and Yeli was uncomfortable with his seven-year-old man-child's request.

So my seven-year-old playmate entered manhood with the name Yeli's Determined One. In the Emperor's language: Yeli's Dono.

It was he, at age nine, who had summoned the dragonmaster before him with three assertive coughs.

The dragonmaster stood before Yeli's Dono, emanating fury. Dono rose to his feet slowly, moving as one does when one's bare foot has inadvertently come within inches of a kwano snake.

The dragonmaster bent a little, for Dono was short for his age, shorter than me by two knuckles. He breathed rage into Dono's face, and I imagined tremors shivering up the boy's legs. I knew what Dono stared into: unnatural eyes marbled white where no white should be.

Dono lifted a hand to his own face and coolly pulled a lower eyelid down. Demanding, silently, to be examined.

A still, giddy moment ensued as everyone absorbed his audacity. Then the dragonmaster threw back his head and roared. I shrieked and covered my eyes. My heart galloped several alley lengths before I realized the nature of the roar: laughter. The cinai komikon was laughing.

I looked at Mother and she at Waisi, and Waisi shrugged but could not conceal a fierce grin.

What? I wanted to ask, as indeed everyone in the temple wanted to shout, for they looked at one another nonplussed.

"Open your mouth!" the dragonmaster bellowed. Like an idiot, I opened mine. So did many within the temple, before we all snapped them shut again, feeling foolish.

"What's this? The gums of an infant?" the dragonmaster roared, and this time there was no humor in the bellow.

"No, komikon!" Dono shouted back, and his childish voice climbed clear to the domes. "Thith ith the mouth of one who didn't wait for time to make him a man. I pulled my milk teeth out two yearth ago; infection rotted the man teeth. A thmall price to pay for claiming my own manhood, hey-o."

Incredulity and astonishment touched every face, even those of the pottery clan, for although the story was familiar to us, the strength and arrogance in the boy's voice was brash and new. The dragonmaster threw back his head and roared a third time. My nerves, jangled about since morning, went taut as the wire a potter uses to slice through a block of clay.

"Sit down!" Mother scolded, jerking me back onto my seat, while Waisi simultaneously whispered, "She's *pissed* herself!"

The dragonmaster's laughter covered our noise, but still my cheeks burned with shame. Waisi shifted away from me. And I realized, with something akin to disappointment yet colored with relief, that the dragonmaster had turned his back on Dono without striking him dead. Indeed, he was walking away, leaving the pottery clan's orphan boy standing there, more naked than if his loincloth had fallen to the ground. He was still cackling, the dragonmaster, still chortling. . . .

Then, as he began to climb the temple tiers, he raised an arm.

Crooked a finger.

Beckoned.

Yeli's Dono had been chosen.

The yolk-brained glass spinner didn't know what to do; he remained oafishly in place until Dono ascended to his tier and clapped him on the back as if they were equals, which they were not; Dono was half the idiot's age and size. Dono then magnanimously gestured for the idiot to lead the way after the dragonmaster, who by then was parting the crowd outside.

"Re spare you, Ebani-basa Caldekolkar," Mother whispered, and I looked from Dono to her. Red rimmed her eyes and tears threatened her cheeks. She caught my look.

"I suckled him alongside you, Zarq. He's my milk son, your milk brother. Pray for him. Pray for his safety. Please."

My milk brother, Yeli's Dono? The pottery clan's fierce little orphan pup? Impossible!

But her words rang true, and, as if buried somewhere deep in my memory, I realized I'd heard such a thing spoken before.

I looked back at Dono, but he had ascended the tiers and walked into the crowd beyond. The toothless nine-year-old man who was my milk brother vanished from my childhood.

FIVE

What happened next is difficult to recount. I don't know where to start. With our triumphant return to our compound from temple? With the press of the crowd and the ululations of women that accompanied us the entire way? Or with the pottery clan men who vaulted onto each other's shoulders like acrobats, bellowing praises to our illustrious bull dragon?

The thing of it is, I remember that afternoon and evening like a series of images hung upon a wall, like one of Mother's famous four-tile panels. Static pictures captured in clay: it's safest to remember events in that manner.

Understand, Temple law states that the clan of a boy chosen by the dragonmaster as apprentice must give away all possessions at sundown on Sa Gikiro, in recognition of all the boy has lost and in preparation for the riches Temple will bestow upon the clan in eight days, as recompense for the life the dragonmaster has taken from them.

Such an event had not occurred to any clan within our zone for more than two generations. We knew what we had to do, as per Temple Statute: give away all our goods. But we did not know how the giving would unfold. Perhaps a blessing, that.

So, the first image in the clay-tile-panel in my mind:

Kobo's twins, Rutvia and Makvia, kneeling on the floor, rolling tikken buds and their hoard of Mombe Taro swatches into their sleeping mats, so as to press the swatches of satin smooth and impart them with the buds' peppery fragrance. Not for one moment do the girls wonder why anyone would want their stained, worn sleeping mats and their swatches of cloth; they are following Temple Statute and offering what they believe to be treasure. Their innocent pride is poignant and sweet.

In the second panel sits a ragged, somewhat greasy lump of sage-colored cloth, featon chaff spilling from a tear. This cloth bundle is my fu-lili, my soft honey, a nondescript stuffed toy that belonged to my sister when she was a child and that had proudly belonged to me since I was two. I was determined not to give *that* particular treasure away, and was furtively stuffing it behind a stack of boxed pigments in the women's pottery shed when Mother found me. We exchanged a look; I thrust out a defiant lip.

"I *need* fu-lili," I said defensively, even though I hadn't slept with the smelly thing, nor played with it, in years. "Some things you just can't give away, Mama."

She nodded curtly, then walked out, leaving me to my crime.

In the third panel stands a group of grinning pottery men, all their worldly possessions laid on mats before their hut doorways: heirloom pipes, burnished machetes, new sandals made of stiff leather, and destiny wheels carved from gharial bone, the wheels' large dice nestled in leather drawstring pouches. The men are swelled with generosity, eager to obey Temple law.

The fourth panel contains one image only. A ceramic figurine, squat and obese and baffling to a nine-year-old girl. The twins and I saw it on Big Grum Grum's mat among a jumble of drinking pipettes, an urn of maska, and a cedar box filled with tobacco. We stared, at liberty to do so because the men had backs turned to us, guffawing over each other's wit. Captivated by the object's mystery, I boldly picked up the figurine.

It was heavy, like a terimelon, but with a tunnel carved through its center. I turned the figurine this way and that. A brooder dragon, that's what it was, but the strangest likeness of a brooder I'd ever seen, for instead of the mottled greens and reds of a real brooder, it was glazed a soft beige, like the skin upon my inner thighs where the sun never touched. Stranger, its thin tail was lifted high, revealing a rump much like my own, complete with an aperture just large enough for me to squeeze all the fingers of one hand into.

I withdrew them, frowning. The tunnel running through the length of the brooder was glassy and knobbed with tiny bumps.

With a grunt, I lifted the object to eye level. Three things immediately became apparent: The figurine was hollow and liquid sloshed within its base, the aperture was a tunnel that gradually narrowed to the brooder's open mouth, and the thing stank, a sour-salt stench that reminded me of the ocean weeds we sometimes burned in our kilns to obtain certain lusters on vases.

"What *is* it?" Kobo's Rutvia breathed, her chin at my shoulder.

"A drinking cup," I announced authoritatively, though in truth I hadn't a clue what the figurine was. "A man's drinking cup. Must be. See, the eyes are cork. You pull them out, like this, to put the maska inside."

"But what's the tunnel for?"

"Oh, *that*," I said airily. "Uhhh . . . it keeps the maska cool? Yes, you know, the air goes in and out, to cool the drink. *Everyone* knows that."

Kobo's Makvia wrinkled her nose. "But how do you drink the maska once it's in?"

"Straws in the eye holes, you cracked egg. Maska straws." I gestured to the tarnished pipettes on the mat.

"Ah," the twins said, finally bowing to my superior knowledge, for it is true; men drink maska through long metal pipettes to filter out fermentation residue.

I turned the brooder figurine onto its back, looking for the potter's seal. I'd never seen anyone craft such an object before and was powerfully curious who might have done so.

"It's leaking," Kobo's Rutvia said. It was.

That's when I noticed the inexplicable: The maska within the figurine leaked from dozens of pinprick holes inside the tunnel. When I hastily turned the brooder right side up again, the maska that had sloshed into its back while upside down now drip-drip-dripped from dozens of similar holes in the tunnel roof.

I knew a ceramic cup could leak by way of a crack, but by hundreds of tiny holes? What strange phenomenon was this?

"It must be really old," I breathed in wonder. "Absolutely ancient—"

"Know what it's for?" a voice said. I looked up and saw Korshan's Rutkar and his cronies leering at me. Ranging from six to eight years old, they were the sworn enemies of the twins and me by mere dint of their ages.

"Wager you don't," Korshan's Rutkar goaded.

"Do, too," I said haughtily. "It's a drinking cup, a maska drinking cup." I lifted it to my lips to demonstrate. "See?"

The lot of them erupted into laughter. The men all turned at once; Big Grum Grum saw his prized "cup" in my hands and roared with fury, and the twins and I shrieked. I dropped the cup on the ground and we fled.

I have since learned the device is used by men during the fertility rite Kana Cinai ki Gourfi, Ride the Brooder's Back. The figurine is filled not with maska, as I'd thought, but warm water—or warm oil, if one is wealthy—and lined with a perforated leather insert. The figurine is said to increase both the fertility and sexual prowess of the user. Odd practice, no? Especially for folk who despise the Djimbi for how they interact with dragons.

I shudder now to recall how I'd so blithely held that figurine to my lips. Big Grum Grum did not often bathe, and that figurine, by the stink of it, had been well used.

Hey-o. I suppose that's more than a static picture of what I recall of that Sa Gikiro, isn't it? Perhaps I remember it in detail so well so as to put off recording what occurred the rest of that day and night. How else might I prolong this avoidance? By remembering Mother, I suppose, and all the other giddily glad pottery clan women, scurrying to and fro, baking sweet cakes, soaking dried plums in maska water and stuffing them with crystallized honey and ground nut paste. Not that we had many plums to stuff, nor honey with which to make sweet cakes, but every last luxury in our cellars was brought forth, and what we lacked we purchased from neighboring clans with promissory notes. Our neighbors knew how affluent we would be in eight days and saw no reason not to give us foodstuffs on credit. . . . With an exorbitant credit charge attached, of course.

The smells that day! The sizzle of renimgar crackling! The heady perfume of shredded orchid rolls! The pungency of liver wreaths!

And I can tell you, the little red congle nuts above the mating shack were scarcely out of their gourds, for in and out the closets went flushed couples all day, putting the nuts on the lintel inside the gourds to request a blessing from Re, should the bull dragon be watching in spirit. Thus a child might take root in the garden of the women's wombs.

Strictly speaking, it was Sa Gikiro, a day of abstinence, so such revelry should have waited until sunset. But just as our clan never fulfilled its Proclamation that day—for how could we slash vines or make coil bottles when so much preparation awaited to honor the bull and fulfil Temple Statute?—so too Greatfather Maxmisha overlooked the comings and goings in the closets.

How quickly the promise of wealth subverts.

So. A portrait of the pottery clan compound on the Sa Gikiro of my ninth year: It gleamed with oiled men and perfumed women; it steamed with the fragrances of cooked rarities and lovemaking; and it glittered with our polished, paltry possessions, laid out for any to take from the courtyard floor at sundown, as per Temple Statute.

When did we potters first notice that the other clan rishi waiting outside our entry arch did not laugh along with us? At what point did the unwavering intensity of their eyes unsettle our nerves, make us pause, bite a lip, and frown? Maybe when those foremost in the crowd outside refused to leave their places even when nature's functions pressed; they chose instead to evacuate their bowels and bladders in full view, right beneath our clan arch, rather than give up the place for someone else. Perhaps it was when one of our women, Kobo's Dash, began reciting statute aloud—understand, out *very* loud, not just her usual mutters, accompanied by a determined, inward look.

I know for certain that as the sharp tangerine sunset stung the dusk clouds purple, the fights breaking out beyond our archway had fixed all our smiles on our faces. Scrubbed clean and dressed in our worst, for our best lay neatly folded on our sleeping mats before us, we stood side by side, ringing the courtyard. Waisi stood on my left; Mother, my right.

As for Waisi, well. She looked breathtaking. Really. The sight of her caught your breath in your chest, where it tangled with your heart and slapped a flush against your cheeks.

She had found face powders and color sticks and blended them and applied them so carefully that she appeared to wear none at all. Yet her eyes, her cheekbones, her lips, her neck . . . ! The threadbare bitoo she wore was far too small for her and hugged her breasts and tummy and rump splendidly, barely reaching midthigh. Even Father couldn't stop staring.

"They won't wait until sunset," Waisi said. "Not much longer now, and they'll charge us like bulls in rut."

"Close your fast lips, girl-who-looks-like-kiyu," Kobo's Dash hissed. "Dare you speak ill against bulls on a holy day?"

"Bulls *do* charge when in rut—"

"Hush, Waivia," Mother murmured, and Waisi for once didn't argue. Mother frowned, chewed distractedly on a lock of hair as she studied the crowd uneasily.

Several heartbeats passed. The crowd at the entry arch had turned into a boiling mass that reminded me of black and red ants at war.

"She's right," Mother said breathlessly. "Waivia, Zarq, go—"

Then they were upon us.

It happened that quickly, Mother looking down at me, speaking my name, a strange urgency on her face as I looked up at her. And then a rush of noise—shouts, cries, screams—and people were everywhere, pushing and grabbing. That fast, it was.

The mob was thick and frenzied, crazed by greed. Mother tried to grab me, but I was shoved beyond her reach. I saw her horror as I fell among the churning feet. A knee hit me in the mouth as I went down; a foot landed on my left shoulder. I screamed and tried to scrabble up, out, away. Strong hands clawed at my shoulders and tried to pull me upright again.

"Stand up, stand up!" a voice shrieked, and then those helping hands were also yanked from me.

Shins, knees, feet. Grit scraping hard against my cheeks, blood from my nostrils. Roaring in my ears. I couldn't breathe.

Then I was yanked up and crushed against a soft, heaving chest. Mother. I clung hold and squeezed my eyes shut.

"Get them under the barracks!" Mother yelled. She tipped over and I wailed and clung tighter, certain she was falling, and she did fall, but only to her knees, and it was deliberate, for now we were under the stilt-raised women's barracks, with the twins crawling frantically before us, after their mother, Kobo's Dash. Big Grum Grum's kids were already huddled in the dark center beneath the barracks. Korshan's Limia scrambled in beside us, her eyes wide and glistening, her screaming baby clutched tight to her breast.

"Go on, follow them," Mother shouted, pushing me after the twins. "We'll be safe under here."

But I refused to move.

"We can't," I said.

She stared at me, stunned.

"We can't," I repeated. "They'll take our things. All our things."

"They're supposed to," she said unevenly.

I shook my head with all the certainty youth can muster, tears rolling down my cheeks. "Not like this."

"Zarq." A pained expression crossed her face. "Some things we must accept, yes?"

"But our pigments!" I howled, loud as the mob outside, suddenly overcome by the injustice of the pillage, thinking only of my beloved fu-lili hidden behind the boxes of pigment in our pottery shed. They would take those pigments, discover my fu-lili behind them, and take my precious toy as well. "They'll take everything—they will, they will!"

My howls froze everyone cowering under the barracks. The adults exchanged uneasy looks. There was truth in what I spoke, for the crowd was so wild with greed, they would take whatever they could, regardless of its worth to them.

And while the adults exchanged those portent looks, I bolted. Yes, I did. I scrambled out from under our safe refuge and hurled myself blindly into the seething mass of legs and feet, intent only on rescuing my fu-lili.

Mother screamed something behind me—at least, I think it was Mother—and someone grabbed at my neck. The cloth of the old bitoo I was wearing tore like wet, rotten twine. On I ran.

Dodging elbows, knocked askew by hip and rump, shoved by hands and trod on by bare and shod feet alike. Noise all around me, disorienting, overwhelming, and motion that seemed to spin me round and about like a bug in a mixing vat of clay slurry. I could have been anywhere, I comprehended so little of my surroundings. Feet and shins and knees, all kicking and churning and scrabbling like bizarre, bedeviled beasts . . .

Then the crowd briefly parted for no discernable reason—just briefly, mind—and I glimpsed our men grappling with each other in the courtyard. The elders were fighting our youngest men, who appeared to be trying to limit the pillage. But our elders, Father included—and this is what scared me most, understand—held our youth back with blows and curses. To allow the holy plunder to continue.

In that terrifying glimpse, in that brief parting of the crowd, I could see where I was, could orient myself in my surroundings. I made straight for the women's pottery shed.

Others were there. Strangers clutching pots of glaze and sacks of white kaolin to their chests, eyes wild with greed. I was stunned that they had dared violate the inner sanctum of our guild clan, had sullied our smooth, fine trestle table with their grasping fingers and wanton avarice when the goods they were taking were of absolutely no use to them.

I darted into the shed and snatched up a dragon's fang, that short, wicked knife potters use for fettling and cutting clay.

"Get back, all of you!" I shrieked. "Get out, get out!"

I slashed at those closest to me; the rending of cloth and the shriek of one wounded graced my ears.

"Out!" I yelled. I leapt atop the trestle table, brandishing the knife in one hand, and hurled a jar of pigment at a pillager. It bounced off her head and she gaped at me for several heartbeats before falling, concussed, to her knees.

"You're not potters!" I screamed hoarsely, passion boiling up from the day's emotional events. "You don't need these things!"

I flung my knife at the nearest person, then sprang monkeylike from the trestle table to the shelves and started hurling jars and amphorae wildly at faces and napes.

I was quite off my head with emotion. Quite. I do believe, had I been capable, I would have readily killed all present and never suffered a whit of remorse afterward.

But Mother appeared, hair disheveled, bitoo torn, one cheek scratched from eye to lip. Pushing through the doorway, she took in the scene with one swift look—me clinging to the shelves like a spider monkey, hurling missiles upon ducking and fleeing pillagers—and then fell to aiding me by screaming at those still within the shed that I was rabid, was demon possessed—run for your life!

People were trying to enter, despite the crush of those trying to exit, and during the melee Mother pushed her way over to one shelf, rooted behind the wooden boxes stacked there, and retrieved my beloved fu-lili.

"Zarq, Zarq, it's fine now. Stop!" She grabbed at my waist, pulled me down to her. Shoved fu-lili into my hands. "Are you hurt? Are you well?"

Even as she spoke to me, her eyes roved wildly over the wreckage of the shed. One hand smoothed my hair too fast, over and over.

"They're going to take everything!" I shrieked at her. I threw fu-lili away, suddenly couldn't stand the thing, wanted nothing to do with it. Just wanted these people gone, our things safe, our life orderly.

My mother's face changed then. Hardened, became something foreign. She took me by both shoulders, shook me.

"I want you to go back to the barracks, understand? Get underneath it. Stay there. You're too small for this. Tell Kobo's Dash and Big Grum Grum's Li what happened here; tell them I need help."

Her expression darkened further. "You were right, Zarq. There are some things one can't give away."

She turned me about, sang out words that sounded like gibberish, like a foreign tongue, like an illicit pagan chant, and pushed me toward the door. Miraculously, the crowd briefly parted, just as it had once before, and I slipped out the doorway and darted through the seething mob outside. Dodging and ducking and sprinting as fast I could, I returned safely to the barracks.

Once there, I scrabbled along cool dirt and around cobwebbed stilts to the very center of the barracks' underbelly. Big Grum Grum's children clung to each other, a knot of snotty tears, and the twins clung to their mother, Kobo's Dash.

I spoke rapidly, my words tripping over each other.

"What can they possibly want with potters' goods?" Korshan's Limia cried, hugging her baby to her breast.

"There's no reason left in them," Kobo's Dash said bitterly. "They just want to fill their arms. They'll strip us bare."

Big Grum Grum's Li pushed her children from her lap.

"Zarq is right," she said. "We must go to the workshop. Hey-o, Limia, give your baby to Zarq and come with us. We have to save what we can. None of us expected this. Not this."

The screaming baby was thrust into my arms.

"Stay here," Limia ordered me. "Don't move." She touched her baby's nose with a finger, and then she, too, was gone.

Gasping for air, clutching the arch-backed babe to my chest, I stared at Kobo's Dash. She glared and began chanting stanzas from Temple scrolls.

Above us, foot thunder and dust rain. The barracks' floor shuddered from a human stampede.

Limia's baby continued to scream in my arms. Fists balled, mouth wide, face puckered, he screamed and screamed. I hated Kobo's Dash, who sat at arm's length from me, squeezing the twins against her, for not taking my burden from me. Obtusely, I also hated her for staying behind, for not going to help my mother and the other women save what clays and tools she could.

My legs cramped. I couldn't sleep. I was too exhausted for tears. The night dragged on.

Slowly, slowly, the crazed swarm outside diminished.

By dawn, it was gone. We stayed put. Indeed, we didn't crawl out from our hiding place until Korshan's Limia crawled in. Hollow-eyed, bruised, and streaked with thin scratches, she hefted her baby from my lap and cradled him to her breast. He rooted languidly, exhausted, then once the milk touched his tongue, he nursed frantically, fists and feet kneading her belly with vigor.

"Where's my mother?" I asked huskily.

"Go with Big Grum Grum's Li. Go now."

"Where's—"

"Go!"

I crawled after the other children.

We emerged into a silent, humid dawn. Big Grum Grum's Li and her goiter-necked mother counted us all. I stared hollowly at the courtyard.

Our men moved about stiffly, through shards of vases and dishes dropped from overfull hands. Eggs, too, had been broken in the crush, and the shattered shells lay upon the ground in a fine confetti trail, the earth churned in spots into an albumen-rich mud that buzzed with flies.

The garden was no more. Every inch of it had been hacked to the ground and carried away, and roots had been yanked up for replanting. Of our fuel stores, so carefully stacked, nothing remained.

The doors had been ripped off our renimgar hutches, and the fat, lizardlike mammals within had been taken away, save for a few trampled corpses. Scraps of torn cloth here and there, a bangle, a broken sandal, a snapped comb, a soiled baby's wrap, spilled pigment, and, inexplicably, a woman's thick, black braid caked with dirt: This detritus was all that remained to us.

It was hard to remember we'd been dragon blessed.

Though we tried, throughout that awful morning, tried to remember we'd been favored by the bull. Over and over we told each other that we had done what was expected of us, as set out in Temple Statute, and that in a clawful of time—a mere eight days—our riches would roll in, wagonful after wagonful, until we would be just as bewildered by our excess as by our current lack. We said these things to each other in various ways as we cleaned, trapped in a listless stupor, loath to touch the refuse yet desperate to see it gone.

Every moment of that horrible day, I wanted my mother. Or Waisi, or even . . . yes, even a glimpse of Father, however frightening and enraged he'd looked last night. For the first time in my life, despite being surrounded by those who'd raised me since birth, I desperately needed to be held by someone in my immediate family: Mother, Father, or Waisi.

But they were nowhere in sight, and no one would answer my tearful questions concerning their whereabouts.

Around midday, Greatfather Maxmisha made a belated Proclamation: The pottery clan would search every corner of the men's huts to see if any mislaid chits could be found. Should any be discovered, our men would purchase from neighboring clans the food we needed to see us through the next eight days.

I looked at Korshan's Limia for an explanation, because chits were for men's hands only, and as no one but a man could enter a man's domicile, what did Greatfather mean by telling us all to join the search? But the high color in her cheeks and the glassy look in her eyes bade me to remain silent.

Of all wonders, quite a few chits were found; it was days later that I realized the miracle only meant the pottery clan men were more canny and less devout than I'd believed. Off a group of them went to purchase food from our neighbors.

That evening, they returned with precious little.

Our neighbors, knowing our plight and fully aware of our impending fortune, had deemed the worth of their foodstuffs, even the goods taken from us during the night, at five times their true value. We had only enough food to see us through a day or two, and nothing else of value to our name.

And Mother still hadn't reappeared.

I found Father, though. I came upon him as he was ducking out of a latrine, tugging his stained loincloth into place. The look on his face was peculiar, as if I'd caught him stealing temple oil. We stared at each other for several heartbeats; then I could contain myself no longer. As bizarre as such an action was between a girl and her father, I hurled myself at him and clung to his waist.

He stank of maska spirits, and his skin was oily and rank. He patted my head awkwardly and tried to extract himself from my embrace, but when he realized no one could see us, he crouched to my level and spoke kindly.

"Now there, Zarq. There really isn't any point soiling the ground with your dirty tears, is there?"

"But Mother's gone!"

"Is she?" His brown eyes, usually so beautiful, were all bloodshot and surrounded by wrinkles. His gaze turned distant. After a brief spell, he shook his head as if he'd had an argument with someone and lost. He cleared his throat. "Your duty is to wait for her in silence. That's the proper thing to do."

"But where *is* she?"

"Hold your tongue, Zarq, hey-o? Too many questions. I'm sure she's around somewhere—you just haven't found her yet. Busy cleaning with the other women." He awkwardly smoothed my cheeks, an atypical gesture for a man.

"But—"

"Look, what have I found?" He plucked from behind my ear a strip of renimgar jerky. I noticed then that underneath the sour stench of his maska breath, he smelled of oily meat. Saliva rushed into my mouth. He pressed the jerky into one of my hands. "Eat up, all to yourself. Good. Now run along, hey-o?"

He stood, patted my head once, and strode away.

I ate the jerky greedily and had the wits to chew on a bitter weed to disguise the smell. I didn't obey my father, however; as twilight settled upon us, I continued to ask others if they'd seen Mother. None of the women answered my inquiries. Korshan's Limia, whom I'd followed all day like a pup, was disinclined to even look my way.

Big Grum Grum's Li finally clouted me. "What are you trying to do, draw attention to the fact that your mother is missing?"

That had been *precisely* what I'd been trying to do. But such a response died in my throat as Big Grum Grum's Li crossed her twiggy arms over her narrow breasts and glared at me.

I curled into a ball on the bare floor of the barracks and shivered. I would never be able to sleep again, never. . . .

I woke to movement, to a sense of an impending event. A clawful of women were rising like mist from their sleeping places and drifting soundlessly out the barracks door. Car Manopu's Wasaltooltic was just rising from her spot nearest me. I sat up, pulse skittering along my veins.

"Go back to sleep," she said, frowning.

I shook my head: no.

"Zarq—"

"I'll scream if you don't tell me what's happening." Instinctively, I knew that whatever these women were about was illicit, and silence was therefore imperative.

She glared. "Why do you want to know? You're a child. You should be sleeping."

"I want my mother."

"She'll be here by morning."

"You know where she is," I said, suddenly intuiting that these silent shadows drifting outside were connected to Mother, to her disappearance, to her decision, spurred by my wild insistence, to save what glazes and clays and tools she could.

"Stay quiet," Car Manopu's Wasaltooltic finally hissed. "This way. Not a word until I say."

I blinked in the darkness, reflexively glanced down beside me, looking for Waisi. Sometime while I'd slept, she must have reappeared, for there she lay, curled on her side, back to me.

"Not *her*," Car Manopu's Wasaltooltic whispered, clapping a hand over my mouth to stifle my cry of relief. "Leave her sleep. Now come."

So I did.

Outside, stars like flecks of fine glazed porcelain glittered upon the dark table of night. I couldn't say the sky looked black, for it was so bright with luminescence it looked as if white slip had been gently swirled through it. Twisted Foot Ryn's Tak, Big Grum Grum's Li and her goiter-necked old mother, and Korshan's Limia awaited us in the courtyard. Nervous as caged mitewings, the lot of them were, save for Goiter Mother, who champed her toothless gums and eyed me with disgust.

Car Manopu's Wasaltooltic made a placatory gesture. Goiter Mother lifted her nose and turned her back on me.

We went off under our compound entry arch, its ceramic liana vines, flowers, and miniature dragon eggs even more beautiful by starlight. The ground beyond was antithetical to the archway: Human waste and detritus from yesterday's mob fouled the earth. We picked our way around it.

Through the alleys of Wabe Din Sor we walked, silent save for the *whisk-rasp, whisk-rasp* of our bitoos snagging upon the brick walls of narrow strictures. I dared speak up.

"Where are we going?"

"Your mother," Car Manopu's Wasaltooltic said, which wasn't helpful, as I'd already intuited that much. The terseness of her reply, however, held in check further questions.

Our little group paused at one juncture and consulted in furious whispers before turning down the narrowest alley we'd yet entered. From the rancid, smoky smells coating the air, I guessed we walked the outskirts of the leather tanners' clan. Despite the stench of dead gharials, my stomach lurched and gurgled. It recognized the smell of meat, however inedible.

The alley ended. Dense black towered before us. Jungle. Just like that.

The black was a solid sheet, yet from the corner of my left eye I thought I saw a section shiver, and maybe also to my right, and also somewhere above and before us. . . .

The whole jungle was alive.

A crick-ben gave a piercing *scritch* near my forehead. I lifted my hands and swatted, expecting the fat insect to whir into my eyes in its quest for a warm, damp place to lay eggs.

Scritch, scritch!

The thing was right above me. I swatted the air furiously. In return, I received a swat from Big Grum Grum's Li. Looking directly at me, dandruff-flaked eyebrows furrowed, she pursed her lips and . . . *scritch!*

"Haaa!" I breathed in admiration. That was some talent, that.

One of her fierce eyebrows twitched, and she turned away.

Then something *did* move at the jungle's edge, filmy and sloth slow. A gigantic kwano spirit! I tried to shriek a warning, but only a squeak came out. Good thing, because heartbeats later I realized it was Mother, stagger-picking her way through liana vines and slippery palm, and over great buttressed tree roots.

I hurled myself at her. She caught me up as though I were much smaller. I burst into tears, then was furious and pounded her with my fists.

"Still, now. I had to leave you, Zarq. No harm done."

"She'll wake the leather tanners. Close those lips, tu-pu!" Goiter Mother husked, calling me little brat as if she were Waisi. "Should never have brought her."

"Better she make this noise at the jungle's edge than back in the women's barracks," Car Manopu's Wasaltooltic said dryly.

"Zarq, listen now," Mother said, setting me upon the ground. "Listening?"

"You shouldn't have left me!"

"I told you I would return. Enough noise for now. Fine?"

I wiped snot across one arm, sucked in a quavering breath, and nodded shortly.

"Good." Above my head, to the others, she said, "We'll form a chain and pass everything along the line, yes? Reduce the chances of stepping on something nasty."

Murmurs of agreement.

"Work quickly," Mother said as she retraced her steps back into the jungle. "Something prowls."

A gasp of dismay from us all.

"A cat?" breathed Tak.

"Stinking afterbirth mess, this," Goiter Mother spat. "Come now, move, move, and let's be done with this place!"

They tried to place me at the safest end of the line, beside the leather tanners' walls. I refused. I wasn't letting Mother out of my sight again. Realizing the futility of insistence, they complied, and so we sweated hard the night through, Mother disappearing back and forth into the ebony jungle, each time returning with a heavy packing urn, the widemouthed kind used for storing palm oil.

That was how it went: Mother would pick her way toward me, hiss at me to stop scratching, foist an urn into my arms, and I in turn would stumble a few feet over crushed foliage and thrust my burden into the arms of Korshan's Limia, while Mother retrieved yet another urn. A thousand biting things eagerly partook of my exposed ears, neck, arms, and legs.

"Stop scratching," Limia hissed at me as she turned and staggered to where Tak awaited, several feet away.

One, two, three, four, five, six, seven urns . . .

"How many more?" I whined. My arms felt soft as undercooked paak, and my legs trembled.

"Courage," Mother grunted.

Her next burden was not an urn but a heavy block of clay wrapped in damp leather. I couldn't carry it; she barely could. The women worked in pairs after that, hoisting huge blocks of clay between them from Mother's cache in the jungle, and I was mercifully exempted from labor.

At last they finished.

"Can we open one, please?" I begged, eyeing the oil urns as we all leaned against a wall to scrape spitfrog foam from our calves and slug slime from our soles. "I'm so hungry."

The others exchanged looks. Sadness turned Mother's starlit face into a clackron mask. "No food in these, Zarq."

"None?" I said in disbelief. "None at all? You hid no food?"

"Food, gaaa!" Goiter Mother spat. "Pigments and glazes, clay powder and gold leaf, fluting and modeling tools and sieves. Things we cannot do without, that's what we hid."

"But we need food!" I felt betrayed that Mother had risked her life in the jungle solely to save the tools of her art and hadn't given a thought to saving so much as a scrap of food for me while she was at it.

"Food we'll find," Korshan's Limia murmured. "Help carry something, little one: Dawn comes."

She was right. The stars were dimming in a clay-gray sky. Mother found me the smallest, lightest urn to carry and tried to stroke my hair, but I ducked out of reach.

We staggered back to our compound, urns balanced on hips and heads and clay slabs hoisted with leather straps over bent backs. Once in the work shed, we unpacked the urns, placing a tool here, a brush there, trying to make them appear dropped and overlooked. The urns of liquid glaze we tipped onto their sides, after first ensuring they were firmly stoppered, and rolled them into corners and under the long pottery table, which was still with us only because of its weight and length.

It was a poor guise at best. Mother felt sure that none of the men would report our transgression to Temple, and the other women concurred, relaying to her in undertones how the men had miraculously found so many chits buried in their huts earlier.

"Ah. So glad to see their common sense is stronger than piety, after all," she said dryly.

Finally, we slipped back to the women's barracks to sleep. No sooner had my eyes closed than a flametail gave its morning cry; moments later, birdsong shattered the silence of dawn.

"Time to get up," Mother whispered. She stroked my hair. I rolled away from her.

In daylight, Mother's overnight stay in the jungle announced itself to all: Her ankles were striated and puffy, as though thin wires encircled them, bites festered on her arms, and one eyelid was swelling to the size and color of a plum. I was aghast. All that from a single night in the jungle?

To my astonishment, no one remarked on her injuries. Children who stared were slapped into looking the other way by navel aunties or mothers. Even Waisi kept her lips closed, though it seemed as if she hadn't even noticed Mother's appearance. Strangely, she wore the twin of Mother's swollen eye, and crimson welts marked her arms, too.

My anger at Mother's disappearance was nothing compared to the cold hostility Waisi showed her. Mother took in Waisi's injuries with a swift, searching look and opened her mouth to speak. Waisi flared her nostrils, spat at Mother's feet, then stalked to the latrines.

I gaped.

"Oh, Zarq," was all Mother said, and she gave a sigh so full of weary ache that my grudge against her dissolved.

Greatfather's Proclamation that morning surprised no one: Our clan would slash vines and make fuel bundles to trade to neighboring clans for food, while a party of potters set off to the Grieving River to collect clay.

Hunger and fatigue had made me featherweight and easy to startle, and during the Proclamation my eyes fixed on one thing and then another, blinking infrequently. I didn't see how I could carry green liana vines. But I was a Clutch serf, born and bred. I accepted my lot without protest. Well, without *much* protest.

No one had yet ventured into the work shed. The "overlooked" treasures that lay in wait still remained undiscovered.

Frayed nerves, hunger, and callous heat: a bad mix. Tempers flared as we slashed encroaching liana vines from the outer walls of our compound.

Liana vines must be thoroughly dry before they can be twisted with dragon dung and resinous macci leaves for fuel. Our labors were worth little in the way of food at day's end, with only green vines to sell. Everyone knew that. Still, we worked the day through, squint eyed and grim, snapping like feral dogs at each other.

Hard work and vine sap disintegrated the bandages around my wounded hand, the one touched by venom from the dragonmaster's whip at Mombe Taro. Soon my palm throbbed, was rubbed raw. Still I worked, the fumes of the bleeding vines coating my teeth and tongue like bitter chalk. The humid air filled with the crush of fat beetles trodden upon, the distinctive wet rasp of machetes decapitating snakes, the whining of hungry children and the arguments of surly men.

I worked with Kobo's and Car Manopu's kin, alongside my friends, Rutvia and Makvia. Old Kobo and his kin had duly laid their machetes upon their mats for giveaway Sa Gikiro night, but all of Car Manopu's kin had buried theirs. As the day progressed, resentment over this grew between the two families. Exhausted from ripping vines from walls with bare hands, Kobo and his brothers began grumbling about the impiety of others. Car Manopu's lot griped about the dismal quantity of vines some had cleared away compared to their own.

Words turned into violence and violence into death when Car Manopu spoke heatedly against the Emperor.

He should have known better, to speak thus before Kobo the Zealot. But it was not for nothing he was named danku Re Car Manopu, Junior Iron Fists of the Pottery Clan, for he was as muscled and rebellious as his legendary namesake.

Danku Re Car Manopu was a broad-shouldered, thick-waisted man with navel ties to the silversmiths' clan. Like so many brawny Malacarite men, the name Iron Fists had been given him during his

Call-the-Name-Out Ceremony. Many Car Manopus lived in Clutch Re, all named after Zarq Car Mano, Malacar's infamous warrior hero.

Perhaps you have not heard of him, though I find that difficult to believe, for tales of his exploits travel with sea merchants and slave traders even beyond the Ocean of Derwent. But as the story of Zarq Car Mano is crucial in understanding Malacar's history, indulge me in a lecture.

Malacar, our beloved, beleaguered nation, has been invaded so frequently that of necessity we Malacarites are able to apply a short view on history and oft use forgetfulness as a survival technique.

We have been invaded twice by those on Lud y Auk, back when that island was known as Messer and its fierce, brown-skinned people were not yet under the Emperor's yoke. We have been invaded repeatedly by the Xxeltekers, the blond foreigners who share our continent yet are separated from our coastal nation by the glacial mountain range to the north of us. Selut y Din, the crescent island westernmost in the Archipelago and home to the throne of the Emperor, has reared our most frequent invaders. There is even evidence that the legendary race that inhabited the rocky isle of Nan y Nan once landed as an army upon our shores.

Yet of all these invasions, none have caused as much strife and hardship to the common Malacarite as the warring of our own people.

We've always had a macabre, almost necrophiliac love of the dead, we Malacarites. Over the centuries, this perverse obsession developed into geographical politics: a man who died in such-and-such a place performing such-and-such a great deed became an icon that forged a small country, solely from the fervor devoted to protecting the hero's sepulchral tower from thieves and rivals. Thus the first Roshu Paras were formed, the private armies devoted to protecting the dead from the living.

Ridiculous, really, but then is there any claiming of ownership of dirt that isn't ludicrous, when stripped of all romanticism? So we fought each other as we ourselves were being attacked, all for the love of cadavers. And borders were formed.

Until Zarq Iron Fists.

Ruthless, arrogant, and immense with muscle—the ultimate

Malacarite man—Zarq Car Mano bullied the various quarreling countries into a single nation and named it Malacar, Land of Iron, in honor
of himself. A feverish time of intense national patriotism ensued; a
time we fondly and erroneously call the Dragon-Blessed Blossom Days.
Under Zarq Car Mano's rule, Malacarite armies even invaded the isles
of the Archipelago, though tales of the battles fought and plunders
gained are exaggerated.

Alas, Zarq Car Mano was only mortal. He died a painful death after
a long, debilitating bout of blood poisoning, caused by poor hygiene,
indiscriminate sexual habits, and an advanced case of mating pustules.
His demise, combined with the ascension of a new, wily Emperor in
the Archipelago, plunged Malacar back into its woeful habit of being
invaded; this time, Malacar was thoroughly conquered.

It was after Car Mano that I was named.

I asked Mother many times *why* she'd chosen that name for me.

"It's a good name, an honorable name. Is it not?" she said.

"It's a boy's name."

"A name has neither breast nor beard."

"Yes but . . . but . . . " It was at that juncture I always gave up. Until one
day, it dawned on me: "It's not *traditional* to name a girl Zarq. It's wrong."

I was flushed with pride at my clever response. Mother was not so
impressed.

"Tradition is always right then, hey-o?" she murmured. "But did not
Zarq Car Mano defy tradition by uniting rival countries into a nation?
Tradition is not something to be followed without question, Zarq. It's
rarely as pure and correct as it's made out to be. All tradition means is
that something has become accepted over time. That's all. It's good to
question such things."

Good to question tradition, Mother? Perhaps. But perhaps only in the
safety of one's thoughts, or with navel kin that one can trust with one's
life. You would have to be a fool to question the current version of tradition before a hungry, devout traditionalist. Worse than a fool to belittle his beliefs if he has just lost everything through adhering to a
particularly questionable custom started by an unloved foreign dictator.

Not that danku Re Car Manopu was worse than a fool. No. He was hungry, muscle sore, thirsty, and sun scorched. His pride was deeply festering from the double blow of watching his clan pillaged by neighbors, and by the refusal of his own navel clan, the silversmiths, to sell eggs and oil at a reasonable price.

And he had that name—Car Mano—to nudge his thoughts against the Emperor's Temple.

Yes, it was at the backs of many potters' minds that day, the thought that if each clan could own an egg-laying dragon, as in the Dragon-Blessed Blossom Days of Zarq Car Mano, then no Sa Gikiro, no eve celebrations, and therefore no resultant eight-day poverty need plague a clan. Perhaps I did not think such things, but then I was only a naive nine-year-old.

But I'd overheard such thoughts spoken aloud elsewhere, by drunk potters sprawled about the courtyard, arguing politics and smoking until dawn.

Many held the belief that dragon ownership should not be monopolized by Temple; there were stories about how, a hundred seventy years ago, dragons were not considered divine. This was before Malacar was ruled by the Emperor, before his theological dictatorship, before Temple decreed how and by whom dragons could be used.

Like all serf children, I was raised with the implicit dream that things could be otherwise; within my blood and with every beat of my heart was the hope—rarely voiced aloud by adult or child—that one day, a clan might own its own egg-laying dragons. Might free itself from poverty and Temple's might. One day.

So in fairness, let it be known that Car Manopu of Re's pottery clan only spoke what had been quietly spoken before, only voiced what many thought about Temple. That he did so to old Kobo the Zealot was the curse of kwano.

It all happened so quickly. I was less than an arm's length away, squatting on my haunches before a bundle of vines. I heard the argument, witnessed the shoving, saw the machete slice into Kobo's flesh. A fine spray of blood misted my feet, my knees, my arms.

Shrill screams. Shouts. The thud of fist striking flesh. Dust was kicked up and vine bundles were trampled and scattered as legs and feet flashed about me. Curses, wails, bellows . . .

Waisi pulled me free. She dragged me through the tight knot of chaos by one arm, as though I were a bundle of vines. She sat me before her, my back to our brawling clan, and fiercely started cleaning my face.

"I hate them," she hissed. "I hate them all. I hope they kill each other."

And she kept saying that, over and over, until I screamed at her to stop.

SIX

Kobo died.

Never before in the history of Re's pottery clan had one potter murdered another. More than grieved, we were appalled. Not so Mother; fury radiated from her like porcupine quills. I'd never seen her so angry. Such emotion belonged to Waisi. I followed her throughout that afternoon and evening like a burr stuck to her hem, fascinated by her rage.

Night fell. Corpse and liana vine bundles lay within our courtyard.

Mother stalked to the work shed and slammed the door on the death keens of Kobo's kin. I slipped in after her. By moonlight, she snatched up the tools we'd artfully arranged earlier and thumped them down on the wooden pottery table. She dropped to her knees, rolled an urn out from its hiding place beneath empty shelving, and heaved the bung from its neck so violently that the resultant pop sounded like a branch snapping.

She didn't drop the cork bung, but hurled it—in my direction. I ducked.

"Stay out of the way!" Mother cried. Then, contradicting herself, "Fetch water."

I scurried to the cistern squatting in the Wet Season corner of the room. It's a testament to how sure I was of my mother, then, for I knew she hadn't thrown that bung at me but had hurled it aimlessly. She raged not at me, therefore I didn't tremble or cry as I heaved off the cistern's heavy wooden cover. Though I did hurry; no need to provoke a bull already in a fury.

While I fumbled in the dark for the cistern's dipper bucket, Mother banged this and that onto the table. I heard another bung squeak-popped from its urn.

"*Water, Zarq.*"

"Can't find the dipper." Of course not; it'd been taken with everything else portable the night previous.

"Use this." She gestured at the large terra-cotta urn she'd just emptied.

Lower that into the cistern to fill? How to lift it out again?

"Never mind. I'll do it." She strode through a shaft of moonlight as she crossed over to me, and the wings of the dead insects caught in her hair glittered like pearls of glaze. She smelled of sweat and bitter vine sap and dust as she bent, grunting, over the cistern's lip. It took the two of us to hoist the filled urn out again.

"Wash yourself. Sleep in here, not the women's barracks."

I guessed, then, that she intended on working the night through.

"Where's Waivia?" she asked coolly.

"I don't know—"

"Find her."

I turned to go, a little unsettled by Mother's abrupt manner. But then:

"Never mind. She'll find us. If she's smart enough."

"Waisi's very smart," I said loyally, turning back.

"She's cunning. A difference, there." She thumped the urn of water onto the trestle table. As if by magic, she'd laid out all she'd needed for the night. She picked up a strong, thin wire attached to a metal bracket: the bow harp.

"Wash," she commanded.

I dutifully peeled off my bitoo. It came away from me like unset clay from a mold, caked as it was in vine gum and dirt. For a brief moment, the bitoo stood upright without me before cracking and folding to the ground.

Mother sank the bow harp into the large block of clay she'd hoisted onto the table. The sinews and muscles on her forearms stood out as she applied steady pressure. The bow harp sank down, down, into the clay.

"Your hand?" she asked.

I was loath to peel off the filth gummed to my wound. I shrugged nonchalantly. "Oh, it's fine. It doesn't need washing."

"Wash it."

"But it'll bleed."

"Better it bleed than turn black. *Make* it bleed."

"But it'll hurt, Mama," I said in a small voice.

"I can do it for you."

I pursed my lips, shook my head, and started washing myself.

It was unnerving, her tone, in that darkness, while in the background death keens pitched and peaked. Tears pricked the corners of my eyes as I splashed the cold water over my face.

"Wash your bitoo as well."

"And sleep wet!"

"You'll sleep dry."

"Naked? But mosquitoes—"

"You'll wear my bitoo. I'll smear myself with clay to keep mosquitoes off."

I did as I was told. By the time I padded, naked and wet, over to the shed's drain pipe to empty the dirty water out of the urn, my thighs and neck and shoulders felt stiff as old leather from the combination of fatigue and hunger.

Mother had stripped. She stood naked and lean at the trestle table. Her full breasts with their massive brown areolae wobbled and swung as she rhythmically kneaded clay. I stared in fascinated revulsion at the pigmentation of her skin, which I had been blind to prior to her heated admission at Mombe Taro: she had the dull green whorls, faint though they were, of a deviant.

"Hand," Mother reminded me, but in her usual voice, the feel of clay beneath her fingers having soothed away her brittle rage.

I swallowed, looked away. "I can wash it in the morning."

"Now please, Zarq. Use this. Tell no one." She tossed me one of the danku's precious sea sponges, favored by Korshan's kin for making decorative designs upon vases. "And hang your bitoo to dry, my littlest. You'll need it tomorrow."

She was Djimbi, yes. But she was my mother still.

I poked a length of my bitoo through one of the many open squares in the work shed wall so that half the long, narrow cloth flapped down outside the shed and the other half within. The holes in the walls had been created by absent bricks, deliberately left out during construction to create the ventilation so necessary during the hot days of Fire Season.

The moonlight stretched my bitoo's shadow long across the floor. It resembled an embalmed corpse.

I returned to the table. An urn of fresh water awaited me, filled by Mother without my help, and reluctantly I set to cleaning my hand. It didn't hurt at first, not as much as I'd feared. In fact, the way the skein of grimy skin slid off my palm to reveal pink flesh below fascinated me. The fascination ended right about the time a bone-throbbing ache set in.

Teeth gritted, I gingerly finished washing my palm. With awkward one-handed maneuvers, I draped myself in the long folds of Mother's bitoo, which was much cleaner than mine, though she'd worked just as hard as I had throughout the day. For my bed I chose the far end of the long, broad table upon which Mother worked. Of course, I wouldn't sleep on the floor, as a woman was forbidden to do so, for fear of soiling dragon-blessed earth with her dirty secretions, be they tears, saliva, breast milk, menstrual blood, sweat, or urine. I didn't curl up on an empty shelf, as Mother suggested, because I wanted to be as close to her as possible, even if that was all of four feet closer.

I lay down to sleep.

Sleep evaded me.

Little surprise. My palm burned and the whole arm throbbed in sympathy. My back and legs were drawing taut with the agonizing stiffness of overwork. I felt as if my body were turning into a bow harp. Without meaning to, I started breathing in gulps and starts, holding my breath from discomfort.

The death keens outside went on. Those shrill cries rose and fell discordantly, full of accusation, anger, and grief.

And then they changed.

The keening reached a strident new pitch, punctuated by harsh, rhythmic chants in a peculiar language. The words seemed somehow familiar. The cadence, the glottal stops, the lilting uplift at the end up each beat . . .

I recognized them. Sort of. They were an eerie mimicry of the

Djimbi-like gibberish we children taunted archenemies with. But the chants I heard now spoke not of juvenile mockery. They evoked malice. Kobo's kin grieved no longer; they plotted revenge with illicit Djimbi magics.

A breeze sprang up, sudden. My bitoo flapped, an unearthly, beheaded thing.

A movement caught my eye above it, just behind my mother's head, on the outside of the hole-checkered wall. My breath caught in my throat; the movement was caused by a shadow, an ever-lengthening shadow that was flowing down from the work shed roof toward the ground.

Python.

My insides went cold and liquid.

"Pay no attention, Zarq, hear me?" Mother hissed, and her voice made me shudder, for her words made real the horror behind her. "Look at me, at me only. It does not exist, that thing you see. Talk not of it."

She began to work her clay with a palpable urgency. She kneaded it, began rolling it out in swift, deft moves. With four strokes of the rolling pin, she had a sheet of an even thickness before her. With a small knife, she sliced her sheet into six square tiles.

Behind her, the snake slid through the blocks of moonlight shining through the wall and cast a shadow over her nape.

She snatched up a teakwood modeling tool, one that narrowed to a delicate, conical point. With loose, quick movements she began to sketch on her clay tiles.

The wind rose. The chanting from Kobo's kin grew louder, harsher, the words heavy as stone.

Mother muttered something in reply. Words sharp, quick, hard as baked clay.

The snake stretched onward. Its head reached the ground, yet still it flowed from the roof, and I knew how high that roof was, for I'd once jumped from it on a dare. No snake should be that length. No snake *was* that length.

This was an otherworld thing, a shadow-serpent evoked by the dark heathen dirge of Kobo's kin.

"I need heat for clay firing," Mother said tersely. She tipped back her long, smooth neck, as muscular as the python behind her, and sang, and the words she used were strange and terrible in their urgency. My heart pounded loud against my throat, so that for a moment I could hear nothing else, save the drumbeat of fear resonating from my chest.

And as difficult as this will be for any to believe—I understand all skepticism and forgive it wholeheartedly—hot air then blasted through the work shed, so hot and dry that the fine hairs inside my nostrils felt sharp as pins.

So hot and dry, it instantly fired Mother's clay tiles to kiln-baked hardness.

The solidity of that otherworld snake wavered for a moment, momentarily became an unstable, gossamer shadow. But Kobo's kin continued their dark chants, and the snake solidified and remained whole despite Mother's magic.

She snatched up a bulb of glaze and swiftly piped a sketch onto her tiles.

The chants outside became barks, no longer remotely resembling our childish taunts.

Mother thumped down her bulb, picked up a brush. Sang again more raw, turbulent words. The air around her began to spin with metallic hues, midnight blue, bronze, silver. She dipped her brush into them, painted her tiles with the unearthly glazes.

Outside, parts of the snake winked in and out of existence. Once. Twice. Thrice.

Kobo's kin screeched their threnody louder. The snake coalesced, then the tapered end of it dripped over the edge of the roof and plopped onto the ground. It began undulating across the ground with violent speed, heading straight for Car Manopu's hut.

Mother threw down her brush, threw back her head, and bellowed at a volume I've never heard before and will never hear again, bellowed powerful pagan words that demanded and commanded, and the dead insects in her hair glittered brilliant silver in the moonlight and rose up like a cloud of stars and flew out into the night.

The snake stopped still.

The chants from Kobo's kin became ragged, syncopated.

Mother sent a summons winging like a white egret into the air.

A jug appeared at her elbow, as sheer as a cobweb. She picked it up and tipped it over her tiles, and from it poured a thin river of luminescent green glaze as real as the blood in my veins. The glaze splashed down, down, down, gracing her clay tiles like holy oil sprinkled from a crucible.

"Heat," she said, or sang, or thought, or bellowed—I don't know; it was all one and the same. The word was puissant and foreign, and I closed my eyes and squeezed my arms around my head an instant before a scorching wind turned my skin into paper.

The blast lasted longer than the other had.

When it was over, I cautiously lifted my arms away from my head. Looked through the checkered wall to the courtyard beyond.

The snake was no more.

No dark shape slithered with sinister intent across our compound. Only star- and moonlight, pure and clean, speckled the ground. And silence, as reposed and sweet as the sleep-smile of an infant, reigned over all. The Djimbi chants had stopped.

"Done," Mother whispered wearily, and her legs gave out and she grabbed the table to remain upright.

Before her shone her creation: a six-tiled panel depicting a scene of three women swimming, one hoisting a plump baby for the others to see. It was an intimate, tender picture exquisitely rendered in a few flowing lines. The green water looked peaceful and inviting; the women soft and supple and utterly at ease. And that baby . . . Why, you knew that baby was loved with deep, delicate care.

In creating that clay panel so full of gentle life, Mother had stopped the evil of the night. The vengeful Djimbi chants Kobo's kin had been employing to evoke evil magics against Car Manopu's kin, and the dark, otherworld snake those chants had summoned . . . in creating that tile panel, Mother had evoked magics of her own and ended it all.

The rest of that week, the pottery clan toiled under a blistering sun, slashing and bundling liana vines and resinous macci leaves that at day's end were traded for a pittance. Kobo's kin hissed and spat when-ever the shadow of Car Manopu's family crossed their own, yet an un-easy truce presided between the two and no more blows fell.

Each night, glassy-eyed with hunger and lock limbed from exhaus-tion, I stumbled after Mother into the work shed. I washed, hung up my bitoo, donned Mother's, clambered atop the table, and fell asleep to her voice. The dreams she evoked—for dreams I was certain they were, because no evidence existed at dawn to suggest otherwise—en-veloped me in calm and soothed away the dizzy wakefulness brought on by hunger.

That six-tiled panel I'd imagined the first night was followed the next by a grandiose platter sculpted in the shape of a pirarucu, that large, predatory fish that is a dietary staple for riverine Djimbi. Daubed with iron and copper chun and spattered with cobalt, the platter was a magnificent piece of bayen art fit for the most illustrious aristocrat.

A temple mirror frame followed that, its twisted pillars and em-bossed, beveled roof tiles bloodred beneath gilding powder. Two ele-gant smoke-fired bottles came next, lovingly and painstakingly decorated.

But each morning, as I said, I awoke to the mundane: a simple hump-molded dish, a functional pot with dragon-tongue handles, a conventional spoon holder.

Waking was like rising through a thick clay slurry, my neck and arms and legs too heavy to lift, my eyelids too weighted to open.

But wake I would, to Mother's insistent nudges. And there I would be, somehow already in my clean and dry bitoo, and Mother in her dust-thick and worn one, the magic that had cradled me during the night and animated my hunger-driven dreams vanishing as I rose.

More than dreams, they were. They were fantasies. A dream ac-knowledges limitations even while attempting to overcome them. A fantasy recognizes no boundaries. A six-tiled panel that can be cre-ated, fired, painted, glazed, and fired again all in one night is the stuff of fantasy. Such a process, in temporal daylight, takes no less than a clawful of days.

And yet . . .

And yet with what detail I remembered the fantasies of those nights! For instance, the elegant smoke-fired bottles with their slim necks and curvaceous bellies and circular bases. I clearly saw in my mind's eye, as I dragged and stacked liana vines the next day, how Mother's strong, square hands had lifted a ribbon of yupplin frond from a bowl of glue at her elbow, the frond ribbon as narrow as the thorax of a butterfly and as long as a bunting's feather. Between thumb and forefinger, she'd strip-squeezed the excess glue off, then slowly pressed the ribbon onto the bottle's surface, her fingers working it slightly this way, slightly that way. Ribbon after gluey ribbon the night through, until the bottle sat swathed in its scallop-shaped bandages.

Contemplative, intense work, that, shunned by most. Mother loved it. She hummed a little as she worked.

Another bottle: Increment by increment, she created a delicate tracework over its smooth, white surface, each gluey ribbon equidistant from the other, each curve clean and sensuous.

That her fingers didn't adhere to the bottle or dislodge the strips she'd already laid down was not the stuff of fantasy. She possessed such skill. But no skill had she to create two such bottles, fire them, decorate them, and smoke fire them in the same eve, let alone carefully scrape off the charred remains of the ribbons after firing to reveal the smoke-black patterns beneath. Certainly, she had no beeswax with which to lovingly burnish the finished bottles.

Yet I saw it all. I did. In just such detail.

I can explain none of this. I'm not saying I *won't* explain it, I'm saying I can't.

All I can do is bear witness.

And Waisi, you might ask? Where was she?

With us.

After that first night, she remained with Mother always, as close as a baby spider monkey keeps to its mother. Right on her heels.

Yet what anger Waisi projected toward Mother, even as she shadowed her every move! Though she never left her side for a heartbeat, Waisi didn't once help Mother if she needed aid lifting a bundle of vines. She never initiated conversation with Mother and never answered her civilly, but instead roared out a reply from a throat so choked with anger her words were warped beyond meaning.

As for Mother, she treated Waisi as one would an ill child. She fussed over her, made allowances for her, and excused her behavior many times to any who would hear. Her manner was that of a mother who believed, illogically, that she was to blame for all the misfortune that had befallen the world and had therefore tainted her child's life. I would have been annoyed by that pitiful obsequiousness if my fear of Waisi's rage had not been greater. As it was, I made myself as small as I could and slinked around Waisi in silence.

At night, in the work shed, Waisi would crawl into one of the empty shelves.

That was an odd sight. Waisi was full figured, and the shelves were narrow and divided into compartments. She had to curl about herself like a newborn babe, legs drawn up to belly and head tucked down to navel. She couldn't have been comfortable cramped up like that all night, especially after such grueling labor during the day. Yet that was what she did night after night, and each morning she awoke more sour, more stiff, and more furious.

I offered one night to trade places with her so that she might sleep stretched upon the trestle table.

"No," was all she said. Just that: no. Such an abrupt, powerful word, so devoid of detail.

I was too deep in stupor to think much about it after that. Food grew scarcer, the sun hotter, and the liana vines heavier than they had any right to be.

I sought refuge in my night dreams and obsessively awaited the miraculous eighth day of our poverty.

It came, that eighth day, sluggishly and reluctantly. The pottery clan women wept with relief, and the men exchanged tight, proud smiles. One of our boys had been dragon chosen. We had suffered. We were virtuous. Now the blessings would arrive.

The rumble of wagons began shortly after dawn. We cluttered the courtyard and crouched on our haunches, eyes transfixed on our compound's archway.

Wagons, wagons, wagons! They rumbled down the widest alleys in our zone, and where a stricture between two walls prevented the continuance of the parade, we heard mallets smash into ancient bricks to create a pathway. Spectators ran, cheering, after those wagons, and I closed my eyes and savored the expectation of what those wagons would soon bring to our clan.

Shiny pots! Crates of dates and sugared nuts! Urns of oil, slabs of gharial meat, bolts of fabric and cured hide. Machetes, combs, hammocks, sleeping mats, tobacco, spools of thread, boxes of seeds, packets of needles, and shiny teak pipes packed in fine sawdust: There was nothing those wagons would not hold.

And the last wagon? It would be filled with plain wooden crates containing a lifetime worth of chits. So many crates, so many chits, and they would all pass into the hands of our clan Greatfather, the number equal to the number of days the average man lived. Equal, then, to the life the dragonmaster had taken from us.

Dawn stretched into morning, morning into noon. Though we heard those wagons and the cheering of those who followed them, none came through our arch.

"It is only right the glass spinners receive their wealth first, because their boy was chosen before ours," Greatfather Maxmisha said magnanimously.

But the first tendrils of apprehension slithered about us as afternoon shadows began to lengthen. Babies cried with the thin mewling of the truly hungry. Mothers dandled them and nursed them and snapped at them. But no one left the courtyard.

Mother was the first. She rose wearily and shot a look at Father. Moving like one twice her age, she shuffled to the work shed.

Beside me, Waisi startled. She looked at Mother's retreating back, then to the entry arch, then back to Mother. She balled her hands and hit herself against the temples. She started laughing.

It was a hoarse, hysterical sound. It broke the stupor that gripped us all. The babies and children began crying anew with vigor. The men scuffed about, formed an agitated group, consulted. I covered my ears, but that seemed like too much work, my arms were that heavy, so I let my fingers slide out my ears and trail down my cheeks and plop back onto my lap.

Dusk settled around us. The rumble of wagons stopped. From the glass spinners' compound many alleys away floated the sounds of celebration.

Father and blood-Uncle Rudik helped Greatfather Maxmisha remain upright. He tottered like a baby learning to walk and leaned heavily upon the knotted stick that had become his cane since Sa Gikiro eve. With father and Uncle Rudik on either side, he shuffled toward our archway.

His malignancy wobbled with every step. It had grown during the last eight days. Or maybe it was only that Greatfather had shrunk. It wobbled to and fro as he walked, in time to Waisi's laughs. It reminded me of the green toggle at the end of the dragonmaster's beard. Gooseflesh erupted over my arms and I shivered violently.

Greatfather went under the arch with Father and Uncle Rudik. They turned a corner. Out of sight. Into the dark.

Mother kneaded clay that night. Simply that; nothing more. Eyes fixed ahead, never once looking at what she did, she pushed and folded the same lump of clay over and over. *Thump-thud. Thump-thud.*

She evoked no dreams for me that night. Just *thump-thud, thump-thud.*

Unwashed and clothed in my filthy bitoo, I eventually fell into a trance that wasn't quite sleep. Waisi never joined us.

Sometime in the depth of night, when dew beaded ground and foliage, Mother stopped. Perhaps it was this that stirred me, the sudden cessation of those thuds. She stood before the table, palms resting on the abused clay, her eyes fixed, for all that I could see, on the exact spot as earlier.

But now she held her head tilted, and a certain tension enlivened her body. She looked like an unclipped yearling poised for flight.

She brushed her hands across her rump—once, twice, thrice, a hand on either side—then left the work shop. I floundered upright, trip-fell off the table, and staggered after her.

She headed straight for the mating closets, rising up the steps as if she were made of wind.

A lone man waited inside the half-open door, his bulk revealed by a shaft of waning moonlight. Father.

He held no candle. Mother stood on tiptoe, found a shriveled congle nut resting on the lintel, and placed it inside one of the congle gourds that perpetually sat there. Father moved inside, into shadow; she joined him and closed the door.

I hesitated. Then I didn't. I lurched as quickly as my stiff legs permitted up the wooden stairs and stood there, holding my breath. The door opened and a hand shot out and grabbed me.

"Not a sound," Mother said, pulling me into the musty dark. Her choice of words was so like those Car Manopu's Wasaltooltic had used to rouse me the night we'd transported the hidden urns from the jungle that I knew that whatever was going to transpire would not meet with Greatfather's approval.

Silently, we three moved through the cramped, dark comb of mating cubicles, passed sliding paper doors half open and the empty, stark cubicles beyond them. No one but us was in there that night; we had our pick of cubicles to choose from.

We went to the back room, to the largest cubicle reserved for First Mating unions and men's pleasure parties, and Father slid the large paper doors closed. The darkness within was so dense it lay like a shroud over my skin. As there were no cushions since Sa Gikiro eve, I sat cross-legged on the wooden floor in a corner. I heard Mother make some sort of movement; I don't know what.

"They said it was an invalid Choosing. They said . . . " Father trailed off into heavy breaths.

Mother didn't speak. A sort of bristling took place, that feeling that comes into the air during a dry storm. The downy hairs on my forearms rose up.

The walls of the cubicle were made from eight layers of woven palm fronds, thus the stifling atmosphere. No light penetrated those layers. Yet suddenly, I could see Mother knelt before Father, both of them bathed in an amber glow.

Crouched on his haunches, Father faced her with his head bowed, his broad shoulders stooped, his huge soft hands clenched between his knees.

Have you ever heard the sound a freshly fired brick makes when carelessly dropped into a puddle? That spitting, hissing noise was my mother's voice.

"I'll petition the cinai komikon," she said.

"Kavarria." Father said her name like a weary plea. "Kavarria."

She rose to leave; his hand stayed her.

"They showed us the statutes," he said. "In the Monsoon Night Scroll. It says just this thing. If a Choosing should be manipulated by the actions of a man so as to win the dragonmaster's attention, such as Dono did, the Choosing is—"

"You can't read."

"Kavarria."

"And Greatfather is blind."

"He sees a little. Enough to read—"

"I'm not talking about that kind of blindness."

Father paused a moment before saying stiffly, "The daronpuis would not mislead us."

"What have they got to gain by telling the truth?"

"There must be some restrictions. If everyone did as Yeli's Dono, why, chaos would reign in the temple on Sa Gikiro, because everyone would try attract the dragonmaster's attention. Everyone."

Silence from Mother, pointed as a thorn.

"So Yeli's Dono will be returned to us?" she asked at last. "As the Choosing was invalid."

"Ah. No. You see, it is not so much the Choosing that is invalid, but the way the Choosing was provoked. Dono will remain in the apprenticeship; however, danku is exempt from reimbursement for the loss. Understand?"

"Oh yes. Yes, I do," she said bitterly. "And I suppose Temple had something to say about everything that was taken from us on Sa Gikiro night."

"Ah. That."

"That."

"Yes, well, it makes sense, doesn't it? We list what was taken by whom. Temple will ensure all is returned. Seeing as the Choosing was, to a certain degree, invalid." He shifted, changed his tone. "This is how it will be, Kavarria."

"If I speak with the dragonmaster—"

"No."

The light around Mother snuffed out, plunging us into a darkness so dense I knew I must have imagined the light. "Darquel, I *must* have food. Please. Don't you see?"

I heard movement, followed by a groan torn deep from my father's chest.

"So you see?" Mother whispered, and to my horror, I realized she was weeping. "We must make things right again, everything, all of it—a new danku garden, replenished fuel stores. . . ." She stopped and sucked in a breath. "But first food. We all need food."

"Greatfather has secured the pottery clan some eggs and oil. Over a month's worth."

"What! How?" Before Father could answer, she cried, "Who? Re show you mercy if it's Zarq—"

A brusque guffaw from Father. "Not Zarq. We wouldn't be able to trade her if we tried."

I didn't like the sound of that, even though I wasn't sure what they were discussing. All I knew was that my worth, in some way, was minimal. Not a nice thing to hear from one's father at any time. But I didn't dwell on it, not then, for Mother again asked, "*Who?*"

I suddenly knew by Father's hesitation that this was the source of his stooped shoulders and bowed head. He felt shame not because our clan had been cheated, and not because he and his father and brother had been unable to secure justice from the holy wardens; he was ashamed of this other thing, this thing that stuck in his throat like a seed husk.

"Waisi," I breathed, not meaning to speak at all. The words rose unbidden from my mouth.

"No!" Mother cried, and I nearly leapt right out of my skin from the sudden movement that accompanied that cry, for one moment she was a stillness in the room's center, and the next minute she was fury in motion.

Scuffles and slaps and something ripped, and Father grunted heavily from the belly.

"Not her, you brute. How could you!" Mother cried.

The mating closet shook and shuddered, and panicked insects scuttled within the walls.

"I'll never touch you again, danku Re Darquel, by the claws of Re—"

"She goes to the glass spinners! She'll do well there!"

"*No!* If you let that happen—"

"Be reasonable, woman! She's of age. She'll do well, eat better than us. They're rich now, the glass spinners."

"She's *my baby!*"

"Hardly that."

"Darquel, do whatever it takes to prevent Waisi from being sent there. Do you hear? You know how they'll treat one such as her, traded under circumstances such as these."

"You make too much noise, Kavarria—"

"And how can you forget the visit from Waikar Re Kratt? He's interested in her. He'll claim her as his ebani yet—"

"We've no guarantee of that. He hasn't returned, hasn't summoned her once. After the way she treated him, little wonder."

"These things take time—"

"He won't claim her, woman! And we need to fill our bellies *now*."

"Bring her back. I give you no choice in this, understand? Take Waisi from me, and I swear, I swear . . ." She broke into sobs.

Suddenly, I was smothered against Mother's bosom.

"Bring her back," she wept against my forehead. "Please, please, bring my baby back."

I thought, in my confusion and fear, that she was begging such a thing of me and not Father.

Only so much later did I realize that yes, I was right. She was.

SEVEN

As soon as dawn broke, we went to see Waisi.

The celebrations that had started when the first Temple wagon had rolled into the korikapku, the glass spinners' clan, were now finished, and the place glowed with the satisfaction of a recently sated python.

The few korikap women who were awake and in the courtyard watched us with heavy-lidded indolence. They were not in the least concerned with our presence. From what I could see of them when I dared glance up from the ground, was that every last one was red eyed from lack of sleep and red cheeked from overeating.

I grew bolder, looked longer.

A cluster of women sat upon the ground amid a luxurious pool of pillows. They lazily raked soft oils through their uncoiled hair with lacquered ebony combs. A little ways off, two women lifted a long sheet of gauzy netting off a table made from upturned paak barrels clustered together; honeyed cakes briefly glittered upon the barrels like dozens of sticky miniature suns. My stomach roiled as saliva flooded my mouth.

Mother approached one of the young women draped across the pillows. The woman was nursing a baby that had recently been massaged with oil; its limbs gleamed as it chuckled at her breast.

"I'm waiting for bull wings to bless the herd of Re," Mother murmured in polite greeting.

"May your waiting end. May bull wings hatch," the woman responded, revealing a horribly yellow front tooth among her upper teeth. It reminded me of a toucan's beak. I was immensely pleased that one so recently blessed had to bear such ugliness throughout her life; not a noble thought, but perhaps you can forgive me, given my age.

"I've come to speak with a young woman known to me as Danku Re

Darquel's Waivia," Mother said, her usual Djimbi singsong held in check by the tight reins of politeness. "She was blessed with the privilege of being allowed to join the korikapku roidan last evening. Is she free to speak with her blood-mother?"

Silence from the toucan, who sucked on her lower lip; it was most unbecoming with that snaggletooth. An old woman who was smoking a pipe upon the stairs of the women's barracks a stone's throw away spoke up.

"Ripe kiyu girl, she."

My heart tripped. Kiyu! The hag had called my sister a sex slave! I waited for Mother to point out that my sister was no such lowly, indentured creature; was instead a free clan woman given the honorable duty of pleasuring the men of her new clan. She merely colored, however, and lifted her chin. "Please, where might I find her?"

Toucan shrugged and looked at her baby, feigning interest in its sleep-snarled hair. The crone answered with a lewd pucker at the mating shack, which sat upon freshly painted red stilts across the courtyard from the women's barracks. Save for the dripping new paint, the shack looked identical to our own, just as boxy and worn. I wondered when they had painted it—last night, inebriated? Why?

With meticulous thanks to both the crone and Toucan, Mother crossed the courtyard in brisk strides. I scurried to keep up and kept my eyes riveted on the fissures in her dry heels, for I could feel everyone watching us with interest now. The interest didn't seem friendly.

Mother paused at the trio of upturned barrels that bore the decadent feast of sweet cakes. To my shock, she lifted the netting and took two. I expected shouts, and perhaps Mother did, as well; her hands trembled as she settled the sticky netting back into place.

No one accosted us. We continued over to the mating shack. With a heavy exhalation that was half sigh, half grunt, Mother sat on the shack's lowest step. She gestured for me to join her. As I did so, she handed me a cake. I sank my teeth into it and, oh, it was sweet! So sweet I broke out coughing and sent a spray of precious crumbs across the dusty ground. Mother whacked my back.

"Eat slower," she mumbled, her own mouth stuffed with honeyed cake.

But I couldn't. I gulped the sweet stuff down, hardly chewing it. At once, I was stricken with painful gas. I folded over my belly with a groan and rocked to and fro. Mother rubbed my back, or tried to, but her hands kept drifting to a stop. She was distracted by her own thoughts.

We waited a long time upon those steps. The sun came fully up, more women flowed into the courtyard, and a little of the morning routine took place before us. Some women fetched water, others sliced paak, another swept the courtyard smooth. Everything was done in a desultory manner. The women's movements spoke not only of a lack of sleep and overindulgence in food, but also of a gluttony of love play and fermented juice. No men had appeared yet, and I guessed they were snoring in their domiciles.

"They've always looked down upon my Waivia, hey-o," Mother muttered beside me. Her distant expression told me she wasn't really addressing me; she just needed to release the words from her throat. "No one has ever liked my Waisi. She's too smart, too quick. Too beautiful."

Even though I wasn't sure whom she meant by *no one*, I was offended because the term included me. "I like her just fine."

She looked down at me as though surprised I was there.

"Ah, yes, you. You're different than Waisi, though. People liked you when you were young. You were normal, average. Waisi, they didn't like her. She crawled and climbed when most babies can't sit. She ran and talked and fed herself when most babies aren't yet on their knees. Always too clever, too bright. At five years, she could recite anything she heard, no matter how long. Word for word she could quote from Temple scrolls, just from hearing something spoken once from a daronpu. You, you were never like that. Lazy baby, like every other child."

"Was not," I said indignantly. "I always worked in the pottery shed with you."

"Yes, yes, you smashed clay lumps into powder, you made nice clay slurry. But Waivia? When she was still young, she made urns and threw pots by herself. Learned skills children twice her age couldn't master. Proud of it, too. All the time she showed off her skills. They didn't like that, the other mothers. One such as Waisi shouldn't be so clever, understand. Shouldn't be so pretty. Not one such as her."

One such as her?

Mother sighed. "That's why I gave you that name, hey-o: Zarq. To separate you from the others in a way similar to how she was separate. So she'd not be so alone."

Mother leaned toward me and clutched my closest wrist with one of her broad, sinewy hands. Her breath smelled odd, like vinegar mixed with raw yolk. I wondered if she'd been ill during the night.

"She should have had roidan kasloo, Zarq. She *needs* it."

"I don't know what you're talking about," I said. "Garden rotations and all that. I think you haven't had enough to eat." A stupid thing to say; of course she hadn't had enough to eat. No one in our clan had.

She looked startled, then a thin smile tugged at her lips. "You don't know what is roidan kasloo mutian, hey-o? I don't mean the garden rotations you're thinking about. There's another type. The mutian, the ceremony. Let me explain it to you, yes?"

Between clans, Mother said, a very important sort of barter often took place. Unclaimed, fertile women were exchanged for wares during a ceremony called roidan kasloo, garden rotations. Not enough women trading between clans resulted in stunted children who matured into lackluster adults.

She tried to make me recall two such woman trades that had taken place during my milk years: apparently, one of Big Grum Grum's girl children had undergone roidan kasloo mutian when I was four, and when I was six, both Kaban's Kavarria and Yanzarq's Dash-li had joined the pottery clan in such an exchange. I must have been a somewhat oblivious child, for I could recall no such sudden appearances and disappearances of women. Mother continued with her explanation, despite my obtuseness.

"A fine ceremony occurs in temple, hey-o, on the eve of roidan kasloo," she said. "The eldest men of the clans involved attend, all the old men who think they know what's best for a woman and her ku. A clawful of daronpuis are there, too, with their rules and high chins and sneers. Behind closed doors, the woman-for-trade is taken into a dark room, and there the First Holy Warden examines her, all by himself, his hands all over her, making sure the quality of woman and wares being traded balance."

Examines her? In a dark room, all alone? My cheeks colored.

"The result of the examination is very important in the bargaining process, hey-o. Very important," Mother repeated. "It says how good a woman is, how much she's worth to her new clan. You see the importance of this, yes?"

She regarded me intently and I knew I was failing her, for I could only nod, hoping the embarrassment I felt at learning about such a shameful process was not evident.

"Zarq, listen now. Open your ears. *It is not uncommon for roidan kasloo to take days and days.* Weeks, even. The woman undergoes examination three, six, sometimes eight times. The more examinations, the better the verdict, yes? Eight is very good. Very good."

She paused again, awaiting my response. I squirmed, wondering what vital point I was missing in my shame.

"Sometimes the moon swells and shrinks and swells again before a judgement is reached." Mother tightened her grip round my wrist. "So much time, so much arguing, so much bragging takes place between clan men during this, to ensure the woman is traded honorably, so she's granted respect in her new clan, so she earns a favorable report from the examining First Holy Warden. All this happens, always. *Always.*"

The jungle vines cleared away inside my thick head. I could see, finally, what she was getting at.

Waisi had been traded overnight.

Unusual, disrespectful, and damaging in the extreme. She would not be given even so much as the lowly status of ebani-basa, my sister, not in her new clan. No. Although she would be required to pleasure the clan's men, she would be regarded as kiyu. An indentured sex slave.

She would be regarded as something less than human.

"That's why I must speak with her," Mother concluded. "She has to understand I had no part in this. I haven't cast her away like a broken pot."

"It doesn't sound like you would have had any part in it even if there had been a proper ceremony," I said. My shame was turning into pique, that such crucial information about what could happen in my future—roidan kasloo mutian—had not been imparted to me prior to now.

I'm ashamed, looking back upon that moment, by how worried I was about *my* future and not my poor sister's fate.

Mother tightened her grip on my wrist, squeezed it in her muscled hand so tightly that discomfort focused my eyes on her.

"We have to buy her back, Zarq. They will despise her here. Kiyu, my Waisi! I won't—"

Just then, someone groaned in the closets behind us. Mother stiffened.

Grunts, a sleep-burred curse, a woman's protest stopped with a sharp slap.

Mother jerked as if she herself had been struck.

Rock-creak, rock-creak: The narrow step beneath us began shifting in rhythm to the movements within the shack. Mother flared her nostrils and closed her eyes.

More noises and movements within the closets, wet and suck-slapping, as well as a guttural stream of barely comprehensible coarse talk. Another slap, far sharper and louder, and someone—a woman—cried out.

Mother's grip on my wrist tightened. My fingers turned puce; the tips throbbed. They were going to split open under the nails and blood geyser out—

A sudden thump. A hoarse, quavering sigh full of glut. Silence.

An unendurable pause.

Male voices in the closets, followed by guffaws. The shack lurched, then the door was abruptly pushed open. Mother and I scrambled to our feet and stepped to the side of the stairs. She released my wrist.

Three young men came down the mating shack's stairs. The door bumped closed after them. The three were all lean muscle and sleep-disheveled hair and love-swollen lips, and they stank of musky sweat and something vaguely like seaweed. They ignored us. Squinting against the morning light, they swaggered across the courtyard and disappeared behind a cluster of huts.

Mother swallowed and stared without blinking at the mating shack's door. I didn't know what to do.

Some time passed. Someone within yawned, so forcibly I heard the crack of jaw and rush of breath from where I stood. A subdued exchange of words followed between . . . two women? Three?

The door creaked open. One, two, three women descended. I was waiting for a fourth—Waisi—when I realized with a start that the third woman *was* her.

But how changed she looked. Taller yet slighter, as if she had been stretched and now could only hold herself together by hunching her shoulders and walking in careful, precise steps. Bruises splotched her arms. Her upper lip was split and bloody. Both her eyes were half closed and purple. Mother cried out and took a step forward, arms outstretched. Waisi looked up.

And stopped dead still upon the stairs.

"What are you doing here?" she hissed.

The two other women scurried away from us.

"Get out of here!" Waisi frantically waved her hands at us, as if shooing away rabid dogs.

"Waivia, let me explain—" Mother began, but Waisi rattled down the spindly stairs and planted herself before Mother, trembling and shuddering as if she were about to vomit.

"How could you do this to me?" she stammered, and that was what shocked me most. Not the bruises or blood, but that wild fragility.

"I didn't know they were going to do it. I had no idea, none," Mother said in a breathless rush, stroking the air inches from Waisi's arms, as if she were too brittle to touch. "I'll buy you back—"

"The last thing I need is to be known as a Djimbi whore's bastard!" Waisi said wildly. "Now get out of here! Go!"

She shoved Mother, actually placed her hands against Mother's shoulders and pushed her away. Mother stumbled backward. Waisi jammed her knuckles in her mouth and bit down hard, to hold back a cry or tears or a curse. They stared at each other, Mother and Waisi, Waisi and Mother, chests heaving, and yet another mysterious veil that had lain over my eyes since birth was ripped away by Waisi's fierce words: *The last thing I need is to be known as a Djimbi whore's bastard.* And I saw Waisi for what she was.

Someone with brown skin, faintly mottled dusty green. Someone who was Djimbi. Like Mother.

Someone unlike me.

And I heard anew the words Mother had spoken not long before, heard them and understood them for what they meant: *"They didn't like that, the other mothers. One such as Waisi shouldn't be so clever, understand. Shouldn't be so pretty. Not one such as her.*

One such as her.

A Djimbi.

Mother clutched her bitoo about herself, turned, and fled the glass spinners' compound.

"Wait!" I cried out, but Mother kept running, stumbling, weaving, and now she was beyond the entry arch and disappearing down an alley, and there stood I, forgotten, abandoned. "Mama!"

I ran after her, bawling.

Didn't get far. Gas in my belly brought me up short.

By the time I made it back to the pottery clan compound, I realized something had changed in Mother, had been ripped right out of her, and that the loss would affect the way she treated me for the rest of her life.

EIGHT

A coughing sickness struck the sesal-pickers' clan, so severely the Temple wardens in that zone placed the entire ku under quarantine. Ripened sesal nuts therefore hung unpicked in heavy ropes in the fields. Monkeys and birds ate the tart widik fruit and oily hintoop blooms that grew vinelike among the sesal bushes, and that which they did not eat began to rot on branch and ground. The seven thousand brooder dragons shackled in the egg stables of Clutch Re lowed in hunger from the sudden lack of fodder.

Egg production dropped. The few eggs the brooders produced bore pale, watery yolks. Shells cracked easily.

Roshu-Lupini Re, the esteemed warrior-lord of our Clutch, proclaimed that any clan that worked the sesal fields would be fed, housed, granted gleaning rights, and paid handsomely. Of the hundreds of clans within our Clutch, few responded to the Proclamation. Only those clans hungry, desperate, or brash enough dared brave the dangers of the sesal fields.

The sesal fields are not fields, understand. They are vast orchards of bush heavy with clusters of nuts and crowded with feral life. Packs of wild curs and troops of howler monkeys live there. Red bees, hawk snakes, and feral cats live there, too. Venomous, mite-sized panpan crawl along the sesal branches, sucking nutrients from the velvety glandular patches under the leaves. Everywhere lurks danger and the threat of death.

Our clan was hungry and desperate enough to face those dangers, to skirt on that knife-edge of death. We journeyed to the sesal fields, my blood-Uncle Rudik acting as clan elder, for Greatfather Maxmisha had fallen into a deathly sleep from hunger and was not likely to wake.

We rode to the sesal fields in wagons that usually transported gharial meat and oil from the Re slaughterhouses, and buzzing flies and the rancid stench of grease and old blood accompanied us the entire way.

In the searing sun, the brooder dragons pulling our wagons stank as badly as the wagons themselves. The old brooders' moss-and-rust-colored scales reeked of decay and regurgitated food, but despite the fetor, I could see the beasts as nothing short of a food source. Throughout the long journey to the sesal fields, I kept inanely hoping a brooder might drop an egg, and that the daronpuis driving our wagons would permit us all to eat it on the spot. Raw.

Even the thought of eating the shell appealed, I was that hungry.

None of the old brooders dropped a single egg during the journey, though. Of course not. Their egg-laying days were long over.

That didn't stop me from crooning to the old brooders, pleading with them to drop an egg. Despite Mother's murmurs that I hold my tongue, I kept up my songs; I was delirious, see, for the hand that had three months ago touched dragon venom during Mombe Taro was now pudgy with rot, the arm streaked crimson. As the hot day and interminable wagon ride to the fields wore on, I slipped into a feverish puddle at Mother's feet, my inane pleas to the dragons unintelligible.

We arrived at the sesal fields at dusk. Murmurs of dismay rose from our clan at the manner of shelter so generously supplied by our warrior-lord: a cluster of slipshod structures, each one different from the next. Mismatched planks, sheets of woven reeds, bolts of improperly cured gharial hide, and mud-straw bricks stacked and strapped together haphazardly had all been used to create temporary housing for the replacement pickers, to protect us from the nocturnal cats that prowled the fields. In my feverish mind, I saw the camp as the ruins of a hamlet, masticated by some great creature, then spat out again upon the earth.

Mother hoisted me over a shoulder as if I were a sack of chaff.

"Hey-o, wake up," she said, pinching me. Three months ago, such a pinch would have made me howl. But hunger had sapped her strength and now the pinch was just a flitting irritation. I closed my eyes. My head bump-bumped against her knobby spine. I just wanted to sleep.

Clunk! The back of my skull thudded against hard ground and my eyes flew open. Mother's face loomed over me. We were in a tent, a floating tent, the gharial hide shifting this way, dancing that way. . . .

"I'll be back," Mother sighed, and then hands were pinning me down, soft large hands smelling resinous and acrid.

A bald woman with no eyebrows knelt astraddle my waist.

"Her hand, is it?" she murmured in a baritone. "Nasty."

I bucked and yawed like an unbroken yearling, trying to throw the woman off, and I grabbed her throat and dug in my nails to rip out her larynx.

"None of *that!*" the woman boomed, and she rose off me in a whoosh of green cloth, turned, and dropped back down on me, sitting bottom-naked upon my face.

Ah. This was no woman. An empty scrotal sac devoid of all hair, and a humid little penis that smelled of astringent soap, squashed roundly against my chin.

The man neatly pinned my arms one apiece under his knees. At his order, someone else sat upon my thrashing legs. Then he started picking at my hand, for all the world like a big green carrion beetle. I passed out.

If it hadn't been for that gelded creature, I'm sure I would have died that day in the warehouse.

Mother had found a chanooi, a proselyte of the Chanoom Sect, administering to the new sesal pickers. All chanooi are castrated, the women circumcised in the manner of convent holy women, thus the man was permitted in the tents of women and children. My hand, with its necrotic flesh, was a clarion call to the chanoom zeal for cleanliness.

What better way to fulfill a holy vow to rid the world of filth than to carve away a child's gangrenous flesh and save the life of the pus-pocked, feverish skeleton?

It's funny to whom we owe our lives, hey-o.

I passed the next few days in delirium.

While I sweated and hallucinated in fever, the rest of my clan picked sesal nuts and hintoop buds and tart widik fruit from the fields. When everyone returned at nightfall, they found me asleep outside, at the entrance of our clan women's tent, my fever reduced somewhat more each day, my arm a little less red, and my hand swathed in clean bandages that imprisoned fresh maggots against my dead flesh.

They ate well, those maggots. My wound began to heal.

Afternoon of the third day, my fever broke.

I became aware of my lucidity gradually, as though stupor were some viscous coating melting off me. I slowly understood that the moans and pantings about me belonged not to otherworld spirits, but to wounded and ill people sprawled, like me, on the threshold of their assigned clan tents, for by midday, each tent turned into a kiln beneath the relentless sun and the heat drove the ill outside. I also realized that no shape-changing demons hovered over me, but instead, clouds of buzzing flies. And no massive carrion beetle was presently picking at my hand, merely the compulsively clean chanooi.

"Feeling better, are you?" he said, and he looked well pleased with himself as he placed fresh maggots upon my wound and began bandaging it anew.

I became aware of a mumbled chanting, now even and clear, now hoarse and unsteady.

Without rising, I turned my head and looked about me. Wending his way through the camp was a daronpu acolyte. With crucible and brazier, he swung droplets of consecrated gharial oil over the ground while intoning purifying stanzas. Every now and then he ducked into a women's tent, then ducked out shortly after, still swinging his holy instruments.

The chanooi cleaning my hand followed my gaze, squinting a little in the bright sunlight, sweating in the oppressive heat.

"To cleanse the earth, hey-o," he said with a sanctimonious sniff. "Roshu-Lupini Re is so concerned about the harvest, he disregards the profanity of women sleeping directly upon Clutch soil. An outrageous sacrilege, that."

I thought the chanooi brave and foolish to so openly criticize our warrior-lord, but I also understood his repugnance; no women's barracks existed in this camp, therefore no stilts and no raised wooden floor separated our womanly waters from the dirt. Women wept tears, nursed babes, and dripped menstrual blood directly upon the soil within their respective clan tents. An outrageous transgression of Temple Statute, that, to befoul Clutch soil with female secretions.

I felt shamed by it, was glad the sin was being corrected by the adolescent acolyte's chants and holy oil.

"Now you sleep," my chanooi said. He patted me on the head with a sweaty hand, rose, and moved to a tent adjacent to ours, to his next patient.

I continued to watch the daronpu acolyte swing oil hither and thither over the ground as he ducked in and out of the encampment's coarse mud-brick structures and lopsided yurts. Gradually, he drew closer to our clan women's tent.

Hey-o, was he handsome! He was the perfect result of Archipelagic and Malacarite breeding: broad shouldered, skin the color of aged ivory, eyes the color of rich, wet loam. His beauty made me acutely aware of my sorry state and my nonexistent hips and breasts.

Our eyes met as he approached our tent.

My gaze lingered overlong on him; I did not drop my eyes as I should have. I couldn't; his beauty held me in its thrall.

Still swinging his oily instruments, still droning stanzas, he came toward me.

He moved with an easy confidence; he knew the power of his looks, and that reminded me of Waisi. Indeed, he was exactly the type of self-assured, attractive young man that would have cast eyes at Waisi while at market, and she at him. But here he was, looking at me, and as he continued to step over the prone sick and pick his way round refuse, a flush started up my cheeks and my heart beat faster.

He stood before me. He continued to regard me, and up close, I could see his look was not what he would have directed at Waisi, not at all. There was too much poise and amusement in his mien, and I knew, in my secret heart, that he was merely diverting himself, momentarily, from his tedious task of purifying soiled ground.

But I didn't care.

I was thrilled by the stir of emotions his attention evoked. His eyes direct upon mine stirred some small animal within me, a creature that not only sought food and light, but seemed, in fact, ravenous. No man had looked at me that way before, in jest or otherwise, and yet here stood the most beautiful young man I'd ever laid eyes on, his whole attention focused solely upon me.

He smiled; my heart nearly burst with joy, and a peculiar heat bloomed near my bladder.

"You're beautiful," I whispered, not realizing till the words left my lips that I would speak.

His smiled twitched. He lifted a foot. Dropped it gently down on my closest leg. Stroked.

I held my breath, was lost in the sensation of his skin gliding over mine and the magnificence of his eyes.

"Like that?" he murmured.

I could not speak, felt faint, would have done anything that he asked of me, instantly.

A bead of his sweat fell slow-slow through the air and landed on my cheek. I touched it with a finger, brought the finger to my lips. Savored the briny taste.

His look altered somewhat, darkened briefly, and his foot fell still on my leg, and I knew, *I knew,* that for that moment I held him in a thrall much the way Waisi usually entranced men. Exhilaration swooped through me; I felt desirable and female and canny with seduction for the first time in my life.

I opened my mouth to ask for more, to again say I found him beautiful, but the words choked in my throat. The moment passed. The acolyte regained his senses. With a curt laugh, he withdrew his foot from my skin, stepped over me, and performed his cursory purification of our women's tent.

I lay at the tent's threshold, staring into the cloudless, sun-seared sky, overwhelmed by a maelstrom of emotions.

The acolyte finished inside our tent. He stepped over me. The smell of male sweat and temple incense flushed over my skin like heat. He walked away, still swinging his brazier beside him. Just before he disappeared behind a neighboring tent, he paused. Glanced back at me. Winked.

And I knew I would never forget him, that daronpu acolyte who'd caressed my skin. I knew I'd treasure forever the memory of how I had, momentarily, entranced the most beautiful man I'd ever laid eyes upon by bringing a drop of his sweat to my lips.

That night, I ate for the first time in days. Jungle weeds, brought to me by Mother from her gleaning in the fields.

At the first nibble of the bitter stuff, I gagged and retched. Mother grabbed my chin and glared into my eyes.

"You will eat these, understand? I don't care how bad they taste. You will eat them and get better and join me in the fields."

"But—"

"You'll get nothing else while we are here if you don't. I mean it, Zarq. Nothing."

I stared, barely recognizing her. Flakes of dried blood clung to her filthy chin and neck, as if she'd suffered a nosebleed while in the fields. Her pupils were tiny black points of fury, her lips sallow and drawn back in a snarl.

Bewildered and frightened, I forced the bitter weeds down. Mother nodded in satisfaction, then fetched a bowl of yanichee from the massive communal cauldrons simmering somewhere in the middle of the camp. Carefully, patiently, she tipped the broth little by little down my throat.

I fell asleep promptly after, as exhausted as if she'd forced me to run laps about the tent.

The next morning, I woke rational and clear-eyed.

The encampment was plunged in that expectant, densely silent gray peculiar to the cusp of dawn. Even the ever present hordes of flies that zoomed round and round the inside of our tent like angry miniature tornadoes clung now to the walls in silence. The snores and heavy breaths of the other women and children from our clan, crammed back-to-back in the tent, seemed quieter in the dawn's gloom, calmer, even.

Mother was sat beside me, one hand upon my arm; she had prodded me awake.

"Today you come with us, hey-o," she whispered. "Pick nuts, earn chits."

Her grip on my arm tightened.

"This coughing sickness is our way to buy back Waivia, Zarq. As long as sesal and hintoop are being gathered, Roshu-Lupini Re disregards the touch of a woman upon his Temple-sanctioned notes. Whomsoever picks is paid. Simple as that."

With a quick look left and right to make sure no one was yet awake and watching, she parted and lifted her bitoo. I was shocked at how thin her thighs had become, at how much her belly protruded. All the pottery clan children, myself included, had a little of that potbellied look. After several months of hard labor cutting vines to sell, without eggs and meat to sustain us and living solely on a diet of coarse roughage that swelled the belly but didn't satisfy the hunger, of course we looked that way. But I hadn't noticed such a potbelly on an adult before.

It was the object strapped above her belly that Mother wanted me to look at, though: a belt pouch, fashioned from some sort of broad leaf that had been stitched together by fibrous strands of a plant. The belt hugged her hips and the pouch hung just above the cinnamon arrow of her sex.

"It works like this, see," she whispered. "One picks sack after sack of nuts and fruit, and these are tallied, and at day's end chits are placed before you at collection table."

She dropped her bitoo, spread it back over her thighs.

"Your father doesn't know I have this pouch. No one from the danku knows. They think I'm too busy looking after everyone to pick, so no one is surprised by how few chits I give to Rudik at day's end. We'll buy Waivia back yet, Zarq! But I need you, understand. I need you to pick for me. For Waivia."

Her speech, her need, drained me. I closed my eyes.

"I'll get you some yanichee, yes? Hot-hot, just fresh made this morning by the camp cooks."

She rose, tiptoed through the tent, and ducked outside.

By the time she returned, people were stirring throughout our tent. Babies mewled and children were asking for food and the latrines. By the time I finished drinking the bowl of yanichee Mother had fetched for me, the ubiquitous clouds of flies once more buzzed above our ears, as if our presence enraged them.

"You stand now, yes? No more peeing in empty gourd for you. I'll help you to the latrines, then we go to the wagons that will take us into the fields. You come picking today."

Leaning heavily on Mother's arm for support, I shuffled to the latrine, which I discovered was no more than a fly-blown trough on the western outskirts of the encampment, running right into the sesal fields.

"Hurry, Zarq," Mother hissed as we both straddled the fetid sewer with our bare feet, along with clawfuls of other women and children. "The men are coming; women must do their dirty business first, before they wake."

"I *am* hurrying," I muttered.

Overhead, dawn stained the sky lavender. Birds trilled and cawed from the sesal bushes surrounding us, and the astringent green scents of jungle foliage vied with the salty aroma of simmering broth and the ashy smell of woodsmoke. The sun sluggishly crested the eastern mountain ridge; instantly, the whole of Clutch Re was plunged in sultry heat.

I didn't feel like working; I wanted only to sleep. Sleep and eat. But I was no longer delirious and I could stand, therefore I was well enough to pick.

Mother wove her way through the chaos of milling men, fussing women, and agitated children gathering round a long line of brooder-pulled wagons. I stayed close to her, overwhelmed by the noisy horde and still weak after my illness. The smell of sweaty bodies and unwashed hair mingled with the leathery reek of the dragons harnessed to the waiting wagons.

Our clan was gathering around two of the dusty wagons in subdued silence—perhaps reminded, by the crowd, of the mob that had descended upon us Sa Gikiro eve. I espied Rutvia and Makvia, and they came to my side, grinning. Though coated in grime, they looked remarkably hale. As did everyone else in our clan.

Everyone save Mother. She alone looked sallow and hollow-eyed, and the neck of her bitoo was stained brown from the nosebleeds she'd suffered while in the fields.

"We've been lining up six or seven times each night for food,"

Rutvia giggled when I pinched her round cheeks. "We eat as much as we want, even if it tastes pretty awful. Which it always does, hey-o."

"But don't try eating more than six slices of paak in one night," Makvia soberly advised. "You'll vomit all over the place. Trust me. I know."

I was itching to brag about my experience with the handsome acolyte, about how he'd actually touched me, actually stroked me. But just then everyone began climbing into the wagons.

Mother pulled me close to her. "Remember," she hissed into my ear. "You pick for Waivia. Pick lots, pick fast."

I nodded wearily and climbed into the wagon alongside her.

Moments later, the daronpu driving our wagon cracked whip upon dragon hide. With a lurch, our cart creaked forward.

NINE

My first day in the sesal fields blurred into a second day, and a third, and a fourth, and a tenth. Mother was well pleased with the number of chits the tallyman handed me each eve, and before giving them to Uncle Rudik, she discreetly tucked two-thirds of what I'd earned into the pouch beneath her bitoo, then hugged me and kissed me and cooed.

"Poor Zarq," she'd later cluck as she handed my pittance to Uncle Rudik. "Still weak from fever. Not picking much, lazy girl. Tomorrow she'll do better, yes?"

As the days raced on, the charade began to irk.

I wasn't lazy, not in the least; as fast as I could I scrambled from bush to bush, branch to branch, snatching at sesal nuts and sticky widik fruit and the oily hintoop blooms with their caustic red stamen. I filled my burlap bags so full that the straps around my shoulders chafed and produced nasty blisters; I picked so energetically because each bag I filled represented a chit, and each chit earned a smile or kiss or caress from Mother.

I was also immensely proud of the fact that I, a mere nine-year-old girl, was secretly earning enough chits that I could soon purchase back my ill-sold sister. In our entire Clutch, no other girl my age could boast of such an awesome achievement.

The price I paid for my dedicated labor, however, was being forced to play along with Mother's charade, which meant that no one but she, the tallymen, and I knew how much I really picked. This chafed at my spirit as much as the straps of the burlap bags chafed at my shoulders, for it became well known among our clan that I was the poorest picker of all. Boys teased me. Father shunned me in disappointment. Even Rutvia and Makvia made the occasional snide remark about my indolence.

Fatigue exacerbated my frustration; each night I returned to our tent too weary to play with my friends or engage in childish warfare with the gangs of camp children from other clans. Still, I had Mother's affection, and that meant a great deal.

Especially as the days progressed.

For as our stay in the fields continued, Mother began to change. She suffered blinding headaches and nausea. It became harder to make her smile, to summon her affection, to elicit a tender response. Blood trickled always from one or the other of her nostrils, a thin seepage that at day's end coated her grimy neck and her filthy bitoo and marked her as one fatally injured.

I knew, and others could guess, that her injury was not the visible kind, nor was it received by normal means.

The other rishi in the camp started avoiding Mother, which took some doing given the nature of our living conditions. Around us as we used the latrines was a void of bodies; behind and before us as we queued for food was a wary space. No one spoke to her save those in our own clan, and she spoke to no one. After a while, no one looked at Mother, either. Their eyes slid over her like a finger over wet clay.

Because Mother, and the very health of our clan, was unnatural, see.

Other people were snake bitten. Those in our clan were not. Other people's skin festered and gave them fever. Our clan had unblemished skin and cheeks that stayed cool. A child was attacked by a feral cat and died from the wounds overnight. Our children scampered, unwatched but unharmed, about the fields. People fainted from the heat, suffered bloody diarrhea caused by tainted food, fell off branches and broke limbs, and still our clan picked, picked, picked, unhindered by illness or injury.

Untouched by fang or venom, toxins or claws, bacteria or accident, the danku of Clutch Re picked.

And Mother bled.

She bled *a lot*.

Each day as our wagon rumbled deeper into the fields, Mother began muttering to herself. Her eyes glazed and her pupils turned to pinpoints that threatened to disappear entirely in her brown irises. The very air about our wagons changed, became denser somehow, the creaks of axle and hoots of jungle monkey muted. When anyone spoke, a barely audible echo answered, as if the entire pottery clan were enclosed in an invisible cave. I knew everyone in our clan was aware of the change by the careful way we avoided each others' eyes, by the way no one asked Mother why she mumbled, by the unacknowledged tension that stiffened necks and locked jaws.

I worried that our daronpu driver might become aware of the change, too.

Then one day, blood-Uncle Rudik announced that he, too, was concerned.

Our clan was sitting in a loose circle, sprawled under the dappled shade of bush and vine, while the heat of late noon turned our limbs soft as melted lard and the air nigh on unbreathable. I felt as if someone were holding a hot, sodden cloth over my nose and mouth. Mother sat by herself, off to one side, bleeding and muttering incessantly.

Uncle Rudik roused us all from our noon-break stupor.

"I have received news from Waidaronpu of Temple Wabe Din Sor. He is impressed by our work in the fields. He has spoken with other First Holy Wardens, and Temple has agreed to lend the danku enough chits to recover from our misfortune."

We all sat upright, exchanged looks, murmurs, hope.

Uncle Rudik held up a hand for silence.

"I have also learned that the quarantine on the sesalmapranku will be lifted in eight days' time. The sesal-pickers' clan has recovered from their illness and will return to these fields. These two thing have made me decide this: eight days from now, danku Re will return to our compound."

Gasps, exclamations, clapping of hands. Tears of relief and joy. Uncle Rudik standing, flushed with satisfaction, among us.

And then one voice, harsh and throaty: "Leave? Why leave? If we stay, we can earn enough so that a Temple loan is unnecessary."

All eyes swung toward Mother. She was standing, fists clenched, cheeks suffused with emotion.

Despite the heat, I suddenly felt chilled, for she was not only arguing with Uncle Rudik, but also suggesting we should stay in the hideous camp, picking in the deadly sesal fields.

"Kavarria," Father said warningly.

She would not be silenced.

"How much have we earned while picking here? Plenty. And have I not kept us all safe throughout? So why leave? We have food, we have shelter. To leave so soon when so much more can be earned—"

"It does not look good that the pottery clan of one of Malacar's most influential Clutches gathers the sesal harvest like common field hands," Uncle Rudik said curtly.

"It looked good enough yesterday and the day before that and the day before that!" Mother cried.

"Re's aristocrats depend upon us for platters and amphorae, floor tiles and tureens." Uncle Rudik spoke as if addressing a wayward simpleton. "That is our trade and responsibility."

"And how tedious and embarrassing it would be if for a short time only Re's First-Class Citizens had to obtain such goods from another Clutch," Mother caustically replied.

"Kavarria!" Father barked.

Her voice rose. "Have we no pride? Will we so glibly accept Temple's offer, an offer that should have been extended months ago when we were truly impoverished? I say no! For it is only now, when we are solvent, do they offer us aid, as if our honor were tainted before by our very lack!"

Mother flicked her thumbnails against her throat as an insult to Temple, then spat on the ground.

The women of our clan sat transfixed in horror by her display. I felt flushed and lightheaded both. Among our men, a sort of bristling took place; if they had been dogs, their hackles would have risen.

"We leave in eight days," Uncle Rudik reiterated stiffly.

Mother took several steps forward, as if she might grab him by the throat. "One month more—that's all we need stay! One month, then we'll have all the promissory notes we'll need to sustain us, without being beholden to Temple, without paying their outrageous loaning fees—"

"You think you can hide what you do here, in these fields, for another month?" Uncle Rudik roared. "Already people whisper, already suspicions are voiced. If Temple should learn of your actions, danku Re will be purged! Not only you would die under an auditor's guillotine, but every man, woman, and child in our clan. Have you thought of that, woman? Hey-o?"

He stood inches from her, his great, calloused hands clenched into fists. I thought he would strike her.

His words, his conviction, his fury deflated Mother. She stumbled back from him a pace. Clutched her head. Made a peculiar noise between a gasp and a moan.

I jumped up and ran to her side and slipped my arms about her waist just as she began to swoon. Her deadweight dropped us both to the ground.

"Everyone back into the trees," Uncle Rudik ordered. "Now!"

He glared down at me as our clan scurried to obey him. "And when your mother rouses, tell her to continue what she does during these next eight days. Understand? Or else I'll send you to pick elsewhere, with another clan, where her Djimbi chants won't be able to protect you."

I swallowed and nodded dumbly.

My fingers became twigs, as rough and scaly as bark. My arms grew into grimy branches. My legs became scabbed and scarred boles. Leaves and cobwebs adorned my hair, and my lungs expelled pure dust.

Pick chits for Waivia. Pick chits for Waivia.

It was my mantra, my food, my air. I never called her Waisi anymore, for the fond diminutive I'd used in the past seemed somehow inappropriate. Both Mother and I called her by her proper name only: Waivia.

Pick chits for Waivia. Pick chits for Waivia.

I was in a race against time, a competition against circumstance, a contest between physical limitations and emotional need. I couldn't pick enough for Mother. At day's end, as we piled into wagons to be transported back to our warehouse, she stared in disbelief at the chits I handed her. Though she never said it aloud, her eyes said it for her: Is that *all?*

Long gone were the days when she smiled as she folded them into her chit pouch.

I wanted to make Mother smile again; I wanted to feel worthy. I so desperately wanted her to notice me, in the very least just notice me, and not have eyes only for the chits I handed her each dusk.

Please, Mother, I'm right here. Look at me.

I never thought it possible to grow impervious to the sight of a deadly green viper hanging a hand's breadth from my face. I never thought the screams of a stricken picker, or the subsequent shrieks of startled birds exploding into the air, could fail to evoke a response in me. Yet they did. I became as wooden as the tree limbs upon which I climbed: still alive, yes, but immovable at the core.

Desperation combined with fatigue do that to a person. Fear becomes an extravagance.

Understand, my mother had always been kind, soft, patient. Ready with a smile, quick to play a joke. She compromised and coaxed rather than ordered and spanked. I knew my place in the world because of her, and I was secure.

Not now.

Now the only possibility that I might receive such maternal affection, might feel an inkling of such security, came each time I handed her my chits.

And as the eight days remaining us counted down to six, then four, then two, the possibility of receiving affection dwindled to nothing at all.

We were sprawled beneath the sesal bushes again, during a sweltering high-noon break. Stopping was a torture for me because it took so much effort to get my aching body moving again. So on this, our second-to-last day in the fields, I didn't sit alongside my clan but remained standing while I sucked the tangy juice from a terimelon I'd found, and gulped down its sugary flesh.

Meal finished, I tossed aside the rind. Picked up two empty burlap sacks, dropped one over each shoulder. Woodenly approached the sesal bush adjacent to the one I'd just stripped bare of dragon fodder.

"What are you doing, Zarq?" a voice asked behind me.

Blood-Uncle Rudik.

I turned slowly, stared stupidly at him. Everyone watched me from where they lay, draped panting upon the ground, their faces bloated and red in the sweltering heat.

"Picking," I mumbled. "I'm picking."

"Rest awhile. We leave the day after tomorrow. No need for you to work so hard, so unnecessarily." It was not kindness that motivated him to order me back, but pique that a young girl should be able to push herself to such limits in such intolerable heat when men such as he could not.

I shot a furtive look at Mother. Her steely eyes bored into mine. Drip, drip, drip went the blood from her nose.

"I'm not tired," I slurred.

Uncle Rudik scowled. "You rebut my words? You are sick with exhaustion. I order you to rest."

"Sorry. Yes."

I leaned against the bushy tree I'd been about to climb and closed my eyes, feigning rest.

I could feel Mother's tension, though, building like a thunderhead. *"Only two days left, Zarq, only two days! If you pick fast enough, if you pick right through noon break, we might have enough. Try for me—try! We are so close!"*

She had hissed the words to me last night before we slept. She'd hissed them again upon rousing this morning. And now, even now, I could hear them echoing round my mind.

I opened my eyes. I had obeyed Uncle Rudik by resting. Time to pick.

I turned, reached up, grabbed a branch with curled, calloused fingers, and made to swing myself upward.

"Stop."

The command arrested me.

"What do you, child?" He was truly angry, and came toward me with nostrils flared. "Did I not order you to rest?"

"I rested. Forgive me, I thought I'd obeyed you well."

He grabbed my shoulders, shook me. "Are you delirious with fever? Sit, I say, and remain sitting till I give word to do otherwise."

I moaned and looked at Mother. Uncle Rudik followed my gaze. His eyes narrowed and he abruptly released me. I almost fell.

He turned to where Mother sat, her eyes riveted on me.

"What do you to your girl child, woman?" he asked, his voice terrible and soft.

She didn't answer, was locked in some sort of trance that was compelling me to climb and pick and pick.

"Answer me, Darquel's Kavarria," Uncle Rudik ordered quietly.

She was deaf to him; I was her only world. Her eyes, and her need, were all that existed for me. The urge to climb the tree despite Uncle Rudik's order was overwhelming. I turned again, reached up and grabbed the branch, and made ready to swing myself up.

Uncle Rudik spun and knocked me to the ground. The fall jarred my wits free of Mother's iron will and I lay there, limp and breathless, and began to weep.

Uncle Rudik descended on Mother and yanked her to her feet.

"What magics do you weave upon her, Djimbi whore?"

"Rudik, really," my father protested, rising quickly to his feet. "My honor—"

"Your honor is challenged by this woman you've claimed. Can you not see she goads your girl child unnaturally?"

"If Zarq wants to pick, let her pick," Mother growled at him. "If she shames you with her determination, then pick also."

Uncle Rudik slapped her. Her head snapped back. Droplets of blood flew like rubies from her nose.

"Take off your bitoo," Uncle Rudik ordered.

"I protest!" Father said, coming forward. His brother turned on him.

"Do you? Then protest *this*." And Uncle Rudik grabbed the neck of Mother's bitoo in both his hands and with a mighty heave tore it asunder. Even as Father launched himself at my blood-uncle, Rudik continued to rip the cloth in two.

Father hauled his brother off Mother, who staggered when released. And there she stood, her breasts and belly and sex and thighs bared to all, the chit pouch cinched round her waist disclosed.

"There!" Uncle Rudik said triumphantly, pointing at the money pouch. "For some days I've watched her, for some time I've questioned each tallyman that has dealt with your claimed woman and your girl child. And look at what she conceals from us."

"This is mine," Mother cried, one hand clutching her bulging pouch, the other wrapping half of her torn bitoo about herself. "I have earned it, by all that is sacred. You know well that I've earned it."

Uncle Rudik shook Father off, who stood staring, flabbergasted, at Mother.

"*You* talk of all that is sacred?" my blood-uncle said disparagingly. "You who use illicit magics daily?"

"To what end do I use them?" Mother said bitterly. "To keep us all safe! How dare you scorn or belittle what I do. Without me, you'd long ago have been struck ill or been bitten or fallen prey to jungle cats. And it's not just these last few weeks I've protected you with all that I know! On Sa Gikiro eve, how do you think so much was transported into the jungle, kept away from grasping hands? How do you think the chits and machetes you buried in your men's huts were not unearthed and taken away?"

She was feral with rage. "And the night Kobo's kin wished harm upon Car Manopu, who stopped the deaths that would have resulted that night? Me. Me, with the very craft that you dare scorn!"

"And who taught Kobo's kin that blasphemous Djimbi filth in the first place, hey-o?" Uncle Rudik asked, voice dangerously low.

"I'm not responsible for how they abused the knowledge they gleaned from me."

Uncle Rudik studied her a moment. The waiting stretched. He turned to Father.

"You are this woman's claimer. You are responsible for her actions. This is Temple Statute, and all present know this."

"Yes," Father said hoarsely, shoulders bowed.

"Take that pouch from your claimed woman."

"Don't you dare, Darquel," Mother swiftly countered. "These are mine, to buy back Waivia. Don't you touch them."

"Take that pouch from your claimed woman," Uncle Rudik ordered.

Father stood a moment, cheeks flushed, his great barrel chest heaving. Then he reached for Mother.

I closed my eyes against the sounds of scuffle, her cries, the slaps, the jagged breaths and the rip of cloth that followed. And then my mother's scream, shrill and heart-stopping.

Overhead, a flock of redaws burst into the air, cawing raucously, and from somewhere not far away, a troop of howler monkeys hooted in agitation.

I opened my eyes to see Father handing all the chits I'd so feverishly earned to his brother, my blood-Uncle Rudik.

Our last day at the sesal fields.

I picked slowly, listlessly. What was the point?

Somewhere down below me, Mother continued to bleed, continued to chant. Not to protect those in our clan, understand. Just to protect me on this, our last day in the fields.

I had to urinate.

Climbing down one of the vine-choked, limb-twisted sesal bushes always required much energy. My legs would tremble uncontrollably and turn soft as overdampened clay. If I had to urinate or defecate, I therefore always did so balanced on a branch, rather than descend to the ground.

I balanced thusly now, and watched my urine splash-bounce down, cascading from one dusty leaf to the next. I watched with the dull, transfixed gaze of one functioning by rote. Even after I finished, I still stared blankly down, my head nodding a little, the heat a humid blanket that bid me sleep.

I don't know how long I stayed crouched, immovable, until my stupor dwindled enough that my eyes focused.

That's when I noticed the skop stems.

Skops grow on the lichen-slick, north-facing branches of most tropical trees. They are hollow-stemmed succulents bearing clusters of tiny yellow flowers. I must have beheaded this particular cluster of skops while climbing; all the decapitated, hollow stems stared up at me, bleeding sticky milk. My urine had splashed a clawful of them. Those were moving.

Slowly, so slowly, writhing and twisting.

Fascinated and now fully aware, I watched.

In moving, the ends of those skop stems split, and in splitting, the ends twisted and coiled in on themselves, forming knuckle-length curlicues and delicate spirals, each unique from the other. I waited until they stopped twisting, then plucked them from their roothold in the sesal bark. The stems made little snapping noises when I picked them, the same hollow pop as when I squashed a cockroach.

Carefully, I strung my delicate treasures on a thin hintoop vine and tied it round my wrist as a bracelet. Thereafter, I deliberately beheaded and urinated on as many skops as I could.

There are a lot of skops in the sesal fields.

By noon break, I was covered in skop jewelry. A clawful of necklaces hung around my throat, two-clawfold of bracelets decorated each forearm, and just as many encircled each of my ankles. Everyone stared as I joined my clan on the ground. I basked in their looks. Till I realized they were not friendly.

People weren't sure what to make of my jewelry, see. They wondered if my bracelets were strange, illicit Djimbi amulets wrought by my mother for who-knew-what dark purpose.

I slinked to Mother's side, then, head down, hoping Uncle Rudik wouldn't notice my jewelry and take it from me. Mother sat at the edge of our heat-battered group, partially obscured by a tangle of nipok treelets. Purple surrounded her sunken eyes, and blood trickled from both her nostrils. Ants crawled over the blood-caked neck of her bitoo.

I silently sat beside her, not too close, lest in her weary despair my presence remind her of what had transpired yesterday, but close enough to still be within arm's reach. In case she should realize that I, too, shared her misery. In case she should want to hold and comfort me.

How I longed for her to reach for me. Hold me. Comfort me.

But I did not deserve comfort, did I?

What had transpired yesterday had been initiated by me going to pick during noon break, despite blood-Uncle Rudik's order to rest. If it hadn't been for that, if I'd only been more canny, timed my departure more judiciously, then Mother would still have her belt pouch full of chits, and instead of sitting here lackluster and vacuous, she'd be glowing with fierce pride in me, euphoric that I'd achieved what she so desperately wanted.

I would have been worthy.

I would have deserved comfort.

But now I did not.

"What—what around your throat, Zarq?"

I startled, hadn't realized she'd been watching me. I looked up from the ground and met her dead-eyed gaze with trepidation. "Jewelry," I whispered.

She pursed her lips, and my heart sank as I realized what she was about to say, so I quickly added, "I didn't steal it from anybody. I made it myself."

And growing desperate, I waggled a hand back and forth in front of her nose. The skop curlicues, dried and cracking apart, rattled like tiny bones. "See? See? Aren't they pretty?"

"Hmmm," she said, her interest waning. "Nice-o."

"They look a little dried out and broken now, but when they're fresh they look real pretty. I can make you one, if you want. It would look nice on you. Sure, sure, it would. We could take it home, dip it in a nice blue glaze, your favorite blue, and it would shine just like a precious stone. . . ."

I was so desperate for her attention. So very, very desperate.

Then, slowly, her demeanor changed. It's hard to say exactly how, but it's as if something inside her was stirring, shaking off sleep, rousing itself, climbing onto its feet and stretching up, up, up, taller and taller. . . .

She grabbed my still-outstretched hand. Fingered one bangle, then the next, riffling through the skops with a mounting intensity that bewildered and scared me.

"How did you make these?" she hissed at last, and oh! how shiny her eyes were and how flushed her cheeks.

"I didn't steal them, honest—"

"I'm not accusing you of such. Just tell me how you made them."

"From skop stems."

"How?"

"You have to snap off the flowers first, then . . . pee on them."

"Skop and pee-pee? That's all?"

I nodded, said in a small voice, "They curl by themselves. From the pee."

"Oh, Zarq," she breathed. "Oh, Zarq."

She stared at me, eyes moist, a smile growing on her face. The smile turned into a beautiful beam, a sun of happiness, and I held my breath, barely believing it.

"Oh, my precious, precious Zarq," she whispered.

She reached for me then, folded me in an embrace that was so soft, so sweet, an embrace that I'd hungered for for so long. She tenderly kissed my leaf-snarled hair over and over. "Oh, Zarq. My precious Zarq."

I was loved again. I didn't know entirely why, but I was.

I clung to her and wept. The next day, danku Re returned home.

TEN

~~~~~

Rain thudded onto the work shed, the noise muffled by the roof's thatch. Damp wind blew through the apertures in the work shed's hole-checkered wall. Deep night blacked everything invisible: Mother, the work shed table, the shelves, the rain vat, the cloaked blocks of clay. Nothing in that bitter darkness existed.

Then Mother spoke.

"Is that all?" she said in disbelief.

I woke up then. The slick urn beneath my naked bottom solidified, became tangible and cold.

Until those awful words—*is that all?*—I'd been functioning in a state of half-slumber. I'd shuffled across the puddled courtyard barely lucid; I'd ignored the pelting rain and the drops sliding down my neck and saturating my bitoo. Semisomnolence had offered some small protection from the wind, had turned me insensitive to the creaking, swaying trees and jungle fronds beyond our compound walls. Deep night during a monsoon squall mattered little to me, enshrouded as I was in the nebulous shell of sleep deprivation.

See, Mother and I were making those trips three, sometimes four, times a night since our return to the danku compound, and even in daylight I moved in a drowsy fog. But those words she spoke, uttered in that tone, woke me up.

"Is that *all?*" she repeated.

I woozily looked up at Mother. I could see nothing in the dark, not even the whites of her eyes. She was just black heat looming over me and the urn I'd just urinated into.

"Did you not drink everything? All-all of it?" she demanded.

My response went unheard in a gust of wind from outside. I shivered violently and hugged myself.

"We must drink more, then," Mother said wearily. "More."

I started crying. Couldn't help myself.

How I hated skop jewelry. I didn't care how brilliant they looked when dipped in glaze and kiln fired to a glassy enamel, or how well the finished bangles and amulets and anklets sold at marketplace. I just wanted to sleep the night through again. No more of this creeping out and drinking jug after jug of cold water, all in an effort to produce as much urine as possible to soak the skops in. The stomach cramps, the bitter rain, the lack of sleep, the dreadful secrecy . . . I was ill from it all.

No one knew the skops curled only when soaked in urine, understand. No one but Mother and I. Therefore, while everyone slept, we drank water and urinated on and soaked and rinsed those hateful skop stems, so that by morning, the pottery clan could dip the dry, delicate whorls and spirals in clay slip—once, twice, thrice—and create the jewelry that had rapidly become fashionable throughout our zone.

Everyone thought the skops curled because of jungle fungi Mother collected and mashed into the soaking urns. In truth, she ate the fungi. Her appetite was enormous. That happens when one is pregnant.

"Rise up, Zarq. My turn." Mother couldn't hear my tears, so weak were they against the relentless rain on the roof.

I didn't move. Couldn't. Was drowning in misery.

"Zarq?"

I wept and shuddered, bitterly cold and exhausted.

Her hands pressed on my shoulders, the weight of her heavy on me as she crouched. Her mushroomy breath blew against my cheeks.

"Sweet littlest, don't cry," she pleaded. Her fever-hot hands cupped my cheeks. "Stop the eye water, please, Zarq. Stop."

She offered no comfort, merely begged; she was as needy as I.

"I can't do it anymore, Mama," I sobbed. "Don't hate me—"

"I don't hate you! What nonsense, this!"

"All you talk about is Waivia—"

"I can't expect you to understand. But I *do* expect you to endure. You *will* endure. You *will*."

"Mama, please, please—" I was sobbing and shuddering, still upon that hateful urn of urine, and I felt alone, worse than alone. Again.

Mother let go of my cheeks.

"Dragon fucker!" she hissed, and a single moth fluttered through the air and landed on one of my juddering, wet knees, a tiny moth the shape of a baby's mouth, all pink and red veined, the likes of which I'd never seen before. It had only one antenna. The other had snapped off, and I knew the moth would die shortly.

Dragon fucker? Me?

Mother rose to her feet, a lumbering, heat-radiating darkness. I didn't move. Held my breath. Was terrified of her. Again.

She started to pace, though I couldn't see her, could only sense her moving in the dark. The moth was the only thing I could see. I couldn't even see the knee the moth had landed on, though it was *my* knee. But I could see the fallen insect, sure-sure. In minute detail.

"Takes all my chits from me," Mother muttered. "*My* chits, those were, earned by *my* labor for *my* Waivia. But no, what is good enough for our Clutch Lord is not good enough for danku Re Rudik! 'Women cannot possess chits,' he spits at me, foaming like a poison frog! *My* chits those were, mine!"

She shrieked like a palm tree uprooted during a typhoon. The moth on my knee dissolved into a wet puddle of red, and I felt it dribble down my leg like menstrual blood.

"Greatfather Maxmisha not yet dead, and your blood-uncle already strutting like a peacock. Some Greatfather he'll be." She spat a globule of brilliant white and it shattered on the ground like a hollow glass bauble. A shard stung my foot and turned into gray vapor.

"So I can't possess chits, hey-o? Then I will make jewelry. Fine bayen jewelry. Trade *that* to glass spinners for Waivia."

She sighed. "But first we make plenty rishi bangles to buy gold leaf and lapis lazuli and silver chain, things necessary for bayen taste."

With one hand pressed against the small of her back, she leaned against the hole-checkered brick wall of the work shed. I could see her now. The wind had blown a ragged tear in the clouds, permitting watery moonlight through. Mother was slumped with defeat, her belly a taut tumor.

"We will tell others," she said in a monotone. "A few. Big Grum Grum's Li. Korshan's Limia. Car Manopu's Wasaltooltic. Kobo's Dash—"

"Not her!" I cried.

"Why?"

"She . . . she . . . " How to explain the woman was like an angry jungle cat, hungry for prey?

"She doesn't like you," I finished lamely.

Mother shrugged. "So? What matters is: Will she tell? She will not. The twins, she wants to keep safe in the pottery clan. No roidan kasloo trading for *her* girls, oh, no. She will do whatever to prevent Rudik from bartering her precious couplets for food and chits."

She straightened, pushed from the wall. "Oh, no, Zarq, make no mistake. She doesn't like me, but she will not tell. She'll pee for us."

Mother was right. She urinated for us. As did the others brought into our dreadful circle of deceit. More than deceit, that. It was blasphemy, for with a womanly secretion, we deliberately fouled plants grown upon dragon soil and then sold the product of that defilement to others.

Temple's Holy Wardens were among our customers.

As aloof as my playmates had been when Mother and I had first returned from the sesal fields, the twins now became downright unapproachable. Their mother, Kobo's Dash, must have told them what we were doing to make the skops curl. Rutvia and Makvia scooted away when I tried to sit by them during meals, and froze like hares under a hawk's gaze if I spoke to them elsewhence. Big Grum Grum's kids also scattered before me, like thrown kernels of featon, though the eldest stopped a safe distance away and stared. Confused and hurt, I retreated to Mother's side and became her shadow.

That's when I noticed that she, too, was receiving a mature version of the same treatment.

Instead of handing their colicky babies to Mother to soothe as in the past, for her touch and voice worked wonders upon the ill, the danku mothers grimly endured the screaming of their infants. Instead of bantering with her at worktable or listening rapt to Mother's fantastical stories, the women spoke only to each other in subdued tones, as if afraid to raise their voices while in Mother's presence. No naughty jokes, no sweet songs, and no friendly gossip filled the women's work shed now.

All throughout my life, I'd grown up with the rhythmic *thump-thump, thump-thump* of clay being kneaded on the work shed table. That resonant pounding was the heartbeat of our clan. Now no more. We didn't knead clay because skop beads required a clay slurry only, which was a good thing, as we had little clay available. But I feared that when we kneaded clay once more, it would produce an erratic, disharmonious sound. Like the heartbeat of something dying.

Eventually, our secret leaked to others. Of course it did. Women sleeping under the same roof as children and nursing mothers and light-sleeping elders could not possibly creep out each night without *someone* noticing.

Our circle of deceit grew larger, and so did the amount of urine collected. For that I was ever so grateful. I was roused only once every fourth night or so to add my dirty waters to the skop urns.

But the atmosphere within the women's barracks changed even more. Women looked over their shoulders constantly, jumped at the slightest sounds, dropped things in distraction, and snapped ceaselessly at their offspring. Anxiety became a permanent, unwanted guest. Urine *had* to be collected. It made the skop jewelry. The skop jewelry fed us. Ergo, the shameful, evil secret had to be kept from the men.

We could not make enough skop jewelry, see. It was as if a fire of fashion were sweeping across our zone and into the next. Eggs filled our cellar once more, and jar upon jar of salted muay leaves and preserved chilies filled the adjacent larder.

Not that it was a time of ease. It was the Wet, the Season of Rains, and thatch that had not been replaced, as was the custom during the Season of Fire, now leaked terribly. Furthermore, we didn't have a store of fuel to see us through the Wet, and so had to purchase dung, dried vines, and macci leaves with wares and chits that should have purchased myriad essentials: unguents and medicines, paak molds and barrels, warm clothes and desperately needed mosquito curtains. Replenishing our fuel stores even took precedence over restocking our

renimgar cages, for without fuel, a potter could fire no wares. But
without meat, one could survive.

So it took a long time for Mother to procure her gold leaf and copper chun to make fine necklaces for the aristocrats.

By then, the Wet was almost over. Greatfather Maxmisha had died.
The pottery clan had lost yet another baby to the mosquito sickness.
I had become a withdrawn, friendless child who dared not even visit
the latrines alone, lest I be cornered by elder children and beaten with
sticks, as had happened on two occasions. And Mother's obsession
with Waivia had grown, swelling as steadily as her child-heavy belly.

When Greatfather Rudik finally deigned to procure precious bayen
materials, Mother set to work immediately. She paused only to eat
and attend nature's call. I stayed by her side, sleeping again on the
work shed table.

The torques and diadems and wristlets she crafted were truly
breathtaking and elegant, so much so that Greatfather Rudik himself
hiked through mud and rain to the Iri Timadu Bayen Sor, the Zone of
Most Exalted Aristocrats, to sell her art at the marketplace there.

A bayen lordling purchased all her jewelry at once. All of it. For an
exorbitant number of chits.

Mother was feverish with joy when Greatfather Rudik returned. I
thought she would demand he purchase Waivia with the profits, and
I think the rest of our clan did, as well. That evening, as we sat under
the temporary roof that had been hastily erected over our courtyard,
as was customary in the Wet, we all waited for Mother to disgrace
herself in yet another scandalous confrontation with our new ku
Greatfather, blood-Uncle Rudik.

She did.

But was it only I who noticed that her shrieks were less strident, her
arguments less clever, her barbs less pointed, than had become the
norm the past months? Or did others also see that Father had to pla-
cate Mother less that time, and that she ended the spectacle sooner
than usual?

I don't know.

Nor do I know if I was the only one who guessed that Mother had
duplicates of those exquisite bayen necklaces tucked away somewhere,

duplicates resplendent in crimson glaze and gold leaf. But I've often thought that this was what finally led to the disclosure of our secret to the men, the knowledge that Mother had the means to buy back Waivia while no other woman could ever buy back her daughter, should she undergo roidon kasloo mutian.

Really, the reason for the disclosure matters little. The past cannot be changed.

"We visit the glass spinners today," Mother whispered, her mouth pressed close against my ear so her words would rouse no one else.

They certainly roused *me*. My heartbeat wobbled wildly as I came awake too fast.

Mother bundled up my sleeping mat and had it tucked onto its shelf before I was even on my feet. She stood in the doorway of the women's barracks, gesturing for me to hurry, a near-term pregnant woman ablaze with impatience in the predawn mist.

First we visited the renimgar hutches, still empty save for a clawful of breeding pairs. The hairless, paunchy creatures within stirred and snorted in agitation at our approach, but settled back into a knot of shivering bodies when no food or hands entered their cage. With a swift look around us that was unnecessary, as we were certainly the only ones awake at that hour, Mother unwrapped her bitoo from her body, draped it over my shoulders, and slowly lowered herself to her knees, clutching the stilts of the hutch for balance.

I wondered how she would get up again, she was that big.

With a great deal of effort and a few grunts similar to those coming from the renimgars, she eased herself onto her back and pushed herself under the hutches. She rolled onto her side, then I heard her clawing and digging away old feces and dirt from the ground.

Her legs trembled as she hauled herself out from under the hutch. It took her several moments to catch her breath. Naked, clutching a dirty oilskin bundle, she waddled to the bathing corner of the danku, behind First Garden, where the ground was sloped from the roofless brick partition walls of the bathing house so the water drained directly into the garden for irrigation.

"When did you bury this?" I asked, as she splashed cold water over herself to clean off fecal matter and mud. Notice I did not ask what was in the bundle she'd placed in my hands. The feel of it had confirmed what I'd already guessed.

"No talk now," she said.

She plaited her long, wet hair carefully, her skin pimpling from cold. I watched her belly as my sibling within moved. A knobby bump appeared above Mother's protruding navel, maybe a knee, maybe an elbow, then slid from view. I hoped it was a girl. I needed a friend.

Mother painstakingly coiled her plaits atop her head, artfully tying them into place with a leather thong she'd worn around her wrist. It was a formal hairstyle, one used only in times of great ceremony. She'd last sported it when Father and blood-Uncle Rudik had carried Greatfather Maxmisha's draped body upon a pallet to temple, to be taken to the gharial basins to be fed to the resident reptiles. That was the fate of all Clutch rishi corpses: an honorable disposal. For each corpse a clan gave to Temple for gharial burial, a notch was cut into the clan burial pole. At year's end, depending on the amount of notches on each clan's pole, Temple gave an equivalent poundage of gharial meat, and the rich, oily flesh was served in a stew known as parfi croidin, ancestor food.

Still naked, Mother took from me the dirty bundle she'd dug. Unwrapped it. Lifted out strands of silver that linked delicate azure whorls and golden fluted tendrils. She washed them as gently as washing an infant and dried them using a corner of my bitoo.

Then and only then did she dress, swiftly, as dawn was nigh and birdsong trilled here and there from the jungle. We left our compound quickly.

Mother wore the necklaces and wristlets. I carried the serpentine biceps bangles, the ones she had crafted from the chunky skop stems she'd deliberately snipped and sliced with a knife prior to soaking, to achieve an undulating, masculine look. Some of those bangles gleamed a glossy crimson as rich as blood. Others shone metallic dark green with raisin-purple flecks, the color of a bull dragon's scales. A precious few of the bangles glinted a milky bluish pink, like fine opals. I didn't know how Mother had achieved such glazes. They were unearthly.

We arrived at the glass spinners' compound just as the korikapku women were starting their morning routine.

The place had changed. It was as if the Wet had never touched their courtyard, it was that smooth and dry, and the three-tiered roof that vaulted over the courtyard was clearly not temporary. That fine roof supported by those expensive hewn posts and beams was there to stay, offering shade in the Fire Season and shelter in the Wet for generations to come.

The mating shack was no more. Instead of the humble structure we'd last seen, there now stood a building the size of our women's barracks. It stood on stilts, so I guessed it was the mating shack. It was painted in garish reds and greens, and lewd figures had been carved onto its walls.

The gaudiness and size of the structure bespoke of a place not where gentle unions occurred in discreet compartments, but where raucous, bawdy parties took place.

Sure, the mating shack in our compound contained a room large enough to host men's parties, but that room was humble, and used during a select few men's rites only. Whereas the glass spinners' mating shack now looked like . . .

. . . A stable. A stable where sex slaves were used ruthlessly, to provide debased entertainments that had little to do with gentle unions or men's rites.

I glanced at Mother and could see the same thing occur to her as well. She stared at the building, color draining from her face.

Then she mastered herself. Lifted her chin, became at once proud yet not haughty, polite yet not humble. As she strode through the glass spinners' courtyard toward their women's barracks, the korikapku women stopped their business and stared. I scurried after her, almost ran right into her when she abruptly stopped. Her eyes fell upon a woman as old as our clan's Goiter-Neck Mother; a look was exchanged between the two. Mother approached the elder.

She stopped an arm's length before her. Bowed slowly, deeply. Straightened.

Then Mother threw her arms high over her head, and the elder reared back like a startled yearling, and several women gasped.

Mother didn't strike the elder, no. Instead, she spread her fingers into a delicate, immobile fan and continued to hold her arms above her head with elbows gracefully, subtly akimbo. It took me a moment to realize what she was doing.

She was performing the infamous Bull Antennae in Full Display greeting.

It was a salutation of respect and honor, used so rarely it had taken on an ambiguous taint. I'd never seen it performed before, had only heard how it had been done by our warrior-lord's First Claimed woman. She'd performed the ancient, powerful obeisance during the coronation of our warrior-lord's favorite ebani, had done it *to* the ebani whom she was known to hate. She'd had little choice in performing obeisance of some sort, but had exercised full will in choosing what form her obeisance would take. Five months later, the ebani had given birth to the warrior-lord's blond-haired, blue-eyed First Son, a child the First Claimed woman had been unable to produce.

And sixteen years later, my sister had vowed to be claimed as ebani by that very same First Son, and I had mistook Waivia's meaning, had thought she'd expressed a wish to be kiyu, a sex slave. And she had mocked me and called me stupid for thinking such a debased fate could ever befall her. . . .

Yet here we stood, Mother and I, Mother trying to rescue Waivia from that very thing.

Slowly, with a dancer's poise, Mother lowered her arms to her sides. All eyes were on her now. Oh yes.

"I'm waiting for wings to bless the herd of Re," Mother boomed, in a voice so impressive that were I our Clutch bull, I'd dare not disregard her hope and at once fertilize an egg with a male-producing seed.

The elderly glass spinner my mother addressed stood there for several heartbeats before clearing her throat and croaking, "May your waiting end. May the wings hatch—"

"Please do me the honor of accepting this worthless token on behalf of your claimer, the venerable Greatfather of the korikapku," Mother said in sonorous tones. I don't know how she'd guessed the elder to be the claimed woman of the clan's Greatfather, but I had no doubt she was correct.

I gawped along with the rest as Mother lifted one of the exquisite necklaces from around her throat and held it out to the old woman. It was the iridescent purple-and-green one, looking for all the world like a delicate chain of exotically sculpted bull scales interspersed with dark amethysts and beryls.

The elder's hands shook as she accepted the treasure.

"And," Mother continued, "I would further beg you to accept this unworthy trifle on behalf of all the glass spinners' women who have suffered in recent months from the presence of a certain unclean woman."

Again, Mother lifted a necklace from her throat, the azure one interspersed with fluted tendrils of gold. I could barely stop myself from crying out. She had only one left, a magnificent opalescent torque.

"Finally," Mother continued in her imposing voice, "I would burden you with this paltry trinket, in thanks for granting me audience today."

As she lifted the torque from her head, there was a collective intake of breath. The dawn's light caught the torque just so, and the enamel whorls looked alive, white tongues of flame glittering with golden-blue veins and clouds of creamy pink.

"Now," Mother said, drawing herself to her full height, which seemed at that moment all of seven feet, "please bring me the ebani who is kept there." She disdainfully flicked a wrist at the sex stable. "I will take the garbage away with me."

The elder stared at Mother, her pudgy, wrinkled hands dripping jewels.

"Forgive my impudence," Mother said, bowing her head a little. "I should not ask you to approach the living quarters of one so profane as she. I will fetch her myself."

A spell hung over us all, a fog as scintillating and pink as the opalescent skops Mother had just raised to the dawn's fire. But it was the Wet. She had drawn on powers not at their prime, for the sun that rose over the Spinal Crest Range was sleepy and dilute. So the spell wavered, like sunlight seen through deep, deep waters.

And just as Mother turned—her hands already reaching out for the baby she'd once suckled, a baby now imprisoned in a state of degradation in a rival clan's sex stable—someone moved among the crowd.

My eyes scraped toward the woman who had moved, dragging over blurred faces like a scoring fork over dry clay. I recognized the crone immediately by the pipe in her maw and the cruelty in her eyes, and I recalled the words she'd spoken with such glee the last time we'd seen Waivia: *Ripe kiyu girl, she.*

The crone tugged on the elbow of the elder who held the jewels. Hissed in her ear. The elder's eyes opened wide, wider, widest, and poof! The fog holding us all in its warm trance lifted up as if blown by immense billows, lifted up and swirled into a tight little cyclone, spinning faster and lifting higher, disappearing into the depths of an ugly black cloud, which promptly unleashed a deluge.

The semicircle of women around us broke for cover. Mother watched them scurrying to and fro. Then she whirled and looked at the sex stable. She ran. Under her footfalls the ground shuddered as if she were a huge brooder on a rampage, for she was big and heavy, an ungainly creature only days away from giving birth. I felt a great fear as I ran after her, fear for her safety and the well-being of my unborn sibling. Up the stable's stairs she thundered as rain pelted down. She ripped open the stable's double doors, actually tore off a hinge, and plunged inside.

"Waivia!" she bellowed, and her voice echoed around that obscene place, and a roll of thunder answered. "Waivia!"

My feet were on the stable's first step as Mother reappeared.

"She's not here," she said in disbelief, and her cheeks were as milky as the opalescent skop beads, but with none of their fire. "Where? What have they done with her?"

Then she was crashing down the stairs toward me. The whole stable shuddered as if it were built of reeds. I leapt out of the way, hit the ground and sprawled, and behind me something in the stable gave way with an almighty crack. The building groaned, leaned inward, slowly began to fold as if it were damp clay being plunged into a vat of water.

I scrabbled to my feet and ran after Mother.

She grabbed one korikapku woman, then another, shook each as if to snap her neck.

"Where is she? Where?"

Where were the *men*? That's what I wondered, wild with dread. But the resonant waves of thunder rolling over and over us blocked Mother's cries from the ears of the still-slumbering menfolk.

Mother had one woman by the throat now, a slender woman with eyes the color of bruises. Did I recognize her? Yes, yes, I did! She'd been in the mating closet with Waivia on that dreadful morning so many months ago. . . .

"Curse your womb with stillborns if you don't tell me! Where? Where?"

"I don't know—" the woman gasped. She clawed frantically at Mother's hands, and her eyes protruded unnaturally.

"Tell me!"

"Gone . . . night . . ."

"When?"

"Long time . . ."

"*When?*"

". . . Before . . . Wet . . ."

Mother dropped the woman. I felt an inane urge to thank her or apologize or something. What I did instead was avoid looking at her as I sidled up to Mother, who was staring at nothing with a stunned look on her face.

"Let's go now, Mother," I said, and I slipped one of my small, wet hands into one of her broad, cold ones. "Come on."

I tugged and pulled. She followed like a wooden toy. No one else did.

It was still raining when we reached the pottery clan compound.

Our men were waiting for us.

ELEVEN

I'd become wise during the last few months: On the way back to our compound, I took the fine bracelets off Mother's wrists and buried them along with the biceps bangles I carried.

I ripped the cowl off my bitoo, blinking and shivering in the rain, and wrapped the beautiful bracelets up. With Mother standing mute and ashen beside me, I dug at the hard earth right there in the alley, dug until my fingers bled and my nails ripped.

With a rock, I then chipped away at the brick wall to mark where I'd buried them. The mark was insignificant, so I chipped some more, then I feared the damage was too obvious. But obvious to whom, signifying what? Clutch Re was a maze of crumbling brick walls. My paltry marks would arouse the interest of no one.

I had to believe so.

"This is where I've buried them," I explained to Mother, pointing as if she had not been standing there the whole while. She nodded vaguely.

I washed my hands in one of the many puddles in the alleyway, and we continued home. The rain was falling so hard by then that the puddles appeared to boil. The air smelled like wet clay.

Greatfather Rudik struck Mother across the face. Father stayed his hand the second time, caught his fist in one of his giant, smooth hands and roared, "She's carrying!"

So Greatfather Rudik struck him instead. Again and again he struck him, and Father did nothing to defend himself, for there in the courtyard, beneath its pathetic roof in the season's last, greatest rain squall, Father allowed our clan to witness his avowal to take full responsibility for his claimed woman's actions.

"Stop hitting my father! Stop hitting my father!" I screamed, and Mother held me back by scrunching up the nape of my torn bitoo in one fist, collaring me like a dog.

Finally, Greatfather Rudik stood back, panting. Father couldn't see out one eye, and his left ear was grotesquely swollen. He stood oddly, leaned to one side. Broken rib.

Our men somberly filed into the men's pottery studio. Father limped in last.

Mother ducked into the women's work shed and began kneading clay furiously. After a while, the rest of the women sidled in. Goiter-Neck told everyone to make floor tiles. They obeyed.

Food was not served until late noon that day. Mother didn't go to the courtyard to eat, so neither did I. Much later, Leishu's Caan thumped a bowl of cold yanichee and grit on the table.

Mother and I shared it, though she left the bulk of it for me.

I often try to remember how my mother had been prior to all this. I endeavor to bring images to my mind that I can share, images of how she cuddled and coaxed, cajoled and kissed, but no specific image will come. How cruel, that time should rob me of those memories and leave me instead with the bitterly detailed images of what she became after that hateful Sa Gikiro.

Is that all that is left us, in the end? That which is most painful and shameful and ugly?

We went to the mating shack that night, and Father told us, wheezing through gritted teeth, smelling of heavy male sweat, that Temple must be informed. Temple *would* be informed. It was the honorable thing to do.

"But," he said, drawing each word out as if it were a long thorn stuck in his flesh, "Greatfather Rudik will wait until my First Son is born."

"Why?" Mother said.

"A favor."

"Peculiar favor."

He offered nothing further.

"What makes you so certain it is a boy?" Mother asked, but her tone lacked fight, and so I realized she, too, knew the child in her belly was male.

Again, Father didn't answer.

After a while, Mother spoke.

"You've been good to me, danku Re Darquel." Her whisper was hoarse. "I'm sorry—"

Her voice broke and she started to weep. He moved, drew her awkwardly to him, though it must have cost him, what with that broken rib. I started to cry, too, though I wasn't sure why. He placed one of his smooth, hairless hands—so soft from all the hours immersed in clay slip—upon the bristle on my head.

We sat like that in the darkness, we three, for what seemed a very long time. More than one night, surely. One night, two nights, a month, a year, a lifetime worth of nights.

We sat there for as long as it took to relinquish, with our embrace, our life as a family.

The following morning, Mother and I threshed featon sheaves to separate the edible grit from the chaff, working as steadily as if nothing untoward had occurred in our lives. When Car Manopu's Wasaltooltic could not get the cooking embers to flare up, Mother helped; that was how normal we behaved. Mother could ignite anything, no matter how green or wet.

We sat in the courtyard with the rest of our clan, gave our ritual response to Greatfather Rudik's communal greeting, and ate our yanichee. Everything was ordinary, and yet it was not. It was as if the entire danku was holding its breath for a certain moment to arrive.

That moment came.

"This danku Re shall perform today to please the dragon," Greatfather Rudik proclaimed.

No rain fell, no wind blew. Instead of chill air, a thin warmth floated about us. Mist rose up from the ground. I could smell citrus ferns unfurling in the jungle.

"Slashing party gathers vines and macci leaves for fuel. Women and children make mud-chaff bricks. Darquel's claimed woman births Darquel's First Son."

I stared at Mother. Other than a slight twinge below one eye, she showed no reaction to this grotesque Proclamation.

In silence, our clan dispersed to fulfill morning chores. I felt eyes upon me, eyes and the wills of those who ruled my world. Only Mother and I remained in the courtyard.

And Kobo's Dash.

I helped Mother rise. Kobo's Dash held something cupped in her hands. This she extended toward us. It smelled like ground pepper.

"What is it?" Mother asked, not even glancing at the neat, leaf-wrapped bundle thrust toward her.

"Keri-peri and tepin."

Mother snorted. "I think Darquel wants the child born alive."

Kobo's Dash stared hard at Mother with glassy eyes. "But you, Kavarria, what do *you* want? Peace, no? Final, lasting peace."

Something in Mother changed then. Her eyes locked onto that little bundle and her breathing slowed and a look of intense craving filled her. With a barely susceptible movement, Kobo's Dash moved the bundle toward her. Mother's fingers twitched.

Then she closed her eyes and shook her head wearily. "I can't. It would kill the baby, too. But . . . thank you."

Kobo's Dash stepped closer, her nostrils flared and her pupils dilated. "You make a mistake not to accept this. Think of your daughter. What future is there for Zarq with you alive? If you die, I can adopt her as my own. Otherwise, her fate is tied to yours and she'll be banished along with you after Darquel dies."

Mother whimpered, glanced from me to the bundle. I could hardly breathe. What did the old hag mean? Why would my father die, why and when?

"This gives her a future," Kobo whispered insistently, again thrusting the bundle forward. "I'll look after her as if she were my own. Darquel will be told the birth went wrong. No one knows what's in this bundle; they all think it's the unguent necessary to safely provoke early labor. Take it; you'll die swiftly, painlessly. For Zarq's sake, take it."

"No."

"Listen, woman! Greatfather Rudik plans to cut the baby from you if you don't birth today! Understand?"

Mother rammed her knuckles into her own mouth and shook her head rapidly from side to side.

"Take it!" Kobo's Dash pushed the bundle against Mother's belly. "You must. Whether you use it or not, take it. He's watching and thinks that I'm offering you the unguent to provoke early labor. If you don't take it, he *will* use his knife on you to get the baby out."

With violently trembling hands, Mother accepted the bundle. "But I need . . . to birth today, I need the proper—"

"In a similar bundle in the woman's second latrine. Hidden upon a rafter. Get Zarq to reach it down for you." Kobo's Dash spat. "Cursed Djimbi fool that you are. Use *this* bundle, for your daughter's sake. Not that one!"

But she didn't. Weeping and apologizing to me for I knew not what, rubbing her swollen belly and cooing to the babe within, Mother used the small, limp bundle hidden in the latrine, not the one given her publicly by Kobo's Dash. Ants swarmed over the latrine bundle, as if it contained something good and sweet. It smelled of licorice and limes and made my fingers tingle. I was bitten several times while shaking the ants off.

This is how my mother brought my brother too soon into the world, then: crouched in a dark, stinking, cobwebbed latrine, pushing bitter herbs mixed with lard up inside her to provoke contractions.

Labor was swift and violent and there was much blood. She leaned heavily upon me at one point and choked, "Now. Back to the barracks," whereupon we staggered from the latrine and crossed the courtyard, leaving a slick red trail upon the ground that would later require expensive purification from a daronpu.

Once in the women's barracks, the hands that would not help us in front of Greatfather Rudik's gaze came forward, and it was Big Grum Grum's Li who caught the babe and Goiter-Neck Mother who cut the cord.

Mother plunged into a delirium that lasted until middle-night. I believe her spirit returned only because I had the presence of mind to press a ball of clay into one of her hands. When her mind had cleared and she'd sipped a little broth, she fell into a deep sleep, the clay still cupped in her palm.

She awoke midmorn the day following. Her hoarse voice dragged me from thick slumber.

"Zarq? Where-where my son?"

Her son! My brother! Re slay me a thousand times, but while I had mopped up the blood oozing from between her legs, and while I had wiped the sweat from her brow, and while I had sat beside her and wept over her wan body while the other women and children slunk around the place, *I had forgotten about the baby*.

And in my look of shock and horror, and in the lack of a baby pulling at her breast or resting in my arms, my mother screamed.

And the day turned to night, yes, it did. Check what historical accounts you may; they will all verify that: The moon blocked the sun from the sky, and all birdsong, all crick-ben calls, all dog barks and ren-imgar snorts stopped. People froze in position throughout Clutch Re while eerie nothingness descended upon us all. The only sign of life, save for the muted thumping of thousands of terrified hearts, was the scream of my mother, and somewhere in Wabe Din Temple, the answering cry of a newborn infant torn too soon from his mother's womb.

Despite the dizzy spells that set her panting like a fevered cat, and despite the blood that fell from her in liverlike slabs, Mother dragged herself through the alleys of Wabe Din Sor, heading for the temple, feral and deranged and determined to find her son.

She didn't make it far. Father carried her back to our compound, and she fought him the whole way, cursing him for being honorable and pious and cowardly and sensible.

For you see, that was the agreement he'd made with Greatfather Rudik: Father's First Son would be given to Temple as an act of penitence for my mother's profane use of clay and skop and urine. My brother would be suckled by a wet nurse and nurtured by pharisaical wardens, and would never, ever know the sweet, powerful love of his own navel-mother.

Thus, my mother lost another child. There was nothing she could do to bring that one back, either.

Why had Greatfather Rudik informed Temple of Mother's profane use of urine when it would only result in the death of his youngest brother, my father?

By telling the First Holy Warden in our zone the truth before rumor did, he'd hoped to limit punishment to Father alone, and by presenting Temple with Father's First Son as an indentured acolyte, he'd hoped to improve the odds that our clan as a whole would escape scandal and punishment. That was what my baby brother became, see, an acolyte not by choice but by bond. No doubt he was cut as an asak-illyas, a holy eunuch destined to be indentured to a bayen lady.

Why had Father not taken Mother with his soon-to-be-born child from Clutch Re? To seek a life elsewhere, in another Clutch, in a coastal city, even among the notorious Forsaken found in meager settlements between Clutches?

Because Father was an honorable man, and as such he had understood his duty: The woman for which he was responsible had committed a grave act against Temple by deliberately and repeatedly fouling sanctified soil with her dirty waters. Therefore, as reparation, he would give up his First Son to Temple and his own life to the insulted lordling.

Simple as that.

Honor, I have decided, is like tradition: not necessarily a good thing.

Another type of waiting began, the waiting that preceded the fall of a whip, the blade of a knife, the claw of a dragon.

It did not last long. Only three days passed from the birth of my brother to the arrival of those four inebriated aristocrats who thundered into our compound on a cloud of red dust. Three days.

Mother spent those three days in the work shed, refusing to come out to eat or sleep. She drank water from the slimy vat inside the work shed and made one wild, violent sculpture after another.

I was wild myself by then. Unwashed, unfed, and not trusting anyone save Mother, I rocked myself in a corner and stared at Mother's face, afraid to blink lest she disappear from me during that instant. At night, Mother's vile sculptures came alive and danced dizzy circles around me, spitting malice.

No one entered the work shed, and no one brought food in, either.

No, I lie. Father attempted both, morning of the first day. Mother vomited an arc of fire at him, and he staggered backward from the work shed, arms batting away flame.

We had flammable liquids in the work shed. Some tinctures were volatile and were never placed near open flame. Perhaps Mother hurled something like that at him, alight from a candle I'd not noticed. It's possible.

But it's not what I saw.

No rain fell during that time, and instead a hidden sun shone, leaden and cloaked in a blanket of fog. The smell of unfurling citrus ferns became a constant taste on the tongue. The Inbetween, the time of mists betwixt seasons, was upon us.

On the third day, the aristocrats arrived, among them the lordling who had purchased Mother's diadems and amulets.

See, Greatfather Rudik had reported Mother's actions to Temple when he gave them my baby brother, and Temple had lost no time in tracking down the owner of the baubles. The simple bracelets our clan had churned out by the clawful were overlooked, though those were buried or smashed when Temple decreed they were objects created in utmost depravity, and the wearers of such would be savagely and publicly remonstrated.

As soon as the lordling learned how his unique jewels had been created, he consumed vast quantities of fine wine and enlisted the aid of the warrior-lord's First Son in seeking retribution.

Roshu-Lupini Re's First Son was rumored to be very good at retribution.

Roshu-Lupini himself, the warrior-lord of Clutch Re, was far away at the time, conducting Arena business in our nation's coastal capital.

I doubt much whether it would have changed things if he'd been home.

Now comes the time where I must record in detail what occurred that day. I find I cannot.

Besides, my narrative at this point is wholly unreliable. I was, in a word, lost. Quite, quite out of my head. Perchance I sought sanctuary in insanity. It is conceivable.

This is what I saw.

Four aristocrats stormed into the work shed, where I was crouched in a corner while Mother still worked at table. They beat Mother and kicked her until the light fled her body in a scattered cloud.

One aristocrat grabbed her hair and drew a dirk and made to cut off her scalp, but was distracted by the trumpeting of the yearling he'd rode into our compound. That yearling was thrashing about in a nervous frenzy, repeatedly slamming heavy hindquarters into the meager wooden pillars that held our Wet Season roof over our courtyard. Distracted by the trumpeting, the aristocrat did not saw off Mother's scalp, but dragged her out into the courtyard instead.

I didn't fight; I didn't help her. I didn't protest; I didn't help her. I ran. I ran and dove under the women's barracks, where I'd already learned how safe its cobwebbed jungle of stilts could be.

From there I saw the rest. Greatfather Rudik kowtowing, banging his forehead repeatedly on the ground at one of the aristocrat's feet as he requested that only the man responsible for the perpetrator of the crime be punished; the aristocrat smiting him; and the hobbled, wing-pinioned dragon at our courtyard's center, beneath our flimsy Wet Season roof, slamming into wooden pillars and sending thatch flying across the compound. The dragon looked as if she would soon break the hobbles round her legs and, too, the muzzle binding her snout. Her whip-thin tail sliced through the air, and the salty, oily smell of dragon fear went deep into my lungs.

Three of the aristocrats grabbed Twisted Foot Ryn and dragged him toward the yearling, which continued to fight against the bolt chains pinioning her wings.

Twisted Foot Ryn's children were not like me. They were not cowards. They fought for their father.

They turned into a pond of viscous sap and encircled the three aristocrats who held their father, and they flowed up the aristocrats' legs and arms and shoved and impeded until the aristocrats released Twisted Foot Ryn. The aristocrats then barked question's at Ryn's woman, who, weeping, pointed at the men's ceramic studio.

The aristocrats stormed off in that direction.

When they reappeared, they held my father between them.

They strapped him against two barrels in the courtyard's center. He was shouting something at Mother, who lay slumped beside a hut. I couldn't hear him above the cries of others and the snorting, thrashing sounds of dragon, but it didn't matter, for by the look on both his face and hers, I knew he spoke words of love.

Two aristocrats managed to hook poles through the yearling's muzzle, and they momentarily wrestled the beast's narrow head still. In that brief moment of quiet, a third aristocrat darted between the dragon's forelegs and unclasped the loose hobbles. I heard the clink of them falling upon ground. *Clink. Clink.* He then darted out of range.

The two holding the dragon's head released the beast. Then the three, joined by the fourth aristocrat who was orchestrating the horror, began hurling ceramics at the yearling.

The yearling reared up and screamed. The muscles in her hindquarters bulged beneath scales green and chestnut; she was a magnificent beast, powerful and enraged and unrestrained.

As the yearling came down, her beautiful, thick, curved talons reached out and embraced my father.

Skop stems spilled from his stomach, glistening white and red with vegetative juices. Blinding shards of screams flew through the air, and talons blazed in the sunlight, and a whip-tail thrashed, and a hut buckled inward under the impact of dragon hindquarters. An aristocrat was caught beneath the rampaging dragon's talons, then a child, who burst into a flock of crimson birds that flew a short distance before flopping wingless, red, and wet upon the ground.

Smells like a blacksmith's forge assaulted me. Hot, moist smells that tasted like rust.

The courtyard filled with dust, clouds and clouds of red dust, and this only days after a monsoon, so dust was impossible. But there it was. Red and everywhere.

I saw my father's tongue, protruded and purple, lying in dirt.

I closed my eyes and rocked.

TWELVE

The aristocrats had to enlist the aid of several dragonmaster apprentices in removing the frenzied yearling from our compound. By then blood and human flesh and mud were one; parts of my father's body, and of the aristocrat and the child who had been slain during the dragon's rampage, were blended forever into earth.

I never once came out from my hiding place during the shouts and curses and havoc of that long day, not until the drugged yearling—the soft, unscaled folds of her throat dewlaps quilled with blow darts like a porcupine—was led out of our compound by six or seven of the dragonmaster's apprentices.

Some time passed then. I don't know how long, and I don't know what I looked at in the interim. I don't even know if my eyes were open. I only grew conscious of my surroundings when Leishu's Caan and Kobo's Dash hooked their arms under my semiconscious mother, who lay slumped amid the bricks of a partially ruined hut, and hoisted her upright.

At that point and that point only did I move. I crawled out from under the barracks and headed straight for her, climbing over crumbled kilns, splintered timbers, and trampled thatch.

Our compound was a rubble-strewn shell. The mating shack lay on its side like a dead animal, three of its four stilts snapped off from its underbelly like broken legs. The women's barracks had suffered damage: One wall and part of the floor sagged down and across the courtyard, spilling struts and lathes and reed wall matting like so many entrails.

It was disorienting, that wreckage where familiarity should have been constant.

A man was sobbing somewhere among the rubble, a deep-chested sound so bald with grief it twisted my lungs. The keening of women crouched in corners—behind the water tower, under the renimgar cages, even within the men's huts—peaked and fell, peaked and fell. Their children neither wept nor wailed, and that is what I remember most from that day: the dense silence of the children's terror.

Leishu's Caan shook her head at me as I approached, tears running freely down her face.

"So you're alive," Kobo's Dash said hoarsely. "Too bad for you."

I picked up the trailing end of Mother's bitoo and wrapped it round a fist. It was a promise of a sort: I wouldn't leave her side. Ever. I stumbled after Leishu's Caan and Kobo's Dash as they carry-dragged Mother toward the women's barracks.

Big Grum Grum's Li suddenly appeared on the slanted steps, the front of her bitoo wet and heavy with blood. She clawed at her own throat as if a bone were lodged there and howled at us. Such a hoarse, raw noise! It froze Leishu's Caan and Kobo's Dash on the spot.

It had been one of her children that had been caught beneath the rampaging dragon's talons.

Big Grum Grum's Li stamped her feet and shook her fists at us. Without a word, my mother's friends turned away from the barracks and instead dragged Mother to one of the only other structures where a woman may bleed or defecate with impunity: one of the women's latrines. The same where, three days previous, Mother had pushed a bitter salve into her womb.

The women's latrines were narrow structures built over deep, foul pits. Each latrine had a brick floor, which was cleaned regularly, and a nasty hole, down which one emptied one's bladder and bowels.

The latrine in which Leishu's Caan and Kobo's Dash placed Mother was an old one. The raised brick floor was pitted and pocked from use, and if Mother had been able to stand upright and straddle the nasty latrine hole, she could have touched all four walls of the narrow structure without moving. But she couldn't stand. Certainly not.

Her friends leaned her against one wall, as carefully as their trembling hands would allow, and pushed her knees up to her chin so the door could be shut afterward. I curled in tight beside Mother, my legs bridging over the dark latrine hole.

"Stay here," Kobo's Dash rasped to me. "Don't come out. For your own sake."

"We'll be back," Leishu's Caan sobbed. She closed the latrine door and entombed us in darkness.

Mother shuddered against my shoulder. Again and again she shuddered, and each time a moist bubbling issued from her broken face. She smelled odd, like a freshly slaughtered renimgar hung belly-open on the drying racks.

Night placed a blindfold over our eyes.

I kept silent and tiny and still. If I tried hard enough, maybe I could make myself and Mother invisible. To be invisible was to be safe.

We stayed in that latrine all the next day, and that night, and the day following that. The light within the latrine during those days was gray and cobwebbed, peeling through the slats and knotholes in the coarse wood walls more slowly than the palm spiders that moved above our heads. The light during the night was so little, my eyes burned as they strained to see.

Beyond our narrow prison, we heard keening and the rasp of wood upon ground as the compound was cleared of wreckage. Once, someone hurled rocks at our latrine and shrieked unintelligible curses. I suspected it was Big Grum Grum's Li.

Leishu's Caan opened our door the third night and gave us a bowl of featon mash. She tried spooning it with her fingers into Mother's mouth, but Mother moaned in pain, and it slopped onto her chest like lumpy drool, so Leishu's Caan stopped. I was thirsty, but she'd forgotten to bring something to drink. She promised she'd bring water later that night. She never did. That was the last I ever saw of her.

Before she left us, though, she spat on a corner of her bitoo and gently tried to clean out the dirt embedded in Mother's cheeks. Again, Mother made an awful sound. Leishu's Caan washed my face instead. A strange gesture, that, when we were sleeping upon the floor of a latrine, but the kindness was apparent. I sat still throughout, frightened by her tender fingertips.

Later that night, my thirst became an obsession.

I *had* to have water. I whispered to Mother what I intended.

Through gestures she asked me to bring her some back. And something else, something else she was asking me, her hands clawing at my thighs, then gripping my wrist, then scratching at the ground.

"The bracelets," I said at last, and she sighed with relief, exhausted by her efforts.

Standing proved difficult. I had shifted about a great deal the last few days, but throughout had remained sitting. My legs had locked up. My tailbone pulsed like a tumor.

"I'll be as quick as I can," I said to Mother, shutting the door on her molten face.

Cold, damp silence waited outside the latrine, and it seemed as if the very night disapproved of me. I stood, shivering hard, for several moments, trying to make sense of my surroundings. Most of the wreckage had been cleared away, but the lack of structures where structures should have stood disoriented me. Finally, I could place everything: the women's barracks, the remains of Yeli's hut, the women's pottery shed.

I headed toward the women's pottery shed.

How frightening to enter it alone, at night, among Mother's weird, broken statues: strewn arm here, head there, across the floor. I thought suddenly of the snake that had muscled its way down from the roof the night old Kobo was slain, and the hacking Djimbi threnody during his wake. I shivered, not just from cold.

Quickly, I went to the small cistern in the far corner and plunged my hands into its algae-slick waters and drank and drank from cupped palms, all the while standing sideways, watching the dismembered statues.

I looked for something with which to carry water to Mother. After some hesitation, heart beating like hummingbird wings, I snatched up a leering, four-eyed clay head from the ground and filled its empty skull with water. Clutching it to my belly, I ran back to the latrine.

Mother spilled all the water trying to drink. Perhaps she drank *some,* for with a burbling sigh, she leaned back and closed her eyes. She kept the statue head cradled on her lap, and I think it was this that had somehow quenched her thirst, the feel of clay in her hands, not the water that had sloshed over her split, swollen tongue and run uselessly between the shards of teeth in her gums.

I left her again, this time to find the bracelets I'd buried in one of the alleys between the danku and the glass spinners' compounds the day Mother had tried to purchase back Waivia.

I went straight to the spot where I'd buried them.

In foggy darkness, in a maze of nearly identical alleys, I went, and on the first attempt dug up the cloth-wrapped bangles. Mother had asked me to find them, so I had. Simple as that.

I tied them into the hem of my bitoo, returned to Mother, and slept for the first time since watching the yearling disembowel my father.

I must have slept long and hard. It was dusk the following evening when Kobo's Dash woke me by jerking open the latrine door. She glanced down at Mother, then looked at me curled tight beside her.

"Get out, Zarq. Now. The men have been arguing. They're going to sell you to the kiyu stables tomorrow."

"I won't leave my mother."

"You will, whether now or when the men bind you and carry you away."

I shook my head no.

She stepped in, wrapped two hands about one of my forearms, and tried to yank me to my feet. I punched her in the ribs. With a hiss, she released me and staggered back. I curled down beside Mother again.

Kobo's Dash glared at us. Then she threw her hands up. "I've done my best, hey-o. I tried!" When that drew no response from either of us, she kicked dirt at us.

"Kavarria, for the love of your child, finish this foul thing you've started and look after Zarq. Understand? Get her somewhere safe before you die—do that much, at least!"

She slammed the door shut on us. Her feet slapped against the ground as she marched away.

Darkness and the sound of buzzing flies laying maggots in my mother's wounds.

Mother made a frothy gurgle and heaved about. It took me several moments to realize she wanted to stand, wanted to leave. But that was beyond her, and then the door opened again, and a giant of a man stood framed in it. He gagged and stumbled back at the stench, or maybe it was the sight of us that so repulsed him.

He half turned away, spat, spat again, and cursed.

"Get up," he finally barked. "Come with me."

Neither of us moved. He looked over his shoulder, licked his lips. Looked back at us. Crouched on his haunches.

In a quieter tone, he spoke again, this to my mother: "Darquel asked me to look after Zarq. I intend to keep the vow I made. Come with me, hey."

I recognized him then: Xxef-keau, the First Son of old Kobo the Zealot. He was a handsome man, as burly as my father and taller, and although he'd never claimed a woman, it was widely known he'd sired children in other clans.

He shifted and looked again over his shoulder. "Look, now, I have food. And a coin-string from the coast. You know what one is, yes? Some believe a woman may use currency such as this. Some of the men feel . . . well. A decision has been made, and those who don't agree with it have approached me and . . . understand? Now come with me."

Mother nodded slow agreement, her head wobbling as if she had palsy. She extended an arm. Xxef-keau hesitated, then reached in and hauled her upright.

He leaned away from her, clearly repulsed. "Can you not walk, woman?" he muttered.

Mother tried to comply, but melted groundward. He frowned down at her, ordered us to wait, and returned moments later with an egg barrow. To me he nodded at an ill-made basket on the ground and said, "Carry that. We leave the danku compound."

He lifted Mother into the barrow and lay her down with the gentle care that is particular to large men and which was so at odds to his look of revulsion. Mother's legs dangled over the sides.

Then he scooped me up, up, up, as I clutched the unraveling reed basket, and placed me astraddle his shoulders. His bare muscles breathed warmth against the skin of my thighs and undulated as he bent and hoisted up the handles of the barrow.

"There's paak in the basket. Help yourself," he said, and I scrabbled inside the basket, hands trembling.

Then, with paak in my mouth and riding astraddle a man's

shoulders, I was taken from my clan compound. Never again would I return.

Dawn floated toward us on a bank of cold mist. It drifted along the alleys and clung to Xxef-keau's hairy calves like the wraiths of lost children. It bejeweled Mother's hair with diamonds and beaded my bare arms like a swarm of mosquitoes. Gray light seeped reluctantly through it.

A cold and timid breeze chased the mist, then retreated. The egg barrow's axle squeaked. Xxef-keau's sandals slapped against hard-packed earth. His breath chuffed from his mouth in clouds of steam.

Suddenly, the noises ceased. I fought my way up from a well of stupor and realized Xxef-keau had stopped.

A plain of fog lay before us, dense and silent and wet. A breeze again, and a glimpse of squat stone podiums, each the height of three men standing atop one another, each with a girth that would require four brooders standing tail to snout to encircle it. Wooden towers with two, sometimes three, tiers, stood atop those stone podiums, and the arcades connecting the highest towers appeared to float on the frayed fog.

I knew this place despite never having seen it before. Geesamus Ir Cinai Ornisak, Dragon-Sanctioned Zone of the Dead. The towers built atop those stone podiums were gawabe, sepulchral towers, and in them resided the kigos, the embalmed wealthy, and their living servants, the makmaki.

A few of those servants of the dead drifted around the great stone podiums and the sepulchral towers above them, going about their morning duties. Shrouded entirely in orange cloth, they were identical, faceless and limbless. They looked inhuman.

My heart beat erratically.

Xxef-keau put me down, rolled his head carefully to and fro to work the kinks from his neck. My legs were equally as stiff and sore and seemed permanently locked in a bowlegged position from having straddled his neck the entire night. Shivering from more than just cold and ache, I watched him lean over the egg barrow and poke Mother until her eyes rolled open.

"Today and for the morrow you'll stay in a gawabe," he said. "I've arranged for a chanooi to visit you on the day after. You're to purchase your girl inclusion in the Chanoom Sect. She'll do well enough with them. They'll accept the coin-string without question. A lot of danku men risked themselves to get that coin-string, understand? For Darquel. So do this thing, and I'll get word of her on occasion and ensure that she's hale." And then, as if it were an afterthought: "Greatfather Rudik has pronounced you nas rishi poakin ku."

Dangerous serf ejected from clan.

Only "ejected" isn't the proper translation for the word *poakin.* *Poakin* describes the muscular movements of a dragon retching up maht, partially digested crop food. When attached to the word *nas,* the phrase takes on a darker resonance. *Nas:* unfit to live with, dishonorable; an unstable, violent person unable to form kin bonds.

Mother would never be allowed within a clan again, *any* clan.

And unless I was separated from her, I would share her fate.

Mother gave the barest of nods: She would purchase me inclusion in the Chanoom Sect.

Satisfied, Xxef-keau lifted me onto his shoulders again, picked up the barrow's handlebars, and entered the Zone of the Dead.

THIRTEEN

After interviewing a number of the orange-shrouded kigos mak-makis, servants of the dead, Xxef-Keau chose for our lodging a sepulchral tower tended by two brothers. With the two brothers behind him, one carrying me, he then climbed the rope ladder leading into their tower, with Mother draped over his back like a sack of chaff. He deposited her on the coarse wooden floor, threw a cursory look about the humble tower, nodded in grim satisfaction, and without so much as a word to either me or my mother, he departed. I never saw him again.

We stayed with the kigos makmakis while the moon waxed, then waned, then waxed full again. With a handsome bribe, Mother turned away the chanooi sent by Xxef-keau the day after our arrival in the Zone of the Dead, ensuring with lucre that should anyone inquire into my whereabouts, they would be told I had joined the Chanoom Sect, and Mother had died.

Between the cost of that bribe and the charge for our room and board in the gawabe, the coin-string given us by Xxef-keau disappeared entirely.

I worked for our keep, then, rooting in the jungle for edibles alongside our hosts or creeping beside them as they set rawhide tension snares. I gutted caught lizards; I gathered fuel. I emptied chamber pots in the morning and lit the cooking brazier at night. I polished wood and cleaned away cobwebs. I made stinking candles from monkey fat and sat with the bodies of the embalmed in our tower, chasing away the brown-fanged rats determined to eat the hanging kigos.

I did not dislike living among the dead.

The family of kigos, the thickly bandaged bodies suspended in their separate vertical hammocks, did not scare me. I knew they wished me no harm. Sixteen of them, there were, most adult sized, though the freshest, cleanest bundle was no larger than a babe, the bandaged head small enough to be cradled within my palms. I was always given watch duty at night, and as I chased rats across the dark floor I chatted to the kigos and sometimes sang to them, even while bludgeoning caught rats to a pulp.

We all agreed, the kigos and I, that rats needed to be thoroughly pulped—their ribs staved in, their organs mashed to jelly—before they could be left for dead.

More than once, one of my hosts, the makmaki brothers, clambered up the ladder to the second tier and bellowed at me to quit the racket; no one could sleep below. A dead rat was a dead rat, no need to liquefy the bastards!

But I knew different. I'd seen a dead rat come back to life once. It dragged its shattered hindquarters halfway across the floor before stopping to frantically gnaw at its own belly. And during my second attempt to kill it, it squealed and bared its teeth at me.

From then on, I knew: dead rats could not be trusted. Better to pulp them.

Xxef-keau had chosen well in picking our two makmakis from the orange-shrouded figures the day we'd arrived. They were brothers, given to quarrels and passionate reconciliations that they took no pains to hide from me, my mother, or their own mother, a bent hag who never took off her shroud or descended our gawabe. The brothers were always stripping to hunt or pick leeches off each other or make love. They looked about my father's age, and were as proud of the gawabe they tended as the rest of the makmakis in the Zone of the Dead were of their own towers.

There was a hierarchy among the makmakis, and our brothers were in the low end of the middle. There were gawabes such as the one we lived in, still in use but lacking the devotion funds of a truly high-status bayen family. There were gawabes that, aside from bats and rats, stood empty, the kigos long rotted, their servants dead or absorbed into another tower. And there were the other gawabes, the ones that blazed with light and life and housed very important kigos indeed.

Within those towers lived many makmakis. They kept the wood and silverware polished and chandeliers lit and dust free. They prepared elaborate meals each evening for the resident dead, and played wood pipes to a table glittering with silver. The food was later eaten by the makmakis themselves or sold to the likes of our brothers, purchased with labor.

No rats in those towers, nor any dust on those embalmed, and the hammocks the dead swung in were made not from braided jungle vine replaced twice yearly but from the finest cords of silk. Frequently, bayen relatives visited those towers and held Geesamus Diroot parties, Entertain the Dead parties, which filled the entire zone with peals of boisterous laughter and drunken music. Should the family of our kigos ever visit, Mother and I were to hide in a chest purportedly used to store the belongings of the dead. But I once looked in that chest and found it empty. I felt sad then, knowing that the dead family's favorite toys and clothes had been traded in market for eggs to feed their makmakis, and sadder still knowing the brothers had dared such a thing only because of how infrequently their gawabe was visited.

A rishi burial—the corpse tossed to gharials and quickly consumed—seemed cleaner and more dignified than perpetual dangling, neglect, and slow rot.

Mother grew stronger. In that worn basket given us by Xxef-keau, we found an herbal paste to ease the pain of her broken jaw. Yet still she could not talk clearly or eat solid food, and she frequently turned away the yanichee or featon mash I and the makmaki brothers' old mother cooked.

On bad days, she couldn't even find the energy to hoist herself onto a chamber pot, and I'd spend my day cleaning first her, then her soiled bitoo, then the floor beneath her, only to start all over again when her bladder loosed once more.

She slept a great deal. She often awoke to her own screams.

But she did grow stronger, and one evening I found her standing up, looking out a latticed wooden window in the lower terrace of our gawabe. She moved her neck carefully to look at me. I found it hard to meet her gaze. That face, with its punched-in eyes and drooling jaw that hung aslant off discolored cheeks, was not *my* mother's.

She gestured for me to come close. I shook my head no. Sadness the color of fog filled her eyes.

With a bubbly inhalation through her open mouth, she stepped toward me. I wanted to flee, wanted no part of her, but everything the way it had once been. She gently cupped my cheeks in her hands and with the balls of her thumbs—now the sinewy digits of a crone—she stroked my cheekbones over and over. Tears burst from my eyes as if expelled under great pressure.

She pulled me against her bony chest, and I buried my face in her flaccid breasts. Crooning, she held me. Rocked me. Twilight descended.

I knew then that we'd soon be leaving the Dragon-Sanctioned Zone of the Dead. I would miss the peace greatly.

Mother showed one of her bracelets to the makmaki brothers that night, and they reacted with none of the wariness of people who had heard the Temple decree against jewelry of its ilk. So she asked them to sell it for her in market, for a coin-string only, because what good would chits be to a woman? They, of course, would be given a quarter of whatever they sold it for.

She also told them to sell it wisely, insinuating the bracelet had been stolen. The brothers cared little how it had been obtained, were only interested in how much they might profit from the transaction. I asked Mother that night why she had trusted the brothers at all; we were at their mercy. They would sell our bracelet and give us nothing in return—

"Trust them," she grunted, and briefly, a tiny firefly of light danced in her eyes. "They are good."

So I convinced myself that she was right, and the brothers would not rob us. By whatever means available to her—Djimbi magic or intuition—Mother had deemed the brothers trustworthy.

She was right.

Thus, we found ourselves, several days later, descending our gawabe, a small coin-string around Mother's neck. A young makmaki from another gawabe jauntily lead us out the Zone of the Dead. I refused to look back at the brothers as they watched us go. I was afraid I would run back to them and beg them to keep me.

After so many weeks living among the kigos, the energy of the living who passed us in the alleys alarmed me. My alarm was reflected somewhat in the eyes of those who looked at Mother's distorted face before they quickly looked elsewhere.

By late morn our young guide procured a ride for us on a dragon-pulled wagon filled with urns of consecrated Temple oil. Then, unexpectedly—Mother and I already in the back of the cart, the daronpu driver plying whip to dragon hide to start the beast—our guide darted into the nearest alley. I made to run after him, but Mother held me back.

We were alone.

By noon, we reached Iri Timadu Bayen Sor, the Zone of Most Exalted Aristocrats.

Its immense temple, Wai Bayen Temple, dominated a marketplace teeming with stalls selling colorful cloth, leather goods, fruit, woven baskets, wall hangings, caged macaws. The temple stood at the center of it all, upon an enormous sandstone plinth perforated with geometrical patterns. The temple was monstrous, a multidomed structure resplendent with copper-scale spires, golden domes, arches, and latticed parapets inlaid with semiprecious stones.

Mother mumbled something incomprehensible.

"What?" I said.

"This is where Greatfather Rudik sold my diadems," she slurred, articulating the words slowly and painfully for my benefit. I saw the temple differently after that, as if a shadow had slid over the glitter and finery.

We tried to find passage out of Clutch Re.

But so many people, so much color, so many smells laden with fat and wealth! And the noise and the conflicting information, enough to turn one mad. I acted as speaker for Mother, asking questions of the women selling wares in the temple square.

As the day progressed, Mother's footsteps grew increasingly erratic and a peculiar, frothy sweat bathed her face.

How easy it would have been just to saunter up to a daronpu or an acolyte and ask questions and receive accurate directions. But a woman could not do such for herself. She would be ignored at best, or beaten for impudence at worst.

Oh, to be a boy.

And then I thought . . . why not? I looked enough like a boy, with my ragged hair and scrawny limbs.

With a precious coin from our already too-small string, I purchased a loincloth from a stall, then crouched to change clothes between two of Wai Bayen Temple's many enameled turquoise-and-white columns. It was dusk by then, and Mother and I had eaten nothing since leaving the sepulchral tower. Her face looked as pale as the wrappings around the kigos I'd guarded.

If not for the dreadful look of her, I would not have had the courage to approach one of the local daronpuis returning to Wai Bayen Temple for the night. I felt panicked by my nakedness, clad only in a loincloth, yet I approached the daronpu with the same swagger I'd seen men use, and I asked where I might purchase a ride out of Clutch Re with the same bold tone. He answered without hesitation or grace, and continued on his way.

That easy, it was. All for the sake of a loincloth.

We followed his directions. Soon we reached the hostels and stables where out-of-Clutch merchants, wagon drivers, and their dragons stayed. We hunkered down in a side alley that stank of urine, and awaited dawn.

The next morn, I sidled into one stable courtyard and studied the traveling merchants as they loaded wares into wagons and harnessed their dragons between cart shafts. One merchant stood out among the others. He had a large family, and though he bullied them relentlessly, I liked the looks of his retinue better than the hired mercenaries accompanying the other merchant trains. They didn't stink of fermented maska, and their clothes were clean and well mended. Furthermore, the merchant's shifting eyes and scarred cheek bespoke of a nature inclined to overlook my mother's state and the questionable elegance of the jewelry I would offer as payment.

Did I trust him? No. Had I another choice? I thought not.

And so, late noon the next day, Mother and I rode out of Clutch Re in one of the wagons of a merchant traveler's train.

How had I known Mother wanted to leave Clutch Re?

She'd told me as much that evening I found her standing by the window in the sepulchral tower. Not in so many words, understand, but in images, bleak sepia pictures without depth or shadow, invading my head like a sickness and pulsing behind my eyes until I shouted against Mother's breast, "Fine, we'll go! We'll go!"

A rishi is not indentured to a Clutch lord, see, is free to leave at any time. But so few do. Why leave a livelihood, one's kin, the protection of a lord, and the blessings of a bull dragon to fend for oneself beyond Clutch boundaries? Such a thing makes little sense.

Once, when I was about five, I found a tiny cat abandoned within our compound. How it had arrived there was a mystery, for it was days old at most, still blind and blunt nosed and unable to do more than paddle the ground uselessly with delicate claws. Mother reached forward to snap its neck between her strong hands, but I begged to keep the kitten. Just until it was old enough to release back into the jungle.

A cruelty to do so, Mother said. A wild cat needed to learn the ways of the jungle from birth to survive. To foist it out of the danku once it could walk was to condemn it to a lingering death. And I knew, even before I asked, that a jungle cat would not be allowed to reach maturity within our compound walls.

I closed my eyes as Mother forced the tiny head backward.

So I wondered as we rode out of Clutch Re, jammed between rough wooden crates filled with Clutch Re wares for trade, if Kobo's Dash had been right. If Mother should have used the keri-peri and tepin leaves to take her own life. If I should have eaten some, too.

Other than the constant terror that my true gender would be discovered, life in the merchant traveler's train was not vastly different than it had been in the gawabe, though the lack of chilies in the merchants' diet left me craving the piquant fruit. I learned that all traveling merchants shunned chilies; chilies disguised the taste of poisons, which a mercenary in the train guard might stir into the communal cooking pot in order to obtain both the wagon train and all its possessions.

I was worked hard and given little to eat in return, and on those nights I was permitted to sleep, I curled beside Mother and the crates in the back of a wagon. Under the dark of night, she would check that my loincloth was wrapped about me in such a manner so that when I bent or was pushed down, my lack of male organs would not be discovered. I doubted whether any boy took as much care with his loincloth as did I.

The stress of maintaining my deception gave me night terrors.

At first, the children in the wagon train tormented me as we walked alongside the wagons during the day, gathering dragon dung and wood for fuel. They didn't pinch or scratch like quarrelling danku children did, but fought with closed fists and well-aimed kicks, and the adults never intervened. But by duplicating their fighting methods and attacking them first, and when they least expected it, the youngest children soon left me alone.

I learned how to be invisible around the eldest.

The members of the five-wagon train consisted of the merchant master, his two claimed women and their sixteen children, a message carrier, one Clutch Re rishi family determined to reach the coastal capital and do better for themselves, and five lanrak paras, soldiers outside of the army. Those mercenaries looked as trustworthy as kwano snakes, but by their gruff familiarity with the merchant master and his eldest sons, I deduced they'd worked together for some time.

I only hoped they'd do the job they'd been hired for—protect us from ambush by Djimbi, bandit, and jungle cat—and not murder us in our sleep and make off with the wares instead.

The dragons pulling the wagon train were cinai satons, literally, "androgynous dragons." Deprived of protein-rich foods and the security of a brooding nest since birth, those lean, cantankerous dragons never laid eggs. Solely because they lacked that ability, the name given them was one that implied ambiguous gender, which was ridiculous, really, as the beasts were as female a dragon as a yearling or brooder. A sterile woman is oft referred to as a saton; it is not a complimentary appellation.

My days in the merchant traveler's train passed in an endless film of cold morning mist, humid afternoon fog, and damp evening chill. Wagon wheels lodged in ruts and had to be pushed and rocked out. Cooking pots had to be cleaned and axles greased. The satons pulling our wagons had to be led along the jungle's edge to forage each evening, and then herded back to camp and their hobbles removed each morn.

I was frequently given watch duty for that, though the merchant master valued his scrawny satons far more than the makmaki brothers valued their kigos, for he didn't trust me to do the job alone. Always his least favorite son accompanied me, a lank-haired lad with webbed toes.

In the dead of night as he and I huddled against the knobby flanks of the foraging satons for warmth, I learned that although Duck Feet's father belonged to no Clutch, the Lord of Clutch Cuhan had loaned him the use of those satons. In return, his father paid a steep tithe to Lupini Cuhan, though Duck Feet thought that was something to boast about rather than a source of anger or shame.

I asked him if his father ever wanted his own dragons. Duck Feet looked at me as if I were yolk brained.

"And end up in Arena as bait? That's what happens to anyone who steals a dragon, you know. You *do* know that, hey-o?"

"That's not what I meant," I said, but I frowned, unsure what I *had* meant. I knew as well as he that no one but a Temple-chosen Roshu, Lupini, or Roshu-Lupini could breed dragons, and that only those under their auspices could ride or work the beasts.

What I'd meant was . . . what I'd been talking about was . . . heresy, of course.

I closed my lips and never mentioned it again.

Throughout those mist-chilled nights filled with stealthy sounds and raw, green scents, and the fog-shrouded days filled with hacking coughs, hard work, and hunger, Mother slept. Always she slept, waking only to crouch behind a bush and relieve herself. When she slept, she frowned hard, as if she were concentrating on something of extreme importance.

I suppose she was. She was concentrating on clinging to life.

One morning as we lurched and rumbled along the rutted jungle path, the merchant master called a halt and ordered me and his brood to lift down a barrel of oil, a drum of maska, and eight sacks of featon grit. As I staggered beneath a sack alongside Duck Feet, I asked him what it was about.

"Tieron," he hissed through gritted teeth, which meant nothing to me.

We placed the foodstuffs beside a mossy cairn upon which a handful of bromeliads had taken root. The eldest sons then wrapped an entire salted and cured gharial in broad leaves, while the rest of us got bitten by spiders and mosquitoes, sweating while we yanked liana vines down from the trees and braided them into a coarse rope. The eldest sons then strung the wrapped gharial carcass up from a bough.

It dangled there like a kigo, spinning slowly.

The entire time, the laniak paras lounged against buttressed roots, chewing thin, tarry maska stems.

By then it was late noon. The merchant master was cursing to be gone. Duck Feet scrabbled up the buttressed root of a gray-boled tree, shimmied along a bough, and *clang, clang! Clang, clang!* The deafening tolling of a rusted bell I hadn't noticed shattered the air.

He rang that bell a long time, and when he stopped my ears hummed as if a hornet were lodged within my mouth.

Mother slowly sat up and eased herself off the wagon she'd been riding on. She would have melted to the ground if I hadn't darted forward and wrapped my arms about her hips. She waved at the cairn, for me to take her to it. Once there, she sank onto the damp stones, took a deep, rattling breath, and lifted her eyes to the merchant master. He gawped at her. *Everyone* gawped at her, myself included. She meant to stay? Here?

"They won't take the likes of you, nor your dragon-bait son," the merchant master said, and he spat in the mud. "But it's your prerogative to stay, of course."

He said this last smugly, pleased to be done with us so soon and happy with our coin-string round his neck and one of our bracelets on his biceps.

He slapped the reins against his saton; the beast lunged forward. The wagon train slowly creaked into action. I watched in disbelief as it trundled into the mist.

"Mama!" I wailed. Overtaken by panic, I grabbed one of her twiggy arms and yanked her upright with all my strength. Surprised and off balance, she stumbled a couple paces before gaining her footing.

"We can catch them—it's not too late." I butted my head into her bony rump and pushed her forward.

She turned and clipped me over the ear. Although she had precious little strength, the blow stopped me cold.

"There," she grunted, pointing at the cairn. Trembling, she sank back on it and looked at me with hollow eyes.

"Why don't you just kill me now and be done with it?" I cried. I threw myself at the base of the cairn, drew my knees to my chest, wrapped my arms around them, and rocked.

The day shortened, then lay down beneath the night.

I stiffly rose to my feet, rummaged about in the gloom until I found a stout stick, and with my teeth gnawed it to a ragged point. Then I unlashed the braided vine that held the gharial carcass suspended out of vermin reach, intending to slowly lower it to the ground. But the carcass was heavy; the vines whizzed through my hands, skinning and blistering my palms, and the carcass landed with a dull thud in the mud.

Mother watched me apathetically. I muttered one of the juicy curses I'd learned from the lanrak paras, shambled over to the carcass, and hacked myself a flake of jerky from it. The dark meat was oily and rich but stank like badly cured leather. I was used to renimgar flesh, not this heavy stuff, for I'd only eaten it before when boiled in a stew during ancestor celebrations. I chewed the jerky slowly, swallowed it, and was rewarded with a sulphurous belch that burned up from my belly like bile.

After eating, I strained and pulled at the braided vine, trying to lift the carcass into the air again. It couldn't stay on the muddy ground; not only would it spoil, but it would attract wildlife. Chances were, the rich smell of it would attract all manner of carnivores, anyway. Mother and I would have to climb a tree to stay safe—

Sure enough, the dense rhododendrons and palm ferns behind the cairn rustled with the sounds of something big and soft footed and hungry.

I hadn't proved very useful to Mother previously in times of crises, and I upheld that tradition; I stood paralyzed on the spot, liana vine slack in my hands.

The beast appeared, standing on its hind legs.

No. It was a man.

No, a *woman*.

A gaunt, almost skeletal woman whose face was visibly jaundiced even in the poor light, her eyes so large they reminded me of eggs. She was dressed in a tattered knee-length tunic made from coarse, undyed hemp, tied at the waist with a braided hemp cord, and an ankle-length skirt beneath it. As she stepped forward, a slit in the skirt divided and I glimpsed impossibly hairy, thick calves. But no, it was not her calves, but leggings made from bark cloth wrapped round and round in strips and knotted into place.

I stood there staring long enough for seven more women to appear from the jungle darkness and gather in a semicircle before Mother and me. The first woman who had appeared—the one I'd stared at as if entranced—finally spoke.

"We don't take boys," she said to Mother.

Mother looked at me. I closed my mouth and shrugged. Mother looked as if the weight of a brooder were straddled across her collarbone.

"No boys," Yellow Face said again. "And we can't take you, either, sister. Sorry."

She didn't sound sorry. She sounded annoyed to have to refuse us, though I had no idea what she was refusing.

Mother grunted, reached into her filthy bitoo, and withdrew the last of our bracelets. She held it in trembling palms and extended her arms. I expected a brilliant shaft of light to illuminate it, such as had occurred when she'd made a similar offering in the glass spinners' compound. But no. Nothing.

Yellow Face reluctantly came forward and lifted the bangle. It was then that the thing looked brilliant and alive, a coiled creature of lapis lazuli and gold leaf. My heart thudded hard against my ears.

Obviously, these women were not Clutch Re rishi and therefore had no idea of the tainted history of that bangle, but still tension strung me tight as a rawhide snare. Yellow Face turned the bangle this way and that, held it close to her eyes, gestured for a short, pocked woman to come forward and study it. They consulted each other with a single look.

Yellow Face turned to Mother. "Where did you get this?"

"We didn't steal it," I said, and immediately was impaled by Yellow Face's gaze. "My mother made it. We're danku rishi, and if she were a man, she'd be a dankomikon, a ceramics master."

"And you've left your ku because . . . ?"

I faltered and looked at Mother. She gave a barely perceptible nod: continue.

"Our Greatfather declared us nas rishi poakin ku," I mumbled.

"Because?"

"Because"—a rush of anger gave me license to improvise, to abbreviate the truth—"because my mother tried to buy back my sister with chits after a dishonorable roidan kasloo."

"Hardly seems a reason to declare a woman and her son nas rishi poakin ku."

"I'm not a boy."

"Speak up, child."

"I'm not a boy."

An arched brow. "Lift your breechclout."

Blushing, I did so. The women around Yellow Face stirred as I revealed my sex.

"Well, now. So you aren't. But I still don't understand why you both were rejected from your guild clan."

"Because my father died, hey-o? For my mother's transgressions. He was punished and he died, and his eldest brother is our clan Greatfather and he never liked my mother, ever!" My chest heaved, my fists were clenched. Tears ran down my grimy cheeks.

Yellow Face's huge eyes released me and impaled Mother instead.

"Because you are Djimbi," Yellow Face said.

The wind soughed through the trees and the sour, heady smell of citrus fern stung my eyes like chili juice.

"Yes," I whispered into a silence that crouched and waited. "Yes. She is Djimbi."

FOURTEEN

Thus began my life in Tieron Nask Cinai, the Dragon Convent of Tieron. Hidden in the jungle upon a rocky hillock, skirted by dry rhododendrons and peel-bark trees, the convent was but a sorry little mill nestled beside a great mossy rotunda, shadowed by the limestone cliffs that loomed behind it. A thin waterfall hammered down from those cliffs, powering the mill wheel and providing water for the onais, the holy women, and their charges. Red and scarlet macaws seethed over the cliff face, eating its salts and minerals.

Between the splatter-drum of the waterfall, the screeching of the macaws, the thrum and creak of the mill wheel and the rasp of the millstone itself, the convent was a very noisy place indeed. The onais communicated in shouts.

"You will be initiated tomorrow," Yellow Face bellowed at me. We stood in the mill's quivering attic, and the thrum of the slow-churning mill wheel ran through the floorboards and straight up my legs to my teeth. I clamped them together, trying to ease the maddening sensation, but that made it worse.

I stared in amazement at the onais sleeping upon the floor about us. How could they, in that noise?

But Mother was asleep, too; the trek to the convent after the night at the cairn with the onais had about killed her. Two of the onais had ended up making a crude device from bamboo and vine, and over this they had draped Mother and pulled her to the convent. It had been an arduous journey for us all, carrying Mother and those sacks of featon grit, and rolling the barrels of oil and maska along the overgrown trail.

I was in such an enervated state that sleep was impossible. Besides, it was only just after high noon.

"Until you are initiated, you don't move from here, the both of you. Understand?" Yellow Face shouted above the noise. "Use that when the need comes." She pointed to a chipped enamel chamber pot.

I nodded dumbly.

Yellow Face crossed the mill attic, stepping round the sleeping onais with as much care as if they were rocks. With a look at me that clearly repeated her directive to stay put, she descended the attic stairs and disappeared from view.

I counted the sleeping onais: twelve. I counted the mosquito curtains drawn up to the attic rafters: seven. I counted the sacks, barrels, food bowls, looms, and coarsely hewn coffers stacked round the perimeter of the attic. I peered through a crack in the floorboards and watched a great wooden cog ratchet round and round below. I used the chamber pot. Unable to sit still any longer, I tiptoed over to the stairs, descended a couple, and peered into the mill below.

I saw the same scene that I'd witnessed upon first being ushered into Convent Tieron: a clawful of onais, holy women in charge of retired bull dragons, were streaked green with stains as they hauled sheaf after sheaf of jungle vines and weeds into the mill from outside. They funneled those sheaves beneath the slow-turning millstone.

At the far edge of my view, I could just see two more onais lifting and turning the resultant green mash with large paddles, occasionally scooping it off into barrels. I watched long enough to see three barrels filled, plugged, and rolled out of the mill before boredom set in.

I walked about the attic then, trying to find a hole in the wattle-and-daub walls to allow me a view of the convent's surroundings. But the walls, although patched and repatched everywhere, and although thick with dust and streaked with viscous green juice, bore no peepholes.

Too bad. I wanted to study the mossy, rambling rotunda adjacent to the mill. Was that where the onais lived, beneath its drafty arches, between its defaced columns, under its crumbling, lichen-coated cornices? If so, why did these twelve women sleep here in the mill attic, during daylight?

Or were they asleep?

I shuddered and scurried to Mother's side. I sat cross-legged on the vibrating floor and stared at the nearest onai.

There I could see it, the rise and fall of her chest. She was alive.

Relieved and finally feeling sleepy, I lay down beside Mother and allowed the hum of the mill to lull me asleep.

I awoke in darkness. The mill wheel was still and silent. My bitoo was damp, I was lying upon my side, and someone to my left was coughing, a deep, wet cough. I was ravenous and thoroughly chilled. I wrapped my arms about myself and curled tight against Mother.

There was a denseness to the silence in the attic, and it took me a while to understand it: The place was filled. With what, sleeping onais? I lifted my head and looked about. In the gloomy light filtering up through the floorboards and the staircase to the ground floor, I saw I'd guessed right.

One, two, three, four, five . . . I counted twice, got nineteen on my first try and twenty on the second.

Twenty-two of us, all jammed into the attic at once! It was a pity the attic was so lofty; the heat from our bodies might have otherwise warmed it some. As it was, the cool of the waterfall hammering into the pool behind the mill contrived with the height of the attic to create as cold a sleeping place as I'd ever lain in. Even in the merchant traveler's train, lying in the back of an uncovered cart between stacked crates and Mother, it hadn't been as chilly as this. At least *here* there were mosquito curtains, however ragged and dusty.

Then I noticed: Just like in the tent at the sesal fields, Mother and I were surrounded by a conspicuous circle of space. No one slept against our backs for warmth.

Someone rolled over. The cougher broke into another long, wet spasm. An onai rose up, stepped around her sleeping sisters, and crouched over a chamber pot. She looked directly at me as she finished, and gave a short wave. I didn't know how to respond to the gesture; was it well meant or an order of a sort? I closed my eyes and feigned sleep.

I began to feel nauseous, I was so hungry. At that point, Mother wrapped an arm about me and tugged me tight against the warm curl of her body.

It was an embrace soft and sweet. Warm. Smelling of paak laced with lime and chilies, of wet clay and tart, white kaolin. Of seaweeds shriveling in the kiln, the bitter, charred stench the price for the swirling metallic hues on our ceramics. . . .

I was falling asleep to dream of such scents. Yet this was not sleep, was nothing like a dream, for I could feel the cold air of the mill and hear the coughing onais still, yet the smells of the pottery compound were as real as my heartbeat. It was as if I were suspended somewhere between sleep and consciousness, the present and the past. Like a drop of water suspended, for a moment, in thick, golden oil.

Like that drop of water, I felt myself sinking down, down, down through the oil, but down to what, I knew not.

I was caught in Djimbi magic. The strongest my mother had ever evoked. Of this I was suddenly sure.

I felt a stab of panic; the golden oil about me grew thicker. I was sucked down faster, caught in a whirlpool, couldn't breathe. . . .

The swirling stopped. Clean morning air smelling of dew and tender bamboo shoots chilled my skin.

I blinked, stunned.

To the left of me stood a kiln: I was standing in a courtyard. But clearly it was not danku Re, the pottery compound of my childhood, for whereas danku Re boasted three beehive-shaped kilns, this compound had but one, and a boxy sort at that. The colors were all wrong, too. Everything was the color of clay. Fired clay, sun-dried clay, limestone clay, earthenware clay, ash clay . . .

The sky was ochre, the ground shades of cinnamon and taupe. The woman's barracks—small, the roof stippled with dark lichen—was terra-cotta, the men's huts rust. And over there, an ash-gray mating shack leaned on uneven stilts.

I lifted my hands into view. They obeyed slowly, blearily. My skin was the mottled green and brown of my mother's.

"Where am I?" I whispered. My words echoed as if from the bottom of a well.

"Danku Xxamer Zu," my mother whispered back. "The pottery clan of Clutch Xxamer Zu. Hush now. No more words. You're safe within me. *Become* me."

And suddenly, I was upon a stool, my left leg pumping a pedal up and down, up and down, and before me whirled a potter's wheel, and upon the wheel sat a large mound of clay, sliding under my fingers, smooth and cool and slick.

I was outside, shaping urns under the shade of a desiccated palm-frond roof. Around me sat the men and women of my clan, a wrinkled Mottled Belly woman to my left with hair like shanks of knotted moss, and a woman who hid her piebald green-and-brown skin beneath carefully applied walnut stain, sitting to my right. That's when I realized who I was. I was my mother, Kavarria. The old woman to my left was my Greatmother, and the woman to my right, my mother.

And this was how we worked in danku Xxamer Zu, outside, men and women together, uncensored by the daronpuis who were far and few between on our destitute Clutch.

Such was the only life I, Kavarria, knew, a life of unity and few walls, and as I shaped clay, I repeatedly looked upon our clan neighbors as they worked across from us potters at their great, hacked butchering slabs, slaughtering renimgars under the sun.

Flies buzzed thickly about their heads, though it was only one head in particular that I searched for.

The tenth son of the butchers' clan Greatfather was a beautiful piebald youth, with muscles that flashed and bulged as he effortlessly wielded his machete, flensing red flesh from white renimgar ribs. He looked up; our eyes met. I drank in his gaze, lapped it up, sucked it deep, thirsted and drank some more. When he looked away, I was amputated, denuded, dehydrated.

Greatmother nudged me with a hot foot; my wheel had fallen still. I flushed and resumed work.

And then . . . oh, then.

His mouth was on my neck and mine on his stomach, his mottled green-and-brown skin ribbed and taut and salty under my tongue. I opened my legs, pushed against him, demanded and bit, but he denied me, rolled me onto my belly, took me from behind where he could spill his seed without growing a child. The pain of him was sweet and sharp, and I pushed against him until he shuddered and sighed into my ear.

After, as the night chill pimpled our skin, I traced my fingers through his sweat, wanting.

No, no, he murmured, as we met again and again behind the water tower. Not that way.

Yes, I insisted.

Djimbi child cursed, he said through gritted teeth.

Djimbi child beautiful, I whispered back. You, me, our child, too—

Birth another man's babe, not mine, he said, and with tongue burrowed between my thighs, he tried to take the sting from his words.

But I thirsted and I persisted. And he . . . he thirsted, too. Oh! I could see it in the edges of his quick-turning glances, I could see it stalking his stride. He wanted it, wanted it like a fire roaring hot on dry wood.

When he finally relinquished—when he stayed atop me and with a gut-deep groan pushed into my womb—a banded noony shrieked in the jungle. Again and again it shrieked. For each of his thrusts into me, the childlike wail rent the night and knifed through my heart.

Afterward, he wept. Said the piebald babe would be cursed. And I, glutted at last, steeped in his semen, denied what in my heart I knew to be true.

Protect us both, then, I finally whispered to stop his tears. Be strong enough to claim me as your woman.

And I placed his hand on my breast and with my legs drew him to me again.

So despite the angry words of kin and ku—for Temple disallowed two full-blood or half-blood Djimbis to unite—he declared to his clan Greatfather that he would claim me as his roidan yin, his garden of children.

The ceremony was short and furious. Held at dusk instead of daylight, men chosen by our two clan Greatfathers wore the yenshik, the ceremonial masks representing the ordeals a claimer might face on behalf of his roidan yin. Each furred and feathered yenshik mask sported a story tree, a lofty pole jutting from the crown, informing the audience which evil the mask represented.

Tarred and braided liana vines dangled from one pole, human teeth clacking together at the end of each braid; those represented kwano snakes and all the danger they posed and the evil they inspired. Clay scales glazed green and blue studded another pole, and from the tip of it hung a thin leather cord; that yenshik represented allegiance to Temple and its wardens. A phallus pole represented mating diseases and bastard children; a stillborn pole, from which dangled the withered limbs of mummified bats, represented the tragedies that might befall mother and child.

All manner of horrors capered about my claimer that dusk, jibber-jabbering from rictus mouths, story poles balanced upon heads. As they capered, they hurled renimgar dung at him and smacked his bare back and calves with paddles.

He stood tall, gazing only at me where I sat upon the chancobie, the throne of submission and apology, which is the seat a roidan yin forever after must occupy in her mind when with her claimer.

But I looked neither submissive nor apologetic as my eyes stayed on his. No, no. I knew too well how I looked, could not keep the hot blaze of exultation off my cheeks. I had what I wanted. Finally.

And although he produced no blood towels for the clan Greatfathers after we coupled in the mating shack at ceremony's end, he tied his loincloth about my waist nonetheless, signifying that his seed, and his alone, had been sown in my garden. No one disputed the claim. We had not been discreet in our visits to the water tower.

It wasn't long after the ceremony—mere days, it seemed—that the smell of baking paak in the mornings slicked me with sweat, and the tenderness in my swelling breasts turned my proud stride into a delicate mince. My Greatmother said the baby would be a girl.

And then. Oh, then.

Word flooded Clutch Xxamer Zu, choking us with a too-familiar fear: Arena wagers had to be paid, but no coin existed in our lord's coffers to pay the debt, nor enough wares in his store holds. Rishi would be given in lieu of lucre. Which rishi, from which clan, would be left to the discretion of Clutch Xxamer Zu Holy Wardens.

A clawful of days later, Roshu Xxamer Zu's paras dragged me screaming from the women's barracks. My claimer kept his vow: He fought for me.

Sixteen, he was. Dead too soon by my lust, his own weakness, the mottled green-and-brown color of our skin, and a para's dirk. As the paras marched me out of Clutch Xxamer Zu with the rest of the chosen serfs, I vowed to love and protect my child with a dedication no less fierce than my claimer's.

But there was one adversary from which I could not protect her. Hatred.

My claimer had been right. Djimbi child cursed.

When my piebald babe cried, no mother in my new clan dried her tears. If she fell, no hands but mine picked her up. Her prattles, however earnest and sweet, went ignored. Sometimes I found bruises the size of an adult's fingers on her underarms.

But I tried, oh, I tried! I loved and caressed and soothed the other children, trying to buy a measure of acceptance for my own babe with those kindnesses. Yet how often can a toddler fall down and be stepped over and walked away from before hurt is a fluid as constant in the veins as blood?

And then the roidan kasloo.

No, no!

I vowed I would protect her—I *vowed* it. I must fix that, try harder, must find her, must make her u—

I awoke to hands shaking me, to a bewildering, body-deep thrum. Unfamiliar eyes stared at me, unwavering, bloodshot, the face gaunt and jaundiced.

"Wake up, child."

I looked about in confusion. Where was I? Where was my girl baby, my Waivia?

No. Waivia was my *sister*, not my baby.

Something fell away from me then, left me cold and disoriented, uncertain of self. The momentary feeling of being in the wrong body abruptly ended, though a memory of it lingered like a headache. I remembered where I was.

"Hungry," I croaked at the woman before me, though I'd meant to ask for water, or ask who I was; both seemed the same somehow.

"Eat slowly," Yellow Face said, but another onai handed me a leather bladder of water.

A semicircle of onais were crouched on their haunches around me, watching. I took the bladder with shaking hands and sucked greedily. The cold water fell like rocks into my empty belly and instantly made me nauseous. I turned to the side and retched it all up again. The onais shuffled back a bit, and I thought I heard Yellow Face cluck irritably, but that may have been my imagination, for the relentless grinding of the millstone below overwhelmed small noises.

"Hungry," I whimpered, and to my shame, I realized I was crying. Hands pushed a bowl toward me. Yellow Face swatted it back.

"She'll vomit again."

"She should have something in her belly first," someone argued, and others nodded in agreement. Yellow Face pursed her lips and shrugged. I accepted the bowl and ate slowly, determined to prove Yellow Face wrong. The cold, clotted stuff had a pasty texture and a bitter, smoky flavor, but I ate it nonetheless.

It wasn't until I was almost finished eating that I noticed the absence of a body sleeping at my side.

"Where's Mother?" I said.

An exchange of looks among the onais. Panic bloomed within me, accompanied by a profound fear.

"What have you done with her?" I clambered to my feet, bowl of mash falling to the ground. "Where is she?"

"Hush, child. Her body has been honored."

Those words: *her body.*

No.

No.

She was not a body, she was my mother! I needed her. Where was she? They'd hidden her—

"Mother!" I cried, and I darted between the women whose hands were all outstretched toward me like twigs on denuded trees.

"Mother!" I cried as I clattered down the stairs to the ground floor and bolted outside. Voices followed me like the raucous caws of feasting buzzards; I ran blindly, tears streaming along my cheeks and taking brief flight in my wake before landing upon parched ground.

"Mother!"

I ran through a field of some recently harvested crop, fallen stalks crackling like crushed eggs under my feet, a rat missing chunks of fur scurrying across my path.

"Mother!"

The air exploded with white.

I froze as wind rushed up from the ground, as hundreds of wings furiously flapped skyward. Feathers rained down upon me; loose down caressed my arms. Chest heaving, I watched as an enormous flock of white pigeons lifted from the field around me and burst into the sky.

But they didn't fly away in panic. No. They circled above me, up out of reach. Round and round they wheeled, hundreds of perfectly white birds, silent save for the flap of wings, the rush of wind through feathers.

Head tipped back, I watched them circle.

"Mother," I whispered. "Don't leave me. Come back."

The birds lifted higher into the sky, their breasts tainted pink with the dawn's light. Higher they glided, still circling, still circling.

I stayed there, motionless, watching, until they were mere specks in the sky.

I stayed there until I could see them no more.

But I knew they were up there still, circling above me. Just because I couldn't see them didn't mean they didn't exist. They were there. Wind rustling through their outstretched wings.

I believe I was carried back to the mill. Or maybe I walked. The memory is blurred by tears and grief.

I do remember finding myself back in the attic, surrounded again by onais, now all cooing at me. Someone rubbed small, gentle circles on my back; another eased me to the floor. A third stroked one of my arms over and over, and a fourth cupped my scarred hand, marked so many months ago during Mombe Taro, as if it were an illborn hatchling.

My tears eventually turned into stupor. A palm against my forehead and hands on either of my shoulders eased me onto my back.

Sleep, yes, sleep. Escape into oblivion.

It was not to be.

Hands nudged my thighs apart. I tried to lift my head to see. The hand on my forehead pressed down firmly.

Confusion flooded me, spiraling rapidly into panic, and equally as swiftly the hands about me tightened and my ankles were grasped and my loincloth was tugged off. I bucked and turned and cried out; the grindstone squealed back. The crouched onais pinned me down by kneeling on my elbows and ankles, which hurt, and something cold and wet was slapped over my sex. Thick, it was, like aloe jelly, and it clung obscenely to me, a strange, invading beast smeared over my crotch and leaking cold against my anus.

I screamed till my throat was a dry riverbed.

The beating of my heart grew louder, louder, until it drowned out my cries. Two things silenced me then: the millstone started singing, and the mosquito curtains, not yet drawn up to the rafters for the day, started dancing.

I was transfixed.

The moldy gauze undulated and billowed, spun slowly and spread wide. Wider. A taste of licorice and limes filled my mouth, and though I knew it not at that time, it was the taste of a powerful hallucinogen, a mighty analgesic, a strange and rare drug: diluted dragon venom. And as the taste blossomed in my mouth, carried there through my bloodstream from the venom jelly spread over my nether regions, the mosquito curtains continued to dance, coalesced into a lovely white cloud that descended upon me with the cool kiss of mist, while the millstone sang in dulcet tones.

I was aware of how cold I was but was indifferent to it. I concentrated on the millstone's voice. There were words there, it was trying to communicate with me, if only I kept still enough long enough, the beating of my heart would silence so I could hear it.

A shocking pain in my sex, a blinding white tug. The cloud and the millstone song vanished.

Burning pain radiated from my groin up into my belly and down deep into my thighs, a nauseating, engulfing never-ending pain that threatened to split my head apart, and it didn't end, it increased, and someone was wailing, a breathless ongoing scream.

Tug, tug, something was ripping my sex out, flensing flesh from bone. . . .

Someone shoved a clot of leather into my mouth.

"Bite down on it, bite down!" a voice yelled against my ear, and the breath that carried the voice smelled of wild allium bulbs, and to this day I've never stomached the smell of garlic.

I was being eaten alive.

White-hot pain, sharp teeth stabbing into me, again and again. It was a raw pain, a barbed agony. I couldn't move or fight or scream to save my life. Pain was all I knew, great pulsing pain with me drowning at its center.

The pressure on my arms and legs lifted as the onais pinning me to the floor rose.

I shuddered with cold. Sweat slicked my spine, ran in cold rivulets down from my armpits. My legs trembled fiercely. I was exhausted but far, far from sleep.

An onai draped a coarse hemp blanket over me. And another.

Oh, Mother! The pain, the pain, waves of it throbbing in hot swells from my sex.

I was going to vomit.

A hand turned my head to the side, held something beneath my lips. I retched up nothing but smoky bile, and as my stomach heaved, the pain below was like a tearing. I wailed.

"Still now," a voice crooned, lips pressed against my ear so I could hear her, for still the millstone ground round and round below. Relentless, malicious.

The curtains danced languidly about me, but I didn't want to watch. My heartbeat drummed loud in my ears, and words were hidden in the rhythm, but I didn't want to hear. I closed my eyes and shuddered with the pain, limp and hurting and desperate for release.

"You are clean now," a voice crooned. "You are onai."

FIFTEEN

It took several weeks for me to recover from the circumcision. Yellow Face checked my wound daily, and I grew to resent her prodding fingers as much as I craved the cool jelly she spread there. The jelly eased the pain and gave me hallucinations and itchy eyes.

She was called Yin-gik, a northern-sounding name that meant nothing to me, so I continued to call her Yellow Face. She didn't seem to mind my hatred.

My name as of the initiation cutting was Zar-shi, according to the first blood patterns my circumcision wound made upon my sleeping mat, interpreted by Boj-est, the convent elder. She'd named all the onais in such a way, I later learned. I suppose it was a kindness that she'd interpreted my blood splotches to resemble my true name.

Crooning Voice turned out to be the young onai who'd waved at me during my first night. Her name was Kiz-dan, and although she slept at my back thereafter, she was impatient with my listlessness. It was she who forced me too soon to hobble to the stairs and descend. My wound reopened and Yellow Face held new beetles against me until they pinched my ragged flesh between their claws, whereupon she decapitated them, leaving their embedded pincers as sutures.

I wondered if Mother had known what would happen to me. I wanted—needed—to know if my anger at her was justified. I felt betrayed not so much by the fact that she'd subjected me to the mutilation, but that she'd conveniently escaped the same through death.

It took me a long time to get over that resentment.

Life in Tieron Nask Cinai, I soon discovered, was one of constant labor and near starvation. If I had thought life in the pottery clan hard, I had been sorely mistaken. What I had deemed essentials in the danku were luxuries at the convent; two meals daily, needles to repair torn cloth, tables and porcelain clay, idle conversation, and tiles or thatch to repair damaged roofs . . . such things did not exist at Tieron.

The holy life was one of subsistence living. Everything done, every waking moment, was to support our lives. No ceremonies or celebrations, no best clothes, no salt or sweetmeats or baking of any sort existed in the convent. No pleasures were ever pursued. I quickly learned that I hadn't experienced poverty and hard labor at all while in Clutch Re. No, not in the least.

In Tieron, I came to understand such intimately.

The onais didn't operate the mill wheel every day; there was so much more to do than make mash for the three aged bull dragons in our care. Encroaching jungle fauna had to be uprooted from the ragged herb-and-vegetable garden that supplied us with our medicines and kadoob, the fat, wrinkled tubers that tasted like bitter smoke and that we ate, nightly, boiled and mashed. Manure from the bull rotunda had to be wheeled out in barrows daily and spread over the garden or dried in the sun for fire fuel, and the aged barrows themselves needed constant repair.

In a pathetic attempt at self-sufficiency, the convent also had a hemp field, and that weed-choked monster consumed far too much of our time and gave precious little in return. It could not be abandoned, though. Precious little was all we had of anything.

Koorfowsi rim maht—jungle weeds suitable for dragon regurgitation—had to be slashed, bundled, and carried back to the mill for the dragons. The mill's roof tiles had to be repaired and chinks in the walls plugged. The locks and channels leading from the waterfall's pool to the mill wheel had to be unblocked and checked daily for wear and tear.

We skinned the hairy peel-bark trees and soaked, beat, and stretched the bark into strips, which we wrapped about our calves as protection against all things fanged and venomous. We laid tension snares along the edges of the garden, caught the occasional fat rodent or scrawny monkey, ate its flesh, boiled some of its bones for soup and carved others into fishhooks, and cut the creature's sorry little hide into leather thongs to make more traps.

We had renimgar hutches alongside the eastern edge of the mill. But we'd often wake at dawn to find a fat python lying right in the hutch among a scatter of renimgar dead from fright, digesting its easily caught meal with heavy-lidded indolence.

We always ate the snake.

Occasionally, Boj-est, our hunchbacked elder, sent a contingent of onais to a tributary of the Grieving River. It was a six-day trek there and back, and when the group returned, they always carried more leeches on their skin and fatigue in their bodies than fish in their baskets.

What with the poor diet and the close proximity of waterfall and jungle, the mosquito sickness and the coughing sickness plagued us constantly. At any given moment, one onai lay in the mill attic fighting death. She did not always win the battle. As we had no gharials to consume our dead during funeral rites, we instead carried the corpses into the jungle for wild beasts to eat. Scattered bones littered the outskirts of Convent Tieron.

We did all that hoeing and slashing and carrying and repairing, hunting and gathering and basket weaving and cloth spinning, sickening and nursing and convalescing and dying, around a rigid schedule of honoring our three bull dragons. I came to know the inside of that mossy stone rotunda very well indeed, what with all the obeisance we did upon its cold slate floor.

When we weren't prostrating ourselves in the bulls' presence, we were straddled across their bony spines, our legs gripped round their ribby bellies, clamped tight over their ragged leathery wings, as we rooted under their scales for kwano snakes. That such small vipers could cause the death of such large beasts never ceased to amaze me.

I suppose I should explain the presence of the bulls at Convent Tieron.

What to do with a senile, impotent bull dragon, hey-o? As magnificent as the beast once was, in old age it becomes a burden, no longer able to enter Arena and provide for its Clutch. Due to Temple edict, a Clutch is permitted only one bull at a time, to prevent any one estate hoarding the rare beasts. No bull ever hatched from an egg laid in captivity; all bulls, therefore, had to be jungle caught. So a captive bull that has reached kuneus, the age of impotence and senility, must be removed from its Clutch before a replacement can be brought in from the jungle.

The old bulls, the cinai kuneus, from Clutches within the Jungle Crown catchment were brought to Convent Tieron.

I remember clearly the first time I laid eyes upon them. Until that day, I—like the majority of serfs throughout our nation of Malacar—had never laid eyes upon a male dragon. I was used to seeing yearlings, brooders, and satons, but of course, those were all female dragons.

Bulls are far more impressive.

Whereas a female stands five feet tall at shoulder, a bull stands seven feet high. Whereas a female's colors blend and do not dazzle, the brilliant emerald and raisin-purple scales of a bull's hide look like polished jewels, the impression heightened by the elegant, olfactory antennae plumes a bull sports. A female bears no such plumes.

Whereas a female's wings are always amputated at birth, save for the wings of dragons in a warrior-lord's stables, a bull's wings are left intact, and no twenty-foot wingspan do they possess, but a wingspan of up to forty feet. Although I never saw such a wing display in all my time in Tieron, I heard tell of it frequently from other onais. The wings of the bulls in *our* care were withered and tattered from age, and did not impress at all.

But of course, their tongues did.

Long, forked, and pale as the moon, those tongues were splotched with black venom, leached from the venom sacks at the back of the bulls' throats. Again, all female dragons save for those in a warrior-lord's stables undergo venom-sack removal at birth. But not so a revered bull.

At first those tongues terrified me, until I learned how tame, how tired, how very old the bulls in our care were. Until I looked in their eyes and learned to see the disturbing sagacity that seemed to exist in their sad, lizard-slitted gaze.

They were a lot of work, those fangless, bumbling beasts. Besides the endless chore of feeding them, grooming them, mucking out the rotunda, and fetching water for them, besides prostrating ourselves before them eight times each dawn-to-dawn cycle and standing guard over them every night, we also had to keep detailed accounts of how much they ate, defecated, and drank. Every month we were required to send a copy of those accounts to the Ranreeb of the Jungle Crown.

That, of course, precipitated a need for paper. Another labor-intensive task.

We always enclosed within those reports to the Ranreeb a list of items we most desperately needed, and that was how I learned to ask unabashedly and repeatedly for charity. There is a shame to begging, yes, I won't deny that. But with practice, one can quell the shame and get on with the business at hand: survival.

How carefully we crafted those scrolls, how long we deliberated over which necessity was most crucial and which could go without mention for another month!

If we had asked without restraint for everything we so desperately needed, the Ranreeb would have refused us everything—we were, after all, holy women who'd forsaken the comforts of the material world to honor the cinai kuneus on behalf of all Malacarites.

Because I was the youngest in the convent by a good fourteen years (Kiz-dan guessed she was about twenty-four, but wasn't sure), Boj-est insisted I learn to read and write. Only two of the twenty-eight onais living at Convent Tieron upon my arrival were literate: Boj-est herself, and Nae-ser, a mustached, gray-haired woman who constantly farted.

Nae-ser had tried to teach Kiz-dan the scribe's art, and Kiz-dan bore the knuckle scars of Nae-ser's bamboo stick to show for it. But something was wrong with Kiz-dan's eyes. She would recognize one simple hieratic, and then further along on the scroll could make head nor tail of the same cursive glyph.

Nae-ser was convinced Kiz-dan's obtuseness was by design, and I confess, so did I; she was a crafty one, Kiz-dan. But I've since learned there are those who suffer the same unreliable affliction, and no amount of beating will correct it.

So in addition to the myriad other chores that ate away my child-hood, I learned to read and write. Both in the Emperor's Archipelagic tongue and native Malacarite. Occasionally, a smattering of Xxelteker and Djimbi, too.

I was awed by the written form of communication. That mere paper and ink could talk to a person who lived leagues away seemed the stuff of Djimbi magic. Nae-ser tried to correct that delusion of mine, that the missives were a form of sorcery encapsulating a fragment of the person who wrote it, but she failed.

As ink and paper were priceless, I learned the scribe's art by scratching on the ground, often at night while everyone slept, save for the required eight onais on night watch in the rotunda.

In the heat of the Fire Season when everyone else repaired cooking pots or spun hemp or fixed barrow axles within the cool rotunda at high noon, Nae-ser and I crouched within the meager shade of the mill and etched hieratic patterns over and over onto the ground. Nae-ser knew not only hieratic, the cursive form of hieroglyphs simplified to be written quickly, but also the scholarly, ancient hieroglyphic art itself. She insisted on teaching me both.

By the time I was thirteen—I refused to lose track of my age as Kizdan had—Nae-ser entrusted me with paper and her inviolable ink-stone for the first time.

I ground the ink carefully, meticulously added the correct amount of water, and wrote my first missive to the Ranreeb of the Jungle Crown, all while crouched on my haunches at garden's edge, a flat rock acting as table. We had no tables in Tieron, not a one.

Other than an eloquent greeting followed by a list of which kuneus had suffered constipation or intestinal worms or what have you that month, my missive was one that politely begged for two new machetes, one hoe, twelve sacks of featon grit, a vat of lye, and a sheaf of writing paper.

I was sick of the smell of wet wood pulp, and Nae-ser, whose eyes were failing, didn't notice me add that last request. Of those items, we received the twelve sacks of grit, a pitchfork instead of a hoe, and a sheaf of fine white paper. I was extremely pleased with myself for weeks after that.

We never knew when the Ranreeb might respond to our requests. Sometimes a whole season dragged by and the rusted bell above the cairn down by the merchant's route remained silent.

And then . . . *clang, clang! Clang, clang!*

It was the onais working in the jungle or the field or along the traplines who heard the noise first. Yellow Face always went with whomever else Boj-est chose to retrieve our goods, for Yellow Face was a relentless worker. It was also she who carried our scrolls down to the merchant's route, enclosed within a cork-bunged section of bamboo, and placed them on the cairn for the next passing merchant to deliver to the Ranreeb.

Rarely did we receive what we'd so painstakingly asked for. In fact, occasionally we received goods for which we had absolutely no use—abalone hairpins from the coast; wine decanters; an immense fur cloak from some exotic animal, fit for the most highly regarded bayen lady; a gilded plaster picture frame. These we hoarded in the mill attic, and whenever a group of Djimbi drifted as silent as mist onto our grounds, we did brisk trade with them.

That became the fate of the bracelet Mother had given the convent in return for accepting me; the tainted bangle purchased no fewer than seven fresh necijunes, the fatty river rodents the Djimbi caught so easily.

Seven fat rodents, each the size of a two-year-old child, for a bracelet that had caused the death of a father, a child, an aristocrat, and ultimately, a mother. I remembered the rich pile of chits her similar bracelets had sold for in Clutch Re. Somehow, the fate of that last bangle—around the biceps of a potbellied, green-haired Mottled Skin—seemed fitting.

One year rolled into the next, unmarked except for the exhausting parade of seasons.

When my rage over the death of my mother subsided somewhat, and the reason behind my screaming night terrors and the irrational fear of being left alone gradually became known, I began to make friends within the convent. But by the very nature of my age, I still often felt lonely. The bulk of the onais were elderly.

I also made foes within the convent, largely among the Grim Cluster, the onais who frowned upon my absolute inability to be as devout as they. Boj-est always put me on night duty with them, and it was torture for us all. I fidgeted during obeisance. I chatted to and swatted and cursed at our three kuneus instead of acting the humble servitor. I got into mischief.

Capturing a wounded parrot and placing it in one of the chamber pots in the dead of night was one prank I played. My knuckles still bear the scars from *that* beating, but it was well worth it, the look on cross-eyed Voe-too's face as she leapt about, tunic up around her wrinkled belly, the urine-wet parrot screaming at her bare buttocks.

There were also sorrows. Tas-urk, a sweet, quiet onai whom I'd loved dearly, died of the coughing sickness. Beb-oly, she of the sly humor, caught her arm in the millstone and died shortly after amputation. Ancient Ter-mii wandered into the jungle one night and was never seen again, despite a lengthy search. Per-tes, our medicinal witch, was crushed beneath kuneus Ka during one of the old bull's rampages.

And a new convert showed up at the cairn.

There had been four other converts prior to that one: two worn, middle-aged sisters bearing dowries of likely stolen but untraceable silver coins; and two years later, a desperate mother and her eighteen-year-old daughter, a huge creature with a vacant mind and shuffling gait. They came bearing dowries of two bolts of leather strapped to their backs, and the mother feverishly promised her daughter would do the work of three if permitted in Tieron.

All of them assimilated quietly and readily to convent life, and it was true: the adolescent worked hard. Unfortunately, she died from snakebite a year later.

I was on the cusp of turning fifteen when our latest convert appeared at the cairn, and at first, her arrival seemed like a blessing, a miracle. With her came a dowry of five coffers, each filled with sandals, slabs of soap, cooking pots, hides, sleeping mats, and urns of oil.

I was overjoyed to see her, not just for her largesse, but because she was only two years older than myself and, unlike the dead simpleton, in possession of all her wits. She'd come to us by choice, odd girl, the inward child of Clutch Cuhan aristocrats. She wanted nothing but to serve the kuneus.

But her circumcision did not heal.

Gangrene set in. By the time my scroll reached her Clutch and family, she was dead.

An inquiry followed in the form of a visit from Daron Cuhan, the

Temple Superior of Clutch Cuhan. He and his retinue arrived upon the backs of five yearlings, flying twice over the rotunda for no reason that I could discern save to impress, before landing in our hemp fields. Our bulls snorted and heaved about in agitation at the scent of the female yearlings, and one of them gashed open his flank in trying to get out.

That Daron was highly critical of everything we did, as were his First Holy Wardens.

It mattered little to them that during the days they stayed with us—they in the attic, we exposed within the roofless rotunda, and this during the Wet Season—they consumed more than all of us combined. Nor did they care how difficult it was for us to keep their hobbled, wing-pinioned beasts from our garden, or how much their yearlings ate of our bulls' fodder. They scorned our poverty even while berating us for harassing the Ranreeb for goods. *How had they known of those requests?* I oft hissed to my holy sisters. But they bade me keep quiet.

Two of the Holy Wardens raped Kiz-dan.

They cornered her one dusk near the waterfall pool, but she said nothing of it until Daron Cuhan and his retinue had departed, for fear of retaliation. She merely explained her gross bruises and swollen eye as the result of a tussle with one of our old bulls, Ka, during a tantrum he had that night. Too relieved by Daron Cuhan's verdict that the aristocrat's death had indeed been caused by gangrene, despite our precautions, we all accepted Kiz-dan's explanation for her wounds without question.

But Kiz-dan changed after that. Became openly derisive during obeisance, raged at our poverty, was obnoxious to the Grim Cluster. She fought with Yellow Face constantly.

About me.

Throughout my years at Tieron, I often wondered if our care of the old bulls was merely a form of cruelty, if by keeping them alive we merely prolonged their suffering rather than provided them with pleasant sanctuary. See, the kuneus at Convent Tieron would have been dead decades ago if not for the enclosing walls of the rotunda and our ministrations. I never questioned the point of keeping the kuneus alive; I understood too well that my sole purpose at the convent was to provide for the bulls, and that without them, I and all the other holy women would have been without roof, Temple charity, and the security of place.

But I did often question if any compassion lay behind our actions.

I was thinking just such a thing, straddled across the ribby back of kuneus Maht, the retired bull from Clutch Maht, when the old dragon sneezed.

I was facing his rump, his tattered, feeble wings folded under my calves. The Inbetween was ending and the sunlight penetrating the weak fog in the rotunda took the aching chill out my bones. Old Maht was enjoying the sun, too. He lifted his snout and waved his scarred head to and fro, scenting the warmed air.

He sneezed again. A bloody glob of mucus splattered against the slate floor.

"You poor thing," I muttered, digging in my heels and giving a rub, the way he liked. "You should be dead, hey-o. You're dying from the inside out. Just rotting slowly."

Drip, drip, drip. Blood splattered onto slate. Old Maht shuddered, dropped his neck, and stared stupidly at the floor. That was how he spent his days and nights, staring dumbly groundward. Pressure blisters had developed on his splayed claws, and the blisters stank with rot. We'd stopped whacking off his talons in our guillotine two months ago; unnecessary, as he was utterly incapable of striking us at that point.

"I don't know why I bother," I growled under my breath, empathy making me gruff. "I should just let these snakes finish you off."

But I continued, anyway, sweeping my snake pole under each partially detached, shimmering dark purple-and-green scale, catching the occasional kwano sucker on my hook, then yank! pulling the wire noose until the serpent's writhing body landed with a splat on the slate floor, its head still lodged in dragon flesh.

Seven decapitated snakes lay around Old Maht's claws, several twisting furiously in their death throes.

I was good at dragon grooming.

Understand, kwano snakes lay their young in between and beneath the scales of a dragon. The young latch their suckers into the vulnerable skin beneath the scales and drink the dragon's blood until the snakes reach maturity, whereupon their mushroom-cap lips and suction-cup fangs alter into the mouths characteristic of a snake, and they detach. Off into the jungle they go, the females returning only when gravid.

As brooder dragons in the jungle retain their wings, unlike Clutch brooders, which have been amputated after hatching, they only suffer kwano infestations during nesting time, when they are stationary, incubating eggs. And as they tend to return each season to the same crown, or treetop nest, the kwano snake returns there faithfully, too. The reproductive cycles of host and parasite are synchronized.

In the wild, yearlings and bull dragons tend not to suffer as heavy infestations as brooders, as they don't lay eggs and therefore are rarely in one spot for long. The few kwano that plague them do little harm. Patches of cloudy scales, pale mucous membranes, shabby olfactory antennae, and sunken eyes indicate a heavy kwano infestation in a bull. The same in a yearling or brooder, though those females have nares only, no antennae. The bulls sport huge antennae to aid in locating a female in season.

It is assumed that in their natural habitat, the sedentary kuneus die from kwano infestation, if younger bulls don't kill them first. How much truth is in this speculation remains uncertain; kuneus are rarely seen in the jungle. The jungle is a harsh place, after all.

"Look at you," a voice purred, "straddled atop that stinking beast as if you enjoyed it."

I grimly kept working, didn't glance at the figure standing behind me at Old Maht's head, though my heart beat faster: Kiz-dan. Heavily pregnant.

"You shouldn't be here," I growled at her. "You'll be caned."

"Befouling the sanctity of this place, am I? With the ill-begotten bastards growing in my belly?"

"That's not what I meant. You're engaging in idle chatter. You're supposed to be working in the fields. *That's* what'll get you caned—"

Old Maht shifted suddenly, lurching back a pace. I grabbed hold his protruding spine for balance. My snake pole clattered to the ground.

"Easy, hey, easy!"

He settled after a moment, shuddering. Kiz-dan came alongside us, her mouth twisted in the bitter smile she wore of late. With some difficulty, she bent and retrieved my pole for me. Despite being only five months with child, she was huge. Boj-est suspected twins.

I reached for the snake pole. She danced it beyond my fingertips.

"Give it, Kiz-dan. Give it over and get back to work."

"Or? You'll hail Ogi-ras to get Yellow Face?" Her eyes sparkled and she made a rude gesture in the general direction of Ogi-ras, who was straddled upon kuneus Ka in another section of the rotunda, rooting under his scales. Ogi-ras was hidden from view by the mossy columns that stood like stone trees in the rotunda—the purpose of which was both to create a disorienting maze for the shambling kuneus, to discourage them from getting at each other, and to prevent them from getting sufficient running space to take flight.

"Will you, hmm?" Kiz-dan taunted. "Tattle-tattle?" But she gave me back the pole.

I said nothing, and fell to grooming Old Maht furiously. She watched in silence.

"Shouldn't you be digging up kadoob or something?" I snapped at last.

She shrugged, and it was then that I noticed the fear shadowing her eyes.

I sat up straight. "What is it? The babies have dropped?"

She shook her head, looked away.

"What then?"

"It'll kill me, you know. This birth."

"Nonsense—"

"The miscarry attempts almost did."

A vivid image of my mother in the danku latrine flashed before my eyes.

"I've got work to do," I grumbled, though I'd meant to offer comfort, show kindness. "What *do* you want?"

Her nostrils flared and she lifted her chin. Despite the sharp relief of her cheekbones and the hugeness of her eyes—the mask of the starving—there was a beauty to her. Something strange, something about the eyes. I'd caught glimpses of it in Yellow Face and a few other onais. . . .

"I want to watch you initiated. Before I die," she said.

"You are not going to die. . . . *What?* I've already been initiated, yolk brain."

"Not that initiation. There's another." And she leaned forward, one hand pressed against Old Maht's salt-smelling hide, her expression intense, her body taut. The hairs on my nape rose, and I knew without a doubt that I was about to learn the reason behind her furious arguments with Yellow Face, arguments that always ended when I appeared.

"There's another initiation," she said, voice low, speaking quickly. "One that's held at night, after Sixth Obeisance. It's the reason you're always given night duty with the Grim Cluster, because they don't partake in such things. Very few of us do. The Grims know what goes on, though, I'm sure of it. Or at least they suspect. It's wrong, of course, what we do. Terribly, terribly wrong."

Kiz-dan gave a high, thin giggle, and those captivating eyes of hers rolled. She clutched one of my calves where it rested upon Old Maht's flank. Even through my birch-cloth leggings, I felt a hot intensity from her fingers.

"Are you ill?" I asked, but she flicked the question away with her free hand.

"Stand night watch with us tonight—you'll see what I'm talking about. Come. You won't have another chance for a month or so. It's rare we take watch together. We can't, it would arouse suspicion. By the time we can do so again, I'll be dead. So come. But you must not tell anyone you'll be watching, not even those on night watch. Not till I say."

She hissed spittle with her intensity, and it was then that I realized what was so different about her eyes, what held me spellbound upon Old Maht, leaning forward despite myself to catch her every word.

They rarely moved.

Really. Those eyes of hers focused on a thing and stayed riveted on it, never wavering. Almost . . . dragonlike. And I simultaneously realized that Yellow Face's eyes did that, too. They locked on an object with the same hair-raising stillness.

Kiz-dan squeezed my calf hard. "Do this for me, hey-o? Come tonight."

"Why should I? I did night watch last night. I haven't slept all day—"

"Zar-shi?" a warbling voice called, echoing through the rotunda. "Quick now! The venerable Ka has taken my snake pole! It's lodged in his gullet! Zar-shi!"

"Coming!" I called. Kiz-dan released me, stepped back. I vaulted off Old Maht and sprinted in the direction of Ogi-ras's voice.

It took a heart-stopping long time to free the pole from the gorge of kuneus Ka, who slavered and bucked and reared and clawed at himself the whole while he choked. He lashed his whip-thin tail about, trying to strike not only me but the six other onais it took to subdue him with blow darts.

At the end of it all, my right arm was swollen from his muscular throat contractions, as I'd repeatedly jammed the length of it down his gullet to try free the snake pole. Bruised, tail whipped, covered in slaver, and my shoulder feeling as if it were dislocated, I staggered to the mill, climbed to the attic, and slept the rest of the day.

Thankfully, no one woke me for Fourth Obeisance, the bull honoring that took place each late noon.

Hunger and the silence of the mill wheel dragged me from slumber around sunset. I came awake as I always did: heart hammering, fear and urgency raw in my veins, a half-formed cry caught in my throat.

My baby, my baby! I have to find her, protect her, they've taken her away from me. . . .

"Waivia!" I gasped.

With the uttering of the name, I shuddered, as always, and something fell away from me, leaving me cold and hollow and disoriented.

You'd think after waking in such a manner night after night, that the disorientation would dissipate, that I'd understand I'd been victim to a night terror. But there was the thing of it, see. It was no night terror. It was real.

Each time I awoke from slumber, I was not whom I was meant to be.

I was in the wrong body. Or rather, someone else occupied my frame, entrapping me in limbo, suspending me in nothingness, and each waking, I had to fight my way back into my body and expel the presence occupying my flesh by giving voice to the haunt's desire: Waivia.

You know whom the haunt was.

Fury and resentment rushed through me, thick as the effluvia in a slaughtered renimgar's intestines. How dare she do that to me! It was my body. She was dead; she should leave me be!

Then sorrow followed, keen as a newly stropped machete. It cut quick and deep, so that at first I didn't feel it. Then it welled up into the cut and throbbed agony throughout me.

The sorrow wasn't wholly mine. Like a bitter aftertaste, Mother's presence lingered within me, departing reluctantly, her love for me and the remorse she felt at causing me such grief rimming my heart and mind.

She would leave me in peace, she promised. She would not return again. No.

But she always did.

Every time sleep claimed me—be it night or day, deep sleep or light doze—she returned. It was as if her obsession were a live thing, commanding, demanding. It was a creature separate from her decomposed body, and she was a hapless puppet-ghost attached to it.

I waited until the cold shudders left me, then rose to my feet. On unsteady legs, I descended from the attic to the ground floor.

The rest of the onais sat about the millstone, eating kadoob and muay leaf mash for their evening meal. I nodded to them, waved away their concern for my shoulder, and went outside.

Ras-aun always cooked the kadoob, boiling the fat tubers in a huge, battered cauldron under the front eaves outside the mill entrance. It wasn't until she scooped a lump of the coagulated mess into my bowl and our eyes met that I recalled the peculiar conversation I'd had with Kiz-dan.

It was Ras-aun's eyes that reminded me: They fixed on mine as if they had hooks, fixed on and didn't waver. Ras-aun was old—almost

sixty—and plagued with palsy. But those uncanny eyes of hers remained still. Like a dragon's.

I ducked my head and scurried into the mill.

While I ate, I chewed over Kiz-dan's request. While I stripped
naked and splashed water over myself with the rest of the onais outside the mill—we didn't bathe in the waterfall pool, couldn't foul it for
the kuneus with our female secretions despite the fact we'd been circumcised and were therefore clean—and while I knelt with stiff legs
and pulpy knees upon the unforgiving cold of the rotunda floor for
Fifth Obeisance under a bloodred sky, I again thought about Kiz-dan's
request.

By the time we all laid out our sleeping mats and settled about our
quiet evening chores, save for the eight onais slated for night watch
in the rotunda, I hadn't yet decided what I intended on doing.

So it came as some surprise, upon setting aside my sewing for Sixth
Obeisance, to realize I had decided to join Kiz-dan.

Yes. I *would* stay with her and the other seven on watch that night.

Of course I would. Wouldn't you have done the same, as a clois-
tered fifteen-year-old desperate for diversion of any sort?

SIXTEEN

Understand, night is the time of the kwano, the moment of the snake. Night is when the One Snake, the First Father, the progenitor and spirit of all kwano everywhere, sends his offspring in search of cold-blooded creatures, so that young kwano may be born beneath scale and leather and thrive upon fresh reptile blood until they reach maturity.

In Tieron, the proximity of the jungle supplied a constant stream of kwano snakes. The small, slim serpents give birth to their young not only beneath dragon scale, but also between the flaps of skin where a lizard's legs join its body, and there are *many* lizards in the jungle. Kwano attach their young even upon pythons, when those great snakes lie in motionless loops over branches while digesting meals. There is no end of the ugly, thin kwano, and it seemed during my time in Tieron as if all of them were destined for the convent's rotunda.

Each night, for the duration of the night, a group of eight chosen onais would therefore walk around the inner perimeter of the rotunda, chanting Temple curses to ward off kwano snakes. At regular intervals during the night, the rest of the onais would rouse from sleep in the mill, stumble into the rotunda, and perform obeisance, and those on night watch would momentarily stop their circumambulations to perform such with them. At dawn, night watch duty ended, though of course obeisance continued at maddeningly regular intervals throughout the day.

Instead of shuffling back to the mill for sleep after dutifully performing the evening obeisance with all my holy sisters, Kiz-dan had asked me to surreptitiously stay behind, to watch those on night watch. That meant I'd have to furtively join my fellow sisters each time they shuffled into the rotunda from the mill for obeisance, for my presence might be missed if I did not.

See, I wasn't at all concerned that anyone would notice that my sleeping mat was empty in the mill when I should have been stretched on it; upon rousing for and returning from obeisance during the dark hours of night, fatigue dulled the senses of every onai in Tieron, and the exhausted self-involvement of each onai as she collapsed onto her sleeping mat ensured that my presence would not be missed. I dared not assume such during obeisance, however: Those from the Grim Cluster were wont to scrutinize me during bullhonoring, regardless of hour, and to later criticize my impiety and impatience with the procedure.

All this was running through my mind as I descended the mill stairs with my holy sisters after dusk and filed outside for Sixth Obeisance, to worship the divine bulls in our care.

Swish-swish went our bark-clothed calves in the silence of night.

Darkness always increased the smells of the rotunda: wet stone, earthy moss, damp leaves rotting in corners upon slick slate; the salty leather of dragon; the warm, pervasive reek of dung; the astringent vinegar of pulped jungle weeds that was not so much a smell as a bitterness coating the teeth.

I was skittishly awake, with Kiz-dan's feverish words ringing in my head: *It's wrong, what we do. Terribly, terribly wrong.* Anticipation goose-pimpled my skin.

Whatever I was about to witness, after all the onais now joining the watch for obeisance returned to the mill to sleep, would be something that would meet with our convent elder's harsh disapproval. *If* she ever found out. I had full confidence in Kiz-dan that such would not transpire; she was a crafty one, Kiz-dan.

Single file, the onais of Tieron squeezed through the narrow entry into the rotunda, the stars above us draped in a gauzy train of cloud. The sky looked overfull to me, as if those glimmers of light far above gathered for spectacle.

I looked through the starlit rotunda for those on watch; they were just now completing their circumambulation, muttering curses to ward off kwano snakes even as they joined the rest of us onais filing in. I saw Kiz-dan, her huge belly distinguishing her instantly from the others. Her eyes briefly met mine. They were fever bright still. She grinned at me.

My answering grin died as I caught sight of the old woman who walked beside her, also on watch. Our stooped elder, Boj-est.

Disappointment welled in me. Whatever mischief Kiz-dan had planned for the evening was surely canceled. Confirming that assumption was the presence of both Yellow Face and my aged tutor, Nae-ser, also on watch. Definitely no roguery of the terribly, terribly wrong kind would be taking place that night with those two on watch.

Crushed, I knelt as meekly as my fellow onais on the slate before Old Maht's stall and pressed my forehead against the floor's cold surface. Somewhere in the rotunda, a dove cooed.

We kowtowed eight times to each kuneus slumbering within its open-faced stone stall: Old Maht dripping blood from one nostril; drugged Ka lying stiff-legged upon his side, wings splayed; and Lutche, the youngest of the three but by no means a yearling, watching us blearily through half-closed lids. Each dragon occupied a stone stall equidistant from the other, and we shuffled from one to the other in silence.

Obeisance over, we all rose and began filing out the rotunda's narrow archway to return to the mill.

It was to be just another night, just another interminable night of sleep broken by scheduled wakings to honor our bulls, wakings haunted by the departure of my mother's invasive, unwanted ghost. I could have screamed from the monotony of it all, from the hopeless, endless tedium that I had been led to believe would be shattered, just for one night, by Kiz-dan's something terribly, terribly wrong.

It was then that I caught Kiz-dan's eye for a second time; it was overbright still, her cheeks flushed despite the damp chill. She looked sharply at two columns not far from us; they stood so close together, they formed a small niche. She meant me to hide in there.

I stopped still. Surely she didn't mean to continue with her mischief, with Boj-est and Yellow Face and Nae-ser on watch? She glared, gestured abruptly. I slipped between the two columns, held still, and waited in silence as the last onai not on watch left the rotunda and returned to the mill to sleep.

My heartbeat sped up and my mouth went dry with excitement. I was stiff from the day's fight with Ka, yes, and I stood hunched to protect strained shoulder muscles. But, oh! I could feel myself coming alive, I could feel youth and expectation flooding through me in a rare and welcome rush.

When the last onai not on watch had departed, the eight onais remaining did not resume their circumambulation within the rotunda. Instead, they consulted in whispers that whisked like the rustle of silk around the stone pillars.

My eyes strained in the gloom as I tried to discern who they all were: Nae-ser, my old tutor; Kiz-dan and Yellow Face and our convent elder, Boj-est; Ras-aun, our palsied cook; Urd-ren, a close-lipped onai; Atl-eri, whom I'd long suspected of hiding a canny intellect behind a facade of good-natured incompetence; and Nnp-trn, a large, mannish onai who doted on Kiz-dan.

As a group, these eight went toward the dragon Lutche, walking fast, taut with expectation. Yellow Face and Nae-ser separated from the group and disappeared into darkness. The others gathered around Lutche in his stone stall. They began stroking him, crooning to him, and rubbing his wing joints in the way all dragons like. He lifted his head, feathery antennae rigid and swiveling, nostrils flaring as he scented the air. He shuffled from one foreclaw to the other. The forked tip of his tongue flicked in and out.

The onais moved away from his neck. Five knelt before him in a half-circle. Big, square-shouldered Nnp-trn stood at his head and latched a muzzle hook loosely into one of his nares. From out of the darkness, Yellow Face returned.

She carried something with her, an immense cloak draped over her arms that shone glossy as a burnished chestnut in the starlight. I recognized it after a moment: It had been one of those incongruous items the Ranreeb often sent us, which we traded to visiting Djimbi for useful goods. Only this cloak hadn't been traded.

Yellow Face tossed its luxuriant folds into the air as though she were casting a fishnet into the sea. As that thick, exotic cloak from the pelt of some northern beast spread out and settled over the slate floor in front of the kneeling onais, I wondered what else had not been traded for necessary goods, but had instead been hoarded for rites such as this.

Moments later, I found out.

Nae-ser came out of the darkness, bearing a fine silver goblet, untarnished by age or use. This she held gently to the lips of each onai, and when those kneeling had partaken of its contents, Nae-ser offered the goblet to Nnp-trn, who had remained standing at Lutche's head, a muzzle pole hooked in one of his nares.

When all had sipped their fill, my old tutor likewise drank from the goblet, then she set it upon one corner of the cloak spread over the slate and joined the kneeling onais.

They began to hum.

Hum and sway, a hypnotic, enticing tune that rose and rose in mellow stages, until the sound became a drone inseparable from the singing of blood in my veins and the whisper of air inhaled and exhaled from my lips. I found myself leaning forward, the music fraught with a tension so sweet, so vaguely familiar, I yearned for it to never end.

From the kneeled women, Boj-est rose to her feet. She did it not as an arthritic crone, but with the fluid grace of a bayen lady. Whatever had been in the goblet had imparted a measure of youth and strength to her limbs.

She stepped onto the cloak and into its center, her feet sinking into glossy fur. As the kneeling onais continued their intoxicating hum, Boj-est stripped.

Her old hemp tunic fell away from her body and slithered to the fur as if made of silk. She wore no bark-cloth leggings, must have shucked them prior to all this, and she stood there magnificently naked.

I say *magnificently*, for that was what she looked. No hunchbacked, cavern-chested, scrawny-limbed crone did I see, but instead an empyreal creature, her naked breasts full and taut, her belly softly rounded, her hips lush, and her buttocks high and ripe. What magics were these, to transform her so?

Or was it my eyes that were transformed, and not the woman who stood on her throne of fur before me?

The humming, yes, that vaguely familiar chanting . . .

Djimbi.

Djimbi magic.

I should have felt fear, but I could not. The music held me in its thrall, was a fire in my heart, a spice on my lips, a yearning on my tongue. I felt swollen and languid and full of growing want. I no longer smelled manure and old moss, but nutmeg and cloves, incense and oranges, rosewater, patchouli, wine, and crisp, new linen.

Boj-est sank gracefully upon the fur cloak. I could almost feel the luxuriant warmth of it caressing my own skin. Old Lutche pulled against the muzzle pole, straining toward the prone woman before him. Nnp-trn leaned against his strength and his head turned slightly from the hook in his nose, but still he pulled forward, his great lizard-slitted eyes upon Boj-est.

His tongue flicked out. Long as my arm, pale as the moon, forked at the end. Spotted with glistening black venom.

Boj-est raised her knees into a child-birthing position. The onais who knelt about her leaned forward, still droning their intoxicating Djimbi chant. They reached out and ran hands lightly over her glorious body. Palms caressed her stomach, fingers trailed over her hip bones, down her thighs, disappeared into her dark cleft.

My nipples hardened; heat pulsed in my groin.

Lutche fought the muzzle pole hooked in his nare. His desiccated wings fluttered, fanning Nnp-trn, who held him still.

Boj-est panted and moaned.

"Now, oh, now," she gasped.

Abruptly, the women pulled back. Nnp-trn unhooked Lutche. The dragon lunged forward, great arrowed snout diving between Boj-est's legs.

I closed my eyes against the terrible sight but could not escape the inebriating Djimbi chants or Boj-est's esctatic gasps, and desire bloomed within me, climbed higher and higher and so deliciously higher—

Boj-est cried out.

Her cry rang around the rotunda, sent a flurry of bats chattering into the night. My eyes snapped open and I found myself panting, sweat slicked, my trembling hands between my thighs.

Nnp-trn hooked her muzzle pole into Lutche's closest nare and pulled back. He snorted and lashed out in protest with his thin tail, but it whacked harmlessly against the stone walls either side him.

Yellow Face crouched at Boj-est's head, kissed her long and full on the lips. Reverently, almost drunkenly, the kneeling onais helped dress the old woman, who appeared boneless and gripped in euphoria. They then placed our elder in a kneeling position in the half-circle. I thought Boj-est would topple; she did not, though she swayed from side to side on her knees, moaning in rapture.

My old tutor, Nae-ser, stood next. Stripped. Lay down upon that fine, thick cloak.

Again the stroking hands. Again the dragon's lunge. Again the woman's cry.

My own heart became the fine, small feet of a thousand scurrying insects, trapped within the cage of my ribs. It became a shattered thing, a singing thing, a thing of instinct and want. It would never be whole again. I could have howled.

Someone did so for me.

Not someone, but something: kuneus Ka. The euphoric cries of the women had woken the temperamental bull from his blow dart stupor, and instinctively I knew Ka wanted to do as Lutche was doing, had performed such prior to this night.

Ras-aun, our palsied cook, lay next before the dragon Lutche.

I pressed my head against the cool of one of my stone pillars and closed my eyes. I felt ill. I felt exhilarated. I felt terribly, terribly afraid.

What I was witnessing, what these women were doing . . .

I could barely grasp the enormity of it. Not only was it bestiality, not only performed without shame among others, but done so with a mortal deity, a *poison-leaching* diety.

What exactly was the venom doing to those women?

I knew the venom of a kuneus had not the strength of that which was leached from a young dragon, had not the strength to cause instant blistering the way my hand had been blistered by the venom-coated whip the dragonmaster had pressed against my palm so many years ago.

But I'd been warned it imparted sting enough.

It was a hallucinogen and an analgesic, and although the kuneus's venom could no longer anaesthetize and paralyze like a young dragon's venom could, it was still poison.

Why, that very day before rescuing choking Ka from the pole he'd swallowed, I'd first inserted my arms into two long, leather gloves. I'd worn a bark-cloth mask to protect my face, had laced the neck of my tunic to the mask's collar. I'd worked in his gorge with eyes shut. All to prevent venom from touching me.

So it confounded me that these women were exposing themselves to the poison in the most bizarre and intimate way imaginable. Willingly.

A stir of noise to my right: The onais who had been asleep in the mill began filing in for Seventh Obeisance. I opened my eyes, realized that the fur cloak and the silver goblet had been spirited away and that those on night watch were completing a circumambulation. They knelt alongside the three old women who'd exposed themselves to Lutche's tongue; those three were already prostrate before Lutche, and so well-timed was the performance of the night watch as they joined them, it appeared as if the three old women had only just likewise knelt.

With a start, I realized I should join everyone. I staggered out from between my two pillars and did so.

That was the longest, most difficult obeisance I'd ever performed. Throughout, I was on the verge of breaking into laughter or tears, or bolting to my feet and fleeing into the jungle. As Seventh Obeisance wore to an end and we kowtowed eight times to Old Maht, I wondered what I should do next.

Return to the mill attic? Oh yes—oh, no!

Stay here and watch more? Oh, no—oh yes!

As we all rose to our feet and began the column-wending walk through rotunda to the exit, Kiz-dan sidled alongside me. Our arms touched through the coarse hemp of our tunic sleeves. One of her hands whisked out, quick as a tongue, and stroked one of mine. The touch of her flesh upon mine was all it took to renew the intoxicating want the Djimbi chants had provoked in me.

I stopped. Bent. Fussed with my feet, pretending to find a thorn there. I let the other onais pass me, then slipped behind my two pillars again.

Thus went my night. I hid, I watched, I surreptitiously joined my sisters for obeisance. Then I hid and watched some more.

I was shamed and horrified by how much the dragon's intimacy aroused me and filled me with want. It was the fault of the Djimbi chants, surely.

Would Kiz-dan lie down last? She would not. I knew then that she loved the babes in her belly, however much she spoke against them and feared their birth.

The night was nigh over; dawn and First Obeisance crept near upon a rose-tinted sky. I knew not how I would work that day, pretending nothing untoward had occurred during the night.

"Zar-shi!" a voice cried out, ringing round the rotunda, startling wits from me, slamming my heart against the roof of my mouth. "Your turn now! Come forward!"

It was Kiz-dan.

She stood near Ka's head—she'd held him as Nnp-trn, last to lie down, had been invaded by the dragon's tongue. The others on watch still knelt in a half-circle before Ka while Nnp-trn moaned before them upon that thick fur cloak. But when Kiz-dan called my name, they all jerked, stiffened, stared at her. Nnp-trn sat upright.

Yellow Face slowly stood.

"What have you done?" Nae-ser said, and my old tutor's whisper sounded laden with tears and horror both.

Kiz-dan's chin lifted angrily. "She can be trusted."

"It's not a matter of trust," Yellow Face snapped. "We've spoken of this before."

"You want to have as much time as you can with the kuneus. You don't want her to take an opportunity from you—"

"Think beyond your narrow little boundaries!" Yellow Face cried. "I don't want her involved because of the danger. She's young. She has her whole life ahead of her—"

"Life? *Here?*" Kiz-dan swept her hand round the rotunda.

"She is present?" Boj-est said, and our elder sounded weary and old, no longer the starlit, empyreal creature I'd witnessed before.

"Yes," Kiz-dan said. "She's been here all along. All along, understand?"

"So she's already involved," Boj-est replied, and she looked down at her wrinkled hands.

"You . . . " Yellow Face took a step toward Kiz-dan. "You untrust-worthy—"

"Still now, Yin-gik," Boj-est barked. "What's done is done."

"But to go against the group like this! Who next, hey-o? What if it's someone we can't trust?"

"Good question. Answer it, Kiz-dan," Boj-est demanded.

"Just Zar-shi. No one else. I'll be dead soon, anyway. You'll need someone to complete your watch. . . ." Kiz-dan started weeping.

Yellow Face drummed her fingers along her thighs, thinking furiously. "Come out, then, Zar-shi. If you're still there."

I was, and the last thing I wanted was to move. After some moments, I did. I couldn't very well cower there forever, could I?

I emerged from between my two pillars and walked toward them. My throat was too dry, too small. I had difficulty breathing; the air was laced with needles. Tremors rattled my vision.

To my shame, I threw myself at Yellow Face's feet.

"Don't make me do it, please don't make me," I begged, as if by begging, I could somehow erase the odious desire I'd felt for the dragons moments ago. What I had felt was wrong; if I railed against the passion hard enough, it would disappear. I would be normal once more, untainted by bestial lust. "I don't want that, what you did with Lutche—"

Yellow Face swatted my scrabbling hands off her skirts. "Asinine creature! No one's going to make you do anything. Now get up."

I rose, couldn't meet her eyes. Wrapped my arms tightly about myself. Rocked.

"If Temple found out," I choked.

A flash of movement, and a hand grabbed my hair and yanked my head back. I stared into Nnp-trn's furiously bloodshot, uncannily still eyes. "No one is going to find out, understand? No one."

"Easy now," Boj-est said, and she struggled to stand.

I spat in Nnp-trn's face. Was instantly shocked that I had done so. Nnp-trn dealt me a ringing blow. I staggered under it, then whipped up straight. All my fear boiled into fury. I struck her back.

Not with an open-handed slap, mind. I ploughed knuckles into nose like how I'd learned while in the merchant traveler's train years before. Cartilage crunched. Blood rushed over her lips, down her chin, was sucked up by the neck of her tunic.

"Zar-shi!" Boj-est cried in ringing tones. "Desist at once!"

But I couldn't. A fury I hadn't felt since my mother's death six years previous frothed within me, turned my mind into a roaring hurricane. I launched myself at Nnp-trn, clawed her, pummeled her, pulled her hair, bit. She staggered back under the attack, then fought, too. She was more than double my age, was a broad-shouldered, large-boned woman, whereas I was sinewy and small. Within moments, I couldn't see properly for the blood running sharp into my eyes.

The others dragged us apart. Kiz-dan stepped between us; of course, we wouldn't strike *her*. Nnp-trn spat a clot of blood.

"You're ill, the lot of you!" I shrieked, meaning myself, too, for having been aroused by what I'd witnessed. "Depraved whores!"

"Shut up, Zar-shi," Kiz-dan said.

"*You* shut up! Deviant!"

"Hold your lips," Yellow Face ordered.

"I will not." My fury focused itself on her, grew hotter. "You mutilated me and took away my name, and now you want to make me writhe like a maggot while a dragon rapes me with his tongue? Why not kill me now and be done with it?"

As I said this last, I realized they were the very words I'd hurled at my mother, down by the convent's roadside cairn. *Why not kill me now and be done with it?* I burst into tears.

"I didn't know she would react this way," Kiz-dan muttered.

"Of course she would; she's yet a child," our elder said. "Go, please, the lot of you, and kneel before Lutche. Dawn approaches. First Obeisance starts soon. I'll talk with Zar-shi."

All save Yellow Face disappeared into the gray gloom of the rotunda. I continued to cry angrily, unable to stop myself.

After several moments, Yellow Face stepped toward Boj-est and murmured something into her ear. Our elder frowned, listened, studied me.

Nodded brusquely.

Then she, too, left. I was alone with Yellow Face.

She gripped my shoulders. I jerked free from her hateful touch.

"You have every right to be angry and repulsed," she said. "What we do here is wrong, there's no denying that. But I can't apologize for what you saw. Can't and won't. I'm neither ashamed of what I do with the kuneus nor willing to stop it. But I need you to understand clearly: The safety of all in Tieron rests upon your complicity and silence."

She reached out, tried to grip me again. I stepped back.

"We are all replaceable, understand," she continued grimly. "The lot of us. You think any would protest if Temple should audit us? No one would even know, and if someone should find out, it would be too late; we'd be dead. We are nothing, understand? For every one of us, there exist a hundred city beggars willing to suffer the holy knife just for the meager charity and sanctuary Temple provides an onai. We could be replaced like that."

She snapped her fingers.

"Understand? Hey-o?"

I angrily wiped snot from my upper lip. "I hate you."

She nodded. "I would, too, if I were you."

"I didn't want this! Any of this!"

"I would doubt for your sanity if you did."

I gave one last hiccuping sob. "I don't know what to do."

She touched me again. The barest brush of her fingers against my arm. "Just be silent, that's all. Be silent. When you want—if you want—we can talk about this again. Now join the others; First Obeisance starts."

I ask you again: What would you have done, at fifteen?

SEVENTEEN

After that memorable night a clawful of weeks passed, during which I worked furiously and sullenly, speaking little. Although my behavior was dismissed as a relapse into my old ways, I felt eyes upon me. Studying. Calculating. Wondering what next I might do.

Eight pairs of dragon-still eyes, finely veined with broken blood vessels.

At all times, one of the eight whores worked alongside me. Hoeing, shoveling dung, working the mill—whatever the chore, there she stood beside me. I resented the constant presence and the threat it implied. As the Season of Fire advanced into searing hot days and thick, humid nights, my resentment built.

I was working in the jungle with a group of onais, gathering bluewood ferns and cutleaf hostas and nipong treelets to grind later in the mill into pap for the kuneus, when my resentment peaked. Yellow Face worked not far from me, her coarse hemp tunic and skirts as grimy as my own, her bark-clothed calves splotched with viper-frog foam, the lace of one of her rawhide boots unraveling and knotted with twigs.

I stood still, machete in one sweaty fist, glaring at her.

Disgusted at myself—how long had I wasted time, brooding?—I slashed at a heliconia bract and stalked over to her, wading through palm ferns and choking ginnies without care for what fangs they hid.

I planted my feet behind her bent form and raked a blunt-nailed hand through my bristle; my hair was cropped short as per convent rules; I was bound to the wretched hairstyle for life, it seemed. Around us onais worked, rustling behind bush and puffing as they swung their machetes.

I opened my mouth to unleash pent-up rancor. . . . And heard it. Faint but unmistakable.

"The bell!" I cried triumphantly, for Yellow Face prided herself on always hearing it first.

Because I stood less than a foot behind her, and as she'd been en-grossed in her labor, my bellow startled wits from her. She shrieked and jumped a hand's span into the air. I grinned.

"The bell," I said, cocking a thumb in the air.

She glared. "I hear it, fool."

"What say you, Zar-shi?" old Ogi-ras warbled from behind a bush. "Is all well?"

"The bell," I bellowed. "Down at the cairn."

Excitement rippled through the onais around us, and within mo-ments, they all appeared from the bushes. You'd have thought the sound of the bell would have provoked only cynicism after decades of disappointing shipments from the Ranreeb. Not so.

"Oh, maybe the leather sandals we requested?" Voe-too murmured, scratched cheeks flushed.

"Eggs? Remember that once . . . ?"

"There'd better be roof tiles waiting down there for us."

Yellow Face waved her machete at the group of us. Despite the sen-iority of several onais present, she took control. As always. "Enough chatter. Zar-shi, Lec-wey, come to cairn."

We returned to the mill quickly.

It was not long after morn, so if we hurried, we could fetch our goods and return before nightfall. We disliked staying overnight by the roadside. Despite the fire we always built during night stays at the cairn, we felt unprotected and exposed.

Back at the mill, Boj-est waited, five other onais gathered round her. She looked tired and leaned heavily against the sheaves of koor-fowsi rim maht stacked alongside the building.

"These go with you, hey," she said, nodding at the onais about her. "Rin-mes has a rucksack of food and drink for your noon meal. Travel safe. Travel as if you had wings."

We murmured our thanks and set off.

None of us expected what awaited us at the cairn. Not one, not two, but *three* young women, all of them not much older than myself, two wild-eyed with nerves, the third tight lipped with anger.

They all wore bayen silk.

We gawped at them, we eight gaunt, travel-sweated onais dressed in homespun skirts and bark-cloth leggings.

I broke the spell; couldn't help it. I let out a whoop at the sight of the three cedar coffers and the clawful of fine leather packing cases gathered round the women. I darted forward and fell upon a leather case, fumbling with its stout strappings and metal buckles.

"Zar-shi!" Yellow Face snapped, scandalized. "Stand here!"

I continued to work at the buckles. "We asked for converts; here they are. About time, too. What's in these, hey?" I flung the question at the nearest young lady. Her expression stopped me cold.

She was looking at me with a mixture of horror and revulsion. One of her companions buried her face in her smooth, tapered fingers and began crying. I'd made a mistake.

"Sorry," I mumbled, flushing. I rose to my feet, shuffled back to where the rest of the onais stood, still gawping. "Thought you'd come to join the convent."

"Close your lips, yolk-brained fool," Yellow Face growled at me. "Can you, hey?"

In the jungle canopy overhead, something heavy moved and a toucan gave its gravelly cry. All three bayen women shrieked, two of them clutching hold of each other. I slapped a mosquito off my neck.

One of the bayen ladies—the angry one, a sloe-eyed youth with luscious breasts and fine, heavy hips and a sweet waist banded with a brilliant green sash—gained control of herself and stepped forward, chin lifted.

"I demand to know what manner of creature you are."

My jaw dropped.

"We are from Convent Tieron," Yellow Face replied.

"This snake grub, too?" Beauty lifted her snub nose at me.

"She is new among us," Yellow Face said by way of answer, and I was pleased she offered no apology for my abysmal behavior.

"Will we have to share sleeping quarters with it?"

"We have but one roof."

A wail from the weeping young lady. Yellow Face stepped forward briskly.

"We have some ways to travel; we must leave now. Lec-wey, Zar-shi, between you both carry the heaviest coffer. Come, sisters, day advances."

I was confused now.

"*Are* they converts?" I asked, but my question went unanswered as the onais stepped forward and began dividing up the leather cases among themselves for carrying.

What should have been a trip completed before dark dragged until well after twilight. The bayen women in their fine, multilayered clothes and delicate leather slippers complained of heat, hunger, and blisters. They wept frequently and swooned often. They were utterly incapable of walking for long without rest and water, the latter of which we shared equally among us and which ran out by high noon.

By the time we reached the mill in the dark, Lady Wringing Hands was a gibbering idiot, her companion had fallen into stupor, and Beauty seethed with fury.

I couldn't wait to open the cases.

Mute Ber-nul met us at the path's end, weeping. We knew at once something was badly wrong. That she'd been sent to meet us—a mute, incapable of conveying her message—only underscored the enormity of the calamity awaiting us.

"Kiz-dan's dead!" I gasped. I started to drop the coffer Lec-wey and I were carrying, to run toward the sickly white shape of the mill crouched at the cliff's base, but at Lec-wey's cry of protest, I instead pulled her forward. Ber-nul waved her hands about and shook her head to and fro.

"What, what?" I cried. "The twins are stillborn?"

"The answer lies ahead of us," Yellow Face said grimly. "Forward now."

We marched on, Ber-nul in front, gesticulating frantically to Yellow Face, who nodded now and then. The bayen women staggered after us, made passive by our fear.

As we approached the mill, the thin rise and fall of keening carried on the sultry night air.

I shivered. Who? Who?

No warm, smoky smell of kadoob cooking; the embers beneath

Ras-aun's cauldron were black as the sky above. We turned the corner of the mill, Lec-wey and I already half lowering our coffer to the ground. . . .

We came up short. Stopped. Stared.

Djimbi. A group of them, crouched on their haunches outside the door. They looked at us without hurry or care and studied us in silence. They didn't rise.

Yellow Face and the rest of the onais caught up behind us. They, too, stopped short.

"Well, then," Yellow Face said after a moment, and she set her burden down. Lec-wey and I did likewise. The bayen women shambled into our midst. They caught sight of the Djimbi—unmistakably Djimbi, the full moon highlighting their peculiar mottled skin, their moss-knotted hair, their nakedness, the bows and quivers of arrows upon their backs—and Lady Wringing Hands crumpled senseless to the ground while one of her companions shrieked and danced about as if a snake were in her skirts. We ignored them.

Yellow Face nodded brusquely to the Djimbi, then swept into the mill. I followed at her heels.

Candlelight, steady and yellow, each candle pointing an unwavering black finger of smoke at the ceiling, the candles themselves surrounding a figure lying too still on the ground, stones upon her eyes. Onais prostrate on the floor, raking their arms with their nails in grief. A cloying smell, vaguely like honey turned bad in heat.

Boj-est, our elder.

As one, the onais stopped their threnody. One addressed us. In the gloom, I recognized her voice before her face.

"She fell down in the garden; was dead by the time I reached her," Nae-ser said.

Yellow Face took a deep breath, let it out as she spoke. "She lived long."

"Kiz-dan's upstairs. We might lose her yet." My old tutor wiped her eyes. "A boy and a girl. Hale, the both of them."

"She gave birth?" I cried. "She's alive?"

"The Djimbi?" Yellow Face asked.

Nae-ser shrugged. "They just appeared. Two of their women helped with the birth. They're with Kiz-dan now. We would have lost mother and children if not."

Yellow Face nodded brusquely and started up the stairs. I followed.

"She's alive, yes? Kiz-dan's alive?"

Yellow Face stopped and glared at me. "It would behoove you to recognize the death of our elder, Zar-shi."

"What?" Then, realizing what she meant, I mumbled, "Oh. Sorry. Yes. Well."

With a snort of disgust, Yellow Face turned and ascended the last few stairs.

Darkness and a moist heaviness in the air. The rusty smell of blood, thick and pervasive. We stood still for some moments while our eyes adjusted to the gloom.

In a corner, two long-haired mounds crouched beside a prone figure. One gently rocked a crude reed basket.

Rrsht, rrsht, went the basket on the floor, sounding like the sigh of a mother hushing her babe.

I had never grown used to the Djimbi. Distrusted, in fact, their silent, unexpected visits. Disliked the resilience in their gazes, the calm in their languid movements. Often, I lay awake at nights after we'd done trade with them, my mouth dry with the dread expectation of their adzes cutting my head from my shoulders while I slept.

Deviants could not be trusted.

My heart stuttered in my chest at the sight of them so close to Kiz-dan, and she so obviously feeble. I shoved past Yellow Face and strode over, planting legs apart, crossing arms over chest, and glowered down at them.

"What have you done to her?" I growled.

Yellow Face puffed up behind me and clipped me upside my head. "For once in your stunted little life, hold your lips shut."

As I sputtered indignantly, she knelt and looked into the basket. Two swaddled babies slept there, side by side and unbelievably ugly, their pug noses whistling a little with each breath, their thick black hair sticking up in unruly tufts.

"What's wrong with them?" I asked in revulsion.

"Zar-shi . . . " Yellow Face sighed wearily.

"They look grotesque."

"They look like newborns."

They did? I'd watched numerous births in the danku. But I must have been away from infants too long, for on second look, Kiz-dan's twins still looked wrong.

I knelt beside Kiz-dan. My knees cracked as I bent, and the sound startled both babies. They jerked in perfect unison, mewled, and smacked their gums a few times. I stiffened, expecting howls. But no, the two sank back into sleep.

Kiz-dan's face looked disfigured, too. Squinting in the gloom, I could make out puffiness and mottling on her neck and cheeks. Like bruises.

"Did they strike her?" I gasped.

Yellow Face shot me a withering look and briskly went about checking Kiz-dan: feeling her forehead, touching the inside of her wrist for her pulse, lifting the blankets covering her and checking between her legs, this last provoking a rush of warm, metallic-smelling air. Kiz-dan stirred and her eyes rolled open, swam about, then rolled shut again.

"So." Yellow Face drummed her fingers against her thigh, studying Kiz-dan. She turned to the Djimbi.

Rrsht, rrsht went the basket.

"Thank you. Yes, thank you," Yellow Face murmured.

"We need new machetes," one of the Djimbi women said.

"You shall have them."

The Djimbi lumbered to their feet. One bent and lifted a swaddled baby out with a speed that alarmed me.

"Careful! You'll break its neck!" I cried, but the deviant ignored me, instead began unraveling a swathe of cloth from her hips with one hand, holding the baby with a frightening casualness in the crook of her opposite arm.

The other woman began unraveling a similar band of cloth from her own hips and crisscrossed it over her back and in front of her long breasts.

"Zar-shi," Yellow Face murmured. "Two of our best machetes, please."

The first Djimbi began tucking the swaddled baby against her naked breasts. The baby began crying. The Djimbi grasped one of her bulbous nipples and poked it into the baby's face. The baby rooted about and latched on. Kiz-dan stirred and her eyes rolled, but again she didn't wake.

"Zar-shi," Yellow Face said more firmly. "The machetes."

The other deviant lifted Kiz-dan's second child from the reed basket and likewise strapped it against her bosom, thrusting *her* nipple into the baby's mouth when it also cried.

"What's happening?" I asked slowly. But I already knew the answer.

"Get the machetes," Yellow Face said. "Move."

"You're giving them the babies?"

She slapped me across the face.

She'd never done so before, had always clipped my head or yanked my ears when driven to physical discipline. Those hands of hers were all bone and sinew, and they cracked against my cheek like a wooden paddle. A nasty pain shot down my neck, hot as scalding oil. My eyes filled with tears, and for a moment I lost sense of time and space. Only a moment, though.

Her face swam before me in the gloomy light crawling up from the candlelight vigil downstairs. Her long, gaunt cheeks were drawn with a fury I hadn't seen before. "Machetes!"

"No," I said, and I was surprised by how calmly it came out. "Those babies aren't leaving."

"They are."

"*They stay.*" No argument in my voice. None whatsoever. I turned to the Djimbi women. "Put them back."

Yellow Face made a dismissive, placatory gesture to the two deviants. Ignore the disturbed child, it said. Continue on your way.

One of my hands shot out and grabbed her bony wrist. Jerked hard. "I said *no.*"

"You have no concept—"

"I'll tell."

Long, long moments passed.

The humid gloom sucked up the sounds of night. No insects

chirruped, no renimgars grunted, no wind soughed through hemp stalks. Downstairs, our holy sisters began chanting a dirge.

Yellow Face flared her nostrils. "You would tell Temple about what I do with the dragons just to keep these by-blows here? We would be audited, all of us; the babes would die with us for my actions, beneath a Temple guillotine. You understand that, hey-o?"

"Not Temple. The others, I'd tell, every onais here. You'd never be allowed to stand watch again together. No more whoring yourself to the dragons' tongues. I would. I'd tell."

The truth of it stood between us like a fine porcelain statue, brilliant white, solid, immovable. Something changed in Yellow Face then. I couldn't see what, but the change was a shift in the air.

When she spoke next, her nostrils flared so wide with anger they curled her upper lip into a bow. "The boy cannot stay."

It was a concession; it was immutable. The girl could stay; the boy would go with the deviants.

"You're a snake," I spat. "A perverted snake. The color of your skin is a reflection of the illness within you."

"You'll cut that baby." Her anger met mine with equal force. She pointed a trembling, joint-swollen finger at one of the babies tucked against the Djimbi women. "Not me. *You*."

I felt a qualm of misgiving then.

If the babe grew up with the Djimbi, it would suffer no mutilation, perform no obeisance, know little of the relentless battle we onais fought daily against starvation and illness.

And if Kiz-dan should die, as looked likely, what then? Who would suckle the infant? What if Kiz-dan survived but her illness shriveled her milk breasts—how then would we feed the babe? With what would we diaper her? Who would sleep with the babe when Kiz-dan performed night watch? And now that we had no medicine witch, what would we do when the child fell ill, as children so often did?

Would it even survive the circumcision?

The enormity of what I was deciding for the child buckled my knees, and I realized I'd made a mistake. Oh yes, it was a cruelty to separate mother from child, but a small one compared to what I would condemn her to. I gazed at my feet, and hot shame swept over me.

Take the child, then. Take them both.

But before the words could leave me, she was there, inside me, her mouth a yawning black cavern of protest filling my vision and roaring in my ears and burning in every vein in my body. *Don't take my baby.*

I reeled, grabbed my ears, doubled over.

"It's not Waivia!" I gasped, but my mother's haunt would hear no argument. It was insane with obsession, it was puissant with conviction: It would not allow the girl baby to be taken from the convent. From me.

Don't take my baby!

The haunt jerked my hands from my ears, thrust my arms toward the closest Djimbi.

The haunt was using me like a puppet, and the violation was hideous; I was entombed within a heavy casing of flesh, I was stifled, couldn't breathe, my eyesight was fading fast in a sheet of viscous blue darkness. . . .

Slash! A red, wet blade carved me free, severed the haunt from me, left me cold and sweaty and shuddering in the mill attic. One of the Djimbi women stood before me, pressed fleshy warm against me, her nose inches from my own, her peppery breath hot on my lips as she muttered aberrant words. Her hands pulled at the air above my head as if she were brushing away a vast cobweb growing there, and she stamped and marched in place as if she were trying to hold something beneath the soles of her bare feet.

I was holding one of Kiz-dan's babies tight against my chest, as if to protect it from the Djimbi. The babe bawled heartily, a raspy cry that was the only pure thing in the attic.

The Djimbi woman jerked away from me, flinging her arms over her head and backward in a long arc. Her shoulder joints popped from the violent, unnatural movement. She shouted something, then looked behind her. Shook her head. Looked back at me. Shook her head again.

I shuddered with cold. I wanted to sit.

"This one haunt ridden, hey-hey. Can't gotta off. Sticky-sure on her."

"Mama," I whimpered, and I started to sob.

After a few moments, Yellow Face took the baby from me.

I didn't see her expression, but I could feel it in the air: pursed lips, furrowed brow, bloodshot eyes unnaturally still and rimmed with anger.

As soon as the baby's warmth left me—and it felt like an amputation—I crumpled to the floor, drew my knees to my chest, and rocked.

Yellow Face gently laid the baby alongside Kiz-dan. Fetched two machetes and handed them to the women. The Djimbi melted down the stairs and into the night.

Even above the hoarse, undulating threnody honoring our dead convent elder, I heard the cry of the child they'd taken with them, as it was separated from its mother and twin.

EIGHTEEN

‿e_℩∽

Fear chased sleep from me that night.

I didn't dare close my eyes. I refused to give my mother's haunt the chance to invade me.

I tried weaving, but the *tock-tock* of my shuttlecock on the loom refused to fall into a steady rhythm. The staccato sound kept my sisters awake, and the cloth I wove was knotted and crude. Yellow Face hissed at me to stop.

So I sat beside Kiz-dan and stared at her babe.

I could still feel the cool waxiness of Boj-est's death-locked skin, where I'd grasped her arm to roll her body onto our corpse pallet. Despite her slight frame, she'd been heavy, as if in dying her body had absorbed every word she'd ever spoken and transmuted it into something physical and spongy. We eight onais who carried her bloating corpse into the jungle grunted under the weight, walking with an awkward hip-shot gait, stumbling often in the dark. The pallet chafed my shoulder raw.

I could still hear the dull thud her body made as we slid it from the pallet onto the jungle floor.

I began to rock the baby's basket to block the sound from my mind.

Middle night was approaching.

I longed for Seventh Obeisance, for my fellow onais to rise, sighing and groaning, from their sleeping mats. In the Wet Season corner of the mill, the bayen women lay together, a heap of slick satin that shone with a nacreous light. We'd dulled their taste buds with pepperfruit as an evening meal, followed by venom-and-herb-laced wine. They slept heavily, their chests barely moving.

I looked over my shoulder. Drew my knees to my chest. Sat hunched.

The look of Boj-est as her waxy cheek had hit the jungle floor and the stones tumbled off her eyes and one of her lids sprang open, revealing a bloodshot eyeball as inert as when she'd breathed—the look of her plagued me like an abscessed tooth. The smile on her mouth no smile at all, but the rictus of death. The short gray hair on her head so thin it revealed her scalp. Delicate and vulnerable and dead and ghastly, she was. Fodder for feral teeth. Her bones would crack easily for those that wanted her marrow.

If she could feel anything, I knew what she felt. Leaden immobility. Stifling oppression. Utter darkness.

I shuddered and wrapped my arms about myself. *When* would everyone awaken for Seventh Obeisance? Soon, surely.

How had that Djimbi woman released me from my mother's haunt? What would have happened if she hadn't? Would I lie now in the jungle alongside Boj-est, the blood-beaded whiskers of a jungle cat brushing my breast as it tore out my entrails? Alive, I'd be, but trapped within my corpse, and no one would know it until it didn't matter anymore, until my last voiceless scream died within me as my skull was cracked open and my brain was feasted upon.

The baby began to cry.

I startled, heart racing so hard against my ribs I couldn't catch my breath. I was certain my mother's haunt was coming over me, that she'd make real the dreadful scene I'd just imagined—

"Pick it up," a voice growled, and the sweet, spicy scent of patchouli wafted over me as expensive satin rustled at my side.

I looked up to where Beauty stood. With hair mussed and eyes shadowed, she looked as if she'd just risen from a lover's embrace and not a hard wooden floor in a convent.

"Sodomized bitch," she cursed at me, and bent to the baby's basket. "It needs to be held. It needs to be fed."

She rocked the basket. The baby's cry continued to violate the night air, a raw sound that set my nerves on edge.

"What do we feed her with?" I said.

"Put it on the teat of the bitch that birthed it."

In another circumstance, my retort would have been scathing. But I was too rattled.

"How?" I said meekly.

She looked at me then. Such a look, too. Haughty, sneering, as if I wasn't worth the spit in her mouth.

"Lay. It. By. Her. Breast," she said, enunciating each word as if I were ludu din din, a foreigner.

I fumbled in the basket, slid my hands under the warm, fist-balled bundle, and lifted the baby as though it were a scalding loaf of bread fresh from the oven.

"She's wet," I muttered.

"Are you dense?" Beauty said, and again she directed another foul expletive at me that was completely at odds with her fine stature. "*Change* it."

Anger reared a hot, horned head in me; the raspy cries emanating from the baby were the most irritating sounds I'd ever heard. "With *what*? And stop calling her an it. The baby's a *she*."

A stirring around us. The lusty cries of the baby were finally penetrating the sleep of my fellow onais.

"Give the piglet over." And Beauty took the baby from me and laid it on the floor. She swiftly untied the green satin banded round her waist. "We'll dress it in this. Fitting, I think; the mark of an adulterer upon a baseborn piglet."

"It's a girl, not a piglet," I hissed, furious.

One eyebrow lifted as she unwrapped the babe. "Is it, now?"

"Yes—"

"Wrong."

She pointed. I stared. A nub of a penis rested on two testicles.

"Oh, no," I whispered. "Oh, no, no, no."

"Oh yes." Beauty removed the soiled swaddling from around the boy and expertly wrapped him in her green satin. "Now roll the little bull's mother onto her side so he can nurse."

"We gave away the wrong baby," I stammered.

Beauty narrowed her eyes, studied me shrewdly. Looked far wiser than the youth of her face. "There were two?"

Of course she wouldn't have known. She'd been outside dealing with her unconscious bayen companion and hysterical friend when the Djimbi melted from the convent with Kiz-dan's girl child.

I could see Beauty digesting the information, and I knew she would use it against me somehow. But I didn't know what to say, couldn't retract the statement, and regardless, the truth of it was apparent in my silence.

"Can't we shut it up?" I growled instead, and Beauty grinned nastily.

"Reverted to an 'it,' has the piggy, now the gender has been revealed?"

I flushed again, got to my knees, and shuffled close to Kiz-dan. I slid my arms under her fevered body and none too gently rolled her onto her side. She moaned and her eyes opened, clouded with confusion.

"Open her tunic," Beauty ordered. "Works better that way."

I flared my nostrils and tugged the neck of Kiz-dan's tunic open to her waist. She was damp with sweat. Her empty belly, so huge and taut only yesterday, was now flaccid.

Someone crouched beside me. Yellow Face. I sensed other onais rising, too. Yellow Face reached for the baby, and Beauty handed him over.

Yellow Face laid him alongside Kiz-dan, took hold Kiz-dan's floor-squashed breast, and manipulated it as if it were a milk jug. After she nudged the bawling baby's face several times with Kiz-dan's nipple, his little mouth twisted sideways and opened wide without a sound. Yellow Face rammed the nipple in with a firmness that seemed inappropriate, but after a pause, the baby fell to sucking, drawing his fists to his chest and his knees to his belly.

The cessation of noise was magnificent. I shuddered with the instant release of tension.

" 'S my baby?" Kiz-dan slurred, wonder growing on her dazed face.

"A healthy boy," I said, before Yellow Face could err. "You have to get better for him, hey-o?"

She gave a small smile and closed her eyes. "Thirsty."

"We'll fetch you something to drink," I said, grabbing Yellow Face's wrist.

Yellow Face remained tight-lipped as we pushed through the onais crowding around mother and child, soft smiles on their haggard faces. A few wept.

Downstairs, in the humidity of a typical Fire Season night, Yellow Face placed her hands on her hips. "What was that nonsense about?"

"It's a boy. We gave away the girl child. It's a boy."

Her breathing quickened. "You're sure of this?"

"His balls are enormous."

She closed her eyes briefly and exhaustion swept over her like a great, dark dragon. When she opened them, they were moist and bright.

"He can't stay, Zar-shi."

"He *will.*"

"No. This nonsense has to stop right now. If it wasn't for you, that child would be safely away from here and Kiz-dan none the wiser. He goes, simple as that."

"It's not my fault he's a boy."

"He goes."

"You gave away the wrong child, not me. He's staying."

"What are you going to do, threaten me again?" Her spittle landed cold on my cheeks. "How many times are you going to use that gambit to get what you want?"

"You're the one with the depraved habits. You can stop any time you want to."

"You call me depraved? You who carry a dead woman's obsession on your back like an old woman's hunch? You who delve into the spirit world each night and rise shrieking like a bat chased from a cave each morn?"

"That's nothing I want. That's nothing I choose—"

"Are you sure of that? Hey?"

"What do you mean?" I blustered, trying to reach for the anger of moments before. No use. It was gone, replaced by fear.

"I remember only too well a child who cried morning and eve for her mother, even while condemning her for what she'd done."

"I was a child!"

"But you've never released that need, that . . . that . . . unhealthy craving that's coupled so perversely with rancor. I hear you. At night, during the day, talking to her, begging her to love you, to stay with you. You do it all the time. Everyone hears it. It's unnatural, child. Let her go."

"She won't let *me* go." I was near tears. "It's not my choice. It's hers."

"Is it?"

"Why didn't she love me?" I wailed.

"She died bringing you to us. What greater love—"

"Not for me!" I thumped my chest hard. "Not for me! For Waivia, my sister. It was all for her, everything. She wants me to find her; that's why she brought me here, that's the only reason she wants me alive. To find my sister!"

A dam of grief and anger and abandonment burst within me.

I threw myself at Yellow Face and buried my face in her shoulder. It was beyond her to wrap her arms about me despite my desperate need, but she did bring herself to pat my back and make clucking noises in an attempt to soothe.

The onais of Tieron Nask Cinai shuffled down from the attic and filed silently past us on their way to the rotunda for Seventh Obeisance.

When the last was gone, Yellow Face spoke.

"Hush now, Zar-shi, hush. Come, Seventh Obeisance starts soon."

"I hate this place," I moaned into her bony shoulder.

"Then you should leave."

That jolted me. I pulled away. "Oh, hey? And go *where*?" I said bitterly.

"Only you can answer that."

"You hate me. You'd do anything to get rid of me."

Her sour face returned. "This isn't about me. It's about you, foolish child."

I crossed my arms in front of my chest. "Well I'm not going to Seventh Obeisance tonight."

She threw her hands up in the air. "Hardly relevant, and I won't be drawn into *that* argument. Stay if you wish. Kiz-dan still waits for her water."

She turned to go to the rotunda. Stopped. Looked over her shoulder. "Give some thought to what I said. And keep an eye on that

bayen beauty of ours. She looks a wily one. I don't harbor much trust
for her."

"You don't harbor much trust for anyone," I muttered under my
breath as I watched her skinny figure stiffly make for the rotunda.

I wiped tears from my face and went to fetch water for Kiz-dan.

Beauty refused to eat her morning gruel. When pressed, she said she
suspected the mess was tainted with a sleeping draft. Her two companions—still fighting stupor from the evening's drugged sleep—
looked up from their empty bowls in alarm.

Too late. Beauty was right. Their gruel had been drug tainted.

Other than myself and Yellow Face, and Kiz-dan, who lay sleeping
beside her baby, six other onais had stayed behind in the attic while
the rest went about the daily labor that kept us alive and clothed. The
locks and channels to the mill wheel were even then being tended to;
water began splashing against the wheel paddles, and the great wheel
began slowly turning, its groans reverberating through the attic.

The youngest and strongest onais had been chosen to attend the
initiation ceremony for our three bayen converts. Nnp-trn was among
them. We gave each other wide berth as we formed a circle around
the seated bayen women.

"A word with the convent elder," Beauty said, lifting her chin.

Lady Wringing Hands gawped at Beauty, her bloodshot eyes wide
and glazed. She opened and closed her mouth like a fish, then
slumped against one of the dowry coffers Lec-wey and I had carried
from the cairn yesterday. The sleeping draft was working already.

Her companion started to weep in a halfhearted manner, then lay
down, resigned, and curled onto her side.

Beauty rose to her feet, managed to look down at Yellow Face
though she was no taller than her. "You are the convent elder, are
you not?"

We exchanged looks, us onais.

The question of who would replace Boj-est had not yet been
broached. Old Voe-too was superior in age, but no one save her gave
a moment's thought to her as elder. Several lackluster crones were
next in line according to their age, but they too were unsuitable

candidates—too slow, too easily confused. Ras-aun or Nae-ser might be chosen, but worsening palsy in the one and ever dimming vision in the other inspired little confidence in most of us.

Yellow Face hesitated, then said, "I'll act in Boj-est's stead for now."

None of us disputed her words. Thus, it was decided: Yellow Face would be the new elder of Tieron Nask Cinai.

Beauty laid a long-fingered hand lightly upon Yellow Face's arm, as if the two were friends heading out for a stroll round the garden. They walked to the far end of the attic for privacy. I followed.

I had an inkling of what was to come and wanted to hear it played out.

Beauty lifted her nose at me. "You're not needed, grub."

I crossed my arms over my chest. "I'm not moving."

"Fine, fine," Yellow Face said wearily, irritably. To Beauty: "Say your piece, child. We've work to do."

I thought that nervy of her, calling Beauty a child. Grudgingly, I admired her for it.

"I know what happens next," Beauty said, color appearing on her cheekbones. "My esteemed claimer took great delight in informing me of the details of my fate. I tell you now: I shan't be cut."

"Nonsense," Yellow Face snapped. "You walk on this soil and eat our food only if you're clean."

"I forbid it."

Oooh. This was going to be wonderful to watch.

Hot color flooded Yellow Face's cheeks. "Then you can march yourself down those stairs and out the door. Temple Statute dictates that all women who serve the kuneus must be clean. I obey that law."

"Do you?" Beauty purred. "Correct me if I'm wrong, but does not Temple Statute also state that a convent must be devoid of the male presence, save for visiting Temple Auditors? And is that child there not unmistakably male?"

"He will be castrated," Yellow Face said tightly, not following Beauty's accusing finger.

"Still male, though."

Yellow Face's eyes bulged. "You will not blackmail me."

"I will not be cut."

"You will leave here or be rendered clean."

Beauty tightened her grip on Yellow Face's wrist; I'd not realized until that moment that she hadn't released her.

"Listen to me, old woman. I'm younger than you by far, healthier, stronger. I can sing and dance and read and write, and I have connections with the most influential families of our nation. You don't want me to leave this place. This sorry little mill, with its rotting timbers and patched walls, I could have it fixed like that, understand?"

She smacked her hands together right under Yellow Face's nose. I thought that terribly nervy of *her*.

"Do you know why I'm here?" Beauty continued vehemently. "Because my claimer loves me. He's madly, wildly in love with me, and he the ugliest little man you've ever laid eyes upon. I could barely stand the touch of his clammy skin, and he knew it. But his brother, there's a man for you. I crept into *his* bed every chance I got. Neither man wants me here, yet neither can stand sharing me with the other. This is their solution to their petty jealousies, see? I've only to whine about my discomforts here and coffers of wealth will appear."

"Unhand me," Yellow Face hissed, and my stomach shriveled at her ferocity.

Beauty released her, stepped back a pace, chest heaving.

"Now *you* understand this," Yellow Face said. "I will not be blackmailed nor bribed. Temple Statute is Temple Statute, and I will have it followed. Whether today, tomorrow, or next week. Stay here if you want. But you will eat nothing of our food nor be allowed a foot outside this mill until I have cut away that evil piece of flesh between your thighs."

With that, Yellow Face turned and walked back to the group huddled round the two unconscious bayen women.

I noticed that Kiz-dan's eyes followed her. She hugged her baby closer as Yellow Face swept past.

I started after Yellow Face. Beauty stopped me.

"What would your dear friend think if she knew that both children she birthed lived, and you gave one away to a group of savages?"

She was stunning in her fury. I wanted to stroke her heaving bosom and feel the heat from her flush. I could scarcely concentrate on what she was saying.

"See to it the elder changes her mind, and I'll play along with your charade that the twin was stillborn," she murmured. "If not, I'll speak the truth."

I swallowed, tried for bravado. "So? Tell. I don't care."

Those lips of hers smiled thinly. "I think you do."

I wrenched my hand from her grasp and joined my sisters.

NINETEEN

I retched up breakfast during the first cut of the holy cleansing knife, turning to the side and heaving even while holding Lady Wringing Hands's head down on the floor as Yellow Face sliced into her. It was not so much the slick whittling of her knife that nauseated me as the jerk-tug, jerk-tug of her other hand, and the way her fingers pinched the hapless bud of flesh, and the triumphant, gritty look on her face as the severed womanhood came away.

"Clean it up, Zar-shi," Yellow Face muttered, as the sour stench of my vomit joined the reek of bird excrement in the attic. The mill always stank of bird scat during Fire Season, when the sun roasted the guano-coated cliffs behind the convent.

Light-headed, I released the unconscious woman and stumbled down the stairs, past the onais already shoveling koorfowsi rim maht beneath the squealing millstone, outside into another hot, windless day. I lingered at the waterfall pool, languid with lack of sleep, and returned with an urn of water balanced upon one hip. Each slosh of the water spilling over the urn's lip penetrated my tunic and ran down my legs pleasingly.

I ascended the mill stairs just as the onais who had assisted in the cleansing rites descended. Not one of them looked upon me kindly as we passed each other.

The stench within the attic burned the nostrils.

"Hurry up, child!" Yellow Face said, puce about the eyes as she fussed between the thighs of the bleeding women.

Beauty had stationed herself as far from us as possible, and throughout the knifework she had busied herself with emptying a coffer. She was meticulously replacing all that she'd inventoried earlier, but wasn't too distracted to shoot me a nasty look. I ducked my head and went about cleaning what I'd retched up.

From her sleeping mat, Kiz-dan muttered something.

"There's water beside you," Yellow Face said. "Serve yourself. We're occupied. And see to that babe of yours, hey? He'll need to nurse plenty in this heat."

I scrubbed and cleaned and watched Kiz-dan rise, wobbling, onto an elbow, reach for the leather bladder Yellow Face had placed beside her, and drink long from it. She looked every day her age and then some, and I was unnerved by the maturity motherhood had overnight wrought in her. It separated us, made more tenuous the friendship I had betrayed while she'd been unconscious after childbirth.

I shot a look at Beauty and jumped; she'd been watching me watch Kiz-dan. Her look was feral. I concentrated on dragging my rag over the wooden floor.

"Aren't you done yet?" Yellow Face groused. "Finish it, hey, and come over. You've got to name these two."

I dropped my rag in the urn. "What?"

"Don't dally, come over."

It dawned on me then: I was the only one in Tieron who could read and write. Nae-ser's eyesight was mostly a memory.

With the realization came a conquering rush. I felt omnipotent, invaluable, indisputable. Opportunity flowered open before me.

On my knees I shuffled to where Yellow Face knelt before the two women. My bloom of exultation immediately wilted. The first task that greeted my new status was interpreting the bloodstains on the sleeping mats of the mutilated women.

I recoiled from the small, congealed slabs on the sleeping mat Yellow Face lifted before me.

"Read them."

"That's disgusting."

"Don't try my patience, child."

I stared at the things in revulsion. "They don't look anything like word characters."

"Boj-est never had a problem interpreting them."

"Makes me question how good *her* eyesight was."

"Zar-shi!"

"There *aren't* any hieratics here."

"Stop being contrary. Read the things." The liverish slabs wobbled as Yellow Face shoved the mat closer.

I batted it away. "*You* read them if you're so wise." Yellow Face flinched and swallowed. Her larynx was an ugly thing to watch. And I realized: She was ashamed of being illiterate. She thought herself flawed, less than me, and was deeply humiliated by it.

The epiphany made me surly.

"Liver," I growled out.

"Ah." Yellow Face said, blinking at the stained sleeping mat. "Well. Liv-her it is."

I felt soiled then. Not only by my surliness, not only by my lie that had in one flippant word condemned someone to the name of an organ, but by Yellow Face's readiness to believe me.

I overcompensated for my spite by naming Liv-her's companion Orchid.

But whereas Yellow Face had accepted the name of an organ without serious doubt, she utterly balked at that of a flower. "Ridiculous. Read it again, Zar-shi."

"Orc-hid," I muttered. "It says Orc-hid."

I rose to my feet and strode from the oppressive heat of the attic, hiding for the rest of the morning in the rotunda, where I groomed Old Maht with unusual vigor.

Beauty remained in the attic that day and all throughout that week.

She ate nothing but what I gave her under the cover of night, and I begrudged her each mouthful but was too cowardly to refuse her anything. I didn't want Kiz-dan knowing the part I'd played in the loss of her girl. Oh, no, I did not.

Yellow Face suspected someone was feeding Beauty. Despite her increasing lethargy, Beauty was not as weak as a starving person held prisoner in an airless attic during the height of Fire Season should be. By the end of the first week, Yellow Face watched me like a bull its prey.

The two young women we'd initiated recovered. We discovered they were Beauty's cousins, sent to us as companions for Beauty. Beauty only resented their presence. She did nothing to comfort them during their convalescence, merely skulked about the attic, helping Kiz-dan when boredom drove her to such a kindness.

She never tried to leave the attic, though. The resentment among the onais over Beauty's continued refusal to be cleansed ensured her obedience, for Yellow Face had told us to stone Beauty if she should step with her unclean feet upon our dragon-blessed soil.

I could see in the parched, sunburnt faces around me that many would readily obey the injunction.

Meanwhile, Kiz-dan and her baby grew stronger. The boy was uncommonly quiet, content to suckle at his mother's breast and sleep. When Kiz-dan was not sleeping alongside him in the cool of the rotunda during daylight, or languidly making the conical bamboo-and-reed hats we wore in the rain, she was fondly watching him nestled at her breasts. She spent hours gazing in wonder at him. Yellow Face was not pleased by such squandering of time. She announced one evening that on the morrow, Kiz-dan would return to the hemp fields.

Everyone protested vehemently. Taken aback by so much dissent, Yellow Face, red-faced and stammering, retracted her announcement.

Kiz-dan and her baby were the darlings of our convent, see. The old onais couldn't keep away from him, constantly touching his tiny fingers and caressing his fattening thighs, even holding his feet to their noses and inhaling deeply, tears running down their cheeks.

And throughout all that—my stealthy visits to Beauty, nuts and peppers hidden under my skirts; the hoeing and pruning and washing and dragon care and millwork—I refused to sleep at nights.

Could not, would not. *Dared* not. I feared the choking might of my mother's haunt, with its taste as jelly-cold and greasy as death. Understand, the unwholesome thing was as elusive yet powerful as that: a flavor, lingering in memory and leaving a nasty aftertaste as it receded, threatening to return should I so much as close my eyes.

So I kept myself awake at night by pacing or weaving or pulling extra night watch in the rotunda. I did this vigilantly and fearfully, dreading each sunset from the moment the sun rose.

I was soon a shattered wreck.

I startled at any sound. Had difficulty keeping my food down. Couldn't hold things properly, couldn't judge distances. My vision blurred. My ears seemed bunged. I couldn't make the most rudimentary decisions, such as which food bowl in a line of bowls to use. I walked in a shuffle and stumbled every fourth step. Cold sweats and nausea alternated with hot flushes.

I began to doze off.

When I knelt in the garden to dig up kadoob tubers, or when I prostrated before a kuneus during obeisance, my eyes closed without me. I had no recollection of them closing, experienced no transition from wakefulness to sleep. I only knew I'd plummeted into slumber when I woke screaming, the chill sensation of Mother's gamy haunt receding from my body.

My screams drew shrieks from everyone, startled the macaws that seethed over the limestone cliffs behind us. Great red clouds of them boiled into the sky with each of my cries, screeching and showering us with crimson down. Crimson feathers formed like mist over the waterfall pool, over the mill wheel, over the hemp fields. Blood dripped from my nose. The onais muttered blood curses to ward off evil. The bats stopped roosting in the rotunda.

One morning, I fell asleep while hoeing.

Standing upright, I was, under a sun that penetrated my bark-cloth hat and set my head to pulsating. I was awake one moment, dully scratching at the dry earth, and the next moment I was asleep.

I landed hard on my face. The impact not so much roused me as befuddled my stupor.

Someone turned me over. A head and broad-brimmed hat blotted out the unrelenting sun in the blinding white sky. Strong arms propped me up, and hands smelling of green weeds and dust pushed a leather bladder against my lips.

"Drink this. All of it."

The bag tipped up. Cool water filled my mouth. I swallowed.

The bag tipped more. I swallowed more. The bag tipped, I swallowed, it tipped, I swallowed. . . .

. . . And coughed. Spluttered as a bitter burning grew like fungus in my mouth and throat. I jerked away, knowing at once from the acerbic flavor of limes and licorice that I'd swallowed diluted venom mixed with sleeping herbs.

"You . . . you . . . " The words congealed in my throat. My eyes focused on the water bearer. Nnp-trn.

"I refuse to listen to your shrieks and babbling one more night," she said quite reasonably, as if discussing the planting of tubers. "This should put you out till the morn after tomorrow."

I gaped up at her, a toothy shadow surrounded by blinding white light, and fear sizzled in my ears like rain against hot embers. I couldn't fall asleep. What had she done? To sleep was to be embalmed alive by my mother's haunt. . . .

Sleep caught me in thick, doughy arms.

I dreamed of color. Of liquid glazes and glass tesserae. Of flavors blood laden and tart. I dreamed of the dusky emotions provoked by the long-gone acolyte. I dreamed in disjointed sensations.

Not once did my mother's haunt defile me.

A barrier shimmered around me the whole while, moist and blue veined, gray and translucent, smelling like salty sun-warmed leather, though slightly rank like a dragon's hide. Even in my sleep I intuited that it was keeping the haunt away, the smell, that taste, those dreams. The venom.

Yes, yes. Somehow, the diluted venom slipping through my blood had created a living membrane round my essence that the haunt could not breach.

But how it tried. It battered itself against the membrane, hurling its vague, clawed shape against the blue-veined wall. Frantic, it was, and wrathful. It howled, an eerie sound too like the atonal, wavering noise produced by the monks' ceremonial water bowls at that Mombe Taro of my ninth year, when I'd first touched venom. Howling. Howling. Uselessly tearing at the membrane with hooked talons, its claws rasping across the surface . . .

But the venom held me safe.

There was no stopping me after that. I needed venom.

I stole it first from Old Maht, scraped it from his mouth with my snake pole and dropped the viscous black stuff into a leather pouch under my skirts, carried just for that purpose. After a little trial and error, I discovered how much water was needed to dilute the stuff to make it potable. Too strong and I'd vomit for days and suffer uncontrollable bouts of diarrhea, which made me as popular as when I'd shrieked without warning during the silence of midnight. Too weak and my mother's haunt could slice her talons through my translucent gray shield. When that happened, when she breached my shell . . .

Well. Terror *can* be a benefactor. I'd wake sweat drenched and writhing, screaming fit to raise the mildewed skeletons of the dead onais scattered about our convent. Old Voe-too took to sleeping beside me, and would whack me with a chamber pot to shut me up.

So I quickly learned the exact water-to-venom ratio and stuck by it zealously.

But a new problem arose. As the Season of Fire tapered toward its end, the venom from Old Maht no longer sufficed. I needed a stronger venom base.

I began to groom Lutche on the sly.

Throughout those long days and humid nights, I worked in a semilucid, hallucinatory state similar to that induced by the mosquito sickness, but without its unpleasant nausea and fever.

Kiz-dan's baby plumped up like a brooder. He went unnamed; was referred to merely as "the baby." To name him would acknowledge his permanence, would remind Yellow Face of his gender. Of castration.

None of us wanted him castrated.

Odd, that, hey? We could so readily pin down a grown woman and cut away from her something profound, yet we recoiled at the thought of slicing off something that a child, by dint of its infancy, might grow up never realizing the lack of, especially when surrounded by women.

But it wasn't only the idea of the cutting that disturbed us; it was the reality that lay behind the deed. No one knew how to do it. It might kill the child.

So Kiz-dan worked far from Yellow Face's presence and became quiet, obedient, and nigh on invisible. She was not the Kiz-dan I'd known, though I was fond of her still in a nostalgic, jealous way. She had grown into her age, had left me and our pranks and quarrels and insubordination behind.

Everyone tacitly aided Kiz-dan's invisibility by washing the boy's swaddlings out of Yellow Face's sight, by never speaking of him while in her earshot, and by going to extreme lengths to keep him happy and quiet when she was about. It was a blessing the boy was so passive.

Nnp-trn dandled him most frequently.

As for Beauty, the trick Nnp-trn had played upon me—offering drug-laced water when my thirst was at a peak and my wits at a valley—Yellow Face played upon Beauty. In retrospect, I believe Yellow Face waited as long as she did not to see if she could break Beauty's will, but because she was overwhelmed by the responsibility of being convent elder. Once her innate bossiness resurfaced, it stayed but good: Yellow Face commanded Tieron Nask Cinai, and we knew it.

I was there for Beauty's cutting. I did not vomit, though I closed my eyes and hummed loudly, teeth gritted. The whole thing ended swiftly, for the emaciated young lady beneath Yellow Face's knife lay still as one dead.

When presented with the bloody stain from her sleeping mat to interpret, I named her Ohd-sli, a name I'd prechosen after long deliberation.

I knew she could read, see, as she'd said so herself, and I was trying to buy her continued silence concerning my part in the loss of Kiz-dan's girl.

Ohd-sli means nothing, of course. It is a sound, as meaningless as the names of all onais. According to convention, the name of a holy woman has to be comprised of two syllables, each formed by a three-stroke hieratic character. That number in our names—six—reminds us we are deficient on two counts, not worthy even in our written names to approach the sacred number 8. Firstly, we're deficient because we are human and not dragon. Secondly, we are female.

The two three-stroke characters that represent the sound Ohd-sli— the open mouth of the O and the tongue slipping behind the teeth for the slick *sli*—look like the stamen in a fluted heliconia. A strong, sensual image, reminiscent of something very human and not so very holy.

I hoped Ohd-sli would enjoy the irony of a holy woman bearing such an erotic name, hoped she would appreciate my subtle insubordination in giving it to her.

Hoped she would continue her silence concerning Kiz-dan's lost child.

When Nae-ser heard the name, she mouthed it silently, forming the hieratic characters in her head. Realization dawned. She stiffened and flushed. Later that day, she called me over on a pretext of helping lift the basket of rocks she'd sifted from the garden.

"This once only, Zar-shi. Understand? Such a prank could slay us all with an auditor's scythe. *They* know how to write, remember."

I muttered acquiescence.

What made me first try to tip my venom-laced brew down Ohd-sli's long, smooth throat? Fear? Infatuation? Equal measures of both, I think. Lust is, after all, a sort of fearful anticipation.

"What is it?" she snarled when I first offered my bowl of venom brew to her lips.

I'd carried the bowl under my skirts precisely for that moment, had planned it days before. My trembling hands sent little waves over the surface of the transparent gel within.

We stood at the base of the limestone cliffs, alone with the odious chore of collecting soiled feathers from the guano-coated rhododendrons growing in clumps in the cliff's shade. The Wet was drawing close, and feathers needed to be collected, washed, dried, and stuffed into the padded vests we wore on cold monsoon nights.

"Drink it. You'll like it, I think," I said, proffering my bowl again.

"Don't presume to know what I like and don't like, grub." Ohd-sli bent and sniffed the brew. The spicy sweetness of patchouli clung to her, even after several months. I inhaled the scent through an open mouth, wanting to taste it.

She reared back, a beautiful yearling full of verve and mistrust. "You want to drug me for what purpose, hey-o?"

"It's not like the sleeping draft Yellow Face mixes. There's no herbs in here. Look, see?" I dipped a finger in the gel. It clung to my skin, formed a peak as I withdrew my finger from the bowl. It dangled from my finger like a thick, dew-speckled strand of spider silk. Clear and lovely.

I inserted it into my mouth, sucked my finger clean. Closed my eyes and savored the instant burn, the tongue-shriveling tartness, the woozy warmth that rushed into my ears and set my eyes itching and nose running and body thrumming. My lungs turned warm and heavy.

I opened my eyes. Ohd-sli was studying me.

"It looks like the poultice Yellow Face healed me with," she finally said.

She'd called her Yellow Face, not Yin-gik. Delight burst into goose-flesh on my arms.

I nodded. "Without the aloe and medicinal herbs. This is pure."

A gust of wind dragged a heavy cloud across the sun and blew spray from the waterfall over us.

"That look on your face when you swallowed that stuff, my cousin looked like that always," she murmured, eyes going distant. "He was a Temple acolyte, trained to be a venom milker. He died young. Rumor has it, from drinking too much of that crap."

She nodded at my bowl.

I shrugged. "I'm careful about how much I use. Come on, try some. Just a little."

"Why?"

Because I'm afraid of you, I wanted to say. Because I need you to be as beholden to me as I am to you.

I shrugged again. "It helps."

A muscle in her jaw twitched and she looked away, toward the mill on its rocky hillock below us, the crumbling, mossy rotunda beside it, the brown, stubble-studded emptiness of our recently harvested hemp field.

"I should have left," she said softly. "Become ebani to some lordling. To a city soldier, even. To a mercenary."

She was talking about the womanhood Yellow Face had carved from her.

"This helps," I said again, and lifted the bowl once more. A drop of rain fell on the center of the gel and slid in a perfect bead to the rim.

"And will it turn me into a shambling, grinning fool like it did my cousin? Like it's doing to you?" she said coldly, turning back to me.

Is *that* how she saw me? I gaped, defenseless.

"I'm not going to be like these ugly crones," she growled. "That's all they are: frustrated old women reduced to straddling dying bulls for pleasure, under the guise of grooming them."

"No."

She snorted. "I've seen them dip their snake poles down dragon throats and lick off the venom to ease their aches and abscesses. Don't think I haven't. That's why the eldest of them groom the most potent kuneus. Its got nothing to do with seniority and honor, and everything to do with needing the strongest venom available. You're turning just like them, sucking up that stuff, and you don't even know it."

Her tirade flushed blood into her lips, swelling them taut and ochre. Rain pattered on us, shivering the dry rhododendrons behind us. Beads of water sparkled on her cropped, glossy black hair like drops of venom gel.

I felt stupid.

All that time I'd fastidiously groomed Old Maht, believing it my place and that when I was worthy enough, I would groom Lutche or temperamental Ka instead. I'd believed in that hierarchy because that's what I'd been taught.

I'd been duped. During her few months among us, Ohd-sli had discerned the real reason behind the dragon-grooming hierarchy of Convent Tieron, and it dawned on me then that the already weakened venom of an old bull *could* be consumed without being diluted in water. . . . Once one had habituated oneself to it, as the old onais in our convent obviously had. Over the years.

I came back with the only retort I could think of.

"You're too prudish to try it, that's all."

Her eyes slowly widened. She threw back her head and laughed. Rain caressed her cheeks. "Yolk-brained twit!"

I loved her laughter, so bawdy and baritone, how it exposed her neck to my hungry gaze. I knew what it would taste like, that neck, all sweet and petal-soft beneath my lips, and I wanted to bruise it with my mouth. Bite into it and feast.

I loved her laughter, yes, but I did not like being laughed at.

"Prude!" I yelled, furious and close to tears.

"You understand nothing," she said. "You're an idiot."

My cheeks flamed and I sputtered for words.

"I have a *child*," she hissed, "a beautiful little boy with chestnut eyes and glossy hair and a hand that fits perfectly in my own. I have a lover, a mansion, closets of gowns, and stores of friends. And here I am in this filth, picking shit-coated feathers off bushes with a grub like you."

"You think you're so special?" I roared. "Take away your gowns and fancy friends and you're just like me."

"You don't look beyond this moment, this day, the next month! As long as you have venom to suck, you're content as a vulture feasting on carrion."

"Words, words, words, that's all you are!"

"I have dreams," she cried. "I *think*."

"Humping your claimer's brother required thought?"

I braced for a slap, for nails, for teeth. She only began sobbing. I left her there and returned to the mill.

TWENTY

The Wet began in earnest.

A deluge greeted us each morn, high winds and rain squalls each noon, thunderstorms each night. Over the next several days, I spent a great deal of time on the mill roof, plugging leaks and replacing blown-off tiles.

Never once did I forget Ohd-sli's words: *You don't look beyond this moment, this day, the next month! As long as you have venom to suck, you're content as a vulture feasting on carrion.*

Weeks passed. The rain didn't stop. The downpour swelled the waterfall behind us into a thundering torrent. We sloshed through calf-deep mud to reach the garden and the rotunda. We hauled the renimgar hutch inside to save our last breeding pairs. The whole while, Ohd-sli's words slithered and swam inside me, as unwanted as liver flukes. As I coughed and shivered and hacked up blood, as I plunged waist deep into roiling cold waters to clean pounding debris out the waterway locks, those words ate at me.

Because they were true.

I *didn't* look beyond one day or the next. I made no plans, had no aspirations.

How could I? Since the age of nine I'd lived on the verge of starvation, haunted at nights by a dead woman's obsession that had taken on a life of its own and would consume me if I let it; by day battling fevers and weather while sifting stones from ground that refused to grow more than contorted tubers.

Dreaming, planning; that required more energy than I had. More hope than I could manufacture. It demanded belief in tomorrow, belief in oneself.

But if pressed . . .

. . . If really pushed . . .

. . . Maybe I could find a tiny seed of a notion lodged under the rock of my heart, on the infertile ground of my spirit, born from the conversations I'd overheard between drunken pottery clan men so many, many years ago, and all the injustice I had witnessed in my life thus far.

But it was a fantasy, that thought. No, it was worse than fantasy. It was a hopeless yearning for an impossibility.

To mention it to Ohd-sli would shatter it into nothingness.

Voe-too. Ron-sin. Yac-sor. Fri-bet and Koh-sei from the Grim Cluster. Rin-mes. Ras-aun. Orc-hid. They all died.

The coughing sickness struck us all, aged and young alike. No one slept for the hacking in the attic.

How it rained and rained and rained.

Our dried and hoarded dragon dung sprouted growth, the air was so humid, so we ate kadoob raw, at first washed and scraped, then later with mud still caked on the skins. We ate our last renimgars uncooked.

Our sodden clothes stank of mildew. Our flesh grew puffy from damp. Fissures striated the skin between our toes, on our thighs, our groins and underarms, the napes of our necks. Night watch and obeisance went unobserved.

The waterfall pool flooded. Our ground floor lay ankle deep underwater, and packets of mosquito eggs floated thickly on its murky surface.

We couldn't tend the garden; it was a lake. Our hemp fields, an ocean.

Huddled up in the attic, the lot of us fought death. We ventured out only to drag a pitiful offering of unmashed jungle weeds to the lowing, desperately hungry kuneus, or to fish rotting kadoobs from the submerged garden, or to empty chamber pots into the lake of filth floating about us.

To Kiz-dan, we gave the most food. She ate without hesitation or guilt, determined to keep up her milk supply for her babe. But he drank a great deal and bawled constantly for more. Too many mosquito bites peppered his body. Some of them leaked pus. We all feared for his life.

It was a Wet like we'd never experienced before, a season that gave us not a day of respite, not an hour without rain.

The strongest of us worked ceaselessly, rinsing out soiled blankets, wringing them as dry as we could, hanging them in hopes they would dry a little before they were next used, but due to diarrhea and bloody sputum, they were always required while still wet. We drank venom openly, frequently, and tipped it down the throats of the ill in place of medicinal drafts.

I, too, drank it. Undiluted. Straight from the dragons' tongues. Over the months, I'd unwittingly immunized myself to gastrointestinal upset through my ever more potent mixtures of venom; drinking venom full-strength now caused little discomfort. But within weeks, I became habituated to the potency of full-strength venom, craved something stronger, thought of a dragon's tongue between my thighs and how such an invasion, upon the delicate tissues of my womb, might fulfill my need, take me to that peak that consumption of an old bull's venom could no longer take me.

And, too, I wondered what the venom of a bull in its prime might do for me. Not that I had much time or energy to indulge in such thoughts.

Ohd-sli and I worked side by side, our spat buried but not forgotten. We slashed jungle vines and wrote frantic scrolls to the Ranreeb. We hiked to the cairn down the treacherous path that had become a rock-churning stream, and we left our precious bamboo-enclosed pleas for traveling merchants to deliver.

No merchants came.

After the third heel-splitting, chest-burning foray to the cairn, we stopped going. All our bamboo-enclosed scrolls rested untouched on the cairn. No one was traveling.

I think all of us would have died that season if the death of one more convent resident had not occurred. It kept us alive, that death, though it set into motion events that altered Tieron forever.

Old Maht died.

And we ate him.

*   *   *

"We have to do this quickly, before the hide is ruined by water," Yellow Face shouted.

Beneath her conical rain hat she looked wild and half dead, her eyes enormous sunken orbs, her skin so yellow she glowed. In the gloom of dawn, she stood over the body of Old Maht and brandished her flensing knife at Ohd-sli, Nnp-trn, and I. Rain hammered mercilessly against our sodden capes. We stood ankle deep in water.

"We have to be careful, hey! No foolishness, Zar-shi. The hide *must* be taken off in one piece." She knelt on Old Maht's neck and began slicing into the puckered flesh around his antennae. "Remove the wings while I sever these. Move now, don't stand there gawping. This has to be done!"

She sounded near hysterical.

Her frenzy transmitted itself to us. Nnp-trn and Ohd-sli jumped forward and began cutting into Old Maht, slipping their knives into the unplated hollows near his neck where the stout wing bones were attached to his shoulder girdle. I clambered over Old Maht's stubby forelegs and grasped a portion of one leathery wing, and I moved the slick tent of a thing up and down to permit them access above and below it. The spidery claws at the end of his wings had curled in on themselves in death. They looked too much like the curled fingers of an infant.

A ripple of empathy shivered over me.

Even though I'd never worshipped Old Maht as divine, and even though I was feverish with hunger and illness, I pitied the beast. He'd once been a proud bull, an impressive creature with a forty-foot wingspan. Years of being grounded in the rotunda had withered his once magnificent wings to a quarter of their original size and reduced the sharp wingtip claws to curled twigs.

Never had Old Maht escaped his roofless prison.

But he'd known freedom had yawned just above his head. He'd stared at the sky ceaselessly, until in his illness, he'd stared only at the ground. By then, he'd been unable to even fold his withered wings along his sides. They'd dragged over the floor like dirty rags, the wingtip claws scratching against the slate like bones, a sad look in his wise old eyes.

Not for the first time, I hoped the look had not been indicative of his intelligence. Better to believe the beast dumb than a sentient, imprisoned creature.

We removed one wing, then the other, slicing down the length of his body where the wing membrane joined his torso. Reduced to his elliptical body, Old Maht looked naked and obscene.

The hammering rain lightened to a sharp drizzle.

At Yellow Face's order, we sliced two wide swathes of leather from each of his wings. She carefully wrapped that leather round the antennae and placed the bundle on a stone.

"Roll him over," Yellow Face cried. Kuneus Ka bellowed at the sound of her voice.

We heaved and strained and used sodden, rotting ropes to roll the carcass over. The body made a spongy noise as we exposed the belly to the sky.

Old Maht was not so big, laid out like that. If three of us lay head to heel alongside him, and we removed his long, thin tail, we'd match his length. His exposed belly reached my chest, his legs, flopped over at the knees, were forehead height.

I felt profoundly weary, profoundly cold.

Yellow Face crouched on her haunches near Old Maht's head and ran a calloused hand over his scintillating, scaly hide.

First she cut from his neck to the root of his long, thin tail, slicing straight down his sternum, right through the leathery black folds of his retracted penis.

"Feed the tail to Ka, Zar-shi. Shut him up. The Ranreeb doesn't require it."

I leaned hard with my knife into the thin, bony rods of the tail, trying to sever it from the carcass. It made a nasty cracking sound. A blister formed on my thumb while sawing through the gristle round the tail root.

Reluctantly, I approached Ka with the thing. Although Statute stated that only a dragon could eat of dragon flesh, and although a dragon was partial to meat despite the bulk of its diet being plants, I disliked the thought of feeding Ka the tail of one of his brethren. But hunger had removed the sad intelligence that always shone in the old bull's eye, replaced by a desperate, primitive glint, and his great arrowed snout shot forward and ripped Old Maht's tail from my hands even as I stood there in indecision.

Ka tried to swallow the tail whole, neck muscles working, eyes bulging, antennae flat along his bony skull. He choked and gagged but refused to retch it up. I left him to his frenzy, the sight of Old Maht's tail dangling from his mouth sickening and saddening me, the small diamond-shaped membrane at the end flapping against Ka's snout as if alive.

It was hard work separating Old Maht's hide from his forelimbs, his breast, his shoulder girdle, his hind limbs. We tugged and sliced, separating the glistening white connective tissue under his hide from his pale rose flesh.

My mouth began to water, my belly growl. I'd eaten naught but jungle weeds for the last several weeks.

Slowly, reluctantly, the beautiful hide came away with a raspy tearing. Even in death, even in the rainy gloom, those green-and-dark-purple scales shimmered as if they were polished emeralds and amethysts. I wept from the hollow beauty of them.

Then we began to eat.

Without looking at each other, pretending not to see, we slipped with shaking fingers tongues of flesh into our mouths and greedily sucked fatty tissue from our palms as we continued to work, cutting the carcass into slabs we could easily carry, slabs that would later be fed to Lutche and Ka.

Or so we told ourselves. That those slabs of rich meat were bound for the dragons' bellies, and not our own.

But as I worked, trembling with hunger, shaking with the horror of what I could not stop myself from doing—I was consuming the flesh of a deity, the penalty for which was death and torture forever after in the Celestial Realm of the Dragon, but, oh! how hungry I was, and, oh! how good the meat—I knew, I knew: Those slabs of flesh would be served to our starving, dying sisters lying in the mill attic.

Flecks of flesh spattered my face, my cape, my bark-clothed calves. My forearms glistened with blood and fat. I felt blessed by what Old Maht was giving me. Food. Life. Hope.

We cut the flesh from the bones, careful not to nick them, as they were bound for the Ranreeb. The bones were light and delicate, most of them hollow, and those that were not had tunnels running through them. Seeing those delicate, hollow bones, I had difficulty remembering Old Maht as the solid creature he'd seemed in life. How fragile and slight his construction looked when exposed by knife and machete.

We filled a wheelbarrow with meat. Another barrow we filled with organs: liver, kidneys, heart, the complex air sacs of his lungs. The stomach with its reeking brown contents went into a third wheelbarrow, along with talons, penis, rectum, bladder, the corrugated neck dewlaps where once Maht stored his food. His oily black venom sacks.

Even his brain we pulled out. So large his skull looked in proportion to his body, yet I could see how very light was the skull's construction; thin spars of bone connecting the braincase, the eye sockets, the jaws.

Darkness descended. It had taken the four of us an entire day to butcher the carcass.

Old Maht was reduced to meat slabs and disconnected bones, parts of an aged, delicate whole. I saw again Boj-est's head sliding face-first into jungle humus.

"We're the same," Ohd-sli murmured beside me in something like awe, though her face was a mask of horror as she stared at the wheelbarrows' contents. "The lot of us. We all look like that under the skin."

Yes. Yes, we did. Rishi and bayen alike.

"I *do* think," I said then, and I laid a cold, bloody hand over hers. "I think about owning a bull dragon. That's what I want, beyond this day, beyond next month. A bull dragon, and a yearling to pair it to. My own Clutch."

My words stemmed from an unacknowledged dream born from all I had experienced, overheard, and witnessed in my childhood.

She didn't reply.

There was no answer sufficient.

Inside the mill again, we set about building a fire.

While Yellow Face whittled shavings from one of the heavy cedar coffers of Ohd-sli's dowry, Nnp-trn and I used large, wet stones to smash apart two other coffers in the attic. Ohd-sli collapsed into a sodden puddle alongside her hacking cousin and fell asleep, over-come, it would seem, by the destruction of her coffers, the last me-mentos of her previous life.

We carried our shavings and cedar boards down to the flooded ground floor and slogged through the sludge of dissolved dragon dung and mosquito eggs to the millstone. We clambered upon that pitted, stained island, and while Nnp-trn and I shielded the shavings from wind and damp, Yellow Face over and over struck gray flint against hard stone.

Finally, a spark.

How we cajoled and wheedled it, desperate for the little thing to flare into life in our shavings.

It did not.

Around midnight, the three of us were so cold and stiff and stupid with fatigue that we functioned without thought.

"Give it to me," I croaked at last, the licorice-lime buzzing of the venom I'd licked straight from Old Maht's stiff tongue wearing thin. "Give it."

Yellow Face's head wobbled as if it were not connected, merely bal-anced on her neck. Without looking at me, she handed the flint stone over.

I opened myself up then. Willed my mother's haunt to enter me. She could light anything, my mother, no matter how wet. I'd watched her do so a hundred times.

I thought of her, called out to her in my mind. Remembered the clay-rich scent of her and the soft-skinned touch of her. Envi-sioned the shimmering blue wall of protection the venom had cre-ated about me, envisioned the sharp talons of mother's haunt ripping through them. Shredding, breaching, reaching out for me . . .

Quick as the roaring, board-splintering rush of floodwater bursting apart a dam, my mother's haunt smashed into me. A maelstrom of emotions swirled in the turbid aura about her: wild love, profound relief, fury, remorse, forgiveness, guilt, apprehension, hope, need. It surged through my torso and down my limbs, memories of danku Re life churning like so much flotsam and jetsam in the turbulence. It spewed from my mouth in a long-drawn howl, it gushed from my nose in a flood of blood, it burst from my fingertips in flame.

Not just a spark, that, but great tongues of flame, instantly charring the cedar shavings to ash. Nnp-trn and Yellow Face fell back, shielding their faces with their arms, and the fire roared from my fingers, blazing hot against the millstone, scorching its surface black.

"On the wood!" Nnp-trn shrieked, and the haunt swung my arms, stiff as the limbs of a corpse, toward the splintered planks Nnp-trn and I had carried down from the attic.

Whoosh! The fire roared up to the underbelly of the second floor, and if the timbers and plaster and interwoven twigs had not been saturated with damp, the mill would have burst into flame. The walls turned bright as day from the blaze, brighter even, for not a shadow danced in the light, and the lake of floodwater turned silver as steel and reflected heat and light back at me.

"Enough!" Yellow Face cried, hugging my calves. "You'll kill us all!"

That was a thought.

How easy it would be to turn my flame-hurling fingers upon Yellow Face, upon Nnp-trn, upon the Grim Cluster. Upon haughty Ohdsli, upon every single onai within those walls. It would be a mercy to release them from their misery. Then I could search for Waisi, find my girl, explain to her, protect her. . . .

"No!" I howled, feeling betrayed and forsaken anew.

I tried to wrench my arms from the haunt's clawed grasp, but it was as if I were fighting hobbles. My arms would not move how I wanted, and as I struggled, my fingers shot flame into the floodwater, set it boiling and hissing. Clouds of steam roiled through the air. I couldn't breathe, was choking on wet heat, couldn't see for the blistering fog. . . .

Later, I learned it was Yellow Face who caught me as I fell unconscious to the floor, a floor as dry and clean as if it were the middle of Fire Season, and not a rain cloud in sight.

Outside, the rain finally stopped.

TWENTY-ONE

"**H**e's coming, isn't he?" Yellow Face said flatly. "That's what it says."

I stared at the creamy scroll in my hands, unraveled it to its full length, seeking protection, assurance, forgiveness. My coarse skin rasped over the smooth paper like a burr against cotton wool. Hieratics undulated in columns down the scroll's length. The black cursive characters exuded oversweet musk; the ink had been ground with incense.

Yes, Yellow Face was right. His Esteemed Excellency, the Ranreeb of the Jungle Crown, was coming to visit Tieron Nask Cinai, along with an Eight Swarm Host of Temple Auditors.

The hide and antennae we'd sent back to him, along with some few details of what we had lost during the Wet, "provoked serious concerns within His Esteemed Excellency." We were instructed to prepare at once for Temple's arrival, and an inspection by an appointed Host.

We'd cured the hide as best we could, had sent it with a passing merchant as soon as the thick mud in the jungle had dried enough to permit travel. Ohd-sli, Lec-wey, Atl-eri, and I had camped down at the cairn for six days, awaiting the first merchant to pass. Unpleased to see us, he'd surlily accepted our woven-reed crate with its holy contents. He couldn't refuse. Temple business.

"Nothing was our fault," I said, looking up at Yellow Face. "We did the best we could."

"He's coming," she repeated again.

"We shouldn't have sent the hide at all. Should never have reported Old Maht's death. We could've kept up the deception for years before it was discovered—"

"We've had this argument before, Zar-shi," Yellow Face said

wearily. "The hide would not have kept well in our conditions. Our deception would have been discovered by the hide's very state when we eventually sent it."

"We could have tanned it—"

"Enough. The hide of a dragon must be treated a certain way, else it loses its scales. The art is known by few. I'll argue this with you no longer."

She was right, and I knew it. But the knowledge galled me. What galled me more was her expression.

I knew by her stricken look that she was thinking about the cauldrons of rich, brown dragon stew every onai in Tieron Nask Cinai had consumed more than a month ago. I knew by the way her fingers drummed against her thigh that she was thinking of Kiz-dan's boy baby. I knew by the fluttering of her pulse, visible in her stringy neck, that she was thinking of the bloodshot eyes of every onai, and the amount of undiluted venom we all daily imbibed as of late, to impart the strength necessary for rebuilding our lives.

So many shared transgressions, all within a single season.

"Temple doesn't have to know," I whispered urgently, though I needn't have whispered. We stood alone in the attic, her at one end, I at the other. The smell of unfurling citrus ferns was sharp even through the walls. Outside, the immovable fog of the Inbetween enclosed everything in its embrace. Each day, the air grew warmer.

It should have been a time of hope, of sowing seeds and expectation. Not a time of dread.

"No one will say anything, not even the Grim Cluster. We *all* ate the meat," I pressed on.

"Temple Statute forbids any but a dragon to consume dragon flesh," she said, and her tone and look terrified me.

"No one has to know."

Her glazed look cleared. Her fingers stopped drumming. "The baby will have to go, Zar-shi."

"Kiz-dan and I can hide with him in the jungle until they leave."

"And after the convent is purged? Where then?"

My heart hammered against my chest, made me breathless. "Don't talk that way."

"It will happen."

"They won't behead us all because of one ruined hide!"

She turned away, wrapped her arms about her elbows. Stared at a wall as if it were a window she was looking out.

"I don't mind the dying, Zar-shi," she whispered. "It's the living that would be hardest. Living without venom."

"Nonsense." Even as I said it, I understood.

"You've never felt the intimate touch of a dragon's tongue. You don't know what it's like, the potency, the transcendence. It creates a need that makes *your* dependence upon venom look paltry."

I opened my mouth to snap that I wasn't dependent upon the stuff. . . . But then closed my lips again. Everyone in the convent was, at that point, dependent upon venom to some degree. We'd used the stuff too liberally, too often, during the last few devastating months.

After a moment, I asked what I hadn't had the courage to ask before, fearing the answer.

"Why? Why do it . . . that way?"

She looked me straight in the eyes. "I think you know the answer, Zar-shi. How do you feel when you take venom? What passions does it provoke in you?"

A flush stained my cheeks. Even remembering the surge of elation, of desire and passion, that swept over me each time I drank undiluted venom caused my nipples to harden and my heart to quicken.

"It's not mere ugly human passion, child. It's something more. It's divine. And when you lie before a bull, when he takes you in that most intimate of ways . . . you become one. For a brief moment, you become the dragon, hear echoes of its thoughts."

"What"—I licked dry lips, cleared my throat—"what would the venom of a potent dragon do?"

Slowly, a beatific smile lighted her face. "If one were accustomed to venom, such as I, no pustules would form from a potent dragon's venom. No fatal convulsions would result. Only momentary transcendence. Pure, perfect transcendence to the Celestial Realm, while one still lived and breathed in mortal form. It's what I've lived to experience ever since discovering the secret rite."

"Discovering."

She shrugged. "It was passed on to me. From Boj-est. And to her from another onai, and so on from time immemorial."

"It's . . . just sex. Deviant sex."

She snorted, looked at me with disgust and pity. "Don't equate what we do with tawdry human wranglings. Not till you experience it yourself. Don't you dare."

"So you have something to live for, yes?" I said, for I had provoked her into this argument not just to assuage my own morbid curiosity about the reasons why she participated in her "secret rites," but to stir some fight back into her.

"You want to one day lie before a potent dragon, be it a bull or a female with venom sacs intact," I pressed, walking toward her, closing the gap. "So stop talking as if we're defeated, as if we can't help ourselves. Prepare everyone, make sure our accounts match, that every onai agrees not to speak of what we ate during the Wet. And those who don't agree, those who find a need to confess our sins into Temple ears . . . " My voice trailed off.

Silence. Yellow Face's expression turned hard.

"Say it," she commanded.

"We kill them," I whispered, though it sounded like a roar, a bellow, the susurration of a thousand butterfly wings.

"How?"

"I don't know. There are ways."

"A knife? Between the ribs, across the neck? When would it be done? In the dead of night, in the jungle during the day? Who would do it, and who would know about it? What of the body?"

"We don't know that we'd even have to . . . do it. I'm just saying that we have to prepare. And make plans. And . . . and . . . not expect the worst."

She looked back at the wall.

"Then you can lie before Lutche again," I said, feeling desperate. "Or Ka. Both in one night, if you want. You can't give up. Fight for our lives, Yin-gik."

"Not you," she murmured, and I had to strain to catch her words. I could hear the scraping of hoes against rock outside and the heavy rasp of koorfowsi rim maht bundles being dragged over ground. But I could barely hear her words. "Yin-gik is not who I am. Never was. Better the name Yellow Face. At least that has meaning."

I stood there in stupid silence and wondered for the first time who she had been prior to Tieron.

"Go find Ohd-sli," she said, still staring at the wall. But her voice was different now. Had reverted to its bossy sting. "Bring her here. Time we utilized those fine alliances of hers."

• • •

For the eyes of Bayen Dinwat of Ginkison Mansion, Iri Timadu Bayen Sor, the Zone of Most Exalted Aristocrats, Clutch Xxamer Zu.

Most Judicious Claimer, greetings.

I write you in a state of contrition and despair.

I have missed you this last half-year. Lest you think my words insincere, let me assure you the arduous life here and the intimate physical loss I have suffered have permitted me to view my time in your household with painful clarity, and I realize now how wanton was my behavior, how contemptible my treatment of your name. Why is it we despise that which we depend upon most?

I cannot ask for your forgiveness. I don't deserve it. Nor do I ask you to take me back, for in my present state I am made unlovely by a holy knife. But I will not prevaricate concerning the desperate plight in which I and my fellow onais find ourselves.

This last season was extremely hard. Eight of us died from the coughing sickness, one of my poor cousins included. A flood from a nearby water source ruined all our food stores, our garden, and fields, and swept away tools and fuel. Despite our desperate efforts, the most aged kuneus in residency died, and the hide which we are of course expected to prepare for His Esteemed Excellency, the Ranreeb of the Jungle Crown, is found wanting in his favor.

I'm sure the upcoming visit by His Temple Host will find none of us lacking in piety, but a few goods, if you could send them this way, will go far to lessen the coarseness of our appearance here and may ease the Ranreeb's doubts concerning our competence at looking after the divine bulls in our care. I include a list of items we most desperately need.

If you could also give my love to your First Son, and tell him I think
of him constantly, my gratitude would know no bounds.

May you be cinai blessed always.
Your most penitent First Garden of Children.

Despite Ohd-sli's outrage, I rewrote the scroll, omitting her request regarding her son. Instead, I inserted a request that her sympathies be extended to Orc-hid's family, regarding the loss of their girl child.

"I don't care about her family," Ohd-sli shrieked. "Arrogant idiots, the lot of them!"

"You don't want to remind your claimer that he has a First Son, that your duty to him is over, that you're expendable. You want to remind him of his love for you, not his love for his son. Understand?"

"He's *my* son, not his! Mine!" She raked her nails along her arms.

I had not known it before then, had never thought to ask, but upon writing that scroll together, I'd learned she was an aristocrat from Xxamer Zu. Xxamer Zu: my mother's birth Clutch, the very same that slew Mother's first claimer, and he but my age.

Perchance it had been Ohd-sli's father, or another Xxamer Zu bayen relative of hers, who had given the orders to send my Djimbi mother from her home and family.

So I ignored her grief.

"Canny," Yellow Face said when I read the scroll to her that evening, the two of us crouched outside in the fog in the exact spot where Nae-ser had first taught me the scribe's art.

That Yellow Face insisted on meeting clandestinely boded ill for the welfare of us all. If she didn't want everyone knowing of her at-tempts to manipulate Tieron's fate in our favor by sending this scroll, if she could not trust us all with that much, then her fear that an onai would confess our collective transgressions to a Temple Auditor was sound.

And terrifying.

Nothing existed around us but fog and fear. The ground itself dis-appeared into gray, luminescent nothingness a hand's span from my toes. I pressed against the mill at my back. Any moment, I feared its solidity would disintegrate. I was balanced on the fine edge of insanity again, swept there by dread.

Fog, fog, cold and vaporous, beading me in damp. I was surrounded, felt claustrophobic. The interminable fog was driving me mad. The temptation to stare into the dense vapor in hopes of seeing beyond it rode like a headache between my eyes. Somewhere above the fog a bloated moon must have hung, for an eerie, liquid light made the fog glare. My eyes bled tears from reading to Yellow Face, my words so much vapor sucked into the impenetrable mist—

"The items you ask for are pitiful," Yellow Face muttered. She drummed her fingers against her thighs. "Subtly enhances our desperation and poverty. Clever."

My stomach roiled from the sour fungi I'd eaten while foraging in the jungle earlier. The taste lay like starch on my tongue.

I cleared my throat. "Ohd-sli believes her claimer will try to mitigate Temple's treatment of us. She's certain he wants her alive and well, however much he scorns her."

"How much influence can he exert if he's a Xxamer Zu aristocrat?"

Xxamer Zu was the least powerful Clutch in the Jungle Crown catchment. In perhaps the whole of our nation. I shrugged. "Maybe enough."

We sat in silence, side by side on our haunches. Not so very far away, the invisible waterfall hissed and burbled into its pool.

"What will they do?" I croaked. I shuddered as I said it, gooseflesh breaking out all over my body.

Yellow Face stared into the fog.

"I was here when Ka arrived," she said softly. "Thirteen, I was, and how the spectacle overwhelmed. Servants swarmed the grounds in glimmering red satins, erecting great white pavilions everywhere. Frothing yearlings bellowed at each other, and daronpuis ambled hither and yon with fat chins tucked low to keep the breeze from blowing off their hats. And there in the midst of it all stood Ka, dwarfing the chaos, scornful of the cinai komikon apprentices bolting his wings shut. They'd flown him here drugged, of course. Feisty one, our

Ka. Impotence came upon him early. He was not the doddering old bull that usually arrives at our convent."

She turned to me.

"Ever seen a bull in full flight, Zar-shi? It's like watching a jeweled mountain gracefully drop from the sky. If you saw such a thing, you'd crave more intimate contact from such divinity."

She shook her head and stared back at the fog.

"The cinai komikon apprentices worked hard that day. A daronpu herded us onais into the attic, but I watched everything through a hole in the wall. Boj-est boxed my ears for disobeying Temple Statute, even though she wasn't then our convent elder. None of us were allowed to view the proceedings, see. Our eyes would defile Hallowed Sanctuary Service."

She drew her mildewed cape tighter about herself.

"By the following dawn, the apprentices had torn open one side of the rotunda, stones strewn about as if belched direct from the earth. My, what a time they had forcing Ka to enter! Blow darts and muzzle poles, chains and yearlings . . . nothing could force him inside. Gaaa, some sacred service *that* was! More like a bloody brawl. Chanting monks, elegantly dressed daronpuis, His Esteemed Excellency the Ranreeb presiding . . . Ka cared for none of it. A clawful of men were injured, you know, trying to get him inside the rotunda. One died."

My heart beat against my ribs like a butterfly caught in a web.

"Three days it took to get Ka inside, us onais the entire time locked within the attic and forbidden to leave, save for at night when we were permitted to feed Old Cuhan, our sole kuneus at that time. We went about as a group, no fewer than eight together at once. Staving off by our numbers what befell Kiz-dan."

Silence.

Her story was over.

Kiz-dan's rape stood stark in my mind, and I was left to imagine the stonemasons walling drugged Ka, impotent while still young, into his prison.

"They will interrogate us," she said, dropping each word in the air as if it were live and fanged and far too heavy. "Separately. In their tents. They will coax honesty from us. The eldest of us may die. Or maybe we won't. So hard-bitten are we, like shriveled nuts impenetrable to the teeth. Maybe only the youngest will die. Too hopeful, too vulnerable."

I tried to swallow, but my mouth was dry as bark.

"Most likely, someone will confess during the interrogation," Yellow Face said. "Confess everything, confess anything. Just to stop the methods they employ while asking questions."

"Or maybe," I husked, "they'll find us faultless. We did no wrong, hey-o. We did no wrong."

"Don't be naive. Look at our eyes, Zar-shi. There isn't an onai here with eyes that don't tell of how much venom we've used."

"That's why we shouldn't have sent the wretched hide right away! We could have all weaned ourselves off the stuff—"

"While the hide disintegrated. Whereupon we'd be in the same situation as we are now. Bull hides are rare, child. Get that through your head. We would still have been held accountable for the deterioration of that precious skin, and therefore punished."

"But not all of us!"

She studied me with her sunken, uncannily still eyes. "If I could, I would save your lives with my own. I would make that sacrifice."

"That's not what I meant."

She laid a skeletal hand on my knee and didn't reply. Even through my tunic, the cold of her penetrated, as if she were the fog incarnate.

I couldn't stop shivering. "We could run away, the lot of us."

"And go where?" she said wearily. "We're old women."

"Not all of us!" I cried again, then felt shamed by my readiness to abandon my fellow onais. My vision blurred.

"Let your tears fall, child. No need to hide your desire to live."

"If the Djimbi can survive in the jungle, so could we," I said, and my tears began to fall.

"Nonsense."

"We could at least try—"

"Listen to me. Listen close. I want you to leave. Take Kiz-dan and her baby out of here. You can pass as a family, you as First Son. We'll dress you right. The deception will work while you travel if you're careful. Return to your Clutch. Join the Chanoom Sect. The both of you are circumcised; they'll take you readily enough."

The words were horrible in their familiarity, overwhelming in the freedom they offered. Daunting in what they demanded.

"I can't just—"

"I'm not asking you. I'm telling." She shook my knee, her grip bruising. "You think I wouldn't have done it years ago if I'd had the courage? I'm nothing but a coward. You *won't* be like me. I have a coin-string buried away. You'll take it with you."

"Oh, no. Oh, no."

"Not on the morrow, but the day after. The Ranreeb will arrive any time now—"

"No!"

"But first I have a favor to ask of you, and it's a hard one. You'll not like it, but I ask regardless." She clasped my cheeks, pressed her forehead against mine. Our breath mingled. She smelled like leaf mold and mud.

"Before you answer," she whispered, "I want you to put away preconceptions and skewed, traditional morals. I want you to think about what you feel when you drink venom. I want you to know the experience is a hundredfold richer than that."

I knew what she was going to ask. Knew it, dreaded it, thrilled to it, wanted to flee from it.

"Allow us to lie before the bulls again," she whispered. "We need you, now that Boj-est and Ras-aun are gone, and I know Kiz-dan won't do it, not now that she has a child. So we need you. To hold the dragon back, to pull him off again."

I shook my head.

Her grip on my knee increased. "Please."

"You don't understand—"

"I revolt you," she said curtly.

"No."

"The act, then."

"No—"

"You've dealt daily with the bulls, Zar-shi. You handle Ka well when he misbehaves."

"I can't—"

"I'm only asking you to hold the kuneus, nothing more!"

"I can't!" I cried. "I'm afraid of my own want!"

She looked at me then. Straightened a little. Saw me for what I was and not just as an instrument to satiate her need. Shame burned through me.

Slowly, carefully, she said, "You don't have to feel ashamed by your desire. Not among us."

"It's wrong," I whispered, cheeks burning.

"The wanting of it? The act itself?"

"Both."

"Who gets hurt, Zar-shi? No one is exploited, no one is forced. It's a divine exchange between beast and woman."

"Deviant."

"Tell me you haven't seen worse elsewhere, worse that is acceptable only because it reaffirms the power-defined relationship of an aggressor over the less powerful. Tell me so and I'll agree."

I thought of roidan yin kasloo, the women trading between kus. I thought of Mombe Taro and how the aristocrats, in all their finery, so gleefully whipped and humiliated the apprentices. I thought of that garish, grand mating closet in the glass spinners' ku, the place where my sister had been imprisoned and defiled.

"When?" I asked.

The entire convent whirred about me and Kiz-dan as if she were a queen bee and I the last nectar-bearing flower to be found.

Terror over the impending purge, shame and disgrace over the sins committed during the Wet, hunger, exhaustion, and illness were all temporarily forgotten in the fervor to spirit Kiz-dan's baby away from Tieron before His Excellency arrived.

It was not just Kiz-dan's baby they were saving, understand. Those women saw their own children in that baby's smile and soft, trusting hands. Babies, siblings, nieces, nephews—those small persons not seen for forty years and more. The onais were saving them as much as Kiz-dan's boy. It was their second chance, an opportunity to say, No, I will not have this child taken from me. I will send it whither I wish.

Kiz-dan's baby represented a love that had been ripped from their hands, but never their hearts, the day someone fated them to Tieron.

Over the next two days those old women sewed good leather shoes for us and fashioned decent clothes from salvaged remnants of Ohd-sli's dowry. They searched for edibles in the jungle and forsook their own meals that they might send us with more food. No one slept. Obeisance went ignored, the kuneus grudgingly fed. All that mattered was the baby.

"If only we had more time," Nnp-trn muttered. Moments later, Atl-eri said the same.

"You're yolk brained if you leave," Ohd-sli hissed, hand tight round my wrist. "My claimer won't let anything happen. A jungle cat will get you if you go. Not that I care, stupid bitch."

Oh, Ohd-sli. Why is it we despise that which we depend upon most?

"Stay out of sight," Yellow Face ordered as she and I knelt side by side, wrapping ill-dried dung faggots in Old Maht's wing leather. "Walk along the road, and hide in the jungle if you hear a merchant train approaching. Don't beg a ride with anyone, no matter how tired you are. Remember, the Ranreeb will be interrogating us, and some-one might let slip that you've fled."

So much advice, so much love. So much fear.

My last night at Tieron, I read again the Ranreeb's scroll. All the women who had become my kin and clan since I'd been orphaned nearly a decade ago worked about me, rheumy eyes straining in the gloom cast by a single, smoking candle illicitly made from dragon fat. The women sewed still, fashioning clothes I had no room to carry, loath to suspend their pointless labors and acknowledge in the result-ing stillness the horror that awaited them.

Kiz-dan's baby suckled, one hand softly, proprietarily splayed over the breast he supped from. His eyes were closed, and his toes lan-guidly kneaded her arm. He'd survived the Wet unscathed; he'd sur-vive this, too. We'd make it so, I and all the other onais of Tieron.

I released the scroll, let it spring back into a curl on my lap.

"We could be making something from nothing," I said. "We don't know the Ranreeb intends a purge."

Old fingers fumbled at whatever task they'd moments before tended so efficiently.

It was that one phrase, see, so vague and portent: *Prepare at once for Temple's arrival, and an inspection by an appointed Host.*

Why the auditors if not a purge? Why the Ranreeb if only a simple inquiry daronpuis could oversee?

Yellow Face broke the silence. She was stropping a machete, the rhythmic rasp unbroken for nearly an hour. The blade edge would be too thin, too fine, for practical use.

"Don't drink from still water," she said. "Check the baby each morn and eve for leeches. Keep a fire burning each night to stave off wild-cats, but don't let the fire smoke."

Silence save for the strop, strop of a too-sharp blade against hard stone.

"If only we had more time," Nnp-trn whispered.

As if it were a signal, the onais in Tieron started weeping.

Middle night, and six onais stumbled blind through fog that slid wet and heavy down our throats. The fog would not part for us, refused to acknowledge our presence with so much as a swirl of mist in our wake. The vapor hung immovable and immutable.

We walked single file, Yellow Face in the lead. Behind her, Urd-ren. Atl-eri. Nnp-trn. Nae-ser. Me.

Without her voice or gaze once wavering, Yellow Face had boldly announced in the attic not moments before that we six alone would perform obeisance, on behalf of everyone else.

"Continue your work here," she said to the onais relentlessly sewing.

And if ever there was a phrase that might damn Yellow Face to death beneath an auditor's axe, she then spoke it. "Your sewing is more important."

The fabrication of clothes that would never be worn more impor-tant than honoring the divine kuneus in our care? How naked our be-liefs lie when stripped of all pretense.

So we six stumbled blind through copper-scented fog, and expec-tation roared within me, made my blood sing, my nape shiver, my fingers quiver. I had already decided what I'd do, you see, wanted it and loathed the wanting with equal intensity. I hadn't informed Yellow Face of my intentions. Was not brave enough for that. Hadn't really thought past the anticipation of hot breath against my thighs and muscular, forked tongue tip sliding between my knees.

Of a sudden, the rotunda loomed out of the fog, only an arm's length away. Before ducking through the crude entrance, Yellow Face stopped and faced us. We huddled in close, all of us gaunt and red cheeked.

"Zar-shi will hold Ka when I go last. And understand, there'll be no night watch tonight. We'll need our strength for the morrow."

"We'd rather guessed as much," Atl-eri said, and, ludicrously, everyone smiled. Suddenly Atl-eri looked half her years. About the age my mother had been when she died.

We went to Lutche first, and the porcelain of my teeth clattered as I fumbled to insert a muzzle-pole hook through one of his nostrils. Nnp-trn stood on his other side, pole in hand.

"We haven't cut his claws for a while," she said.

Yellow Face paused, looked at us all.

"Anyone unwilling?" she asked. No one replied.

Yellow Face had prepared a venom draft earlier in the day, on the sly; no fine silver goblet contained it, but instead a coarse congle gourd. We all drank from the gourd, drank it dry, myself included, and though I knew not the Djimbi chants the women next intoned, I hummed along with them, instantly intoxicated by the magic.

With some help, Nae-ser lay before Lutche with all the dignity of an aged aristocrat reclining on a divan. She folded her hands across her sunken chest and sighed heavily, closing her blind eyes.

"Allow him to take me completely, Yin-gik," she murmured, while the rest of us chanted and hummed in the background. "Please. Don't pull him off of me until . . . until I'm gone."

Yellow Face shook her head. "Suicide would taint the rest of us, Nae-ser, would make it look as if you had good reason to expect the worst. I won't jeopardize the chance that some of us may survive the Ranreeb's visit."

Nae-ser inclined her head slightly, her naked scalp sliding over damp slate. "Of course. You're correct. Please excuse my selfish request."

"There's nothing to excuse," Yellow Face murmured. "I'm sure all of us here long to escape tomorrow by succumbing to the dragon's poison this night."

The chants of my sisters grew stronger, to chase away the darkness Yellow Face's words provoked.

Then it was time for me to release Lutche.

I was shocked at the strength in the old bull's neck as he lunged at Nae-ser. One of his shriveled wing claws scrabbled like a large spider against my back as his hind limbs rock-pushed him forward, his stubby forelegs with their too-long talons splayed either side of Nae-ser.

Urd-ren lay down next. Hollow boned and lithely built the bulls might have been, but dragging Lutche off Urd-ren was hard work. She didn't help, thrusting herself at him and begging for more.

Sweat ran freely down my spine and under my arms, pooling around my tunic sash, as I pulled the bull off the delirious woman.

"Ka next," Yellow Face said, helping me secure Lutche in his stall. Her eyes were bright, her pupils mere dots, and she moved with a speed and deftness I'd not seen in her since the year prior.

Ka threw back his head and trumpeted at our approach. Nnp-trn threw back her head and howled in reply, startling wits from me.

"Me first," Nnp-trn said. "I want him like this. Angry and hungry and impatient."

I looked to Yellow Face for guidance, but she looked only at her hands, a thin smile on her face.

"I'll help hold him back," Atl-eri whispered to me.

But we couldn't.

No sooner did Nnp-trn lay before Ka than the tempermental bull attacked. He grabbed her in his gumless mouth and lifted her hip first off the ground and shook her like a cur shakes a rat.

Nnp-trn screamed, and I lunged at Ka with my muzzle pole and tried to insert it into one of his nares. Yellow Face pulled me away.

"Let him feast his fill," she shouted, eyes riveted on the dragon. "Don't stop him."

"He's killing her!"

"Such a beautiful way to die."

"Atl-eri, help!" I cried, wrenching away from Yellow Face, and Atl-eri and I danced about Ka, muzzle hooks slashing about the bull's snout like scimitars in battle, until at last we had him secured in his stall. It took an eternity; it took but heartbeats. Dragon blood dripped from the slashes my hook had made on his snout; Nnp-trn's blood dripped from his jaws. Yellow Face danced about me, flapping her twiggy arms like an emaciated crow.

"Release him!" she cried. "What are you doing?"

"What are *you* doing?" I shouted back.

"Is it not what she wants?" Yellow Face gestured at Nnp-trn, who lay facedown on the slate. Though the faint noises she made were ecstatic gasps, too much blood slicked the slate around her. I dared not look at her groin.

"You said suicide would implicate the rest of us," I growled. "Yet you'd kill us all to watch such a thing?"

"How dare you judge what you don't know, what you've never experienced. Those two were one, don't you understand? That sacred dragon and that lowly woman, they were *one*. You'll never know such intimacy, such a holy union—"

"I will."

"When, if not now?"

"Now, then!" I cried. "You hold Ka back and I'll lie before him. Go on, do it! Give up your turn for me!"

We stared at each other, both out of our minds by the violence we'd witnessed.

Atl-eri stepped forward. "Not Ka, Zar-shi. If you want to lie before a bull, chose Lutche. Ka has gone feral."

"If she wants Ka, let her have Ka," Yellow Face challenged, eyes locked on mine. "Let her experience the full glory of divine passion."

I glanced again at Nnp-trn, facedown at our feet. One foot twitched over and over. She'd fallen silent. I felt ill and feverish. It had all happened so fast, I could scarce grasp it.

"Not Ka, then," I whispered. "Lutche."

Yellow Face made a deprecatory noise and lifted her chin at me.

"Go, then. Do what you will. If you were truly my daughter, you'd want Ka."

Who was this old woman standing before me?

"I was never your daughter," I whispered.

"I've loved you like one."

Love? She called what she'd shown me *love*?

But the words lodged in my throat as Yellow Face began weeping. Stooped and bowlegged from ill health, jaundiced and emaciated, her age somewhere between fifty and a hundred, that delusional old woman wept and turned her back on me.

"Go. The two of you. I'll see to Nnp-trn."

Atl-eri took me gently by the elbow and led me to Lutche.

"You wish to lie with the dragon?"

Her words were soft, her breath sweet against my face. I was upon my back, the cold of damp slate penetrating my tunic and chilling my bones. I stared skyward into midnight fog.

"Yes," I replied to Atl-eri.

She stroked my forehead. "Remember this night always, hey-o. Wheresoever this life takes you, whatsoever should befall you, carry this night in your heart always."

She slowly unlaced my tunic, began humming her intoxicating Djimbi chant. She trailed her fingers gently over my belly, cooed to me, dipped her tongue lightly against my lips. I felt myself arching toward her, craving the taste of venom, the clear, soaring exhilaration it provoked.

"Please . . . " The whisper escaped me without my knowledge.

She didn't obey, continued to caress and kiss.

"Oh, please, please, now." I was nothing but ache, nothing but desire. My hunger needed to be sated now, now, now.

She stood, a whisper of shoddy hemp tunic, and drifted to Lutche's head.

"Be gentle with her, good bull," she said, or maybe I imagined her words, for my heart raced loud in my ears.

I raised my knees. Gooseflesh pimpled my trembling legs. I spread my knees apart, offering the bull my desire.

I closed my eyes. Did not want to see him charge at me, great, muscular tongue snaking out his snout, feathery antennae arced high and quivering over his scaled brow.

Time slowed and stretched. All I could hear was my own rapid breaths.

Then warm, moist air blasted over my knees and my exposed belly, air that smelled of limes and licorice, and talons slid over wet slate either side of me, sending minute vibrations through the clay rock beneath me. Dry, scaled skin shoved my knees farther apart, the movement brusque and powerful, and another moist blast warmed me. Scales rasped coarsely over the tender skin of my inner thighs. I smelled salt and manure and leather.

I held my breath and tensed, fingers gripping hemp cloth, and then Lutche roared, his mouth a thumbnail's length from my sex, his firm gums brushing my buttocks, and the roar resonated through me as if I were a bell that had been struck, had become a vibrating liquid in my veins, shaking every sinew, rattling every bone.

My eyes snapped open. I stared into one great amber eye cocked sideways, its lizard-slitted pupil staring right at me, right through me.

There was sentience there. Oh yes. Whatever I'd needed to believe in our inhuman imprisonment of the old bulls, I knew differently now. The dragons *understood*.

Lutche blinked, pleated citrine-and-purple eyelid slowly closing, slowly opening. He drew back above my knees. Again his coarse scales rasped over my tender skin. His nostrils flared, sleek and glossy as burnished mahogany.

The forked tip of his tongue protruded, trembling, testing the air, flicking my belly, leaving a venom-slick trail across my skin. It was not warm, that tongue, neither was it cold. It was like a breath released heartbeats ago, carrying a memory of warmth but as cool and satiny as the stamen of an orchid. The venom on my belly throbbed, swelled my desire into a sweet, unbearable peak.

Again Lutche roared, and I could see into his throat, could see the red, wet muscles corded and vibrating. The top curve of one of his talons nudged me, and there was such strength in that accidental prod, in that uncontrolled movement, that his talon bruised my rib and slid my whole body over a space.

My ears resounded with Lutche's hoarse bellow.

He sucked in a breath. It inflated the corrugated dewlaps of his throat crop. Then his tongue shot out, thick, sure, a corded, searching muscle, and with unerring certainty, the forked tip entered me.

Wondrous pain, blinding burn.

I screamed, arched away.

And then . . .

. . . The rush of venom through my blood, a flood tide of fire surging, billowing, heaving, peaking through my body. I would take flight, I would ignite, I would explode with divinity and puissance and joy.

And then . . .

. . . I heard whispers.

The memory of voices, strange and incomprehensible and beautiful in their power. Images flitted through my mind, as well, too blurred to be more than hazy color. Those otherworld whispers, those hazy images, they were the dragon's thoughts.

Ancestral memories, passed on from time before humans, passed on when dragon bull mounted dragon brooder, when dragon brooder regurgitated crop food to dragon hatchling. Somehow, through the exchange of semen and saliva, ancestral memories were passed down the generations, from dragon to dragon.

And I, I was almost privy to them.

If only I could fly higher, if only I could understand those thoughts and see those memories, I would be truly one with the dragon. I would be whole for the first time in my life.

"More," I cried, ecstasy shaking me like a leaf in a gale.

But Atl-eri pulled Lutche away.

"No!" I gasped.

Did she not understand? I wanted him, I *needed* him, and he needed me. I could almost hear him talking with each agitated snort, his words buried in dragon breath, and if only I held my own breath, if only I stilled the racing of my pulse and the beating of my heart long enough, I might comprehend those mysterious, divine whispers that were so compelling, so alluring. Maybe then I could talk with the divine. . . .

My hands tried to replace the lack of dragon tongue.

Though my fingers slid in and out so sweetly, the powerful unity I'd experienced and the otherworld whispers of dragon voice I'd been on the cusp of understanding could not be reproduced by my hands.

Slowly, the magnificent flame within me died to a glowing ember. My hands fell still.

I wept, utterly bereft. Yellow Face crouched at my head.

"So now you understand," she said, and her wise old eyes carried within them the grief of the world.

TWENTY-TWO

Before sunup, Kiz-dan and I left Tieron Nask Cinai, her babe wide-eyed and silently gumming the swaddling that bound him to her chest. No one came down from the attic to see us off; Yellow Face forbade it. She alone descended to the mill floor with us.

Upstairs, the old women who'd pressed around us, weeping and touching the babe for one last time, began keening.

Yellow Face held a greasy black bladder the size of a mango in her hands. "You'll be needing this, I'll warrant."

Venom. I didn't confess that I'd already hidden some in the ruck-sack on my back.

Ever since the night when fire had spewed from my fingertips, my need for venom had dwindled; it was as if the debacle had spent the haunt. That didn't mean I believed my nights would always belong to me. I feared the haunt's revival, knew it would return as surely as dark followed each day, and I wanted to be prepared. Thus, the venom hidden in my pack.

And, too, I yearned to hear the dragons' compelling ancestral memories once more, to experience the ecstasy and oneness that lying before Lutche had momentarily blessed me with. Could I replicate the experience with venom and my own fingers? I prayed I could, doubting it even as I hoped for the impossible.

"Mind now," Yellow Face said, fussing with the foul bladder, not quite ready to place it in my hands. "It marks you. Your eyes, under-stand. Anyone who knows anything about dragons will see how much you've used, and anyone who knows of the rite will guess how inti-mately you've received it."

I nodded, plucked the gift from her hands. "Thank you."

"Take this, too. Carry it with you always. Sleep with it, carry it when you wash, make it a third arm." She handed me the machete she'd stropped to a fine edge. I hesitated before taking it. She'd promised to keep the blade to assist the other onais in suicide if it looked like the suffering provoked during Temple's interrogations would only end in wholesale slaughter of the convent.

"Take it," Yellow Face said again, and so I did, and at her insistence, I promised I'd carry it with me always, though it was a promise I did not intend on keeping. "You have the coin-string I gave you? The currency may be used by a woman, so if anything should happen to you, Kiz-dan may use it with impunity."

Unlike me, Kiz-dan could never pass as a young man when disguised, and for the first time, I truly realized how responsible I would be for her life.

We both looked to where Kiz-dan wept bitterly at the mill door. She was furious with Yellow Face over Nnp-trn's death; her fury was lending her the strength to leave. For yes, Nnp-trn had died from Ka's mauling.

"What will you do with the corpse?" I murmured, looking at my feet.

"What we always do with our dead."

"Take the body *deep* into the jungle. So no one from Temple finds it. The dragon marks between her thighs, upon her groin—"

"I'm no fool, child."

That raised my hackles, and my eyes met hers. "Did you lie with Ka last night? After seeing to Atl-eri with Lutche?"

Her lower lip trembled and she lifted her chin. "I lay with Lutche. Urd-ren held him for me, when she was recovered enough to stand. I had long to wait; it was near dawn before I received the dragon's tongue. But I risked the others discovering me at it; could *you* have denied yourself one last time with the dragons, knowing now what you know? Having felt the divine as you did?"

"No," I whispered.

Did I hate her? I couldn't decide. Love, madness, hate, need; it was all wrapped up so tightly for me. Yellow Face professed to love me, and my mother, who had once truly loved me, had treated me in the end no better than curt, austere Yin-gik.

That's when it struck me. How to save us all. Convent, onais, our lifestyle, our boy baby.

Mother.

I had summoned her haunt once, had channeled her gift with fire for our benefit. Surely I could do it again.

"What?" Yellow Face said sharply. "What is it, Zar-shi?"

"I'll fight them off," I said, dazed the idea hadn't occurred to me before. "With fire. Like the night we cooked Old Maht—"

"Nonsense."

"I can! It would work. You saw what I did. I could do the same. Burn down their pavilions, send them running into the jungle, surround Tieron in a moat of fire—"

"Are you mad? To what end?"

"To save us."

"Stupid child. *Think*. Can you stave off Temple's might? No. How many auditors and wardens does the Ashgon of Ranon ki Cinai control? Strike down the Ranreeb of the Jungle Crown, and that's who you deal with next, my girl, the Ashgon himself of the Temple of the Dragon. And beyond the Ashgon, in the Archipelago awaits the Emperor and his legions of warriors."

"But someone has to stop all this! We did nothing wrong." All right. So maybe I didn't hate Yellow Face; I was sobbing, my heart was breaking, and *we had done nothing wrong*.

"Listen to me, Zar-shi." She gripped my chin in one hand. She only reached that high, my chin, and I was not so tall. I hadn't realized it before then: Yellow Face was small.

"You are cursed with this obsession over your mother, understand?" she said. "Be rid of it as soon as you can, or it will dominate your every action, whether you know it or not. *Get rid of that haunt*."

I tried to turn my face away but she held it tight, shook me.

"Don't cave in to the anger memory can provoke, hey-o," she hissed. "Don't be seduced by the fury and might of that haunt."

"But—"

"You can read, you can write, you work well with dragons. You've been cleansed, you have a bright, quick wit about you, you know about the secret rite. Use *those* if you wish to change things.

Don't burn what you would destroy. You'll only choke on the ashes."

She snapped her hand away from me, shoved me in the chest. "Now go."

With that, she turned and walked away.

"Wait," I said breathlessly.

She stopped, did not turn back.

"Have you . . . have you ever understood the dragons' thoughts?"

She shook her head. "The divine mystery has always remained just beyond my reach."

I felt the grief behind those words as if it were my own.

"Have you ever been able to replicate that transcendence? Using just venom and your hands?"

She turned, then, and looked at me, tears streaming down her cheeks.

"No," she said hoarsely. "The gift must be given by a dragon, Zarshi. I don't know why. Now go. Go."

"You're making a mistake!" Ohd-sli shrieked from the top of the attic stairs. "Don't leave!"

I tucked the bladder of venom into my waist sash and approached Kiz-dan.

"Ready?" I asked, weeping.

She nodded and stepped out of the mill.

The journey back to Clutch Re was as difficult and wearisome as when I'd left it nearly a decade ago, only instead of living in dread of my gender being discovered, I feared the sudden appearance of an auditor. Instead of suffering blows and beatings from children my own age, I suffered leeches and hunger and the festering bites of a thousand unseen insects, because instead of sleeping draped in an old hide alongside my mother in the back of a traveling merchant's cart, I dozed fitfully at night beside Kiz-dan and her baby in the jungle itself.

How pitiful my carefully tended fires seemed against the stealthy sounds that stalked us in the darkness.

Morning and night, we spread upon the baby a waxy concoction the onais had given us, to stave off the sickness spread by mosquitoes. We used it carefully, needing it to last our entire journey. On ourselves we spread only hope.

The Inbetween ended. The Season of Fire began.

Our food supplies ran out.

We ate the grubs I found beneath the bark of dead branches, and bitter leaves and fibrous tubers that gave us gas and turned Kiz-dan's milk so sour her baby complained when he nursed. If not for the time spent munching the koorfowsi rim maht my mother had foraged from the sesal fields, I would not have recognized even those bitter leaves as edible, and we would have starved.

After little over a month—the both of us lank with heat and hunger and riddled with parasites and bites—we reached the valley of Re, under the stern brow of the Spinal Crest mountains. We would not have survived the jungle for much longer.

Sometime, the road we'd followed must have forked from the main trunk leading to the center of Clutch Re, for we entered the Clutch at the gharial basins. I stared stupidly at the fenced ponds stretching before us like enormous framed mirrors.

A swirl of emotions threatened to reduce me to tears: I was home. I had no kin or clan to return to. This was where I belonged, and yet I was unwanted.

"We'll rest first," I said hoarsely, turning away from my birth Clutch unsteadily. "Wait until high noon, when everyone rests."

Kiz-dan dully nodded agreement.

We rested in the muggy shade of a liana-choked tree, shared an unripe avocado the size of a plum. My dark emotions formed a sour knot in my stomach. I refused to acknowledge them. Denial was a powerful tool and the only one I had at my disposal.

When the heat of high noon reached its peak, we took off our travel-stained convent tunics, pulled on our disguises, and stepped out from the jungle onto the raised road leading into Clutch Re. A great carrion bird of an indeterminate blue lifted off a nearby tree and flapped lazily into the sky. It followed us in long, wide circles.

Dikes bordered either side of the road. Beyond the dikes, woven bamboo fences encircled waters corrugated with long-snouted ghari-

als. Not a person walked the bridges and walkways suspended between the stilt-raised huts in the basins. High noon in the heat of Fire
Season was a good time to travel unseen by man.

We were watched, though. A thousand pairs of eyes riveted on our
backs as we walked. Like a slow wave, the gharials turned toward us,
began belly sliding as close as the fences of their respective ponds
permitted. Unhurried. Intent. Drawn by the scent of our skin.

"Will those fences hold?" Kiz-dan asked.

I shrugged, kept a wary eye along the road, looking for loose gharials, for inquisitive wardens, both equally dangerous. "The sooner
we're through here, the better."

Dressed in the tattered finery of the cobbled-together disguises
Ohd-sli had delineated, my hair only inches long and Kiz-dan's own
naked scalp covered by the gauzy bitoo cowl the onais had fashioned,
we looked like rishi from a lordling's mansion. Two such rishi had no
reason to travel in the gharial basins.

Halfway along that straight, raised road, a clawful of daronpu
acolytes filed out one of the many raised huts shimmering in the heat
of the basins. They walked along a suspended bridge; two pushed a
cart. Even from that distance, I knew what filled it.

"Keep walking. They aren't interested in us. Don't stop," I said.

Chanting and dashing the agitated gharials below with consecrated
oil, the acolytes dumped their cart of corpses into a gharial basin.

The water boiled alive. Teeth flashed. Jaws clapped loud and staccato across the flat basins. The gharials in the pools either side of us
thrashed and snapped at each other in sudden agitation, knowing others were being fed. The baby watched wide-eyed.

Kiz-dan stumbled over a rock, transfixed by the grisly scene.

"Keep walking," I repeated, looking only forward at the shimmering row of brick buildings at the road's end.

The carrion bird continued to wheel high above us in lazy loops. I
shivered each time its shadow crossed over me.

We reached the string of fly-blown buildings at the road's end.
Slaughterhouses, they were, and the stench of blood and raw meat
made me dizzy with hunger. We skirted the dark brick buildings
quickly, avoiding the gaze of the rishi we passed until I realized

such a stance bespoke of guilt, whereupon I glared at any who looked our way.

It was with great relief that we finally entered the maze of alleys so typical of Clutch Re. Anonymity lay within those crowded alleys.

At the first ku compound, I stopped.

"Wait here," I told Kiz-dan. "I'll be right back."

Exhausted, she sank against the ku entry arch. It was a dismal, unadorned arch, not extending welcome. I guessed from the compound's proximity to the gharial basins that the clan worked the slaughterhouses.

I approached an old woman who was using her teeth to soften reed fibers for weaving. To mask my feminine voice, I spoke in coarse grunts. Rocks in my empty rucksack weighted my female gait. For all intents and purposes, I looked like a soft-faced boy.

Without hesitation, the old woman sold me paak slathered in sesal nut paste, in exchange for one of the smaller coins on the string of coastal currency that Yellow Face had given me.

After years of eating the oily kadoob tubers with their noisome, smoky flavor, the chili-laced paak disappointed with its blandness, and the nut paste cleaved in an unpleasant way to the roof of my mouth. Kiz-dan ate wearily, passing no judgement on what I gave her. The baby spat the paak out in a crumbly spray but worked at some of the paste with a series of puckered expressions.

The emotions knotted in my gut snarled tighter as I ate. The old compound walls felt like a familiar embrace; the maze of alleys and the smells of cooking paak were the sights and scents of a childhood long lost. I was not home, no. I was somewhere else, somewhere I could never return to, and I wanted to weep with the loss.

Overhead, the great carrion bird still wheeled.

Under the guise of scratching my balls, I dipped a hand into the venom pouch at my waist beneath my tunic and sucked the stuff off my fingers.

Good thing the sun shone so fiercely and that many walked about squinting from the glare. Unless someone looked close, my eyes looked no different than everyone else's.

Or so I told myself.

*   *   *

By dusk we reached our destination. Geesamus Ir Cinai Ornisak, Dragon-Sanctioned Zone of the Dead.

Sweaty and dust coated, Kiz-dan stared at me, fear stark upon her worn face. She dared not speak, lest the acolyte driving the wagon we rode overhear. But she clutched her babe close to her chest as the cart trundled over brittle brown weeds and shot looks of dread at the great stone foundations of the gawabe, the sepulchral towers, surrounding us. I'd told her where I'd planned to sequester us, and she'd agreed; now I could see doubts flitting through her mind.

I thought it a good thing that we'd arrived during the Fire Season and not during the Inbetween. The spectacle of fog swirling around the gargoyle-carved arcades that connected the superior towers would have elicited tears from her. They had me, years ago. It was a good thing, too, that dusk was nigh and the orange-shrouded tower keepers, the makmakis, were out of sight. I remembered the terror their shapeless forms had inspired in me, and although I'd forewarned Kiz-dan about how the makmakis dressed, I think the unusual sight might have snapped her fragile nerves.

Our wagon creaked to a stop. The dragon harnessed to it snorted and rooted at the ground. The driver, a cleft-jawed acolyte, sat for a moment, yawning hugely.

How small his female dragon looked to me, after so many years of seeing only our convent kuneus. How slim and delicate, how naked without antennae, how bland with her scaled hide of russet and moss instead of the iridescent dark green and raisin-purple of a bull.

Her wings had been amputated as a hatchling, of course, as were all the wings of every Clutch Re dragon save for those in Roshu-Lupini Re's private stables. Her venom sacs likewise would have been removed at the same age. Yet even so, I found myself looking at her with a fondness borne from my intimacy with the bulls. More than fondness; I felt bonded to her. I knew her to be not merely a divinity used, due to her sex, as a respected beast of burden, but as a sentient being with ancient memories linking her to her ancestors and all living dragons, a bond we humans could never obtain with each other.

I caught her eye. Wisdom resided in that sad, weary gaze. Yes. Wisdom akin to the looks I'd seen in the eyes of captured monkeys clutching their tiny babes to their breasts.

I wondered if Temple knew about a dragon's ancestral memories. I doubted it. For them to know would mean that somebody from Temple had at some point participated in a rite similar to what I'd undergone with Lutche. And such intimacy, for a man, was anatomically impossible. And all in Temple's hierarchy were male.

Unless somewhere, somewhen, a woman who'd undergone the rite had told a man, and he in turn had told Temple. What had Yellow Face said? "Anyone who knows of the rite will guess how intimately you've received it."

"Give a hand with the urns, then," the acolyte who'd driven us to the Zone of the Dead sighed, as if expecting me to refuse. That had been the barter I'd used to purchase the ride, that I'd help unload his cargo once at his destination; I was still playing the part of a young man, see.

Kiz-dan joggled her sleeping baby nervously while I sweated and labored alongside the acolyte, unloading urns from the wagon. I couldn't help but study the temple as I worked, for no braziers burned within its sunken amphitheatre. No smoke coiled from its unadorned chimney. No acolytes swept away the dust that had drifted in, and no daronpuis strolled about in clackron masks, reading from scrolls. Even in the gloom of twilight, I could see the temple was an austere, neglected place, the mud-brick columns and broken-tiled roof worn by sun and rain.

"What've you got for me, blood, blood?" a hoarse voice roared. "What have you got?"

On the far side of the wagon, Kiz-dan instinctively crouched out of sight beside a rutted wheel. From the gloom of the sunken amphitheatre a rangy giant appeared, the chatelaine round his daronpu robe dragging like a tail. His beard was cleaved in two down the center, and each half he wore over a shoulder like a mantle. Part of his skull sported tufts and bald patches; the other, corded black hair. He staggered like one drunk toward the crates we'd unpacked and began sniffing them. He delivered an angry blow with his cane to one. I leapt near out of my skin.

"Insufficient! Inferior! Take it back, blood, blood!"

The acolyte ignored his superior and nodded wearily at me. "Down into the temple proper with everything, hey-o."

Trembling, I nodded and bent to heft an urn into my arms. While crouched, I hissed under the wagon, "Stay out of sight. Stay quiet."

I could see only Kiz-dan's haunches, but they shifted in acknowledgement.

I glanced at the daronpu bellowing curses at the unpacked goods. "If he comes after you, run. He's too drunk to chase you. Don't run far or I'll never find you."

"Come *on*," the cleft-jawed acolyte said to me, and I hastily hefted the urn into my arms and followed him.

Down the eight tiers of the amphitheatre we staggered. I glanced behind me when we reached the ground floor; the drunken daronpu still bellowed curses at the packing crates. I reassured myself that he had no idea Kiz-dan crouched on the other side of the wagon. She was safe as long as he continued focusing his ire on the crates.

I shifted the weight of my burden and followed the acolyte through an archway, down a short flight of stairs lit by a single smoking candle lodged in a puddle of tallow on a middle stair, and into a dark underground antechamber.

The first thing that hit me was the stench of charred wood, as if we stood in a place that had been devoured by flame years ago.

"I can't see," I said, blinking in the acrid darkness, and by the sound of my voice I knew the antechamber was neither huge nor empty.

"Put the urn here," the acolyte said by way of answer, and I heard his own burden thud upon the floor.

I shuffled blindly toward his voice. My hip bumped hard into something. Things cascaded groundward with a clatter of bamboo.

The acolyte cursed. "Don't move. If you step on one, he'll kill you."

I froze, neck and shoulders burning from the weight of the urn in my arms.

"Wait here." The acolyte brushed by me, smelling of male sweat. After Tieron, the pungent musk was strange, frightening and appealing in its rich strength. He returned moments later holding a candle lit from the one on the stairway.

I blinked about the antechamber.

Scrolls lay everywhere. Some were carefully bunged within bamboo pipes, some lay exposed to air and dust. They littered crates, covered urns, were scattered upon two worn hammocks swinging from the low stone ceiling. They covered a stool, a table, were even strewn over the top of a potbellied iron stove devoid of a stovepipe. I realized that was the source of the smell of the antechamber; the stove, presently unlit, kept the scrolls relatively dry, yet due to its lack of a pipe, spewed smoke into the chamber.

More scrolls were slotted neatly into an old cabinet. A lurid clackron mask leered at me from the top of the cabinet; a bamboo-encased scroll protruded from its crimson lips.

"Put the urn over there and pick those scrolls up. Stack them back on the table, and be quick about it, too, in case he comes down here."

With that the acolyte shoved by me and left the antechamber.

I thumped my urn down where he'd indicated. My back muscles were so tight and angry I couldn't straighten again. Hunched, I staggered over to the table, knelt awkwardly, and began picking up the scrolls and bamboo pipes.

One cracked and yellowed scroll lay flat upon the table; it looked as if it hadn't been rolled up for many a year, as if it would crumble if forced to do so. Its very age invoked reverence, begged curiosity. I gingerly picked up the brittle paper. Couldn't help myself.

Beautiful hieratics lined the scroll, faded from black to brown, running in perfectly straight columns. Elegant sesal-flower motifs blocked off the scroll into sections. The cursive glyphs invoked the memory of me and Nae-ser crouched beside the mill, drawing with twigs in the dirt. Grief coursed over me, and I swiped tears from my eyes before they fell upon the fragile paper and bled the ink.

Heavy breaths and labored footsteps descended the short stairs at my back. I hastily laid the paper back on the table, knowing I shouldn't have touched it.

Too late. I'd been seen.

"What are you doing?" the acolyte cried. "Put that back. Don't mess with it. Do you know how old it is?"

He dropped his crate near my foot.

"Stupid rishi bastard," he growled under his breath as he studied the ancient paper, hands hovering as if to shield it from my very presence. "I told you to pick up the scrolls from the floor. That's all. Just pick them up."

My cheeks flamed. "I *was* picking them up."

He snorted, picked up a different scroll, rolled it tight, and jammed it into an empty bamboo pipe. "Ignorant, the lot of you. Completely unable to follow orders—"

"You put that in the wrong casing," I said hotly.

"What?" He glared at me from beneath a fringe of black hair.

I gestured at the bamboo pipe in his hands.

"That scroll doesn't go in there," I snapped. "But what would I know, hey-o? I'm just an ignorant rishi bastard."

Slowly, he teased the scroll out the casing he held. Unraveled it. Read its ornate title, then looked at the title engraved on the bamboo casing for long moments.

They didn't correspond, the title on the scroll, the title on the casing.

A muscle along his square cheek bulged and flattened.

I realized then what trouble I'd got myself into. The average rishi was illiterate.

"You can read," he said quietly, not looking up.

"A little only," I said, trying to keep my voice steady, casual.

"How?"

I thought of Ohd-sli. "A bayen lady taught me, in the house I served. In return for certain favors."

He looked up. Studied me.

We were inches apart. Surely he could see I was female, even in that gloom. My breath came too fast, too shallow.

"Why are you here, then?" he asked.

"Her claimer learned of us," I said hoarsely. My heart thundered against my rib cage.

He nodded, looked down at the scroll in his hands. After a moment, he pushed it toward me. "Read."

I swallowed, could barely find the spittle necessary to do so.

" 'Eight and eight and eight days did they wander therein, seeking the dragon's lair,' " I read, and my dry, unsteady voice helped disguise my fluency. " 'Eight and eight and eight times daily did they look starward, seeking a nesting Clutch in the jungle's knotted crown.' "

I could read no more. My hands shook the paper too badly.

After several moments of silence, the acolyte nodded.

"You could join Temple, you know," he said, looking again at me. "Better than becoming a kigo makmaki. If that's why you've come to this zone, to serve the dead."

"It is," I said hoarsely. "I . . . I like women too much to join Temple."

"Too bad."

He turned away from me, gestured at the scrolls still scattered on the floor. Turned brisk. "Finish picking these up and help carry the rest of the crates down. And good luck to you as a makmaki."

He ducked out the chamber and disappeared into the dark temple.

After a restless night spent huddled against the great stone foundation of a gawabe, we set about looking for the sepulchral tower tended by the makmaki brothers Mother and I had boarded with a decade before.

But each inquiry to the orange mounds of cloth swishing about the zone, carrying jugs of water on heads and hip, upon backs wood for cooking, and jungle-caught jambas impaled on sharpened branches, sent us in a different direction than the last. Kiz-dan shuffled wordlessly behind me, her deeply lined face and the crying of her baby reproach enough.

It wasn't until late noon that I realized the huge carrion bird from yesterday followed us still, flapping from one tower to the next, resting on the tetrahedral rooftops.

The bird raised the hairs on the back of my neck; not only was its behavior odd, but it was a peculiar bluish color, a species of vulture I'd never seen before. I quickened my pace, tried to avoid it by walking opposite to where it landed. I was doing just that—dodging its skulking presence—when I recognized the gawabe directly before me. It was the sepulchral tower the makmaki brothers tended.

I glanced up at the carrion bird perched on the upswept eave of the gawabe behind us, and realization swept over me.

"It herded us here," I said, and I went cold and my heartbeat tripped, and of a sudden I recognized the creature. Its queer color was that attributed to the mystical carrion creatures said to guard the skies of the Celestial Dragon Realm. In other words, the vulture was a Skykeeper, but shrunken to the size of a mortal buzzard.

"A Skykeeper," I hissed. "Look, there!"

Kiz-dan ignored me and sank wearily against the stone foundation of the brothers' gawabe. "I need to rest awhile, Zar-shi. Just awhile."

"Zarq," I said, turning back to her, and I felt the bird's eyes bore into my back. "Call me Zarq now. Please."

Far above our heads, the carrion bird lifted off and flapped slowly toward the jungle. From the corner of my eye I saw it go, and the *rsht, rsht* of the wind through its wings invoked a nameless, powerful dread.

No. Not so nameless. It was the same sound my mother's haunt had made when I'd consumed venom back at the convent to keep the obsessive spirit at bay. It was the same sound the haunt's claws had made as it had tried to rip its way through my venom-induced shield.

I shuddered.

"Well?" Kiz-dan asked.

"That bird." I pointed at its skylit silhouette. "What was that bird?"

She stared at me. "What does it matter?"

"It wasn't natural. It was an otherworld. . . ." The words died in my throat at the expression on her face.

"Never mind," I muttered.

Perhaps I'd been mistaken, in my fatigue. That was most likely. Yes. I had to believe so.

I whistled at the stone foundation that I recognized as the one tended by the makmaki brothers who'd harbored me and my mother years before. But no head poked out the door high above us, and no corded ladder was thrown down in invitation.

"They must be out hunting," I said wearily, sinking onto my haunches. "We'll wait. They'll return before nightfall. I don't want to go in without seeing them first."

Kiz-dan said nothing. She slowly unwrapped her baby, removed the soiled moss bound under his rash-riddled bottom, and tossed it aside.

Neither of us voiced the thought that the brothers might be dead.

A naked foot in my kidney woke me sometime later.

"Vermin. Get away."

My eyes flew open. In the twilight gloom, two men stood before me. It took but a heartbeat to recognize them.

They looked the same, incredibly so. Perhaps more gray in their wiry black hair, perhaps more creases on their cynical faces. But they looked beautifully, beautifully the same.

"It's me," I whispered, unexpected emotion overwhelming me. "The potter's brat. The rat bludgeoner."

I could barely make out their expressions in the gloom.

"Speak up; we can't hear you," one snapped.

I rose to my feet, suddenly cold despite the sultry evening.

"You always put me on night watch," I said hoarsely, and I couldn't stop myself; the tears ran freely down my cheeks. "I made too much noise killing the rats. My mother . . . my mother . . . we both stayed with you."

I was sobbing like a child, and I badly wanted to hold them, be held by them, those two men who had been nothing more to me than landlords for a brief spell.

They exchanged looks, studied me anew, glanced down at Kiz-dan and child, then looked back at me.

"The danku rishi tu?" one of them said at last. "You?"

I nodded.

"What do you want?"

"To board with you again. I can pay, see?" I fumbled for Yellow Face's coin-string; it broke and the coins spilled from my fingers onto the ground. "I'll stand night watch again, clean and hunt like I used to. I'm better with a knife than before."

"You. The danku rishi tu."

"Yes."

"That"—a nod at Kiz-dan—"is not your mother."

"She died." I could barely get the words out.

"A miracle she lived as long as she did," one remarked tartly.

"Will you take us as boarders?" I whispered.

"The three of you?"

"Please."

They looked at each other, communicated with their eyes. One shrugged, turned back to me, and nodded.

I threw myself on him and hugged hard. Couldn't say why and couldn't stop myself.

"Thank you," I wept.

He extracted himself from my embrace as though I were something dead. "No rat pulping. A dead rat is a dead rat, understand?"

I nodded.

"Fine," the other brother said. "Let's get inside and eat."

He pulled a thin cord I'd not noticed and that hadn't been present a decade before, and unloosed the ladder to the tower.

I dreamed that night.

No, I did not dream. I was visited.

She came to me as a sharp-beaked bird, a Skykeeper of the Celestial Realm shrunken to the size of a mortal vulture, her blue-feathered wings tipped with claws, her eyes beady and red. Each of her long, scaled legs ended in talons dripping blood. She opened her beak; it was lined with thin, curved teeth. She reeked of carrion.

I knew what she wanted. Her favorite nestling. Waivia.

"Go away," I whispered, and the blue light luminescing from her pulsed stronger, casting a nacreous sheen over Kiz-dan and her child, asleep beside me.

The bird cocked her head, eyed Kiz-dan angrily.

"Leave them alone," I said, heart thumping against the dry roof of my mouth.

That wicked beak stabbed forward, a hairsbreadth from Kiz-dan's breast. I bolted upright and fumbled in my waist pouch for venom.

The bird squawked, a raspy, shrieking sound that filled the gawabe. Kiz-dan's baby woke and then began wailing. The footsteps of the makmaki brothers thumped across the floorboards above.

"RAWK!" the bird screeched again, moved closer, spread its wings, pulled its neck back for another deadly blow with its beak, and that's when I realized it looked not at Kiz-dan but at me, at my waist, at the venom pouch.

And then it dived at me.

Not to wound, understand, not directly. Intending instead to steal my pouch of venom, and leave me vulnerable to its obsession to find Waivia—

I thrust an oily glob of black venom in my mouth and swallowed feverishly. Choked on the burn, the nasal fire, the tears streaming from my eyes . . .

The vulture shrank to the size of a pigeon, then flew out an open window on a dewy cloud of blue.

I explained the noise to the makmaki brothers as a bad dream. Nothing more. Promised them it wouldn't recur; I'd sleep with my mouth bound if I had to. I avoided Kiz-dan's eyes as I stammered out the explanation.

I didn't sleep the rest of that night.

I spent the hours vowing to never again fall asleep while on Clutch Re without first mixing black venom with water, then drinking down the resultant translucent and lovely gel.

Returning to Clutch Re had somehow freed my mother's haunt from its ethereal world inside me, had given it more power. The thing was very alive and very whole right now.

The next morning, I found blue feathers on the floor where it had stood.

TWENTY-THREE

Kiz-dan detested the brothers. She didn't like their cynicism, their lewdness, their intimacy. Her revulsion provoked the two. They often coupled in her presence.

"Get us out of here," she'd growl at me, white about the lips. "This is bad for the baby."

"Go upstairs while they're at it. They only do it to goad you."

But Kiz-dan shunned the second tier of our tower, with its embalmed inhabitants; the smallest kigo, no larger than Yimyam, especially disturbed her. She turned sour, harped at me constantly. Daily she aged, like a fig left out in sunlight. I avoided her.

While she griped and cooked and cleaned, I foraged in the jungle, fetched water from the local well, gathered firewood for the cooking brazier. While she wove sleeping mats and washed soiled baby wraps, I stood watch over the familiar mildewy kigos on the second floor.

Don't misunderstand me. The brothers didn't laze about after our arrival. Hardly. Poverty permits no such leisure. They checked their snares in the jungle daily, and with the few monkeys and rodents they caught, they bartered for paak and essentials in the dismal market held weekly outside the zone's decrepit temple. Our presence eased the brothers' days, yes, as their ancient mother had died several years ago and their workload since had been great.

I wore their mother's makmaki shroud when going about, disliking the heat of the worn orange cloth but secure in the obscurity it offered. I wondered how many other kigo makmaki were fugitives hiding beneath those shrouds.

I relapsed into using venom daily and nightly.

Because, you see, each morn I found feathers upon the narrow gray window ledges of our tower. Brown feathers that when held in a certain way to the light shimmered milky blue.

Mother's haunt was stalking me. Of that I was sure. Each day, the moment I walked outside, the great shadow of the carrion bird slid over me. I took to slinking from gawabe to gawabe, staying close to each stone foundation, one hand upon the venom sack at my waist beneath my shroud, the other holding the keen machete Yellow Face had given me.

And I dreamed of Waivia.

Even with the venom humming giddily through my veins, I dreamed of her. Of the bruises on her chubby, infant arms. How in her childhood no one but Mother had picked her up and soothed her when she fell. How she'd looked descending the mating closet in the glass spinners' compound.

The sobbing I'd heard while the glass spinners' closet had rocked at my back haunted my sleep, and when I woke—once, twice, thrice a night—the weeping revealed itself for what it was: the scratching of talons against the wooden lattice windows of our tower.

Always, always, a carrion bird circled above our gawabe. Night and day. Day and night. My use of venom increased.

My breath stank of licorice and limes. My fingers trembled and my body twitched. My eyes watered incessantly from infrequent blinking; dragon eyes, oh, yes, I had dragon eyes now. I didn't care. I needed venom.

I craved its sour taste and slippery viscosity; from the moment I swallowed it down, I waited anxiously for my next drink. Everything I did, everywhere I went, marked the passage of time until I could next indulge myself. I was never satisfied. The haunt was out there, alive. Stalking me.

No more did I associate venom with the divine ecstasy I'd experienced lying before Lutche, with being one with the dragon and hearing its ancient, profound memories. No. I drank venom solely to stave off my mother's presence, her obsessive strength, which was growing stronger each day I remained in Clutch Re.

Waivia was here. That's what my mother's haunt believed. Waivia was here, somehow, somewhere, in our birth Clutch, and Mother wanted me to find her. That much was obvious by how frequently I dreamed of Waivia, by how potent mother's haunt had become since my arrival on Clutch Re.

So I drank venom.

After a month in the gawabe, my venom was nearly gone.

"You've swallowed more, haven't you." It was a statement, not a question, and Kiz-dan's perpetually sour expression puckered even further. She had weaned herself off venom long ago, had gone through the painful withdrawal symptoms upon discovering she was pregnant. She'd not wanted her breast milk tainted by dragon poison, and even during that last devastating Wet Season in the convent, she'd used it only when at her very sickest.

"You've swallowed more," she said, with all the disgust that only someone reformed can muster toward one not yet freed from self-enslavement.

"You wouldn't understand," I growled.

We sat across from each other, sweating in sultry, still air, her scrubbing a pot clean with sand, me trying to repair a damaged snare. I say try, because my fingers refused to operate how I wanted. Upstairs, the makmaki brothers slapped and sucked each other in the descending twilight.

Hot, frustrated, and badly wanting more venom, I threw the snare aside and leapt to my feet. The baby followed me with his eyes from where he lay belly down and naked on his mat. I patted him perfunctorily on the head on my way to the closest window. I started to close it for the night.

"Don't you dare," Kiz-dan snapped. "You'll stifle us all."

"It's almost dark. It'll cool shortly."

"Keep the window *open*."

"Mosquitoes."

"Draw the netting down."

I glared at her. Didn't know how to argue further, my thoughts were that disordered.

"It's rats, Zar-shi. I hear them, too, sometimes. It's nothing but rats," she said. I'd made the mistake of telling her about the noises, about my theory concerning the carrion bird that lurked outside our windows at night.

"Explain the feathers, then."

She clanged her pot down, wiped her split-nailed, sooty fingers wearily across her bare thighs. She wore a short wrap, more a loincloth, really, made from the tattered remnants of her convent skirt. The remains of her convent tunic covered her breasts. Our disguises had been torn up for use as baby wraps.

"All manner of birds roost in the eaves," she said.

"None with those blue feathers."

"There are a starfold kind of birds in the jungle."

"You said yourself you've never seen feathers like that."

"And I never saw two brothers act as perversely as these do, yet they existed before I witnessed their obscenity." She scowled up at the faint cries issuing from above.

I grabbed a fistful of my hair—short but undeniably present for the first time in a decade—and yanked in frustration. "I need to find more venom, hey-o. I've got to get some somehow."

It was a conversation we'd had a clawful of times. She stood and pulled one of the brother's shrouds over herself. The baby started wriggling upon the floor in anticipation.

"Where're you going?" I asked.

"Out."

"Obviously."

She bent, lifted her baby up, and pulled him under the shroud with her. Elbows and the writhing of the baby bulged beneath the orange cloth.

"Are you going to help me, or just stand there and glower?" she snapped. I stormed over to her, flipped the back of her shroud up, and with a long length of cloth helped bind the baby to her back.

"Why do you always put the shroud on first?" I grumbled as I worked. "It'd make things easier if you waited until he was strapped on."

"He hates being strapped on. If he thinks I'm going without him, he doesn't fuss as much."

The baby babbled and slapped at my hands, trying to grab one and bite. Little arrowhead teeth peeped through his pink gums.

"Where're you going?" I asked again.

She sighed. "To fetch water."

"*I* did that this morning."

"You forgot."

"I did not," I replied hotly. I tied the last knot, checked that the baby was secure, and angrily tugged the shroud over his grinning face. From within, he complained and started batting at the cloth.

"Lower the urn down to me, hey," she said wearily.

"I don't see why you're going to get more water when I filled it this morning."

"You didn't, Zar-shi. And you didn't do it yesterday, either. You said you would and you went outside with the urn, and you returned later with it empty." She lifted an urn from the floor and pushed it into my hands. "It'll be a blessing when your venom is gone."

I gaped at her, stunned she could wish such malice on me. Then, slowly, clarity dawned.

"You've been stealing it from me while I sleep," I said. "You've been throwing it out. That's why there isn't much left."

The orange mound before me snorted in disgust. "You're a mess."

She turned and walked over to the terrace door, hem hissing along the ground.

"You've been stealing my venom!" I shouted at her back.

"Lower the urn to me," was all she replied, opening the door and tossing the braided vine ladder outside. It slithered down in a whispery rush.

I followed her, watched her descend. Outside, the muggy night air was just as stifling and oppressive as within the gawabe. Bats darted this way and that after insects.

"I trusted you," I railed at Kiz-dan's descending form. "How could you, knowing what happens if I don't get it? Brooder bitch. Whore. Thieving—"

She cried out, started writhing around. "No! Oh, no, no, no!"

"—dragon-sucking—"

"Zar-shi!" she screamed. "He's falling!"

It took me a moment to grasp what she meant, what the peculiar movements under her shroud represented. Then I dropped the urn on the floor and grabbed the rope adjacent to the ladder, the one used to lower and raise the ladder from below, and I wrapped my palms round it and slid down, fast, the rough twine burning as Kiz-dan shrieked *No, no, no.* I plummeted to her side, reached out, grabbed air and old orange cloth.

"Zar-shi!" she screamed, and my fingers touched something, a leg, an ankle, a small arm, and I held on hard, but whatever I held wasn't him.

He fell, light as a feather.

Down.

Down.

"NO!" My heart shattered with my cry as he hit the ground.

"Don't let go of him, don't let go!" Kiz-dan sobbed.

"No!" I screamed.

Then one of the makmaki brothers was there, naked on the ladder above Kiz-dan, reaching for me.

"Give him to me. It's fine, it's fine; give him over," he said.

I couldn't understand, felt dizzy, felt rope sliding through my fingers.

"Let him go, Zar-shi," Kiz-dan screamed. "You're falling!"

"I've got him now. Release him," the brother bellowed, and his foot struck me on the head, and then I was sliding away from them all, twine burning my palms.

I landed hard on the ground, that fast it was, my knees driving right up into my chest and knocking me half senseless onto my back.

I stared at them on the ladder above me: an orange mound of cloth that was Kiz-dan, and the makmaki brother standing above her. He was clinging tight to the ladder with one muscular arm, his free arm clutching the bawling baby against his gray-haired chest.

And above them, in the star-peppered twilight sky, wheeled a large vulture.

I turned my neck stiffly.

No small broken body lay beside me. Only white empty swaddling.

Swaddling my drugged fingers had failed to tie together.

*   *   *

That night, I refused myself venom. I stood night watch with the hanging dead instead, loathing myself and all I'd become. Reliving the harrowing image of Kiz-dan's baby falling, feather light, to the ground.

Pace, pace, pace. I could not stand still.

I wove, over and over, through the sparse forest of vertically hanging dead. My shoulders brushed their ashy bandages, my feet wafted dust from the coarse floor planks. My agitation stirred the smell of the kigos, that murky, mildewy, vinegary reek peculiar to the embalmed.

The kigos' pallid bandages hung like accusations in the air. For the first time, I was struck by how similar to a baby's swaddling those bandages looked. But for the quick response of that makmaki brother, Kiz-dan's baby would now be as gray and lifeless as the kigos those bandages bound.

How had it happened? Surely I'd tied that swaddling tight, surely. . . .

I stopped still, thudded knuckles against my temples, confronted my reality: I could no longer function among those I loved while the dragon's poison sang in my veins. I had to give the stuff up, lest someone die from my venom-induced ineptitude.

I had to give it up.

Oh Re, lend me your strength.

I had, at best, a clawful of days' worth of venom left, *if* I used it nightly only, and *if* I diluted it very thin. I had, therefore, just enough venom to begin the excruciating process of weaning myself off the poison. And I would do it. Yes. I would do it.

Had to.

A whimper escaped me. I resumed pacing. Trying to outrace my need, my fear.

But a thought chased me, insidious and silent as a haunt: I could obtain more dragon venom instead of giving up the habit. Use it more judiciously. Perchance, somehow, somewhere, I could find more. . . .

Self-revulsion washed over me. Had I not learned, was today's near-tragedy not lesson enough?

A wave of shudders swept over me. My teeth clacked together and a sour, cold sweat trickled from my armpits and slid over my ribs. I pushed the thought of seeking more venom aside—that tempting, se-ductive thought—and wrapped my arms about myself to still the next wave of venom tremors.

"I *will* give it up," I vowed to the hanging dead. "I will."

A rat poked its head out a ragged hole in the wall, looked at me with protruding raisin eyes, and, as I'd not been attentive during my night watches of late, dismissed me as no threat. It scuttled low bel-lied across the floor.

I flew at the creature, roaring as if it were the source of my crisis. It darted back into its hole and my bludgeon stick thudded on nothing but wood.

Bile flared up my throat. Ulcerous pain radiated from my belly. I shuddered, broke into another cold sweat. Sank unsteadily to my knees. Retched.

This was not going to be easy.

Anger welled within me then. It wasn't fair. I'd served the kuneus well for so long; to be cut off now, from all dragons, from all venom and at the mercy of my mother's haunt, was unjust!

And how *would* I survive that creature, without venom's shield?

I wiped my mouth against the back of a hand, staggered over to a wall. Slid down it and sat there shuddering.

Without venom, I would have to do the haunt's bidding and find Waivia. Or . . . I could leave Clutch Re, forcing the haunt to return to its dependent, ethereal state within me.

Never that, oh, no! The memory of the haunt's gamy touch, of its obsessive rage, of being held hostage within my own flesh as it took over my body and used me as a puppet—

My stomach torqued and I doubled over in agony. Stars lit the dark behind my closed eyes, and those shards of light flashed, turned into a monsoon of gold, orange, and red the color of rust, of flame, of lips, of blood. The colors rained about me, drumming in my ears, thun-derous, deafening.

Slowly, my vision cleared. The roar in my ears decreased to a susurration, then to a rhythmic, small wet sound. I lifted my head from between my knees: That low-bellied rat had returned, was lap-ping up my bile from the far corner.

I retched again.

When I finished, I closed my eyes, rested my head against the splintered wall at my back. Anger washed over me again, wearily this time.

When had my life ever been mine? When had I not been governed by starvation or grief or the madness of my mother? Not since that Mombe Taro of my ninth year. Not since the subsequent visit of that aristocrat with hair the color of liquid honey and eyes glass-clear blue.

A short, sharp barb of hatred stung me. The emotion provoked another paroxysm of tremors, more intense than the last, laying me out flat upon the floorboards so that I stared wild-eyed at the kigos dangling above me as my heels drummed briefly, frighteningly, against the floor.

Panicked, sweating profusely, I rolled to my knees as soon as the convulsions stopped. Crawled to the hatch that opened to the floor below. Scrabbled with the heavy, rusted ring bolt and lifted the trapdoor with difficulty.

With each passing moment, panic grew within me. I couldn't do this; I couldn't live without venom.

But I had to.

I needed Kiz-dan. I needed help.

Weeping and shuddering, I tried to clamber down the rope ladder. But the ladder defeated me. I could not find the cursed rungs; the wretched thing swayed too much, was nigh on insubstantial. I slid down its length, landed with a jarring sprawl on the floor. The thud woke Kiz-dan and the brothers, I heard them stir.

Crawling belly down like that bile-eating rat on the floor above me, I reached the spot where Kiz-dan and her child lay, formless shapes in the meager moonlight slipping through wall cracks and beneath window ledges.

"Help me," I sobbed, meaning, really, Give me venom, ease my want.

Two shadows either side of Kiz-dan abruptly sat upright, and I almost shrieked, but realized, even as another paroxysm of tremors gripped me in an epileptic-like fit, that the shadows were the makmaki brothers, that they'd taken it upon themselves, for the first time, to sleep either side of Kiz-dan and her child.

To protect them.

From me.

Mercifully, Kiz-dan understood from my slavering, teeth-clacking, juddering state what I needed; moving efficiently in the dark, she mixed some of my precious venom into an empty gourd while the brothers did silent sentinel duty on either side of her baby.

She cradled my head in her arms as though I were an infant and tipped the blessed venom down my throat.

Oh, hated, most desired taste! I savored the licorice-lime burn as it spread peace throughout my body, as my bones melted like wax in Kiz-dan's lap.

When I was able, I spoke.

"Don't give me anymore after this, hey," I whispered, my voice raw and shaky and uncertain. The baby I'd almost killed earlier sighed sweetly, suckled air in his sleep. I spoke again, with more conviction. "I have to give it up."

"Yes. You do," Kiz-dan replied. Her eyes, in the dark, were glistening hollows.

"Will you help me?"

A pause. A nod I felt but could not see.

"But don't touch him again, Zarq," she said, steel in her sibilant voice. "Don't so much as lay a finger on him ever again. Understand?"

I understood.

And I realized then that even freed from venom, I would never be to her what I'd once been. I was Zarq now. Not Zar-shi, her holy sister-in-vows, but Zarq. Someone quite, quite different.

Thus began an eternity of torment. Or so seemed the interminable days and nights that followed, blurred into never-ending misery by a constant wash of nausea and cold sweats and tremors.

When I wasn't ensnared in exhausting, ponderous sleep, haunted by visions of Waivia being mistreated and defiled, I was vomiting, shivering, hallucinating, sobbing. Kiz-dan tended me with the brusque fastidiousness of one dutifully performing an unpleasant though necessary act. She emptied my chamber pot and held me down during the worst of my withdrawal tremors, forced me to swallow gruel, and cleaned it up after I vomited it moments later. The makmaki brothers offered to look after her baby, take him out while they tended their jungle snares. At first, Kiz-dan refused. But as the days bled into weeks, she relented.

The brothers aided Kiz-dan in other ways, too.

Ignoring my flailing fists and snapping teeth, they bound my legs and arms with rough twine so I couldn't charge out the gawabe and plunge to my death, deranged by need for venom. On certain days, one of them watched me while the other worked the traplines alone, so that Kiz-dan and child might have some time together outside the madness in our tower.

The brothers took to washing the child's swaddling cloths, mashing his food, rocking him to sleep. The three were forming a bond since the near-tragedy on the ladder, the baby at the center.

On those days that I was left alone with one of the brothers, I schemed. Couldn't help myself. Although I'd decided to rid myself of venom, another part of me—a feral, desperate part—craved it still.

"Please untie me," I'd beg. "I'll be good. I won't go anywhere, just . . . just . . . " Rage, instant and unstoppable. "Untie me! Let me out of here. I'll kill you all when I get free. I will, you'll see!"

I tried other tactics, too.

"I know you like sex," I'd whisper to the makmaki brothers. "You can have me any way you like. Untie me and I'll pleasure you. I'll do whatever you want."

Busy whittling darts for hunting, the brothers didn't even glance my way.

"Grow a cock, girl, and we might consider it," one of them eventually grunted.

One day, addled beyond all reason, I offered the same to Kiz-dan.

"Kiz-dan," I hissed, my wrists chafed raw and my fingers cold from the twine that bound my hands. "Untie me. I'll touch you as Lutche did, I'll pleasure you that way—"

"Shut up!" she screamed.

She threw aside the monkey carcass she was skinning, slapped me once, twice, thrice, then snatched up Yellow Face's machete, the one I'd carried faithfully since leaving Tieron, and waved it in front my face.

Eyes shadowed from lack of sleep, fingers streaked with monkey blood, she snarled, "Speak that way to me again and I'll cut your filthy tongue out. Understand?"

I did.

Never again did I try to bribe her or the makmaki brothers with my skeletal, stinking body. Instead, I concentrated on what I'd set out to do: recover. For I was determined—in those moments of lucidity between bouts of madness—to overcome this, to get well.

During those lucid times, I wept pitifully and thanked Kiz-dan for all she suffered on my behalf.

"Whatever I say, don't untie me till this is over," I'd whisper hoarsely. "I want to get better, Kiz-dan. I do."

Purse lipped, she'd remain silent. Bracing herself for my next descent into madness.

That hot, oppressive Season of Fire dragged on and on. I turned sixteen.

It would not end, my misery; it would not release me. My bones ached, my flesh withered, my mind became a dank cavern.

Blue feathers littered the floor about me, I swore they did; strange claw marks grooved the wood. I screamed during my sleep because the moment my eyes shut, my mother's haunt appeared, bringing visions of Waivia being defiled by cruel men. Memories haunted me, too.

Blue-eyed, blond-haired ones.

How I grew to loath that fine, arrogant face, those detail-rich memories.

But slowly, as the Season of Fire drew to an end, my moments of lucidity increased in length and frequency. Slowly, I was able to eat more and keep it down. Kiz-dan untied me, and I tottered about the gawabe like an emaciated crone, performing the simplest of chores. And though the haunt continued to invade my nights, I learned how to master my fear, how to lie alone and silent in the dark until the terrible images passed, my heart hammering so hard against my ribs it felt like some wild thing that didn't belong within me.

It was then, as I began to heal from my abuse of dragon venom, that my cravings for the stuff altered.

It crept over me, this cruel alteration, so subtly I didn't notice the change until it was puissant. See, I no longer desired venom just to indulge my body's addiction to the stinging, heady warmth, nor just to shield myself from my mother's haunt.

No.

I now remembered the powerful ecstasy provoked by the dragon's tongue. I now recalled the alluring whispers of the beast and the mysterious ancestral memories that had skimmed elusively just beyond my full comprehension during the erotic rite. I now craved those things, not just the quick, sweet burn of venom's sting.

I realized my cravings had altered when I found myself nightly plagued with the memory of the dragon's tongue, when lust burned in me so furiously that I awoke drenched in sweat, hands between my briny thighs. Even during daylight I was filled with desire for the brutal strength of the dragon, and I would creep to a secluded corner to indulge myself, hoping desperately to provoke the transcendence and oneness I'd felt when joined with the dragon.

A desperate, futile hope, that.

Of course, I knew in my heart that those numinous sensations were directly tied to venom. But those who are desperate will try anything to ease their need, and I was very, very desperate.

No matter how I tried to slake my lust and replicate the joy and the unity the bestial exchange had provoked, I failed. And with each failure, my yearning to hear again those mysterious dragonlike whispers—secrets that promised to open the Celestial Realm to me—increased.

Like Yellow Face, I didn't know why my attempts to replicate the dragon-provoked sensations with my own fingers met with failure. In despair, I eventually came to the conclusion that the transcendental state achieved during the secret rite had something to do with the dragon itself, with the divine living presence and the exchange of bodily fluids that occurred between human and holy beast.

With this realization came resignation. Acceptance.

No, I lie. I never accepted *that* particularly cruel loss, never transcended the newly remembered desire for the questing greed of the dragon's tongue between my thighs and the numinous liminality such intimacy provoked. Instead, I buried the desire. Buried it deep, deep within me.

Deep beneath my growing hatred for Kratt.

Kratt.

As the monsoons of the Wet turned sections of the Zone of the Dead into small lakes, Waikar Re Kratt became my new addiction, my substitute obsession. Specifically, the death of Kratt.

See, while I worked about the gawabe, stacking wet wood to dry, stirring bones in bubbling broth, I thought of him.

About how he had looked during the Mombe Taro of my ninth year, whipping the youngest dragonmaster apprentice with calm, methodical sadism. That same look upon his face when he watched Waivia kowtow to him, her sauciness only inflaming his intense, calculating stillness. That look again upon his face, magnified a thousandfold, as he beat health and justice and hope from my mother when he ordered Father bound before an agitated yearling and whipped the young dragon into a savage bloodlust.

For every cooking-brazier fire I lit, for every rat dropping I swept up or pound of featon grit I soaked, there grew in me the conviction that Kratt represented all that was evil in the world, was the catalyst for all the wrong I'd witnessed and all the suffering I'd endured.

I began picturing him choking on a songbird's bone at banquet, his face turning puce, his eyes bulging, his hands clawing futilely at his swelling throat. I pictured him in bed during a fire, his legs tangled about the silken sheets as smoke curled thick and black about him and fire consumed his ornately carved bed, as tongues of flame devoured his embroidered pillows and turned his wheaten hair into a fiery halo, the skin on his screaming face black and bubbled.

Viscid and persistent, hate followed me, and I welcomed it, reveled in it, quickened to it.

I was not idle during those times. As the Wet continued, I grew stronger, began once more to earn my keep. I cleaned and gutted game caught in the brothers' trapline of snares. I gathered fuel and decanted the urns placed upon our tower's window ledges to catch drinking water. I foraged what edibles I could from the jungle's dense snarl, washed baby swaddlings, pounded featon kernels into flour, scrubbed pots, whittled hunting darts.

At first, Kiz-dan and the brothers treated me with a caution that barely masked distrust. But as my lucidity remained intact and my unpredictable rages and bouts of madness became a thing of the past, they gradually relaxed in my presence. I won't distort the truth: a certain tension still existed between us, and I learned not to approach the baby too closely or babble with him too long, for Kiz-dan or one of the brothers would pluck him from my presence under some pretext.

Their message was clear. I could not be trusted with the little one, even though I was obeying Kiz-dan's injunction to never, ever touch him again.

And not cradling that child, not tickling his round, soft tummy or dandling his pudgy weight on my knees, cut deep.

He was a sweet baby, with a smile that poured his heart onto his face and a laugh that bubbled deep from his belly. The makmaki brothers doted on him, called him Waitembakar, First Cousin's Son, though Kiz-dan called him Yimyam, after the white bunting that trills so sweetly each dusk. I adored the boy, but had to show my love primarily by fulfilling mundane chores. Each lizard I caught substituted a warm embrace. Each urn I set outside the gawabe as a rain catcher supplanted a cuddle, a kiss, a rough-and-tumble game on the floor.

I envied the brothers. Not only did they have the love of that growing little boy, but they also had formed a close friendship with Kiz-dan, who no longer looked bitter and shriveled and weary, despite the challenges of life during the Wet, despite the recent ordeal of tending me during my withdrawal. Somehow, the four had made a family of themselves. Their contentment was obvious.

Envy would have consumed me if not for my obsession over Kratt. That bitter anger, that swelling hatred, kept me centered, gave me purpose.

As for that carrion bird that housed my mother's haunt, it followed me still. Some days yes, some days no. I accepted its presence as one accepts a deformity.

As for the night terrors about Waivia, I suffered them still. Most nights yes, a few nights no. I accepted them as one accepts a recurring abscess.

Hatred for Kratt helped me accept those plagues, helped me quell my loneliness and seclusion.

As the fog-shrouded days of the Inbetween replaced the Wet, my obsession over Kratt reached a feverish pitch. Hatred now adhered to me like a clot of old blood, like a scab that I constantly pick-pick-picked at and made bleed. Ruination, destruction, chaos, incoherence, amputation, blindness, disembowelment—I wished it all upon Kratt. I fed off the pain I envisioned for him, yet the images I created in my mind's eye no longer sufficed. I wanted—craved, obsessed over, *needed*—to make the fantasies real.

That festering boil eventually burst.

It happened this way. One fog-dense morning, the makmaki brothers discovered a rare jungle cat caught in their trapline. The pelt of the tawny, black-spotted feline was worth a handsome sum of chits; the brothers rejoiced. But in the process of killing the feral cat without damaging its pelt, one of the men received a nasty blow to the leg. The cat's claws nigh on crippled him, slashing 'cross the back of his left knee and all but severing the tendons found there. It was left to me and the unhurt brother to transport between us the heavy carcass of the cat to the inrakanku, the furrier clan, for of course we would not skin the carcass ourselves; such a pelt required the skills of adepts.

Leaving Kiz-dan to tend the wounded brother, the remaining brother and I wove our way through the alleys of our neighboring zone, both of us shrouded in makmaki orange, the pendulous, ponderous weight of the cat strung to a pole carried between us. By then it was high noon, though you'd have known it not from the gloom of the fog-engulfed day. The air was heavy with the tang of citrus ferns unfurling in the jungle, and my shroud clung to me like a caul, damp and smothering. My shoulder was already chafed from the pole I carried. A thin seepage of blood drooled out the cat's smashed jaw, which swung a hand's span from my belly, and its one remaining eye stared unblinkingly at me. That's how the makmaki brothers had ended up killing it, see. By bludgeoning it over the head.

The smell of the beast—that freshly dead reek of sour bowels and blood—threatened to gag me.

As we neared the furrier clan's compound, a small parade of children skipped about us. They, too, knew the worth of the pelt, and their excitement was infectious. I found myself grinning. That is, till an evil thought slithered into my mind: With the chits this pelt would procure, surely I might be able to purchase some venom from someone, somewhere.

Hating myself, I gritted my teeth and banished the thought.

The makmaki brother proved very adroit in the negotiations that followed; we left the inrakanku with a plump chit pouch. We headed directly to the nearest apothecary, for the wounded brother would require palliatives and restorative balsams more potent than what we had in our pitiful store of medicaments back in the gawabe.

It was as we were winding our way through fog, basket-burdened women, and children at play in the alleys that we heard the clangor of bayen bells. We flattened ourselves against the coarse alley walls to make way for the oncoming litter of a First-Class Citizen.

A figure appeared in the fog, a young boy no older than ten, dressed in the pleated rose gown of an asak-illyas, a eunuch indentured as a holy steward to a bayen woman. The youth's brow was furrowed as he rang his bell, walking the customary sixteen paces before the litter of his lady. Mist beaded the bristle on his shorn head; his wide eyes looked this way and that, as though he were seeking something, and he walked with an uncertain gait. He looked on the verge of tears.

This was the first time I'd seen an asak-illyas since my childhood. Suddenly, I was swept back to the past, back to when my newborn brother was stolen from my unconscious mother's breast and given to Temple as an asak-illyas.

This bristle-headed boy before me could very well be my brother.

I found I couldn't breathe.

The boy shuffled by us, followed by an elegant litter carried by six stocky servants naked save for loincloths. The litter smelled like velvet and crushed grapes.

Clang, clang. Clang, clang.

I stared after the back of the departing litter, now blocking my view of the boy leading it.

"Move on," muttered the makmaki brother, nudging me in the back.

But then a drape was abruptly jerked open on the litter and a slender, feminine hand waved to and fro, and a woman cried, "Where *are* we? Stop right now, stop!"

The litter bearers shambled to a halt. The bell ringer—that uncertain boy wearing the gown of an asak-illyas—hastily stumbled to the litter's side. Words were exchanged. I heard them not; the asak-illyas shook his head vigorously, backed up a pace, vehemently denied whatever accusation had been hurled at him.

At an order from within, the servants set down the litter. How their muscles quivered as they strained to smoothly place it upon the alleyway!

The asak-illyas backed even farther from the litter, clutching his bell to his belly. He was biting his lip. Was he crying? Hard to see from where I stood, with mist swirling between us.

A head and boot appeared from the litter. Flaxen head, black boot. Kratt.

I guessed it even before I saw him fully, even though I had not seen him since he was an adolescent and I a wide-eyed child. I knew it was he, just by the abrupt tension drawing the air taut and the Xxelteker blond of his hair. My heart slammed against my throat.

Moving with languid grace, Kratt unfurled himself from the litter and stood before the hapless asak-illyas. Again, an exchange of words, a shrewish interjection from the woman still draped within the litter. Again, the frantic denials from the asak-illyas. The boy clutched his bell tight to his belly, as if it were shield and mother both.

Kratt struck him.

Raised an arm and backhanded the boy with the full strength of a grown man.

The sound instantly imprinted itself on my memory, and I hear it now in the most unexpected ways. When a sailor slaps a heavy, fresh-caught fish onto the deck; when a ripe terimelon falls to the ground and splits open upon impact; when a sodden gown is whacked against a laundering slab by a washerwoman.

The blow picked the asak-illyas off his feet and sent him sailing several paces through the air. He landed, deadweight, upon the hard alley floor, arms splayed outward, and I felt the impact through the soles of my feet. His bell landed with a metallic thud an arm's length from his loose fingers.

My heart split in two and each piece lodged in one of my ears, and the pounding deafened me to all else. I started forward; the makmaki brother held me back. I was dimly aware of his iron grip around my waist, of the adhesive cling of his wet shroud, joined to mine where he pulled me tight against his chest.

Kratt approached the fallen boy with coiled, languorous grace. Prodded him ungently with a boot. The boy looked so small, so thin and crumpled laid out like that, his pleated rose gown rucked up round his knobby knees, exposing spindly legs.

Kratt had killed him. So easily, so casually.

Kratt barked something at the dead boy. The corpse twitched, stirred. Groggily, the boy pushed himself up on an elbow.

Alive! I almost swooned with relief.

Wobbling like one drunk, the asak-illyas clambered to his feet. Looked about, muddled, blood spilling from his nose. Espied his bell. Shambled over to it, picked it up. Staggered to the front of the litter and resumed his place sixteen paces ahead.

Kratt gave an order to the litter bearers; they bent and lifted it, calf muscles bulging, muscle-corded backs quivering from the strain. Their napes suffused a dark red and their veins protruded. They settled the litter onto their shoulders as carefully as a mother settles an infant onto its sleeping mat.

Kratt joined the asak-illyas at the fore of the litter. As if harnessed to him, I moved forward when he did, pulling against the makmaki brother. The brother's hold about my waist tightened; I pulled sharply. He released me and stepped back, not wishing to draw attention to ourselves with a struggle.

I moved forward as if made of mist, to keep the asak-illyas in sight.

The young boy stood in front of the litter, staring fixedly ahead. He recommenced ringing his bell, the rhythm uneven.

Kratt stood just behind him to the left. Only a father should loom over his own young son that way, and only with protective intent. But threat was explicit in Kratt's presence. Threat and menace.

They started moving forward, asak-illyas, Kratt, litter bearers, and the woman draped within. And although I followed them to the end of that alley, I did not stay with their retinue longer. My footsteps slowed and the litter trudged ahead and that small, stricken boy—mutilated at birth to be an indentured holy servant for life—went forward into his dismal future, leaving me behind.

It was not much, what I'd witnessed. But it shook me badly. The boy's naked fear, his impotence, his vulnerability, his youth. The possibility that he could have been my brother, a babe I'd sung to in my high, childish voice as he grew in my mother's belly.

And Kratt. Seeing him again, after all this time, after all I'd wished against him, after my obsessive, repeated fantasies . . . It appalled me that yet again I'd stood by and done nothing as Kratt enacted more cruelty on the defenseless. It galled me that despite many months of brooding hatred, of plotting his death, fear of the man had numbed my mind and limbs when an opportunity to fulfill those dark dreams had presented itself.

The makmaki brother and I returned to our gawabe at dusk.

Yimyam was asleep after a busy day of wreaking havoc, and Kizdan, exhausted and harried, was insistent that we bring the wounded brother to Temple Ornisak on the morrow, for he'd fallen into a fever and his wound still wept blood and serum. She feared that even with our expensive apothecary medicaments, infection would set in unless the wound was stitched together.

I barely heard her whispered consultations with the hale brother as I readied myself for sleep.

But sleep did not come.

Long after everyone else breathed the deep, even breaths of slumber, I lay awake, hearing again and again the wet, resonant sound of a man's hand striking a boy's cheek. I tossed, I turned, I clenched fists and teeth alike, heart racing. No visions haunted me that night; memory manufactured images enough to stave peaceful sleep from me.

What a long, dark night.

Occasionally, the wounded makmaki brother groaned or cried out in his sleep. Kiz-dan or the hale brother would rouse, mutter soothingly, mop his brow, give him water to sip. Once Yimyam babbled in his sleep, a string of incomprehensible words.

How slept that asak-illyas? I wondered. And how had I let him walk away from me, when he might have been my brother?

How slept Kratt?

I could have so easily killed him there in that alley! Run up behind him with a heavy rock from the alley wall, pounded it into the back of his head. I could have done the deed and fled before the slow-moving, thick-skulled litter carriers ever reacted.

But no. I had stood there and done nothing.

Nothing.

Toward dawn, a rainsquall burst overhead. The relentless drumming on the roof enervated me no end; I rose. I could lie there no longer, would remain inactive not one moment more. From its usual resting place beneath my mat, I retrieved the machete Yellow Face had given me upon leaving Tieron.

I ran the blade along one edge of my mat; it cut clean and deep. Good.

Good enough for Kratt.

I stalked over to the gawabe door, lifted from its wooden peg the worn makmaki shroud that Kiz-dan and I shared. Pulled it over my head. Quietly opened the door.

The air outside was so dense with humidity from the thundering squall that breathing was like trying to draw sodden chaff into the lungs. Rain poured from the eaves in silver ribbons against a backdrop of gray morning sky. I leaned out the tower and unlashed the rope attached to the damp, heavy ladder that was drawn up under the shelter of our tower's lower eaves. With one tug, the heavy ladder went slithering past me, slap-slapping the stone on its way down.

I picked up my machete, knotted it to the hem of my shroud, and descended the gawabe. At the bottom, standing in an ankle-deep puddle in the murky dawn light, I laboriously hauled on the rope, tugging the folding ladder back up to its shelter beneath the eaves.

By the time I'd finished securing the ladder's rope, I was drenched.

I didn't care. The weather could hurl what it wished at me; I had a mission that scorned mere rain.

I unknotted my machete from my hem, tucked it underneath the thin, clinging curtain of my soaked shroud, and set off. Heading toward Cafar Re, the sacred palatial grounds of the warrior-lord of our Clutch.

The squall petered to an end. The sky lightened somewhat. A songbird warbled a lonely soliloquy.

The ground began sluggishly sucking up the rainwater, and the astringent tang of citrus ferns bled into the muggy air. Vapor rose in ragged fingers, pulled upward into the gloomy sky. Other servants of the dead descended their gawabes, going about the daily business of life.

On I walked. Steady as a heartbeat, determined as vice.

The mist coalesced, turned into dense, low fog. I could see no farther than a dragon's length ahead. The suck-suck of my feet in the mire echoed loud off the surrounding gawabes.

A wall loomed before me, sudden. Long, straight, man height, a clot of ancient rust-colored brick and rock. I'd reached the end of the Zone of the Dead. I walked alongside the wall till I reached an alleyway that in the gloom gawped at me with the clouded white of a blind man's eye.

I entered.

My footsteps sounded like sibilant whispers, the swish of my shroud's hem upon hardpan like insects scuttling over the waxy cheeks of a cadaver. Specters of mist swirled about me. A cold, gamy draft scolded, shredded the mist, separated ethereal figures and sent them hissing on lone journeys elsewhere.

People appeared in the fog, real people with urns on their heads or babes tucked in their bitoo cowls or massive bundles of burlap-wrapped wares strapped to their backs and foreheads. The sounds of industry began echoing from wall to wall: the wooden *thok* of mallets, the *thump* of pestle in featon barrel, the orders of men and the squeals and wails of children at work and play.

I fed off the noises, let the vitality of rishi at work fill me with energy.

I caught a ride on a Temple egg-delivery cart pulled by a brooder so old, so work worn, her life spirit followed in her wake like a defeated child. The cross-eyed acolyte who drove the cart didn't hesitate at accepting me as passenger, for I was a servant of the dead and to refuse a makmaki's request was to invite misfortune. Nor did he question my shrouded gender, for of course I was male; a female would never address a Temple acolyte.

The egg-delivery cart wound down this alley and that in the fog.

I soon lost patience with the meandering journey and its frequent delivery stops and walked instead, following as best I could the instructions given me. Hungry, I fed off the brooding certainty that before middle night, I would be at Cafar Re. Thirsty, I drank from a dark well of expectation.

The sun did not show itself that day.

The impenetrable gray of late noon sank slowly into the gloom of dusk, which in turn was dyed black in a vat of deep night. Damp, chilled, and determined, I reached Wai Bayen Temple, in the Zone of the Most Exalted Aristocrats, in the silence of middle night.

My water-wrinkled soles slapped against the cobblestones of the sprawling, empty market square surrounding the temple, and the sound echoed off the temple's tiled pillars. Even without the luminosity of star or moon in that fog, I caught glimpses of the temple, disjointed images revealed by lamp and candlelight.

Fog-shimmering patterns, cast from light gleaming through the geometric designs carved into sandstone balustrades and walls, hung suspended in the dark like motionless birds. Faceted, muddy light glimmered through beveled lead-glass windows. Lances of tarnished light shone from minarets and glinted off the copper-scaled onion domes below them.

The gross amount of that light spoke of a luxury that renewed my anger and resolve.

Beyond the market square: inns and taverns, stables and shuttered shop fronts catering to traveling merchants, all clustered together in a stench of urine and cooling gharial grease. I'd been here before, of course. With my dying mother. When we'd fled Clutch Re almost a decade before.

Raucous laughter and music bulged from one tall, narrow inn, and three drunken men spilled from the doorway and staggered across cobblestone. One of the three stopped to vomit, hands gripping knees as he bent over his own feet. I waited until he was through, then approached, safe beneath my orange shroud.

"Cafar Re?" I muttered.

Pudge eyed with drink, he made ready to hurl insult. But he bit his tongue as a shaft of tavern candlelight revealed me as a servant of the dead. Rearing back, he pointed.

"Down there. Left. And down again."

I descended the steep, cobbled street. Tavern fug and mist trailed behind me, a slipshod duo. Then a warm, heavy, citrus-scented wind blew and sloughed away fog and tavern reek both. And against the sudden brilliant, star-spattered black of night, I saw Cafar Re.

Cafar Re.

Literally, Bastion of Tears.

Understand, that was the name of our Clutch bull, in the Emperor's tongue: Tears. Every bull dragon throughout Malacar was named after a bodily secretion, was called something base and vulgar and contemptible. Such a name camouflaged the divine beasts so that the One Snake, the First Father, the progenitor and spirit of all kwano everywhere, would overlook our sacred, scarce bulls.

Clutch Re, Clutch of Tears. Cafar Re, Bastion of Tears.

The bastion encompassed the entire hill across from me. Domes and galleries and gardens, fountains and pavilions and arcades: With the clarity afforded by hilltop and full moon, I saw the roofs of it all, even the fronds of tall palm trees caressing the balconies of some of the Cafar's uppermost floors. Glazed ceramic tiles covered the tetrahedral rooftops, gleaming like tarnished brass. Undulating clay dragons, silhouettes sharp and small in the moon's glow, crested each upswept eave.

I remembered the danku, my birth clan, the pottery guild, making such dragons. Once upon my youth.

The fog descended again, as sudden and complete as its departure, and I found myself running down the cobbled street, down toward the base of Cafar Re, my heart too hot, too heavy, the blood in my veins poison, the machete in my fist a hungry thing. My breath scraped along my throat; it was hot as metal in full sunlight, coarse as desert sand. My makmaki shroud flapped tight against me like the wrappings round an embalmed corpse.

At the bottom of the hill, the fog parted again, affording me a view of a fine avenue stretching away to right and left like a paved moat at the base of Cafar Re's hillock. Majestic bayen manors enclosed by fenestrated sandstone walls lined one side of the avenue—the far side, so that the manors looked up at Cafar Re. On the opposite side of the avenue, a wrought iron barricade encircled the Cafar's hillock.

A wrought iron barricade interspersed with guardhouses.

Beyond the guardhouses, beyond the wrought iron barricade, a stately cobbled drive carved switchbacks up the hill to the Cafar proper, disappearing here behind lush fronds and dense tangles of heliconia, reappearing there. At the top of the drive another wall, this one solid sandstone, only glimpses of it visible from where I stood at the Cafar's base.

Well, then. That iron barricade, that sandstone wall, had to be penetrated, yes?

Fog again, sudden, chill, redolent with the heavy sweetness of cultivated blooms, and I could see nothing save myself and dense gray.

Then the slick, rolling whisper of carriage wheels, the brisk click of dragon talon-nubs against cobblestone. I held still, exposed yet hidden in fog.

The carriage was approaching from my left; I couldn't see it, but its advance was clearly audible. The creak of fine leather, of oiled axle. The deep "Hey-o" of the driver slowing his beasts. The snort of dragons, the manure-and-leather smell of them.

I'd forgotten that smell.

I was at once overwhelmed and lifted high by that odor, and the conviction that someone must die tonight returned, hot as steam and scalding my heart, for the scent of dragons was the scent of the convent that had sheltered me, was a reminder that a group of feeble, emaciated women might have been slaughtered by Temple scythe.

Movement from the guardhouses flanking the huge, gated drive into the Cafar. Grunts, clank of metal, all submerged beneath the creaks of leather and dragons whuffing as the carriage loomed out of the gray.

It rolled past me in a whoosh of air and swirl of fog, so close my shroud caressed its great wheels. The yearlings tossed their snouts against their blinders, the brass of their harnesses jangling. The carriage driver had his body turned toward the guards at the gate; the carriage itself blocked me from the view of the guards lumbering out of their pillar boxes into the fog.

I was unseen.

The carriage stopped a body's length from me. A voice called from within.

That drawl conveyed lazy superiority, confidence, ennui, belonged to a face I'd memorized in fear and loathing. I *knew* that voice.

Or so I thought; so obsessed with my goal, I heard only what I wanted.

That voice muttered something, and I was certain of who sat within that carriage. I felt indomitable. The machete in my hand, omnipotent. Certainty roared in my ears: This was my destiny.

The spirit of Re, the fervor of my mother, had placed me here for this.

The guttural exchange of words between carriage driver and gatehouse guards, the grating of gates being laboriously swung open, blurred into the background.

Light as smoke, I drifted toward the carriage. One hand closed around the lacquered carriage door handle. The brass estucheons on the sable wood were cold against my palm.

With the slightest of pressure, the door snicked open. A tiny sound. Like a raindrop falling upon a swan.

I launched myself toward the wheaten-haired person draped in porphyry and emerald silks upon the overstuffed carriage seats within. He turned in a miasma of alcohol and perfume and grilled meat, and as his eyes widened and his mouth opened, my machete slashed forward, across his long, golden neck, but my shroud, my makmaki shroud that had protected me and camouflaged me thus far, hindered my wild slash, and my blade slashed not across his throat but across one smooth, rounded shoulder, and as the momentum of my strike carried me forward and I fell against the person I would have killed, I realized it was not Kratt, was not even a man.

We struggled a moment, me and that fine, drunken bayen lady, the luxurious folds of her gown and my slashed and worn shroud hampering our movements. Forever it seemed we were entangled thusly, me sprawled upon her in a parody of a lover's embrace, her hot, soft, heaving bosom separated from my cheek by the thinnest of orange cloth.

Then we were apart. I spun, launched myself out the carriage, hit the ground running, stumbling, my machete still gripped in my fist.

And as I ran into the fog, feet slapping against slick cobbles, she inhaled and screamed.

TWENTY-FOUR

Panic.

Inability to breathe, to think.

Run, run, run!

Up the steep, cobbled hill across from the Cafar, stumbling, lungs as loud and ragged as frayed bellows.

Quiet, quiet; I had to be more quiet!

Behind me the clatter of sandaled feet, the hiss of swords being unsheathed. Voices shouting, exchanging directions and orders. Into one fog-shrouded alley I ducked, away from those voices, my feet slap-slapping on slick cobblestone, echoing off walls. I was too loud, needed to be silent, but to be silent was to be still, to be still was to be caught. I had to run, run, run—

A small hole in the wall to my left, a dog hole, a child's hole, ancient bricks fallen onto the alley. I slid to a stop, hesitated. Threw a wild look behind me, trying to gauge how close my pursuers were in that dense fog. Close, by the alarming sound of heavy breathing and pounding feet drawing ever closer.

I scrambled over the jumble of spilled bricks and pushed into the hole. Got stuck halfway through. Writhed, ignored a crunching pain in my ribs, the abrading of skin, scraped out onto the other side, spilled onto slick cobblestone, chest heaving.

An empty square before me, crowded with mist, silence, and the smell of dragon. I was in the courtyard of an inn for merchant travelers.

To the left of me, the stables.

I scrabbled to my feet, ran toward the low building. Fumbled with the wooden latch of a door. Slipped within the stable's pungent darkness.

I took several cautious, silent steps inside, my ragged breathing overloud. The door creaked closed behind me.

Old, cobwebbed timbers. A row of stone stalls housing muzzle-tethered brooders to my right, a single chain slung across each stall opening. Work-worn dragons shifted listlessly in the loose boxes, disturbed, but not unduly, by my appearance. Flagstone and scattered bedding chaff underfoot. Overhead, low floor of a loft. To my left, a pitchfork stuck upright in a pile of manure. A hillock of clean bedding chaff loomed in the dark behind it.

I would stay here the night and the following day, hidden in the loft, and slip out the night thereafter. . . .

But no.

No.

It suddenly struck me how profoundly I'd erred by ducking into the stable, lured by the panic-driven desire to hide, for surely every building in the area would be searched before dawn and I'd be routed out like a rat from a burrow. I'd made a dreadful mistake. I'd cornered myself—

A man's grunt.

I held still, held my breath.

And again the noise, loose and phlegmy, and again, from somewhere in the darkness not far from me.

My first instinct was to run, but even as I was turning to take flight, the significance of the sound sank in. Heart hammering, I fought the urge to flee, instead strained to see through the gloom. I gradually made out a single, indeterminate shape sprawled upon the hillock of clean bedding in the dark rear of the stable.

A stable hand, asleep on the chaff.

Cautiously, I approached, hand clenched round my bloodied machete. As I stood over him, recognition dawned: Before me lay the same pudge-eyed drunk who'd given me directions to the Cafar not long before.

Merciful Re.

I fell upon him then, tugged and pulled at his worn pants. He mumbled incoherently and his eyes opened, rolled in his head. He reached for me; I slammed a fist against the bridge of his nose. A soft crunch, a splatter of blood. He fell into the chaff, unconscious.

Shaking, I pulled off my shroud, dropped it, and began dressing in his rank tunic and pants.

The slap of sandaled feet in the courtyard.

I froze.

After a pause, the sound of footsteps resumed, grew louder as they neared the stable.

I cast about. Where to hide? Up in the loft, among the stored bedding chaff. A ladder, where . . . ?

Too late, the sound of feet right outside the door at my back—

I snatched up my machete, scrambled toward the nearest dragon's stall, and ducked under the chain. The fat brooder within tossed her head, snorted. Shifted. Rolled her eyes, fought her muzzle tether. I made futile placating motions with my hands.

The brooder's disquiet spread along the length of the stable, and the rest of the dragons blew air out their nostrils and shifted about.

The stable door creaked open.

I sidled alongside the fat brooder, a beast whose shoulder blades reached my chin, whose girth was almost too much for the stall, whose length was twice my height. She snorted in agitation as I disappeared into the hindmost part of her loose box, and she tossed her head and fought her muzzle tether, trying to see where I'd gone. I ran one hand reassuringly along her leathery, scale-knobbed flank. In answer, she pushed hard against my touch, shifted her weight as though to crush me against the wall. I ducked behind her rump, crouched low. Her thin tail whipped this way and that, slapping stone and my knees both.

I held my breath, strained to hear.

Above the dry, raspy sounds of talon nubs shifting through bedding chaff, of dragon snorts and rumbles, of tails whacking against stone stalls, I could hear . . . nothing. Nothing of my pursuer. Could only picture him cautiously entering the stable, prodding the unconscious drunk with one foot, narrowing his eyes at my too-small shroud puddled on the naked man's chest. Could only imagine the set of my pursuer's jaw, the straightening of his shoulders, the tightening of his grip on his sword as he pieced together the evidence that confirmed my presence in the stable.

And then he was there, standing before my brooder, a huge, muscular shadow with shoulder shields and breastplate that glinted in the dark, his sword held ready. Could he see me, crouched here in the corner with nothing but fear and desperate hope and the dragon's shifting bulk to hide me?

"Drop your weapon and come out."

I thought I would faint.

"Drop your weapon and—"

I lunged for freedom alongside the brooder's opposite flank. The guard skirted round the dragon's head, blade held high to meet me. I dived beneath the dragon's chest; the beast trumpeted, tried to rear. I scrambled to my feet on the other side of her, turned to flee. . . .

A blow landed across my shoulder and back, hurling me against the stall wall.

I hit the wall hard, slid down it to the ground, sprawled upon flag-stone, stunned. The brooder shifted this way and that, the guillotined talons of her hind claws rasping along the floor inches from my face, the diamond-shaped membrane at the end of her tail stinging my cheek, tossing chaff into my eyes.

Clank of metal: the guard ducking under the stall's chain. He was sidling alongside the agitated brooder. Coming toward me, blade raised.

I willed it then. Willed the power of my mother's haunt to surge through me, willed fire to pour forth from my fingertips as it had once in Tieron, but the otherworldly magic did not come, for the haunt no longer resided in me, had taken the corporeal form of the carrion bird that roosted even now on the window ledges of the makmaki broth-ers' gawabe, back in the Zone of the Dead.

The brooder dragon shifted abruptly.

Threw her entire bulk against the guard. Pinned him against the stall. Where I lay sprawled on the floor at her rear, one of her feet landed half on my right arm. I ripped it out from under her crushing weight, scrabbled yet again beneath her belly, scramble-crawled along her far side, and collapsed outside her stall.

The guard, pinned beneath the brooder's flank, pushed ineffectu-ally against her weight. She pushed back, eyes white ringed and rolling, foam coating her muzzled snout. The guard's eyes protruded unnaturally. A burbling exhalation escaped him. His metal breastplate screeched against the wall as the brooder began slowly, steadily rocking to and fro, trying to smear him into stone.

I staggered to my feet and limped from the stable, leaving a thick, red trail behind me.

He had struck me, the guard.

That had been his blade that had thrown me against the stone stall, that had sent me sprawling on the floor at the rear of the dragon.

Although his strike had been hindered by the dragon's tossing head, the blow he'd delivered was a fatal one. I knew such, even without seeing the wound in its entirety. The amount of blood running down my calves, the chill in my body, the growing numbness in my legs, and inability to think as I staggered through the dark told of how badly I'd been maimed.

And the agony, ever growing as dawn approached and the fog about me lightened, that seared deep through my back, as though something were trying to rip my shoulder blades free of my flesh.

I did not make it to the Dragon-Sanctioned Zone of the Dead by morning. Instead, I ended up passing the day huddled in the unused back of an ironmonger's forge, among barrels of water that stank of the molten iron that had been plunged into their depths to cool on days previous. Agony locked my muscles rigid, and I rode under and over waves of consciousness.

Oblivious to my presence, the ironworkers tended their fires, worked their bellows, hammered at steel and sweated beneath their heavy leather skirts while I struggled with the process of dying.

But I did not die.

As night fell and the ironmongers left for the warmth of their huts and food and women, I came to the dull realization that I'd survived the dreadful day. I was at once consumed with the groggy determination to die in Kiz-dan's arms.

The hardest thing I've ever done in my life was to haul myself upright that night.

Forcing myself to walk was just as difficult. But I managed. Grit-jawed and small eyed with pain, I staggered out the forge house, into the fog of the Inbetween. And that fog, mercifully, lifted shortly thereafter, and so by the stars' positions, I managed to navigate through the maze of alleys and stagger home. I reached the Zone of the Dead by dawn.

Great swathes of it had been razed.

I stood there, dull witted and swaying, and stared at the destruction. Gawabe after gawabe had been burned down to its skeleton, and the stones of some foundations had dislodged in the heat and tumbled into smoke-blackened rubble. Strewn about the charred beams and sooty boulders lay heat-warped shutters, cracked eaves figures, shattered urns, cooking braziers distorted into violent, twisted shapes. The sprawling pyre reeked with tart fumes, glowed in places with the incandescence of smouldering flame, elsewhere stood as black as the belly of an empty furnace. The finer gawabes stood largely untouched, their multitiered, tetrahedral roofs blackened here and there from smoke, their stone foundations dripping oily black dew.

The whole place was eerily still save for the gray smoke rising in fingers and clouds, carrying delicate wafers of soot into the ashy sky. Still, but not silent. Cinders popped, embers cracked, timbers groaned, steam hissed, dying flames licked fallen beams.

Stiff and sluggish with blood loss, I shambled into the Zone of the Dead.

Hot embers crunched under my feet like soft, fermented eggshells. Blisters bubbled upon my soles. Heat from the dry, tart air turned my eyes into balls of chalk, drew the skin on my cheeks taut as drum rawhide, set my wound to throbbing anew. The tang of charred wood filled my mouth with a flour-dry bitterness. No one else moved about the charnel as I made my way toward the makmaki brothers' tower.

As I walked, I saw bodies among the glowing cinders and smoke-blackened shards of urns. Bodies mummified by heat into gray, leathery figures. Bodies freakishly untouched by flame, smut-covered faces gazing unblinking at the sky.

I reached the remains of the makmaki brothers' tower. No heat-shrunken, charred bodies here, nor evidence of wooden shutters or eaves. The fire had blazed hot and complete here, consuming all in its wake.

But there were bones.

Scattered skeletons, shattered into shards by heat and falling stone.

Resting beside one sooty boulder at the far edge of the rubble—cowering there as if hanging on to a mother's skirt for protection—lay a skull. A small, small skull.

It could be cupped within my hands, it was that small. But I didn't pluck it from its place, didn't soothe it in my palms. Didn't place a kiss upon the cracked brow or whisper the name of the small white bunting that trills so sweetly each dusk.

Instead, I staggered a short distance away, then stopped, swaying. The ground swooped up to the sky, and I collapsed.

The sword wound across my back and shoulder blazed with hot agony. I couldn't feel my feet, my legs. A peculiar dampness was flowering across my chest. From where I lay, I could still see that small skull, hazy, wavering, watching me with plaintive eye hollows.

How had he died? Crushed beneath a falling, flaming timber? Choking on smoke, his eyes wide and uncomprehending? Or did Kiz-dan make it to the ladder with him, frantically begin climbing down its burning length, only to fall as flame severed the rope from the gawabe? Did she drop little Yimyam as she fell, or did she clutch him protectively to her breast, ever the loving mother, only to crush him with her weight when they thudded against the ground?

"Let me die," I croaked, as smouldering embers snapped and hissed about me. "Let me die."

And it appeared before me then, that great carrion bird that housed my mother's haunt.

She stood before me.

Rank and bloody. Maggots writhing in its eyes and plopping out the nasal cavities of its beak onto the ground. Huge, it was, its long, scaly legs towering above me where I lay. Strips of nacreous gray flesh were tangled in its talons; more such rot hung like ropes of slime from its shimmering blue breast feathers.

In its eye sockets, beneath the gory veil of writhing maggots, red orbs glared. The bird reared back its head, opened its beak, let loose a cackling cry that rattled over the Zone of the Dead.

A tongue protruded, thick and black. It undulated out of the bird's throat in powerful surges. It was not a tongue, but an engorged snake. A giant kwano.

I screamed.

The snake sprang. Fangs buried into my shoulder and cool muscle slid round my neck. I grappled with the thing, but my fingers ran through it, sank deep into viscous, cold gel, and I fought to breathe, was choking, and then the Skykeeper attacked and tried to give me what I'd asked for only moments before. Release. Freedom. Death.

I lifted a hand to shield myself from the bird's assault; it slashed my flesh from hand to elbow. The snake squeezed, enclosing my vision in a dark cave, the cave constricting tighter, darker, heavier. The bird attacked again, ripping me out of the cave, out of darkness, bringing me back into the misery of life through the agony of wounds.

And then a giant stood above me, swinging a cane like a scythe, bellowing like an enraged dragon. His beard was cleaved in two down the center, and each half he wore over his shoulders like a mantle. Part of his skull sported tufts and bald patches; the other, corded black hair. He was naked, all sinew and nerve, with a great, dense matting of hair cradling his sex.

The Skykeeper staggered back under the giant's attack, stabbing this way and that with its razor-toothed beak, but the giant parried each blow with his cane and a roar.

The snake unwound from my neck, rose up onto its tail, a stout column of quivering rage crushing my chest, forcing wind from me anew. But the giant swung at it with one ropy arm even while swinging his cane at the bird with the other.

And he spoke. Words I recognized, though I did not understand them.

Djimbi.

The Skykeeper screamed and shook its head like an enraged baboon. The snake collapsed in coils onto my chest, *thud-thud-thud*. I couldn't breath. Darkness threatened. Immutable, irreversible darkness.

"Choose!" the giant yelled at me. "Pain or ease!"

Life or death.

I understood then that the Skykeeper carried death within her in the form of the kwano snake, but that she herself was life, however painful, however fear filled. That's why creatures such as she protected the Celestial Realm for immortal dragons: Skykeepers held both life and death within them. Painful life, painful death.

I wanted neither. I wanted life without pain, without the memories, without the evil. I wanted death without the lonely, infinite void.

"Choose!" the giant bellowed, and Yellow Face appeared beside me, looking like death herself, arms outstretched to gather me to her breast, and I knew then that the convent *had* been purged, that my holy sisters had died under Temple's scythe, died for saving their own lives by imbibing in medicinal drafts laced with dragon venom, died for improperly curing a bull's hide for a sanctimonious Temple superior.

Temple. That mighty, faceless power that crushed lives so indifferently, that espoused piety yet generated duplicity, that monopolized and tyrannized and dictated. Temple was the cause of all the misery I'd witnessed and suffered in my life. Temple was the reason I'd never again lie before a dragon and experience transcendant lust, would never again hear the secrets of the Celestial Realm whispered in the dragon's mysterious tongue.

"Choose!" the giant bellowed again.

The vision of Yellow Face grew clearer, her death-waxy arms reaching for me. I reached for her in turn. To escape a life where Temple and misery and oppression ruled as an omnipotent triumvirate.

As my fingertips brushed the slick, bone-cold ones of Yellow Face's specter, memories I would leave forever flashed before me: the softness of my mother's cheek as I buried my face against her long, smooth neck, the heavy fall of her hair sweeping over my shoulders like wings. Waivia's mouth pressed against my ear in the dark of middle night, my sweaty hand clenched about hers as we curled together on our sleeping mats and she whispered exhilarating stories to me. The stark horror in my mother's eyes when she realized her boy infant had been stolen from her breast. The piercing blue eyes of a handsome young man, his wheaten hair sweat plastered against his forehead from the effort of concentrating on my mother's head, which bounced a little against the hardpan floor each time he drove his boot heel against her jaw. Slam, slam, slam. With deliberate, measured blows, he drove his boot heel against her face. Over and over and blood-spattered over . . .

I hesitated midact of receiving Yellow Face's death grip, remembering that blond-haired, blue-eyed aristocrat who'd beaten my mother near to death and killed my father.

I had lost everything because of that young man. Father, mother, clan. My womanhood, my health. Reason. Dignity.

Kiz-dan's baby had died not because of me, but, ultimately, because of Waikar Re Kratt. Temple might be faceless in its enormity and might, but Kratt was not.

And one last memory played in my mind then. A memory of staring at dragon bone and sinew, at the guts and brains of a slaughtered bull named Old Maht. I remembered the ambition I'd had, the fantasy-dream, the impossible goal I'd dared voice to the holy sister that stood next to me.

"That's what I want, beyond this day, beyond next month," I'd said. "A bull dragon and a yearling to pair it to. My own Clutch."

My own bull dragon, my own dragon estate.

Kratt's death.

These, then, were what I wanted.

"Choose," the giant yelled a fourth time, and my hands fell away from those of Yellow Face's ghost.

"Life," I said hoarsely.

Yellow Face shattered into a thousand shards of light. The Sky-keeper dived at me, but instead of rending me in two, it shoveled the snake into its beak and took flight.

Blue feathers showered down on me, luminescing softly.

Pain descended on me full force. Hot. White. Edged with bloody black. Up and down my body it blazed, stealing my breath, arching my back, drawing an endless scream from my throat.

The giant shook his cane at the departing haunt. Then he turned to me, talon-slashed chest heaving.

"Sun tomorrow, hey-o. Sun, sun, Season of Fire comes." As if we were best of friends with little to do but engage in idle gossip. He leaned on his cane and studied me, panting heavily, the slashes across his chest dripping blood onto the ground. "So you're the Skykeeper's daughter, hey-o? Ha!"

He turned, inflated his rangy chest, and roared over the acres of smoking ruins, "I've found her, Emperor Fa! Hear me? I've found her!"

And as the giant's battle cry echoed over the destruction, I closed my eyes and sank into oblivion.

TWENTY-FIVE

Throbbing pain, swelling, swelling. Receding.

Descent into sleep.

Pain again, swelling greater, the agony deeper.

Sleep fled from me as the pain became immediate and keen and I woke with a gasp that turned to a long-drawn cry as fire roared up and down my arm, burning right into the marrow of my bones. I couldn't see; darkness all around. Was I blind?

A movement at my elbow. The cool, smooth wood of a bowl nudged my lips. "Drink this. It'll dull the pain."

I sucked frantically at the offered liquid, spluttering and dribbling. Finished drinking with a gasp.

"It hurts, it hurts—"

"I imagine it does," the voice said, and a hand pushed my head back against whatever I had been laid upon. "Lie still. Give it time to take effect."

"It hurts."

"Deep breaths. In. Out. In—"

"I'm blind."

"It's night; there's no light. Breathe, now. In. Out. In. Out."

I focused on those breaths, fervently copied the rhythm. The darkness grew muggier. The voice began to fade. The pain dulled.

I mumbled something, I knew not what. The voice replied with words that elongated, warped, became slow, unintelligible.

Sleep cradled me in gentle arms.

Daylight.

I came to quickly, as if shaken awake, and stared about me in a daze. My eyes darted this way and that as I tried to process what I was seeing.

I was upon one of two hammocks in a low-slung room that appeared to be hewn from rock. Light came reluctantly through a squat, open doorway and crept sluggishly over smoke-blackened stone walls and a hardpan floor littered with bamboo casings. Across from where I lay stood a cabinet crammed with scrolls, topped by a leering clackron mask. Beside the cabinet was a desk; parchment, quills, pigments, pots of ink, mugs, and candles crowded its surface, and someone dressed in the white tunic and green scapular of a Temple acolyte sat on a stool before it. I stared at him, recognizing his profile from somewhere, somewhen. . . .

That cleft jaw, the dark hair hanging over those dark eyes: This was the acolyte from whom I'd bartered a ride into the Zone of the Dead when Kiz-dan and I had arrived at Clutch Re a year ago. With the recognition came the realization that I was in the underground antechamber of decrepit Temple Ornisak.

Even as the realization seeped slow as melted lard into me, something else nagged at me. Some strange emotion, some latent memory trying to intrude on my consciousness. . . .

Yesterday's battle with the Skykeeper.

How could I have forgotten?

And then I remembered the choice I'd made during that battle, and the reasons behind it: I would live, so as to fulfill my silent vow to kill Waikar Re Kratt and avenge my family. I would live, so as to fulfill my dream of one day owning a dragon estate.

But I couldn't own a dragon estate, not now, not ever! I was rishi, I was female, I had native Djimbi blood in my veins. Never, ever would Temple grant me the honor of acting as overseer of one of their Clutches. Never, ever would they sanction the breeding of brooder dragons who lived on such an estate.

What had I been thinking?

Better to bury that impossible dream beneath what *was* attainable. Better to inter it in a tomb of hatred for Kratt. That I could readily do. Hate Kratt. Focus on my vow to kill him and avenge my family.

My family . . .

Fire. A small skull.

"Kiz-dan!" I gasped, for how had I forgotten *that*? Kiz-dan, her baby, the two brothers, the razing of the Zone of the Dead . . . oh, Re, have mercy! Make it all untrue, all a bad dream. They had to be alive, they had to be. . . .

At my cry, the acolyte turned from his work at the desk.

"Don't get up," he said, rising to his feet. "You'll be sick."

"But I . . . the fire . . . "

He none too gently pushed me back against the hammock. Pain flared across my back, a crackling agony that I welcomed because I deserved to suffer, I did, I did.

"You'll be fine," the acolyte said brusquely.

I remembered the gentle voice from last night, so different from the acolyte's clipped tone: the mad giant who'd rescued me from the Sky-keeper must have tipped the wooden bowl against my lips in the dark and murmured reassurances to me, not this acolyte.

The acolyte's cool, long-fingered hands briefly dipped upon my brow, checking for fever. His skin smelled of wood ash and bitter ink.

"Drink this." He turned his back on me, retrieved a bowl from the crowded desk. Held it against my lips.

I turned my head away; I deserved no such respite from pain.

He misread the reason behind my refusal and said impatiently, "It won't harm you. It's an opiate, to dull the pain of your wounds. You drank some last night. . . . Look, I'll drink a little. See?"

He sipped the draft, then tipped the bowl against my lips. "Drink."

I had no reserves to refuse further. I drank the cloyingly sweet stuff.

The moment I'd emptied the bowl, he turned away from me.

"I took away your machete," he said, setting the bowl down on his desk. He sat again upon his stool and drew inkwell and quill close to begin the ceaseless chore of copying decaying scroll onto new paper. "I'll give the blade back to you in time. For now, it's hidden. Safer that way."

He'd taken away the gift Yellow Face had given me. How dare he!

But then my ire died and fear rushed into its place: He'd hidden my machete. Ergo, he *knew*. Somehow he'd guessed I was the attacker of the bayen lady, the reason behind the Zone's razing. . . .

No. Everyone owned machetes, all rishi, regardless of trade. Just because he'd discovered such a common blade upon me did not indi-cate that he knew I'd tried to murder a First-Class Citizen.

But not everyone bore the wounds that only a Cafar guard's sword could make. Like the wound 'cross my back.

I couldn't keep my eyes open. The draft I'd swallowed was dragging me down into sleep.

Last thing I saw was the acolyte biting into a pomegranate, the red juice running down his chin like blood as he regarded me beneath his dark fringe of hair.

Thus began my days in Temple Ornisak, the crumbling, neglected temple in the Dragon-Sanctioned Zone of the Dead.

I healed quickly from my wounds, far too quickly for the acolyte, whose name was Oteul. By the second day, the bone-deep wound upon my back was all but closed over, leaving only a jagged scar that ran from my nape to the bottom of the ribs on my left side. The scar luminesced a most peculiar blue; I saw the sheen of it reflected in Oteul's eyes as he gaped at my back. The color was identical to the underbellies of certain riverine fish. Or the feathers upon the breasts of legendary otherworld birds.

As for my other wound—the one the Skykeeper had inflicted upon my arm—it disappeared entirely overnight, leaving no scar whatsoever. Oteul regarded me charily after that and gave me wide berth. Daronpu Gen, however, beamed as if I were a prodigy and handed me the worn robe of a Temple acolyte, along with the green scapular that denoted the lowest rank in Temple's hierarchy.

"Wear this now," he'd ordered. "Too dangerous otherwise, hear?"

Daronpu Gen: the rangy, odd-bearded giant who had rescued me from the Skykeeper. I rarely saw him the week following the Skykeeper's attack, as I lay in the hammock, weakened and lethargic from both the blood I'd lost and the grief over the deaths of Kizdan and her child. Daronpu Gen swept in and out of the antechamber, reeking of smoke, debris entangled in his divided beard, soot blackening his face, and blisters bubbling his hands. He'd bellow for more bandages, more medicaments, and knock scrolls flying as he looked for them. Then he'd order me to remain in the antechamber, give me a piercing stare, and depart in a flurry of charred robes.

Oteul went with him, after both seeing that scar upon my back and discovering I was female, and I was left alone in the antechamber.

Alone, save for my grief.

Alone, save for my hatred for Kratt.

I could not bear those long, lonely hours filled with the harrowing images of a small skull and scattered bones that haunted me whether I slept or lay awake. I think I would have gone mad if not for the scrolls.

I began reading them.

Lethargically at first, the words running through my mind as mere distraction, with no meaning attached. But gradually, the lilting, archaic prose snared my attention and I found myself eagerly escaping my misery by delving into the history of Ranon ki Cinai, the Temple of the Dragon, and the parables woven within.

The stanzas I liked best were those that evoked the sharp, green scents of the jungle and the salty, leathery smell of the dragons. As I read, I recalled the sentience I'd oft glimpsed in the sad eyes of the kuneus I'd tended in Tieron, and I wondered how Temple could produce such wise, evocative lyrics and view dragons as divine, yet treat people and beast so abysmally.

These thoughts pricked at my conscience, threatened to penetrate the tomb where I'd interred my impossible dream of one day owning my own dragon estate. But I could easily divert myself from such unsettling thoughts by remembering Kratt and all that he'd taken from me and all that he stood for. I could readily submerse myself in hatred for him and thus keep entombed my impossible dream.

In between reading the scrolls, I would therefore think upon Kratt and the many ways I might fulfill my vow to avenge my family, until the thinking of such grew too hot for me, provoked too many memories of all that I'd lost, and I'd dive quickly into the scrolls again.

And then one morning, end of my second week during my stay in Temple Ornisak, a scroll I'd not noticed before caught my eye.

The scroll was sitting upon the crimson tongue of the wooden clackron mask that squatted atop the antechamber's weevil-ridden cabinet. Hauling myself off the stool, for I frequently sat at the desk and copied the old scrolls onto new parchment, doing Oteul's work as he helped Daronpu Gen salvage the lives of the inhabitants of our zone, I approached the cabinet. I don't know why I hadn't noticed that scroll before—it stood out prominently, balanced as it was so precariously in the mask's maw—and I briefly entertained the thought that perhaps it had been placed there purposely that morn, to catch my eye.

As I plucked the encased scroll from its spot, I saw the gleam of metal beneath the mask.

I nudged the mask aside: Yellow Face's machete winked at me. Aha, so that's where Oteul had hidden it! Pleased at my finding, I left the blade hidden, as it was safe, and now that I knew where it was, I saw no reason to move it. Instead, I took the scroll to the desk to read.

I popped open the end of the bamboo casing and tipped out the scroll within. Immediately, the musty fug of old age filled the air.

The scroll was floury, brittle, and yellow with age. As I carefully unrolled it, pieces of the frayed edges flaked off onto the desk.

The hieroglyphs within were beautiful. Extravagant and richly detailed with inks of crimson, porphyry, and emerald, now faded. I knew this must be a very old scroll indeed. Such archaic glyphs—many foreign to me—were no longer in use.

I began to read, guessing as best I could from the context of the stanzas what the antiquated glyphs meant.

> And so shall it be, by the immutable, divine will of Emperor Wai Fa-sren, that servants will tend the bull's every need.
>
> The bull will have servants to cleanse him and servants to feed him; servants to ride him much and far, that his strength grow and his wings not wither; and servants to stoke his ire, that he be vigorous, and mate. There is nothing a servant shall not do to please the bull, and the servant will willingly give blood and life in the course of such duty.
>
> Only the uncontaminated may serve the bull thusly, that the bull's pleasure be not tainted by perversity and evil, and these herein are named: Any reincarnation of the Emperor Fa, who is but an aspect of the Divine Bull, and any of his First Sons; any ordained Holy Warden

from the Temple of the Dragon; any Roshu, Lupini, or
warrior-lord who owns and controls a dragon-breeding
estate sanctioned by the Emperor Fa.

My heart began beating faster as I read, and the fine hairs on my
arms rose. This old scroll—the Scroll of the Right-Headed Crane, according to the hieroglyph engraved on the bamboo casing—clearly
stated who could serve a bull dragon. Again, I felt tendrils of ambition
and hope trying to penetrate the tomb in which I'd interred my impossible dream.

I read on, as if compelled.

Any dragonmaster who has earned such title through
pure service to one or more bulls in lands governed by
the Emperor Fa may also serve the bull; any komikonpu
who have earned the privilege of apprenticeship to such
a dragonmaster, and any inductees and servitors chosen
on Sa Gikiro by the bull-directed will of that dragonmaster may likewise serve; and any from the Chanoom
Sect, or any similar persons rendered clean by holy knife
may, under the sanction of Temple or dragonmaster,
serve the bull when necessary or needed.

These and these only may serve the bull, now and forever more, near and far. Heresaid by Emperor Wai Fa-
sren.

I stared at the stone walls.

I had been rendered clean by a holy knife; *I* had served the kuneus,
the retired bulls, in the Temple-sanctioned convent of Tieron. Did
that mean I could serve a bull dragon as did the warrior-lord of our
Clutch?

Shuffling noises behind me. Grunting. A man's scream, Daronpu
Gen's muttered response. I hastily replaced the ancient scroll in its
casing and was just rising from my stool when Daronpu Gen stumbled into the antechamber, half supporting, half dragging a man
along with him.

"Give me aid, boy!" he bellowed at me, emphasizing the word *boy*. "This man needs help."

I put the encased scroll on the desk and went to his side, nervously checking that my scapular hung correctly about the neckline of my tunic, hiding my meager breasts.

The man the daronpu carried was dressed in the charred and tattered remains of a makmaki shroud, the head of it cut raggedly off to create a tentlike garment hanging from his shoulders. The man was coated in smut; his eyes looked like white nuts beneath the thick, oily grime. Blood ran heavily down his right calf.

"Damn fool cut himself scavenging in a ruin near here. I came across him on my way back for more—move those casings there, boy, before we trip on them! Help me lift the man onto the hammock—come on, come on!"

The wounded man screamed as we hefted him, stomach down, onto one of the two hammocks in the antechamber.

"Shut your noise, man!" Daronpu Gen bellowed. "Where's your pride? It's only a scrape."

It wasn't. The gash was deep, directly behind the knee, and the exposed tendons and bones glistened like white, wet porcelain against the soot-blackened red of bulging flesh.

All at once I remembered the makmaki brother who'd been wounded by the jungle cat in a similar manner, the morning prior to my bungled murder attempt.

And all at once I remembered Kiz-dan's insistence, during the night I'd decided to kill Kratt, at taking the wounded brother to Temple Ornisak come morning.

A wild, desperate hope sang in my veins: Maybe they hadn't been in their gawabe when the Zone had been razed! Maybe they had been here in Temple Ornisak.

"What are you gaping at, boy? Fetch me water, fetch me bandages. . . ."

"Did you treat a man suffering a wound like this the morning of the razing?" I asked, rooted to the spot.

"What?"

The man on the hammock squealed like a wild pig.

"Did you treat a man—"

"Does this look like the time for idle chat, boy?"

"I need to know," I choked. "A man, a twin of another. He would've been brought here by a young woman with a baby, a boy just learning to walk—"

"I've no time for such reminiscences."

All self-control exploded from me. "Answer the question! For the love of Re, answer me! Did you treat a man suffering a wound like this on the morning of the razing?"

Daronpu Gen stared as if seeing me for the first time. Slowly, he nodded.

"Deep in fever, he was, but not so far gone as to be lost."

My heart skipped several beats. "Where . . . where are they?"

Daronpu Gen shook his head: He didn't know.

I staggered as if punched in the gut.

"Many fled into the jungle that day," he said softly.

"But they haven't returned," I said.

He snorted. "Wise of 'em, no? Look, I've heard rumor that those makmakis who were able purchased themselves a new life in neighboring clans. Perhaps they . . . ?"

I nodded, unable to speak. Yes, they might have done that. With the small windfall of chits the furrier clan had given in exchange for the jungle cat's pelt, they would have had enough to purchase themselves inclusion in another clan.

Kiz-dan, alive.

Her baby, safe and well.

But that skull, that small skull . . .

One of the kigos, of course. The skull of the smallest embalmed dead in the brothers' gawabe, the kigo that had disturbed Kiz-dan so much just because its size was so close to that of her own babe.

In danger of swooning, I clutched the daronpu's arm to stay upright.

"They're alive," I said hoarsely, tears hot in my eyes. "I thought . . . I thought . . ."

He harrumphed, patted my hand with his filthy, blistered one. "So, then. Are you ready to work now?"

I nodded.

*   *   *

And work I did.

Placing orphaned children in the households of untouched gawabes. Racing with crudely made shovels to the nearest smoldering timbers that had burst again into flame, to furiously shovel dirt over the new fire. Apportioning food and water to those without shelter. Carting rubble and wreckage to the jungle's edge. Setting the bones and healing the welts of those who'd been wounded, either in the razing or in the bayen-wrought interrogation process I learned had preceded the fires.

I worked so hard, I scarce noticed the passage of time, the change of seasons, save to one morning awaken with the thought: It's Fire Season again. Oh. I'm a year older now. I'm seventeen.

Seventeen I was, dressed in the acolyte's green collar and tunic Daronpu Gen had procured for me, smeared in soot, splattered with food stains and poultice and the blood of the wounded. I toiled ceaselessly alongside the rangy giant and Oteul, trying in my small way to right the wrong I'd caused to the innocent inhabitants of the Zone of the Dead. With my hair hacked short by my own machete, and with the grime that coated me like tar, I looked very much the part of a worn, devout acolyte, albeit a somewhat effeminate one.

Regardless of the authenticity of my disguise, I always hid from the daronpuis who oft visited our zone, investigating the attack of a makmaki upon a bayen woman.

Heart hammering, fear buzzing in my veins like hornets, I'd slip away during those visits and hide either in the jungle's edge or in the antechamber at Temple Ornisak. There I'd remain, staring fixedly ahead, until Daronpu Gen or Oteul retrieved me.

More often than not, it was the daronpu who retrieved me and not his quietly pious underling. Oteul avoided me at all costs; I feared he was not as trustworthy as Daronpu Gen assumed, and that one day the daronpuis leading the investigation would appear in the antechamber to get me, Oteul hovering behind them.

Temple's investigation revealed nothing, however; in the end, they deemed the attack upon the bayen woman as the random act of a lunatic disguised as a servant of the dead. The surviving makmakis were exonerated from my crime. And though Oteul continued to regard me charily, I reasoned it was due to my gender and the sacrilege of wearing my disguise. I no longer worried that he'd guessed I was the attacker and that he'd act upon that knowledge.

And so I worked hard, and did some good to those who had suffered so abominably for my attack upon the bayen lady. But no matter how long the hours or how grueling or heart-wrenching the labor, I thought often of Kiz-dan. Where was she? How fared she? And little Yimyam, her babe, was he talking yet? I waited for their return, believing they'd come back for me, if only to inform me which of the hundreds of guild clans in Clutch Re they'd joined.

But they never came.

And I realized, at one point, that they never would.

Hurt and loneliness accompanied me always as I worked thereafter, though I learned how to channel those feelings against Kratt. This was not the mad, obsessive hatred that had gripped me prior to the razing, understand. No. This was something cool, something rational, something far more complete.

It was not just Kratt's death I wanted, by then. It was what that death would change. Waikar Re Kratt was to inherit Clutch Re upon his ailing father's demise; if his half brother, Rutgar Re Ghepp, were to inherit the estate instead, surely Clutch Re rishi would be treated better than under Kratt's dominion. Surely.

From what little information I managed to surreptitiously eke from Daronpu Gen about Ghepp during the daronpu's frequent midnight rants against Temple and life in general, I learned that Ghepp was reputed to be a somewhat passive, conservative man.

A far better overseer for a Clutch than a capricious sadist, to be sure. If one were to remove said sadist from the line of Clutch inheritance.

One such as me.

By the time a contingent of the Chanoom Sect arrived in the Zone of the Dead, determined to rebuild the ravaged lives of its inhabitants, I had decided upon a course of action.

I'd come to the decision slowly, with great care. Yes, the end result of it would be my death as well as Kratt's, but I accepted that. Understand, I was bone tired, a fatigue not just of the body but of the mind and soul. Realizing that Kiz-dan had survived the razing but had felt no need to learn if I'd likewise survived renewed an ache I'd thought I'd long come to terms with: that searing feeling of being abandoned. Day and night I recalled that day when my mother had fled the glass spinners' compound and left me behind.

I'd been left too often. The loneliness was too much to bear. I would kill Kratt and avenge my family, and in doing so secure for all rishi a better life on Clutch Re. And I would die for it and have peace at last.

I began stropping Yellow Face's machete to a keen edge.

You may ask: What *had* Daronpu Gen meant, upon helping me overcome the Skykeeper by choosing life, when he'd bellowed, "I've found her, Emperor Fa! Hear me? I've found her!"?

And how had he found me lying in those acres of ruins in the first place, and how had he seen the Skykeeper for what it was, when no one else I'd known ever had?

I did not ask Daronpu Gen those questions, did not dwell on them. Refused, in fact, to ask them of myself. For since that day, I'd not seen the Skykeeper once, nor suffered any gut-wrenching dreams or graphic visions about Waivia. I was enjoying the relative peace this granted me, was cherishing it fearfully, and I was, therefore, afraid to ask any questions concerning the haunt, lest the answers suggest that my relationship with the creature was far from over.

So I never asked those pertinent questions as those grueling days rushed on, and indeed, I was so very preoccupied by my elegant, simple plan of how to kill Kratt that it was easy to disregard such germane questions for a short while.

And that was all I needed, you see. A short while. A clawful of weeks.

Because then Mombe Taro would arrive. Mombe Taro, when dragonmaster apprentices chosen in years previous were inducted or reinstated into the dragonmaster's apprenticeship through public flogging. Mombe Taro, when the warrior-lord of our Clutch, along with all members of his family, walked unguarded along the Lashing Lane, whipping eight times whichever apprentice they wished.

Mombe Taro, the time when I could easily, swiftly, step onto the lane and bring my machete across Waikar Re Kratt's throat.

Only until that day did I have to overlook, ignore, and stave off questions that might have pressed at me if I let them. Only until Mombe Taro arrived.

After that, those questions would not matter, for I'd be executed for murdering the Roshu-Lupini's First Son.

TWENTY-SIX

I rose early on the day of Mombe Taro, determined to leave the Dragon-Sanctioned Zone of the Dead by dawn and secure for myself a certain spot at the coveted halfway mark of the Lashing Lane.

Hollow eyed and dressed still in my worn, sooty acolyte's tunic and scapular, I was sure no one would recognize me. Not the bayen lady I'd forever scarred with a holy woman's machete several months ago, nor any guard who might have glimpsed my face during my subsequent flight from the Cafar. Not that I cared if I *was* recognized, as long as I could first do what I had planned to.

Oteul was asleep, stretched out on his hammock with one soot-covered hand flopped over the side. He looked so harmless like that; I almost regretted the suspicions I'd harbored about him. Since Temple had concluded their investigation concerning the murder attempt, Oteul and I had worked side by side more often, and I'd realized that he was a calm, devout young man, believing strongly in the good of Temple though able to recognize its faults when pressed to do so by his unorthodox superior.

Nevertheless, I kept one eye upon him as I retrieved my machete from beneath the clackron mask. As I said, I *almost* regretted the suspicions I'd harbored about him. Almost.

Daronpu Gen was awake, waiting for me outside upon Temple Ornisak's uppermost tier. He was leaning on his cane, each half of his cleaved beard tossed over either of his shoulders, and was chatting to a bat hung upside down from one of his fingers. I ascended the temple tiers to his side. The bat burst into flight.

"How much passion in a queen ant, hey-o?" the giant asked me, head cocked.

I had no time for his inane behavior, for yet another of the peculiar questions he constantly asked of air and earthworm. "You chose life," he growled at me when I didn't answer. I met his gaze levelly.

"I'm choosing when and how and for what purpose I'll die," I said. "When it comes your time, will you have that luxury?"

And I tucked my machete up under my tunic and walked briskly away from him, before he could engage me in debate.

By the time I reached the Lashing Lane, a crowd had already lined its length. Children jostled at the fore, and the red dust of Clutch Re coated the monks sitting cross-legged along the men's side of the lane. The sun glared hard off the monks' water bowls as they struck them over and over, producing discordant, atonal sounds.

I pushed to the front of the crowd on the women's side of the lane, elbowing children and mothers aside with all the command of a man, dressed in my acolyte clothes. I found the location I wanted: the place across from the whipping bar where the youngest dragonmaster apprentices always stood, where the terrified inductees cried and screamed and fainted.

The place I expected—*knew*—Waikar Re Kratt would stand, to choose the most vulnerable, most terrified apprentice to strike. I was that certain of Kratt's character, at that point. I took my place with cold satisfaction.

And it was then that the smell of the nearby dragon stables slicked the inside of my mouth like thick oil.

A shiver erupted over me, then another, and another. Saliva rushed into my mouth, my stomach torqued, and my diaphragm spasmed. I bent double with a cry. Alarmed, those near me pushed back a pace.

What was happening to me?

Realization dawned: It was that smell, that dragonish smell of urine and manure and regurgitated crop food laced with the smell of licorice and limes.

That oh-so-forbidden tang of venom.

For yes, these were the warrior-lord's stables where uncut dragons resided, and the tang of venom—so distinctive, so provoking— hung like a nagging memory in the air, and it was as if my painful withdrawal from venom had never occurred a year ago, as if it had been only yesterday that venom had stung my throat with heady warmth.

The parade of our most eminent Clutch Holy Wardens began down the lane.

Reeling, I struggled to master myself, to fight the terrible feeling of want that was creeping, insidious as sickness, through my veins. I straightened with difficulty. Gripped tighter the machete concealed beneath my tunic, pressed flat and cool against my ribs.

The inductees and servitors started walking the lane next. How small those boys looked.

Yes, I knew they were not boys but men, having lost all their milk teeth for adult ones. But their small, rounded shoulders, their twiggy arms, their slight chests so devoid of muscle, and their bellies as smooth as cooked albumen clearly delineated them as boys. Kiz-dan's child would look like that, in six years' time.

Sweat glossy and shuddering still, I looked about the crowd, saw a range of emotions on the faces. There was dismay and fear, yes. There were nausea and anger, too, also grief and terror revealed by keening and hair rending and arm raking. But more frightening than those was the pride I saw on the faces of some, and the rivalry and resentment and bloodlust burning on the faces of most.

Those boys-who-were-men were not human to that crowd. No.

They represented all the wealth Temple had given to each boy's clan, or the wealth Temple should have given for the same but had not. They represented Temple's might and wealth and corruption, made worse by how the boys would learn to arouse the Clutch bull during their apprenticeships.

Understand, a bull dragon must undergo shinchiwouk, ritual combat with another bull, before it achieves erection. But due to the scarcity of bulls, no Clutch lord would risk his beast in such a confrontation. Thus, the apprentices—trained and led by a dragonmaster—replicated ritual combat with a bull at Arena without seriously damaging the beast, so as to bring the bull to full arousal.

Dragonmaster apprentices: Temple's dragonwhores. That's what they were, those small, terrified boys who walked the lane.

It wasn't right that such youngsters be symbols for the inequality and injustices of rishi life. It was not right.

I gripped my machete tighter.

Another paroxysm of withdrawal shudders jerked me like a disjointed puppet, and I almost lost my grasp on my blade.

Oh, Re, *I* was a dragonwhore, only in a far more absolute way than these boys ever could be, for I'd lain before a dragon in a profane act of bestiality, I'd oft imbibed dragon venom, and all these last months while laboring in the Zone of the Dead, the memory of those experiences had been buried deep in my womb, in my psyche, in my spirit.

And now just the whiff of venom had restored all my old want with the flood burst of a dam exploding apart.

The servitors came next down the lane, young adolescents bearing the scars of previous Mombe Taros. Some showed fear. Most concealed it with bravado. Behind them walked the veterans.

I did not snicker at their erections as I had done when nine years old. Oh, no. I understood them, understood them well, was filled with seething, nauseating envy that their venom lust would soon be satiated by poison-drenched leather. I struggled to turn that envy into hatred, funnel the hatred where it belonged, against Kratt, but the smells of uncut dragon whirled around me, addled my mind, confused my conviction, and all I knew was want—

And there walked Yeli's Dono.

I was not looking for him, had not connected his inclusion in the apprenticeship nearly a decade ago to his possible presence during this Mombe Taro. The familiarity of him caught my muddled attention before recognition dawned.

The wide, almost astonished eyes, the narrow face, the short legs and the impatience apparent in how quickly he walked the lane, right on the heels of the young man in front of him, focused my gaze several heartbeats before I recognized who he was.

I gawped.

Yeli's Dono had grown into a man. His erection was as prominent as those of his peers. His muscled torso bore the scars of every Mombe Taro he'd participated in, to be reinducted into the dragonmaster's service, since joining the apprenticeship nearly a decade ago. Stubble shadowed his sharp cheekbones, as if he'd shaved carelessly. Lean and sinewy, impatient and expectant, he could have been my twin.

Could have been, if not for all I had been through and all he had not. And he would soon be whipped, soon experience the hallucinatory warmth of venom's touch.

Anger overwhelmed me, made me sway.

He had ruined my life, that young man, with his audacious request to be included in the apprenticeship, with his actions that had impoverished our birth clan and led to Father selling Waivia and, ultimately, to Mother's death and my current suicidal situation—

But no.

No.

Not Yeli's Dono, but Kratt. Kratt, the one who had altered my life so violently, who had placed me here, now with a machete in my hands and my execution for murdering the warrior-lord's First Son a certainty.

Yes?

I struggled to regain my equilibrium, to seize my sense of purpose, but it felt as nebulous as mist and all I knew was that already I had failed, for all I wanted was venom, venom, venom, and I was despicable for that want.

The dragonmaster of our Clutch began walking down the lane.

He'd aged since I'd last seen him, the skin on his chest now folded a little, his thin goatee braid now gray, though he looked as tensile with strength as before, and he chattered still to himself.

Odd, but he no longer looked demented to me. No. To me, he now looked normal.

And there, glistening in the dragonmaster's arms, lay corded leather dripping lovely black venom.

I couldn't tear my eyes away. Even above the odor of dust and human sweat, I could smell the licorice-lime scent of venom in all its glory. Saliva flooded my mouth anew, and my groin pulsed hot.

Gone was my purpose, my reason for being there. Gone was my need to kill Kratt, avenge my family, and secure for Clutch Re a better overlord.

The dragonmaster drew closer.

Whip me, whip me, whip me.

The refrain sang through my veins regardless of the fact that no serfs from the crowd were ever whipped during Mombe Taro. But my craving did not recognize reality, refused to accept fact. It was a song, a passion, a requiem, and a request, an antiphony to the tolling of the sacred water bowls.

The dragonmaster's steps slowed as he drew nearer me.

Whip me, whip me, whip me.

The women either side of me tensed and held their breath. The children jostling about them froze. The dragonmaster stopped right before me.

His blood-marbled eyes burned into my own, and the heady smell of venom became my everything. And, oh! how I wanted him to lay whip to my flesh, how I craved the pain for the venom that would accompany it.

A feather drifted down through the air. Slowly. Lilting one way, drifting another. It landed on one of the dragonmaster's whips and luminesced briefly before dissolving into air. A shadow slid over him. Over me.

He looked skyward, the dragonmaster. I knew what he saw without moving my eyes from his face: a massive otherworld bird from the Celestial Realm of the Dragons. A Skykeeper. My mother's haunt.

No one else looked up. It was as if that bird, that shadow, existed just for the cinai komikon and me.

Then the dragonmaster looked from the carrion bird to me and impaled me with his gaze, and I knew he could see me for what I was: a woman dressed in acolyte's clothes. And images flashed before me then, red and fast and furious: images of me defying Temple and becoming a dragonmaster's apprentice; of me lying before a dragon and reveling in the thrust of its tongue, rejoicing in the transcendant ancestral memories of the beast; of the outrage of the populace, the hostility of Temple, the roar of thousands of Malacarites chanting for my death in Arena . . .

The dragonmaster turned away from me, and I reeled, overcome by the magnitude of the enmity I'd glimpsed in his eyes.

And then the dragonmaster lifted his arm. Beckoned. Silently dared me to accept his challenge and become his apprentice, despite all I'd descried in his gaze.

I was not brave enough for that! Who could be? To tackle tradition and theocratic law, to defy the might of Temple and the will of the Emperor himself, required a strength and purpose and resolve far greater than I possessed.

Yet . . .

Yet I remembered then.

Remembered what I'd read, some time ago, in an ancient, crumbling scroll in Temple Ornisak.

. . . And any from the Chanoom Sect, or any similar persons rendered clean by holy knife may, under the sanction of Temple or dragonmaster, serve the bull when necessary or needed.

I had been rendered clean by Yellow Face's knife. And as of this moment, I had been chosen by a Temple-sanctioned dragonmaster to become his apprentice, for reasons known only to him.

I could, therefore, serve the bull. By Temple law, I could. And therefore, by extension, I might one day own my own dragon estate.

Would I dare accept the dragonmaster's challenge?

I had come here seeking vengeance and death, not challenge and life. And yet . . .

Of all that I'd glimpsed in the dragonmaster's eyes, one image stood sharpest before me, and that image imbued me with the desire to live beyond that day: the image of me lying before a dragon again, experiencing transcendental carnal intimacy, hearing divine whispers, glimpsing the ancestral dragon memories that promised to open the Celestial Realm to me. . . .

Yes.

Yes, I would. I would dare accept the dragonmaster's challenge. Once more, I would choose life over death.

I did the unspeakable, then, and the obvious: I stepped onto the lane and began following the dragonmaster.

A stir from the crowd. Uncertainty building. Indignation in those who knew that Temple law forbade a low-status, green-collared acolyte to walk upon the lane during Mombe Taro.

Along the length of the lane, the syncopated clang of the monks' water bowls grew ragged. Fell silent.

The crowd stilled, tensed.

The dragonmaster stopped. He stood with his back turned to me, and I stopped, too, fearful and uncertain.

Slowly, the dragonmaster turned. He studied me as the whips draped in his arms dripped beads of venom onto the dust.

Oh, let me lie naked in that dust while dragon poison dripped upon me!

"Strip," the dragonmaster ordered.

No.

No, he didn't mean it. I couldn't reveal my gender before this crowd. Was he insane?

Yes. Yes, he was.

And he meant it.

His eyes, his stance, his fierce grin challenged me to obey, and I knew then that this was a test I could not fail should I want inclusion in his apprenticeship. And now that it had been offered to me—the unimaginable, the impossible—I wanted it more than anything I'd wanted thus far in my life.

While still holding my machete beneath my tunic, I reached behind my nape with my free hand. Unclasped my green acolyte's collar. Let it fall.

Keeping my eyes on the blood-marbled ones of the dragonmaster, I bent slightly, grasped the hem of my tunic, and in one swift, fluid motion, pulled my disguise up over my head, lifting my hand that held the machete along with the garment so that steel remained hidden in cloth.

I dropped cloth and hidden steel to the ground.

I stood straight, shoulders back, and looked only at the dragonmaster. My cheeks felt wet. Did I weep? Yes. I wept for want of venom, I wept because I had failed—

But had I?

As the shocked crowd began to stir either side me, I wondered if I had, indeed, failed. If I might not yet, as a dragonmaster's apprentice, be able to take Kratt's life and place his brother Ghepp as overlord in his stead. If I might even, one day, become dragonmaster of Clutch Re.

I had first to survive this day, though.

The crowd began to cry out, jeers and insults conveying outrage, and within heartbeats, the outrage terrified me as faces contorted with fury over my profane presence upon the lane. A stone glanced off my shoulder, a sharp, quick sting that jerked me forward a pace. A sandal slapped against my belly and knocked the wind from me. Only the Temple precepts that delineated who could and could not step upon the lane during Mombe Taro prevented everyone from surging toward me and beating me to death.

Another rock struck me in the back; I cried out, leapt, half turned, was struck on the forehead, again on the back. . . .

The rain of rocks grew thick, bounced off spine and elbows and breast, dizzying, terrifying, and I stumbled under the barrage, staggered, fell to my knees as something bounced hard and sharp off my head so that my ears rang and my vision blurred and I knew not up from down. The roars of the crowd reached a new pitch and fear sang cold and dreadful in my blood as I covered my head upon the ground—

And then a sound, a furious sound coming up from behind me. *Clud-thrish, clud-thrish,* the sound was both a ripping and a pounding. The ground beneath me vibrated, and as I half turned, arms still cradling my head, a magnificent yearling bore down on me, galloping from the stable end of the lane, her green-and-rust-colored scales brilliant with health and vitality, her pleated dewlaps a beautiful milky blue.

The caped rider was leaning down over her flank, reaching for me as he thundered closer.

I scrambled upright, broke into a run.

A wrenching snap of my spine from the momentum of an arm scooping me up, the dizzy rush of ground beneath my feet, wind and pumping dragon neck before me, the muscular rhythm of dragon gallop beneath me, an arm tight around my waist.

Within moments, we galloped the length of the lane.

At the lane's end, the rider hauled back on the reins. The yearling tossed her snout and trumpeted. Slowed. Came to a lathered, fretful stop in front of the parade of astounded Holy Wardens.

Ungently, the rider hauled me onto the saddle before him; I caught a flash of a crimson shirt, unlaced at front, and a deep blue cape as I scrambled astride the yearling. Metal saddle ornaments gashed my naked thighs. Then the rider wheeled his beast around, and I scrabbled for a handhold, lay half over the dragon's thick, short neck and clutched it tightly as we rode back down the lane, returning to where the dragonmaster stood.

Waiting.

Grinning fiercely.

We stopped before him, our yearling snorting and shifting about.

"What do you, komikon?" the rider behind me bellowed above the crowd's noise.

"The will of Re directs me," the dragonmaster replied, eyes gleaming, fierce grin replaced by dark determination.

A string of curses from the rider.

His breath hot on my neck. His thighs warm against my rump. The sound of his voice ice round my heart.

Slowly, I looked over my shoulder. Looked upon my rescuer. Upon the possessor of that familiar, dreadful voice.

Waikar Re Kratt.

My stomach lurched and I thought I might vomit. Kratt barely glanced at me, stared hard eyed at the dragonmaster. "A woman can't apprentice."

"You and I already agreed on this: I'm directed by the will of Re."

"She was dressed in the robe of an acolyte—"

"I'm directed by the will of Re."

"There are laws, man!"

"*It is the will of Re!*" The dragonmaster's cry was a boom, a roar, a tempest that swept over the entire lane, and from overhead, an answering shriek, throaty and chilling, an otherworld sound that filled the sky, and every head present tipped up, looked high, and saw the inconceivable: a massive carrion bird luminescing with strange blue light.

A Skykeeper from the Celestial Realm.

Screams. Panic. People scattering, stumbling, falling, fleeing. The yearling I rode reared, trumpeting; I was unsaddled, landed heavily on the ground as wicked talons each the color and length of a machete slashed the air above me.

Kratt fought to control his beast; I scrabbled away from it, back, back.

The crowd continued to scatter as above us the Skykeeper, visible to all, wheeled the length of the lane, shrieking, claws extended.

Then the bird fell silent, and Kratt regained control of his dragon, and by the time I looked up, my mother's haunt was no more than a silver shimmer disappearing high, high into a solitary cloud in a clear blue sky.

The crowd had fled. Dragonmaster apprentices, monks, rishi spectators, and attending eminent Holy Wardens had run for cover. At the stable end of the lane, the stalled parade of elegant bayen carriages sat entangled with each other, several overturned and splintered, the dragons harnessed to them lowing in fear.

Mombe Taro was a shambles.

"Get up, girl."

I looked up at the flushed face of the dragonmaster.

"Get up!"

I scrambled to my feet, legs unsteady, my breath thready and cold and insufficient.

"Walk over to the bar."

I swallowed. Understood then that the dragonmaster meant to whip me, to continue with the annual ritual of Mombe Taro whether or not he had spectators and apprentices. With or without the pageantry and ritual. The dragonmaster still meant to induct me into his apprenticeship.

I walked over to the whipping bar, my bare feet raising clouds of the red dust unique to my birth Clutch. Behind me, I heard Kratt exchange words with the dragonmaster. Heard him ride his beast over to a section farther along the whipping bar that ran down the median of the lane.

As I gripped the smooth wood of the bar—slick with consecrated oil, furred with dust, carved with contorted, vaguely human shapes— I saw Kratt tether his lathered, exhausted beast to the bar a distance away from me.

I was going to get what I wanted most now.

Venom.

And though that venom might be imparted by a whip, a whip wielded by someone I had vowed to kill, someone I feared and hated, someone who had murdered my father and mother and destroyed my childhood, I would be receiving that which my spirit craved, what my flesh cried out for. What I longed for with every drop of my blood.

And it would gain me inclusion in the dragonmaster's apprentice-ship. Would give me unlimited access to the dragon's heady poison, to the questing greed of a dragon's tongue. Would allow me to again hear the incomprehensible secrets of the dragon's ancestral memories.

And that whip, by granting me inclusion in the dragonmaster's apprenticeship, might allow me, somehow, one day, to exact the vengeance I'd vowed to exact, and change for the better the lives of all Clutch Re rishi.

But for now, for this moment, I would suffer. Oh, yes, I had no doubt of that. Waikar Re Kratt would cut me slowly, torturously, to ribbons.

He would not kill me, no. But he would make me suffer.

I gripped the bar tighter and braced myself for the whip's fall.

ABOUT THE AUTHOR

Janine Cross has published short fiction in various Canadian magazines and was nominated for an Aurora Award in 2002. Her nonspeculative fiction has appeared in newspapers and a local anthology, *Shorelines*. She has also published a literary novel.